PRAISE FOR DEVRI WALLS AND
"WINGS OF ARIAN"

Whenever I couldn't read it, I was thinking about it, I love when books are that engaging!

~ Meagin Ramiro

Devri Walls' debut YA fantasy novel is a richly imagined tale of destiny, lies and promises, epic quests, pain, heartbreak and finding your own place in the world. It's a high fantasy novel, and a really good one at that. With an interesting premise and unique approach to the concept of good and evil, it's a novel that really stands out; a memorable and enjoyable addition to the genre.

~ Evie Seo, Bookish Blog

I enjoyed this book immensely. It jumped right into the action from the very beginning, and there was never a part where it began to drag.

~ Emma Nilsson

I read a lot of young adult books because I have a 12 yr old daughter and a 14 year old sister who love to read. Plus, honestly, YA books tend to be clean and more fantasy, thus a better escape, than adult books. Since I purchased my Kindle Fire in March I can think of about 3 or 4 books off the top of my head that I really, really loved, enough to pass along to my other sisters (5 total), friends, even my mom. I just finished this book today and it's going into the keeper pile.

~ AK "Amythyst"

... I found myself in love with each one of the well described characters. I was very much emotionally attached. Such a great read and I would highly recommend this book to anyone and everyone.

~ Jessica

Devri does an amazing job weaving a story! The characters are compelling and they grow and adapt to what is happening around them as the story continues. The characters wrap you up and the story line is so much fun to read.

~ *Rachel D.*

Love Love Love this book! I was engaged from the very beginning and had a hard time putting it down. The characters were well developed and easy to fall in love with. It was creative, witty, and full of adventure. I can't wait for the second book to come out.

~ *BroncoGirl*

This book blew me away. I loved it from the first page and was thrilled to be reading something so richly creative and engaging.

~ *Booklover*

WINGS OF ARIAN

Book One in the Solus Trilogy

DEVRI WALLS

This novel is a work of fiction. Names, descriptions, entities, and incidents included in the story are products of the author's imagination. Any resemblance to actual persons, events, and entities is entirely coincidental.

StoneHouse Ink 2012
www.StoneHouseInk.net
Boise, Idaho 83713

First Paperback Edition 2012
First eBook Edition 2012

ISBN: 978-1-938426-52-0

Book cover design copyright © 2012 Phatpuppy Art
Layout design by Ross Burck

Published in the United States of America

There are far too many people to thank in this endeavor. To my Father, who read the very first version of Wings of Arian and encouraged me to continue despite its rough state. To my Husband, who had endured more tears, hysterics and frustrations than any man ever should. To Ciera, without whom I can honestly say this would not be happening right now. To all my early readers and cheerleaders: Jen, Lindsay, Amber, Rachel, Caryn, Ashley, Caitlin, you were there when I needed you. And I really needed you.

I would also like to thank Aaron at Stonehouse Ink for taking a chance on me. And Claudia at Phatpuppy Art, for the amazing cover.

I would like to dedicate this book to my amazing husband who has supported me in every crazy thing I have ever tried to chase. I cannot imagine a more supportive amazing person to have by my side. You give me strength beyond my own.

WINGS OF ARIAN

PROLOGUE

BOOK IN HAND, ALERIC headed quickly towards the king's study, his footsteps echoing down an empty stone hallway. Turning abruptly to the right he pushed open two large doors, giving a passing nod to the guards at each side. Purely ornamental, the guards were a tradition from times long past.

Behind his desk, the king casually leaned back, his crown slightly askew on his graying hair. "What can I help you with, Aleric?"

Aleric deliberately, and somewhat dramatically, dropped the book onto the table with a bang. The dust billowed out and around the king's head from its tattered pages.

The king swatted at the onset amidst a fit of coughing. "Are you trying to kill me?!"

"Of course, my king," Aleric replied dryly with a shrug. "Lucky for me, your guards failed to check for dusty old books carried by murderous old men."

"Very funny," he said still swatting at the dust cloud. "Now what is it that you..." His eyes widened as he noticed, through the clearing dust, the symbol on the front of the book. Two wings set on a stand, the one reaching for the other, leaving an empty circle between them.

"I see you recognize the symbol of the Ancients."

"Of course I recognize it," the king snapped. "Why did you bring it here?" he shifted uncomfortably in his chair.

Aleric should have relished this moment, but he couldn't. Being right didn't make it better. He cleared his throat. "It is time, the prophecy has come to pass my king. It is coming."

The king's eyes began to bulge. "That..." he gripped the arms of his chair tightly as red flushed over his face, "that is not possible."

Aleric was usually even tempered, but at the moment anger bubbled up within him. "It is, of course, possible. We have been telling the royal family for hundreds of years that evil would return and yet you have refused to teach the people. We have warned of the dangers and you have ignored us. The prophecy was given, recorded in here." Aleric tapped forcefully at the book. "And then, hidden in a corner of the library where it could acquire a thousand years of dust."

The king's face retained its usual redness that appeared whenever he didn't like what he was hearing. Looking at the book as if it were a viper about to strike he said, "*How* do you know that evil is returning?"

Aleric let out a deep breath. "I felt it. It's what we of the magical community call a 'thread.'"

The king looked at him as he normally did whenever magic was discussed, like Aleric had sprouted a second head.

"This world is inhabited by many creatures, both magical and non-magical, all with threads. It is the essence of our life force. These threads," Aleric explained, clasping his hands behind his back, "weave themselves together in a beautiful tapestry. Each thread shines with different intensities; each is unique to its master.

A thousand years ago, after the battle and before Arian made his prophecy, the dark threads that had been woven in were finally silenced." Aleric frowned. "But this morning, one wove itself back in."

The king relaxed back into his chair, crossing his arms calmly in front of him. "Just one? Is that all this is about, Aleric?" He shook his head with a half grin. "One is easily contained, don't you think?"

"No, this was not any thread, Your Majesty. This was *the* thread." He could still feel it, like a black snake weaving itself in and out of the other threads, marring the tapestry he knew so well. "The power was…impressive. I have no doubt it was Dralazar. He will call his people to him, and then everything you have tried to hide from this people will be marching through the village square," Aleric gestured out the window, "including magic."

Shoulders tight, the king breathed heavily through his nose. "What does the prophecy say? How are we to defeat this 'Dralazar'?"

"There is one who will be called to fight just as one was called in all past battles; the prophecy refers to them as the *Solus*. This Solus is monumentally important," Aleric stressed. "The prophesy states that if evil is defeated it will be the *final* battle. I need to find and train this Solus."

"Who is it?"

"I have no idea!" Aleric wasn't sure if it was the situation that was infuriating or the king's complete lack of knowledge on a subject that he had willfully chosen to withhold from the people. "I have to find them first and then they will need to be trained on everything! They will not know evil, or magic, or anything that goes along with either of those because you have forbidden it!" He clasped his hands behind his back again to prevent an accusing finger from flying forward.

"Watch your tone!" the king warned, leaning in. "Generations have passed away living in nothing but peace and harmony with each other, not ever knowing evil. Thousands have benefited from this choice."

"Yes, I am very familiar with the Kings of Meros' opinion on the matter. And as I have consistently argued, you cannot control how that choice will affect future generations." He closed his eyes for a moment, taking deep breathes. "How many of them will pay for the simplicity of life the others enjoyed?" He continued, "This people…they are trusting, they believe anything you tell them. What is going to happen as evil starts to infiltrate and tell lies? What will happen as it tries to turn neighbor against neighbor? And they will," he emphasized, "I have seen it." Aleric stepped closer to the king's desk. "Don't you see? Evil stayed gone this long to lull them into a state of ignorance ripe for the picking! And now, how many generations will fall under evil's control because of the ignorance of their parents?"

The king's face had grown red again under Aleric's rant. "There is nothing that can change what has been done, we will find the Solus and train him, and he will defeat Dralazar just as Arian did a thousand years ago."

"Are you trying to convince me of that, or yourself?" Aleric walked over to the window that looked out into the village shaking his head. "It is not going to be that easy."

"You will train them and they will do what they have always done, defend the people," the king said with a nod, clasping his hands together in front of him.

Aleric leaned on the windowsill, his white hair falling forward as he took a deep breath. "How can we expect them to do as they have always done, when nothing is as it has always been? Look at them, Your Majesty, they are like children." He waved out the window with exasperation.

The village teemed with people moving from the bakers to the farmers market and everywhere in between. Running in every direction, children waved colored ribbons in celebration of summer. There were no unkind words or worrisome glances from parents wondering if their children were safe. No concerns over whether they had received proper change or not. No, they were a people happy in blissful ignorance. It was a beautiful, unnatural sight.

The king was silent, his knuckles white. "We cannot go back," he finally repeated. Flexing his fingers, he added, "There is no purpose in lamenting our situation. How will you find this Solus?"

Aleric walked back over to the table and pointed to the picture on the front cover. "The Wings will tell me who it is. They are located in the Forest of the Ancients. If— " he stopped, pushing his lips into a thin line, "If I can convince this Solus to accept the calling, we will return to the castle and begin the training."

The king jerked forward, "Why the castle?"

Aleric turned away from the king, taking a deep breath. "I have to start somewhere. Dragging them into the forest to see Guardians, pegasus and magical golden wings seems a bit abrupt." His sarcasm was biting. He knew the king's patience was waning, but so was his. "I will keep them here for a few days, long enough for them to begin to grasp the idea of doing magic. After that I will have to take them to the Guardians, and then, the Wings."

The King peered suspiciously at the cover of the book, "What good will the Wings do?"

"The Wings show the past, present and, occasionally, the future." Aleric walked back over to the window, leaning again on the sill, staring at the innocence beyond. "Trying to explain evil will be like me trying to explain black to someone who has only ever seen white. The true density of it would be incomprehensible. The Solus will need to see it, all of it…" Aleric shuddered, "…every vile thing that has ever been committed by man under evil's name. One cannot fight what one does not understand."

CHAPTER ONE

The Wings

IN A CLEARING SURROUNDED on every side by the encroaching forest, the smell of pine on the air, Kiora stood before two of the most beautiful things she had ever seen. Two golden wings stood sparkling in the sunlight, so large they were humbling.

"They're so big." Kiora said craning her neck upwards. Each wing must have reached some thirty feet in the air, arching around, reaching for the other. They were separated at the top by just inches, leaving a sense of longing, one wing for the other.

"Yes." Aleric said. He had been very quiet since Eleana had announced it was time to visit the Wings.

Turning her attention back to the structure before her, Kiora ran her fingers over the fine craftsmanship, each feather on this masterpiece was unique, slightly varying from the next. The space between the two wings sparkled and shimmered like a mountain lake. Her dark hair and green eyes rippled with it, dancing as if her reflection was secretly amused about something she didn't understand. She smiled back at it. Leaning her head back, she closed her eyes feeling the sun on her face and the cool breeze as it tickled her skin. It had been so long since she had felt free, without the watchful eye of her sister.

And then Eleana approached, her copper hair flowing down her back.

"Are you ready?" she asked.

"The magic is so strong. I can feel it pouring through me." Kiora whispered, her fingers still lingering on the feathers.

"It is." Eleana gently set her hand on her back. "Perhaps you should sit down."

Kiora turned back to the three chairs Eleana had called out of the ground, her fingers reluctantly dropping back to her side. The chairs were a mess of twisted roots and grass bent to Eleana's will, beautiful furniture set neatly in the middle of the clearing and facing the wings. Aleric sat smiling with a smile that did not reach his eyes. Kiora frowned, it was strange. Aleric's eyes usually twinkled when he smiled. It was one of her favorite things about him.

Suddenly nervous, she said, "I still am not sure that I understand why we are here." She searched Aleric's face for clues as she sat down, gripping the twisted roots that served as arms for their chairs.

"Since evil does not exist in the world you know, we must show it to you." Eleana explained again. "The wings can show us the past." Reaching out she touched them, instantly the void between the wings snapped into solidity with a thunderous crack. Kiora jumped. Pictures of the past began to roll in front of her, more horrible than she could have ever imagined; even more horrible than her old visions. She turned her head away with a gasp as Eleana moved to sit in the last remaining chair.

"Kiora," Aleric touched her arm, his voice thick with guilt, "Please, you have to watch, it's necessary. As the Solus, you must understand what it is we are fighting."

Kiora looked up at him, bewildered. His blue eyes were laden with apologies.

The Solus. Up until now it was just a title; one that had finally enabled her to make some sense of her past. But now, she had seen what Aleric had been hinting at. With great effort, she turned her eyes back.

In a towering picture a man stepped over his wife, screaming, spittle flying over her and the room. With a grunt of anger, he pulled his hand back and slapped her across the face, sending the woman flying. Kiora recoiled in her chair as if she had been slapped. Her mind was reeling, searching for understanding where there was none.

The wings moved on to the next scene, a man stealing into the home of another in the middle of the night.

"What is he doing?" she whispered again glancing back and forth between Aleric and Eleana, who were not watching the scenes before them but watching her instead.

Eleana's head turned reluctantly back to the pictures, focusing Kiora back on what was playing before her.

Pulling a dagger out of his shirt, the man stood over his victim,

Her hands flew to her mouth, "No." she whimpered looking frantically at Eleana and back to Aleric.

The man plunged the dagger silently into his victim's heart, swiftly, deftly and without remorse.

Kiora groaned in pain, wrapping her arms around her stomach.

Aleric reached over again touching her arm in reassurance. Blood was seeping out of the dying man's wound when the picture changed.

"Aleric, I can't," she groaned. "I don't understand."

"It was the only way," his voice cracked, "to show you evil, to help you understand."

She could tell he felt pity for her, but it didn't stop the pictures. On and on they rolled. Pain racked her body with each terrible event rendered before her. Her stomach lurched, threatening to empty itself, her muscles aching with tension. Lying, stealing, hatred, murder, detailing things that had been no more real to her than the fairy stories she had been told as a child. The happiness she had felt as she trailed her fingers across the wings were now gone. She was drowning in a sea of pain that was so much deeper than she had believed possible. How could something so beautiful show such evil?

The wings moved on, a small child was being sold into slavery. Men moved around him probing his body, examining his teeth as they would an animal. The boy's terror was palpable to Kiora as though he were next to her. The boy's new masters soon prepared a brand, searing it into his tiny back.

"No!" Kiora screamed, surging to her feet. "Stop!'

The wings ignored her pleas and the pictures marched on relentlessly before her.

"Kiora, please," Eleana begun reaching for her.

But Kiora didn't hear the rest. With a whimper of panic she turned, and ran.

She could hear Aleric and Eleana shouting for her; she didn't care. All she cared about was escaping. Soon their voices vanished, then their threads vanished, and all that was left was the wind whistling past her ears.

KIORA RAN FURTHER AND further into the forest. The branches reached out in an attempt to stop her, ripping at her clothes and hair. She tripped, stumbling over fallen tree limbs and rocks as she ran. Her pants were ripped and her knees were probably bleeding, but she didn't care. Sobbing, she pushed through the branches, her throat and lungs burning with the combined effort.

In her naivety, she hoped that escaping the meadow would mean escaping the pain, but no matter how far she ran the pain would not stop. The screams and cries of those she had seen rang in her ears, and the memory of it ran with her, side by side, holding her completely and utterly hostage.

Lurching to a halt, she finally she gave in with a scream, collapsing on the ground, sides heaving with exhaustion and pain. She sobbed into the forest floor, pounding her fists into the ground until they ached. With a groan, she wilted, allowing the numbness to grab hold.

Limp, she lay there on the ground with pine needles and rocks digging into her face and hands; wishing silently to reach into her mind, pry the images from her brain, to wipe her memory. The thought almost made her laugh. That was the problem with memories; they were impervious to any attempts to erase them. No, memories nag at you, never allowing you to forget. She had learned that lesson well.

A new hopelessness drug itself over her like an unwanted blanket. What she had just seen would be with her, always. She had never known of her own innocence, but it had just been stripped, taken, and she was acutely aware of its absence.

The next day dawned and Kiora was pulled out of nightmare-filled sleep to singing birds. She blinked a few times before remembering where she was; she hadn't remembered falling asleep. Groaning, she rolled over, aware of a throbbing in her face and hands. She brushed at the pine needles and rocks she had ignored yesterday that were now firmly embedded in her skin from the long night on the ground. Once the offending objects were removed, she recognized the tiny thread slipping through her heart. This one was magical, good, and belonged to a Guardian. The Guardian's threads vibrated faster than anyone else's she had come across.

She looked up to the trees, squinting at the slivers of sun breaking through the foliage. "Is that you, Malena?" Aleric had said she would eventually recognize individual threads, just as one would recognize a face upon seeing someone; but they were all so new to her still, and there were so many.

A small creature no bigger than the palm of her hand flitted down on shimmering wings, her silver hair lying perfectly between them. She was stunningly beautiful; her eyes were big and blue with a perfectly sculpted nose and red lips—a contrast to Kiora's dark hair, green eyes and subtle features. Malena's striking features and pale silver hair were a perfect fit to her shapely, albeit tiny, body. When Kiora had first met her she had half expected the tiny creature to giggle and blush incessantly.

"Kiora, Arturo is waiting for you."

Kiora stared at the ground, chewing on her lip. "I can't do this, Malena!" she blurted. "I thought I could, but I can't." A tear trickled down her cheek and she angrily brushed at it. "I can't even watch evil, how can I possibly fight it?"

"Kiora, it is the goodness of your heart that qualifies you for this calling," she said gently. "This is also why it hurts so badly. Goodness is pained by evil. It is the way of things."

Kiora gripped her head, sagging. "I can't, Malena. I can't stop this evil, maybe there is someone else, maybe..."

Malena interrupted. "There is no other, Kiora. You have been with us only a short time and it has already been proved time and again."

Kiora peered up at her through her hair, scowling, "What are you talking about?"

"Levitation?" Malena prodded.

Kiora snorted. "Levitation took me three days to learn. When I finally did get that stupid rock to move, it was because I was mad at Emane. I aimed it at his head." She gingerly touched the bruise on her own forehead; it had almost faded in color but was still incredibly tender. "I missed."

Malena fought back a smile. "That is what you get for using magic in anger. Regardless, three days is miraculous. I believe Aleric said it took him a month."

"Really?" He hadn't mentioned that.

"More importantly, we were all most surprised to find you could speak to Arturo."

"Everyone can speak to Arturo," Kiora said, pulling her knees to her chest and resting her head with a defeated sigh.

Malena flew closer, putting her finger under her chin, forcing her eyes up. "No, Kiora, they can't. He is telepathic, as you know, but only a few magical creatures can communicate with pegasus. And humans? Well, you are only the second to have that ability."

Kiora stared at her for some time not sure what to say. "Who was the other?" she finally asked.

"Arian."

"As in, the 'Wings of Arian' and the 'Prophecy of Arian'?"

"Indeed. He was the last Solus and the one who set down the prophecy concerning you." She smiled, "He was also Aleric's grandfather."

"Aleric's grandfather? But that would make Aleric..." she trailed off trying to do the math in her head.

"Older than most. Magic keeps us young, Kiora."

Kiora reached down and picked up a pine needle, twirling it absently between her fingers. "Malena, are you sure? That I am the Solus?"

Malena turned her head to the side, "You do not believe it?"

Throwing the needle away, she sighed, "I don't know what I believe."

"Kiora, whether we believe it or not is of no consequence, it is a choice you have to make. Our faith in you will not garner faith in yourself."

"Faith in myself," she murmured. "It is hard to have faith in yourself when your own sister..." she stopped.

Malena raised her eyebrows

Shaking her head, Kiora asked, "Is it always going to hurt?"

Malena's eyes filled with sadness. "Yes, it will always hurt," she said, reaching out a tiny finger to Kiora's cheek.

Kiora looked away, her chest aching and her eyes burning with the tears that had sprung up. She was so foolish to have hoped that Malena's answer might be no.

"Kiora, why did you accept this, in the beginning?" Malena asked gingerly.

Kiora mulled that over, chewing on her bottom lip. "Because," she ventured. "It explained everything. It explained the visions I would have, it proved that I wasn't crazy." *And that my parents' death was not my fault*, she thought.

"Sometimes things hurt, Kiora, but we do them anyway. Your people are depending on you."

Kiora battled within herself. The pain of last night was still raw and the thought of enduring

more or being acquainted with it on an intimate basis made her want to run screaming; but what of her people? Could she allow them to become the victims in this nightmare?

"What are you thinking?" Malena finally ventured.

"What if I try to save them, and I'm not good enough?" she blurted. "What if I fail and it happens anyway?"

"What if you don't try to save them at all?" she answered

simply.

"Malena, I have never been...anything."

"Don't be ridiculous, Kiora, we are all something. You just never knew what lay within you. Now that you know, you must choose. Will you ignore it and go back to pretending that you are nothing? Or will you embrace it and become the something that you were meant to be? You have been blessed with all the tools to fulfill this calling, Kiora, you just need to find them."

Kiora fiddled with the torn edge of her pants, weighing what she had just seen with what Malena had said. "Being different has always been...bad for me. She thought of her sister's disapproving glances and shuddered.

"Being different will now be painful for you, but it will be worth it. One step at a time, Kiora," Malena added.

Swallowing, she sighed. "Where is Arturo?"

"He is waiting for you to call." Malena smiled while brushing a wisp of dark hair out of her face. "You are extraordinary, Kiora; you just haven't seen it yet."

The little Guardian fluttered into the trees, her silver wings glinting briefly as the sun caught them, leaving her alone again.

Arturo, she thought.

Are you ready? The tenor voice reverberated, not in her ears but through her mind.

No, she thought before she remembered he had just heard that. "Sorry," she said out loud, "ready as I'll ever be."

As she waited alone in the woods, the memories from the wings tiptoed back into the forefront of her thoughts. Shoving them back, she clenched her fists and pushed herself to her feet. "You could always go back home," she growled to herself. "But you don't want that either, do you?"

It wasn't but a minute later that the low hum of Arturo's thread announced his arrival. Shortly thereafter, he flew in, landing a few feet away from her. He was always beautiful, but today in the sun he was glorious. The pegasus was not white but rather opalescent. When the sun hit his outstretched wings, the colors danced and spun across them in a beautiful water ballet. Greens, blues and pinks swirled across each feather.

"More training?" she asked out loud.

No, more tools for more training. Climb on. We have a ways to go.

Pulling herself on, she settled in front of his massive wings. He stretched them out, flexing a bit before he pushed into the sky. She grabbed at his mane, fighting to keep herself from tumbling backwards as he took off.

Hold tight, he instructed.

They exploded out over the canopy, the world stretching out before them. The mountain range surrounded them on all sides, marking the end of the world. The trees flew by beneath them and Kiora breathed in deeply, enjoying the moment.

"Why can't you talk to humans?" she asked after a few minutes.

Pegasus can read the minds of anything that has the capacity to think. But to communicate with us, they must be capable of telepathy; humans are not. You have something different about you that allows you to hear me.

"I'm different?" she wrinkled her nose in distaste. "Am I telepathic?" she asked.

I doubt it.

"Hmmm," she mused. "I don't know if I would like knowing what everybody was thinking all of the time."

I have never known any different, he answered simply.

Looking down, the thick wooden areas of the forest were disappearing and were replaced with lone trees, grass, and rolling hills. A river wound its way back and forth looking like a snake wiggling through the valley. In front of her, the mountains pushed themselves up from the ground stretching into the clouds.

The mountain range that surrounded the land gave it a rugged beauty that she had always treasured. There was just one dark spot in that mountain range; it was a source of continual visions for her, as well as a constant reminder that she was indeed, different. Just to the right stood a section where two giant peaks flowed down to meet each other almost at the valley floor.

You have visions about those peaks? Arturo asked.

Kiora started, and then covered it with a laugh. "Sorry, I am still not used to the fact that you hear everything I think."

What did you see?

"I always see a gate in between the two mountains, there." she pointed. "It's huge, the metal swirls and moves in a way I've never seen metal worked before. Anyway, they are affixed to the mountain blocking the pass, and locked in the middle. Sometimes in my visions, I would grab at it and rattle it, trying to open it."

And could you? Open it?

Kiora paused; there was anxiousness to Arturo's tone that was different. "No, there is always a man, with dark hair." Even recounting the vision, she felt dark and cold inside. "He laughs and then he always says the same thing, 'I shut it, but I could not have locked it without her help.' I don't know who 'she' is, and it feels like it's important, but I can't make any sense out of it."

Arturo was silent for a moment. *Sometimes visions don't always make sense at first.* "Yes." she took a deep breath, she did not want to let the past ruin this amazing ride. *No more thoughts of visions, of wings or of evil,* she told herself.

Throwing her arms out, she laughed. "This is amazing!" she shouted into the wind. This type of experience was exactly what had allowed her to throw herself headlong into being the Solus. She looked out over the world, from Meros in the south, to the Sea of Garian in the east. Her world was edged with a barren rocky land that butted up to the magnificent mountains. In stark contrast to the mountains lay her valley; there was a forest of magnificent pines, grassy hills, small lakes and winding rivers. She could see the castle turrets poking up at the edge of the forest, glittering in the sun and marking where Meros began.

On they flew, coming closer and closer to the mountain range. In fact, Arturo seemed to be flying straight at the face of the mountain without the slightest indication of deviating. Kiora's heart thudded.

"Where are we going?" Kiora yelled.

Arturo did not alter his course, nor did he justify the question with an answer, but continued to fly straight at the face the mountain looming over the top of them, threatening them for their boldness. Kiora's heart pounded faster as they were enveloped in its shadow. Arturo swooped in at the last second, pulling his wings back to slow them, and landed neatly on a large boulder jutting out of the side of the mountain. He knelt for her to slide off.

She sat there for a moment, her sweaty hands clenched firmly around his mane, staring at the ledge.

Don't be silly, Kiora. We just flew all the way here and much higher than we are now.

"I know, but I trust you."

More than you trust your own feet?

"At this height? Yes."

Arturo snorted and stayed as he was, waiting for her to dismount. She slid down slowly, placing her feet carefully and wiping her hands on her pants.

"What are we doing here?" she asked, turning her eyes away

from the ledge.

I cannot help you with this, Arturo said, settling himself onto the rock ledge. Clearly, he expected them to be here a while.

Placing her hand on her hip, she scanned where they were. They were surrounded by rock on three sides; the fourth side was just a lip of stone that stuck out over the cliff. The view was magnificent, although nothing of any magical importance struck her eye. Leaning against the rock wall, she crossed her arms and stared out into the world, wondering what the point of it all was.

"Why does everything with magic always have to be cryptic and horrible?" she pouted.

You don't believe that; you have been thrilled with your magic, he corrected.

"I was, before the wings."

People may do whatever they wish with magic, Kiora; that is what makes it horrible, not magic itself. You know that, you can feel that. And much of what you saw in the wings had little to do with magic and everything to do with evil.

It was true, evil threads did feel distinctly different.

"Fine, but it's always been cryptic. Aleric always left me nearly without any instructions when we were at the castle."

The pegasus smiled to himself. *Because if we showed you everything, you would learn nothing.*

"Come on," she shivered, wrapping her arms around herself. "You fly me up the side of the mountain, strand me here with nothing and then tell me to figure it out?"

Kiora, have I ever told you how exhausting it is to project into a human's mind?

"No. It is?"

No answer, just a look.

"Fine," she huffed, pushing herself back up. "You know, I could still learn if things were explained. For example," she said walking back and forth along the face looking for anything that might justify their trip here, "you could have just explained threads without having me traipse through the forest all day."

But you learned, Arturo pointed out.

"Yes, but I could have learned faster if you would have explained what I was feeling." She had stood there forever looking into the forest with no idea where to go. But then she had felt it, the thread. Something poked its way through her heart vibrating like a guitar string that had been plucked.

Perhaps, but what will you do when there is no one to help you and you must rely on your own feelings?

"So, I am looking for a feeling?" Kiora pressed.

Arturo looked at her with an almost parental glance of disapproval before he fell silent again.

"All right, all right." She nervously tiptoed closer to the edge of the rock, she laid down gingerly, pulling herself the final few inches to peer over the edge. The loose rocks dug into her thighs and stomach, but she was not going to look over this edge standing. At this height, even lying down made her dizzy. She closed her eyes to clear her head and took a deep breath. Opening her eyes again she scanned the valley below. It was breathtaking: the river crawling around the base of the mountain, the trees spotting the countryside going on for miles. However, beside the obvious beauty, she could see nothing else. Not one sign of civilization, magical or otherwise.

I must be missing something, she thought. She was slowly learning that in magical lessons the answer was never obvious. She stared intently, except for the breeze rustling the trees below, she saw nothing. Not even a bird soaring above the treetops. She finally rolled over and looked at Arturo. Who appeared to, once again, be smiling at her.

"What's so funny?" she asked, sitting up to brush the rock bits off her palms.

He just shook his head and turned to look at the back side of the rock face.

Kiora stood up and walked over to where Arturo was looking. "I don't know what you want me to do, Arturo. There is nothing here!"

She walked back and forth looking for anything unusual.

"It would be really helpful if you would just talk to me and let me know what it is that you want me to see." Her voice trailed off as she felt a low hum coming from the side of the mountain. "What was that?"A gust of wind blew her hair into her face, nearly obscuring her view. She pawed it out of the way wishing she had braided it.

She walked back and forth again in front of the rock face. As she passed by the middle, she felt it again, the same low hum, similar to Arturo's but without his pulsing. "Is that magic?" She looked at Arturo.

He nodded his head again towards the area she was looking at.

"I know. I feel it. I still don't know what to do, though. It's just rock." She turned to look at it again with her hands on her hip. Cocking her head to the side, she noticed something. Squinting, she looked closer. Some sections of the rock were not as crisp looking as the rock surrounding it. They looked...fuzzy around the edges. She frowned as she slid one hand across the rock face, it all felt like stone.

"Arturo! What is it?" She slammed her hands against the rock in frustration. As soon as both her palms hit the wall, it evaporated before her eyes. Then she was falling into a large stone room slamming her hands and elbows into the floor.

Kiora moaned in pain, pushing herself back to her feet.

Arturo trotted by her into the cavern as if to say, it's about time! "Thanks, Arturo, glad you're concerned." She brushed off her pants, tucked her now tangled hair behind her ear, and looked around. It was bare with the exception of a very old looking wooden table in the center of the room. On the table sat a large book, candlestick, an ink bottle and a quill.

She gingerly brushed off the dust and cobwebs that encased the book. Placing one finger under the cover, she carefully opened it. It smelled of dust and old paper. Inside, set on top of the bound pages was a loose piece of parchment with very small precise handwriting. She pulled the piece out and squinted trying to make out the words.

"I need light," she mumbled. And with that, the candlestick ignited. Kiora shrieked and jumped back, nearly dropping the paper.

She looked at Arturo with wide eyes. "Did I do that?" She motioned at the flame flickering away at the top of the candlestick.

Read.

"Right. Sorry." She walked closer to the candle and held the parchment up:

Solus,

This book is a collection of instructions; it contains everything that you will need to know in order to keep evil at bay. It is valuable both to you and also to Dralazar. He will do all he can to obtain the book. You must be vigilant in preventing this. He is already very powerful, and to add more to his arsenal would be foolishness.

Kiora stopped reading. "Dralazar?" she asked Arturo.

Evil's master.

"Why haven't I heard his name before?"

There is much you have not heard, Kiora. When we return to the Hollow I am sure we can show you who he is, but for now please focus on the task at hand.

Kiora continued reading.

This book has been enchanted by the Ancient One to be used as a tool of training. It possesses things that are both powerful and dangerous to the untrained. It will only show you what you need to know and nothing more. This allows you to learn at a safe pace within the realm of your capabilities. Keep it safe, and it will keep you safe.

Evil has spent centuries trying to gain a foothold in our land. We have now been fighting the evil for five years and I am not sure how much longer this battle will continue. Many lives have been lost, more than I dare count, for I fear the number will be more than I can bear.

I have seen your day and I fear for you and your people. I have seen visions that I do not understand and I worry that the gate may be falling. I do not know if this is a good thing, but I pray that the battle will be short lived. Whatever may come, know that you are capable of whatever you are called to do. You would not have been called otherwise.

God be with you, Solus. Fulfill your destiny, follow your path, and find those who are placed in your path to help you on your journey. The key to victory is finding what evil does not possess.

Arian

Kiora sat down slowly on the ground, her hands shaking. "Five years. He said he had been fighting the evil for five years," she moaned. Putting her head in her hands, she cried.

On the flight home she struggled with her emotions and chose to deal with it, again, by not dealing with it at all. Instead, she clutched the book in her hand and stared. The sky seemed a little less blue with numbness as her new companion.

Kiora, stop it, Arturo demanded. *There is much to do and not enough time for self-pity.*

"I am not pitying myself," she said aloud.

Kiora assumed they were headed for the Hollow, the home of the Guardians. But they flew right over the section of forest that Kiora was reasonably sure it was hidden in.

Blinking, she looked around before asking, "Where are we going?"

The Wings of Arian.

"What?!" she shrieked, nearly dropping the book. "Arturo, no! Put me down. I won't go back there. I can't go back there, especially not now." The thought of five years' worth of fighting was still tumbling around in the back of her mind where she had tried to hide it.

They are waiting for us, Kiora.

"I don't care." She stopped. "Who's waiting for us?"

Eleana, Aleric and Emane.

She nearly fell off his back. "Emane! What is he doing here?" she demanded.

That is why we are going, to figure that out.

CHAPTER TWO

THE PRINCE

WHEN THEY LANDED IN the meadow where the wings stood, Kiora could see a familiar shock of blond hair splashed against one of the trees. She clenched her teeth. Prince Emane. She found herself wrapping Arturo's mane tighter around her fingers.

Relax.

Kiora tried to relax, but even the way Emane stood drove her crazy. He casually leaned against the trunk of the tree with his arms crossed in front of him, one leg swung over the other, announcing to everyone that he was supremely sure of himself. It was nearly the exact pose he had pulled right before she had aimed that levitating rock at his head. Her cheeks flushed. Although annoying, it was less annoying than the hysterics he fell into after the rock smacked her forehead instead. There was no denying he was handsome, she had tried, but—he was. His eyes were a stunning shade of blue that pulled you in and threatened to never let you out. He was tall with a lean muscular figure and blond hair that always fell over his forehead. Everything about him was perfection, his high cheekbones, strong nose, and feathered hair. Perhaps it was his knowledge of his own perfection that made her crazy and not the perfection itself.

She slid off Arturo, still clutching the book, and waited for Emane's signature cocky look, through half-opened lids, but instead saw his blue eyes widen at the sight of Arturo. Smirking, she silently relished the moment. It wasn't a victory really, but it still felt good to catch him off guard.

Aleric placed a weathered hand on Emane's shoulder and leaned into him, whispering something in his ear. Aleric was a little shorter than Emane with shoulder length white hair that was receding on the sides, and white bushy eyebrows. His skin was wrinkled with age, permanently carving laugh lines into his cheeks and around his eyes. Kiora loved him.

Emane had unfortunately, regained his composure as they neared, and was now staring at her contemptuously. Kiora pulled the book tighter to her. Aleric, on the other hand, looked amused, his blue eyes twinkling beneath his bushy white eyebrows.

"What is she doing here?" Emane asked.

"What am I...?" she sputtered. "What are you doing here?!"

"I am here at request of the king, and Aleric," he added, motioning to her mentor unapologetically.

"I don't know what good you could possibly do here," she said, lifting her chin higher.

He chuckled. "What's that?" he asked, motioning to the fading bruise on her forehead, cocking his head to the side. "Run into a tree? Oh, wait...no. I seem to remember what caused that."

"That's quite enough, you two," Aleric interjected. "We have work to do. Kiora, bring the book with you."

Emane smugly nodded at her before following Aleric to the four chairs that now stood in front of the dreadfully beautiful wings. She glared at Emane's back, squeezing the life out of the book in her arms as he sauntered off. She hissed to Arturo, "Do you think I could hit him with a rock? I am sure I could get it right this time..."

No, Arturo thought back. *And be careful with that book, it's a thousand years old.*

Kiora started. Looking down at the book, she forced her fingers to relax before kicking at a blade of grass. Grumbling, she made her way to the wings.

Emane glanced backwards, "What? The horse gets invited too?"

Kiora stiffened but heard Arturo's voice resonate through her mind. *Perhaps one rock might do him some good,* he quipped before spreading his wings and making a quick exit.

Kiora burst out laughing.

"What's so funny?" Emane demanded.

"Nothing, Prince, nothing at all," she said sweetly. Satisfied, she sat smugly back in her chair, putting the book in her lap and placing her hands neatly on top.

Emane rolled his eyes before crossing his arms to look at the spectacle before him. "Well," he asked, "what does it do?"

A voice came from behind, "Its shows us what we need to know."

Emane turned, Kiora did not. She was focused on Emane's face; she really just wanted to see his reaction. He didn't disappoint. As soon as he laid eyes on Eleana, his jaw went slack and his eyes bulged.

Eleana was the guardian of the Guardians, as near as Kiora could tell. She really didn't know what she was. She had heard the Guardians call her a Protector before, but had never gotten around to asking what that meant. Where the guardians were tiny— hummingbird tiny—Eleana was nearly as tall as Emane and more beautiful than any human could possibly be.

She was also more graceful than Kiora could ever imagine

anyone being. Eleana glided towards them so smoothly, Kiora could scarcely believe her feet were touching the ground at all, and in a gown that looked to be made of nothing more than gold dust, glittering and moving with her like a second skin.

Emane's eyes moved from her dress to her hair, which flowed down her back in a waterfall of spun copper. This backdrop of gold and copper was a perfect canvas for her eyes, which were an indefinable, glittering blue that exceeded even Emane's. Eleana looked very much human, yet her beauty was unearthly. It had taken Kiora off guard as well when she had first met her, but Emane was going to need someone to help shut his mouth if it hung there any longer.

"Kiora, Prince Emanc," she said sweetly. "We have details of the prophecy we need to discuss."

Kiora leaned back in her chair but Emane leaned in closer. "The prophecy regarding the Solus, I assume?"

"Yes."

"Have we found him yet?" Emane asked.

Kiora choked. Eleana looked surprised as well, and they both looked over to Aleric.

"Um, yes." Aleric answered, sitting straighter. "The Solus has been found."

"Excellent. My father will be pleased to hear it." He looked around expectantly and finally asked, "Who is it?"

Aleric said nothing and instead answered with a sweeping arm in Kiora's direction.

Emane looked between Kiora and Aleric incredulously. A smile spread across his face. "You are joking."

"I am afraid not," said Aleric.

Emane leaned carefully even further forward in his chair, his eyes staying clear of Kiora. "You told my father that she was someone that might be of use during the war and that you were training her *while* you looked for the Solus."

"I know your father well enough to know that he would not have been able to look past the fact that she was a girl," Aleric answered unapologetically.

The smile had dropped off. "Her!" he yelled pointing at Kiora. "You are really telling me that the Solus is her? Isn't the Solus supposed to be able to actually do magic?! Not just knock themselves out trying?"

Kiora gripped the sides of the chair, her throat tightening.

"I assure you, Emane, Kiora is quite adept to the calling." Eleana said.

"How do you know it's her? What if you're wrong?" Emane pushed. "And you lied to my father?"

"The Wings of Arian brought us to her," Eleana said, motioning to the giant structure before them, deftly moving past the issue of Aleric's lie. "I assume you are familiar with the Wings?"

"My father explained what Aleric told him." He grumped, throwing himself back in his chair, "Have they ever been wrong?"

"Never," Eleana answered. "And I have never seen anybody pick up the needed skills as fast as Kiora has. She has a strength of character unequaled in this kingdom. Her magic is proving to be very strong, and will eventually be a force to be reckoned with." Emane crossed his arms, staring skeptically at Eleana. "She also has the gift of sight; of visions. She still has much to learn, but the distance she has traveled in the short time she has been here is impressive by anyone's standards."

"If she is so wonderful," he said with an angry flip of his hand, "then why did you send for me?"

Kiora suddenly became very interested. What did they need him for?

"There is another part of the prophecy; a part that I have not shared with anyone until this afternoon," Eleana explained. "Aleric, would you please explain to the Prince what I shared with you today?"

Kiora and Emane's attention turned to Aleric.

Before he could answer, the void in the wings cracked and turned solid, just as it had the day before. Kiora's mouth went dry and she clutched the arm of the chair, terrified of what the wings might show.

To her relief and slight embarrassment it showed, instead, pictures of her. It showed her moving things with her mind, mercifully leaving out the part where she smacked herself in the head with a rock, as if the Prince needed to see that again. It showed her finding the book, riding Arturo; Aleric showing up on her doorstep to collect her. They flowed in no order she could find, next they flashed up a picture of her sobbing on the ground, watching her parents drive the wagon away for the last time. Kiora looked away, swallowing back a whimper of grief. It showed her hanging laundry as her eyes rolled back in her head and she collapsed on the ground in the middle of a vision. Her sister paced angrily back and forth in front of her waiting for her to wake. Then it moved suddenly to a picture of Emane standing next to her, holding a sword and shield before it went blank.

It was silent for a moment before Aleric began. "The second half of the prophecy that Eleana shared with me this afternoon..."

"Wait!" Emane held up his hand. "What do you mean, 'that Eleana just shared with you'? The prophecy is in the book. You read it, my father read it."

"We read Arian's prophecy, that is true." Aleric clarified, "But he was not the only one with the gift of visions."

Eleana intervened, "This vision was of monumental

importance," she explained. "This may be the last battle that will require a Solus. As such, the Ancient One, Epona, also received a similar vision and recorded the details, some of which were missing from Arian's account."

"Who is Epona?" Emane protested. "What is an Ancient One?!"

"Suffice it to say she is a very magical being that has been around for a very long time," Eleana said with finality. "Aleric," she said, indicating that he should continue.

Aleric sighed, looking weary. "Epona's prophesy states that the Solus is not to go this alone. As is tradition, a Protector will be assigned. The prophecy gives some clues as to who this Protector may be." Aleric continued, "It is…unfortunate that I was not aware of that particular part of the prophecy earlier." He glanced to Eleana with obvious frustration. "It is prophesied that that Protector is to be of royal blood."

Emane and Kiora seemed to understand at exactly the same moment. They both came flying up out of their chairs.

"Him?" Kiora shouted. Her finger shaking as she pointed.

"You want me to protect her?!" Emane objected. "The only thing she needs protecting from is her own mouth!"

"You're one to talk!" she shrieked. "You can't be serious! He would probably push me off a cliff before he protected me!"

Emane turned to her, seething. "How dare you! I would never harm anyone!"

"Really?" She took a step closer to him, tired of him throwing his weight around. "Because all you've done since you met me is to make it obvious how much you despise me."

He laughed, stepping in closer as well. "Oh, that's rich! You march into my house like you own the place, and then have the nerve to tell me that I don't know how to run my own kingdom."

"You don't! From the moment I arrived you've been mad that I didn't follow you around like a puppy dog." Her cheeks flushed at her own boldness.

"I have not..." he stammered, "I don't need you or anybody else following me around! I was trying to be cordial, my intentions were good."

"Well, you can take all your good intentions and go back to your castle," Kiora snapped, "because they don't seem to be a doing a lot of good here."

Emane's head jerked back as if he'd been slapped. "I'll go back to the castle when I want to go back to the castle and not a moment before!"

"Of course, my prince," she yelled with an exaggerated bow, "We wouldn't want a lowly peasant girl telling you what to do!"

"You are impossible!" he yelled. He turned to Eleana and Aleric with nostrils flaring. "I'll do it. I'll be her Protector." Looking back at Kiora he sneered. "My duty demands it." He turned, his sword swinging at his hip, and stomped through the meadow, disappearing into the tree line.

Kiora stared after him, her mouth gaping. "WHAT!?" she finally shouted. Turning, she shoved the book into Aleric's hands charging off after Emane.

Aleric started to chuckle. "Well," he said, clearing his throat. "That went well."

THE DARK PEGASUS FLEW over the valley approaching a land that time had forgotten. He soared close to the earth, hoofs skimming over boulders, and his shadow gliding beneath him. With a quick turn left, he soared into the largest shaft and followed it down deep into the earth.

The rock narrowed inward the deeper he flew, and he was

finally forced to land. Folding his wings flat to his back, he made his way to a large cavern, where a dark haired man sat upon a stone throne, twirling a large silver ring around his first finger.

The pegasus approached and bowed. *My Lord, Dralazar.*

"Raynor," he nodded. "What did you find?"

Arturo and Eleana have both emerged. Their threads appear only to disappear again. I am assuming they are hiding in the Hollow.

"Of course," he said, twirling the ring back and forth with his thumb. "And the Solus?"

I don't know. Raynor's head dropped lower, his eyes not leaving his master. *I have not picked up anything powerful enough to suggest that they have been found.*

Dralazar breathed out slowly, his eyes closed. "Of course they have been found, Raynor. Why else would those two be moving around?" he said through clenched teeth.

I am sorry, my Lord.

Dralazar surged to his feet. "Of course you are sorry, Raynor! But your apologies will be of little consequence if we lose this war. If we wait until they are powerful enough to determine which thread belongs to this new Solus, it will be too late!"

With all due respect, my Lord, they are untrained. Surely we have time.

"I will not take any chances!" he yelled. "I thought we had time from the beginning, I thought Eleana had sealed her own fate. But we have failed time and time again." He punctuated each word stepping closer and closer to the dark pegasus.

Raynor bowed his head, his eyes fixed on the floor. *What will you have me do?*

Growling, Dralazar swung past Raynor, moving to a pewter basin sitting on a stone table. Running his fingers over the silver snakes that worked their way up the long spindly legs, he breathed out in disgust. The magic was so weak compared to the Wings of Arian, but Eleana had done a masterful job of whatever spell she had initiated to prevent him from using them. That was not the only spell Eleana had masterfully concocted, he thought, and he would hate her for it until the day he died. He was forced to stay here, using this basin. It was weaker, more subject to her blocking spells. He passed his hand over the liquid inside. The snake's ruby eyes peered in as it began to bubble. "Show me the Solus!" he demanded.

A shadow emerged, but that was all; a useless shape to define the threat. "Curse Eleana!" he yelled. Batting the side of the basin, he sent it clattering to the floor.

My lord, we already knew that she had...

Dralazar slowly turned his head to the side, his green eyes narrowed to slits. "Enough, Raynor."

Leaning forward, he put his palms flat against the stone table. "This time, Eleana, it will be different," he breathed out. Turning his head to Raynor, he growled, "I have spent the last thousand years hiding, creating the perfect storm for my return—an innocent people and untrained Solus. I will not let this slip through my fingers when we are so close!" he slammed his fist into the table. Breathing heavily, a thought occurred to him and a dangerous smile flitted across his face. "Come with me, Raynor." The two walked through the labyrinth that the cave system had naturally provided. "We need to find the Solus, and I would like to make a point while doing that."

What point would you like to make, my Lord?

Dralazar turned the corner into yet another tunnel. As he did so, the sound of barking and snarling began to reverberate off the cave walls. "That when I find the Solus, I will kill him."

The farther down the tunnel they traveled, the louder and louder the sounds became. Near the end a magical barrier rippled and shimmered, keeping its prisoners quite contained. Dralazar stood before it, looking at the message he was about to send the Solus.

My lord, Raynor bowed his head in respect. *The Hounds are widely unpredictable. Are you sure you want to use them already?*

Dralazar's eyes were gazing at the weapon, his eyes dancing with excitement. "Yes, Raynor, I am. Last time we did not use them to their full potential. Besides, Raynor, look at them." Dralazar turned his head to the side, a sly smile dancing upon his lips.

The Hounds were huge. At the shoulder the smallest one measured four foot high. The obvious leader of the pack measured more than five. They were all black and their hair was long and matted, their mouths were filled with excessively large canines, leaving their faces coated with thick white goo. Their eyes gleaming with hate. The leader of the pack strode through the rest, approaching the barrier, baring his teeth at Dralazar.

Dralazar laughed. "Speak, you mutt," he commanded. "It took me a long time to give you the gift of speech."

Broken and garbled words came out of the Hound's mouth. "Whaat u waaaant." Each word was long and drawn out. It sounded like a demon was trying to speak with a mouthful of gravel.

"That's better," Dralazar cooed. "I assume you and your mangy friends are hungry." The pack's barking immediately resumed as they pushed each other closer to the barrier. Dralazar held up his hand and the barking immediately ceased. "I have a job for you."

The Hounds, salivating in anticipation of the promised hunt exploded out from the mouth of the cave with Raynor right behind them. He took to the skies to lead the pack back towards the forest. The giant Hounds leapt over rocks and boulders with such ease they might not have been there at all.

Dralazar replaced his basin on the table, brushing his hand across the top, he called the liquid back to its place. Leaning over

it, he whispered his enchantment. A picture began to appear and
he could see the rocks and boulders as the leader of the pack ran
through the gauntlet of stone that surrounded the caves. He was now
looking out through the pack leader's eyes. This way he could see
the end of the Solus as if he had done it with his own hand.

KIORA HAD TO KNOW why Emane had agreed to be her
Protector. He had done nothing but openly despise her from the first
day. He was fast, but it didn't matter. Using threads, Kiora had just
become the best tracker in the kingdom.

Moving through the trees, she focused in on Emane's thread,
feeling and following. His thread felt the same as those who had
sided with good, but vibrated at a much slower frequency than those
with magic. It also seemed thinner. She had followed him for some
time before the ground began to slope downward underneath her
feet and she was forced back on her heels, using her hands to keep
from tumbling end over end. The land was alight with sound—birds
chattering, bugs humming and the sound of running water getting
closer. As the sound of water increased so did the strength of the
thread, and she knew she was getting close.

Thankfully, the ground leveled out as the vegetation thickened
and she moved her hands back to the front to protect her face
and eyes. The trees grew closely together here, their branches
intertwining above her head, and the bushes had no intention of
letting her pass. Trying not to make too much noise, she pushed and
weaved, breaking through the heavier part of the tree line. Once out,
she could see the outline of the Prince standing next to a shallow
but fast flowing river. Startled, she quickly dropped to her knees to
avoid being seen.

There from her knees, she watched him pacing back and

forth in front of the river, his lips moving, muttering something underneath his breath. He picked up a rock and threw it as hard as he could into the river, then another, and another.

She settled in, watching him pace. He walked as a prince should walk: tall and straight with an air of royalty. His features were strong, unlike Kiora's, and in the sun his blue eyes seemed even bluer, a perfect combination with his sandy blond hair. He reached back, pushing his hair off his forehead. She felt an odd thud in her chest and shook her head. It really was a shame, she thought, that he was such an ass.

Prince Emane stopped, staring absently at the river as all the natural tension he usually held dropped away, as if it had been peeled from him. His shoulders drooped, his head lowered and he looked, for the first time since she had met him, vulnerable. Kiora felt her cheeks flush, feeling as if she were intruding on some deeply personal moment that he never would have allowed himself to have had he known she were watching, but she couldn't tear her eyes away. He just stood there, looking weighed down. The posture, although not familiar on him, was familiar to her. Feeling guilty for yelling, she closed her eyes scrunching her face up, dreading the inevitable. She had followed him all the way out here, but an apology was not her original intention. Reluctantly she stood and began walking quietly, closer to the Prince, the sandy shore padding her approaching steps.

She cleared her throat, "Prince Emane?"

The prince jumped and pulled his sword as he turned, pointing it right at her throat. Kiora took a step backwards, swallowing hard, looking at the blade.

"Kiora!" He dropped his sword back to his side. "What are you doing here?" he shouted at her.

"I'm sorry" she blurted, her hand brushing over her nearly

skewered neck, she glanced back at the blade now hanging at his side.

"I could have killed you, Kiora, I can't believe..."

Lowering her hand, she repeated slowly, "I'm sorry." She fixed her green eyes evenly on him.

He slowed as her words registered with him, "What?"

"I am sorry, Emane."

He sheathed his sword and turned away from her with an irritated hiss. "Sorry for what? Telling me that I can't run a kingdom or for insinuating that I would rather push you off a cliff than help you?"

She cringed. "I judged you before I knew you. I still don't know you. Aleric has insisted, though, that you're worth knowing," she said with a halfhearted smile.

Emane snorted. "And when did he insist that? He has spent years telling me all the things I need to improve on." He reached down and threw another rock into the river with a grunt.

"Do you remember when we first met?" she asked, folding her arms in front of her. "You mistook me for a servant, handed me your laundry, and then was angry with me for not agreeing to do it anyway."

He smothered a smile, "Most girls would have done the laundry."

Her mouth twisted ruefully. Shaking her head, she said, "I knew that was the problem."

"That you wouldn't do my laundry? Please, Kiora, I have more than one..."

"No, you aren't used to anyone standing up to you."

"That's ridiculous," he scoffed.

"Really? You still seem to have problems with me standing up to you; or at least failing to grovel at your feet." *Like all the other girls*, she thought.

He looked at her for a long while before walking past her to a fallen log by the river's edge and very un-majestically plopping down on it. He leaned his elbows on his knees and looked back in Kiora's direction.

"So, you're the Solus."

She shifted uncomfortably, "That's what they tell me."

"Wonderful," he said dryly. "How long have you known?"

"I have lost track of time, the day I came to the castle. A week, maybe two."

"A week!"

"Maybe two!" she said defensively.

He shook his head, "Look, Kiora, I don't want to fight; a week just doesn't seem like a lot of time to fulfill your destiny."

She dropped down cross-legged in the sand. "I know."

His blue eyes narrowed, "What brought on the sudden change of heart?"

She shrugged. "We might be spending a lot of time together now that you have agreed to be my Protector."

"Hmm," he grunted. "Can you really do magic?" he asked with a strange mix of curiosity and lingering suspicion. "I mean, besides hitting yourself in the head with a rock."

Kiora smirked. He asked. What was she suppose to do? Focusing in on a rock near his foot she willed it to move. Lifting off the ground, it hung there for a moment before flipping him in the knee.

"OW!"

"Sorry," she said, trying to suppress a giggle. "I'm still learning."

He raised one eyebrow, leaning towards her, "I think you did that on purpose."

She didn't try to hide her smile, her green eyes twinkled with laughter "Of course not, Prince."

"Lying is not becoming, you know."

"I never lie," she said, pulling on her most solemn face.

"All right then, tell me what you were laughing about earlier," he challenged.

She covered her mouth with her hand, trying to stifle a laugh. "Oh, Sire, I don't think you really want to know."

"I do."

She turned her head to the side, evaluating him. "All right, I had asked Arturo if I could throw a rock at you." Emane sat straight up. "It was after some rude comment you made," she said waving him off.

"Wait," he held up his hands, taking a deep breath. "You asked the horse?"

"The pegasus happens to be telepathic, so watch what you think. You will be pleased to know that he told me I most certainly could not throw the rock."

"I like this horse already. Why is that funny?"

"Pegasus," she corrected. "Because after you insulted him he decided that perhaps one rock would have done you some good." She started giggling. "I'm sorry, it just wasn't like Arturo. He is normally so calm and distinguished when he talks. And you did insult him."

She glanced up at Emane. He had a gentle smile on his face, looking out at the river again. She grinned to herself, it was a start.

"He talks to people?"

She shook her head. "No, just to me."

"Why just you?"

"He didn't really explain." Well, he had tried but Kiora was still confused about it all.

Emane bent over picking up a handful of pebbles. "What's it like when he talks to you?" he asked, letting them rain down through his fingers.

"Different," she said thoughtfully. "It's like I can hear him, but not with my ears. It's just inside my head."

They sat there in awkward silence for a while.

"Well, this is nice." Emane said, clearing his throat as he shifted on the old log "I think we have gone five whole minutes without biting each other's heads off."

"It's a start." Tucking her hair behind her ears, she said, "I have a question for you as well."

"Go ahead," he said.

"You didn't seem surprised about all of this. Aside from the fact that the Solus was me," she amended.

"I wasn't." He rubbed his knees, evaluating her. "I grew up with Aleric shoving history lessons down my throat."

"You knew about..."

"About all of it, yes. Evil, the Solus. Aleric lived in the castle to watch for the fulfillment of the prophecy and to teach the royals what to be expecting. I have trained in combat since I was a little boy with nowhere to use it." He shrugged. "To be honest, I never thought any of this would matter. Now here I am talking to the Solus and have been assigned to one more thing."

"I don't understand. Why didn't they tell us?" Her pulse rose as she realized the implications. "You should have told us!"

"Knowing something and believing something are two different things. I don't think anyone fully believed it would happen again. I know I didn't. Aleric had his hands full trying to teach me. I thought it was an enormous waste of time," he said with a groan, pushing himself back to his feet.

Before she could stand, a handful of threads slipped through her. At first it was just uncomfortable, but within seconds their full force hit. She slumped over, her hands at her chest. They were dark and cold and struck through her heart with needles of ice.

"They're coming!" she gasped, clawing at her chest.

Emane ran over to her side. "Kiora, what is it? What's wrong?"

"Evil. Evil is coming. A lot of them." Her voice was raspy as she tried to speak through the pain.

"Are you sure?"

She nodded.

He grabbed both her arms, "Do you know who it is?"

She shook her head no, "It's different than I have felt before. It is magical but it doesn't feel human." She looked up into his eyes, her heart pounding. "They are coming, really fast."

"Come on, we have to get you out of here."

He put his arm under her and lifted her to her feet. She stumbled along the sand underneath the Prince's support.

"Kiora!" he yelled at her. "You have to control this!"

"You don't understand," she gasped, her legs dragging like noodles beneath her.

"You're right," he grunted, trying to pull her forward. "I don't. I have no idea what you're feeling right now. But if what you are telling me is true, then we have to leave, now! And if I have to carry you the whole way, we won't be moving very fast!"

Kiora took a deep breath and nodded, trying to clear her head and take control of her frozen heart. The threads were getting stronger and stronger as whatever it was kept getting closer.

"Come on, Kiora, get a hold of yourself," he repeated, jerking her forward again.

Setting her jaw, she willed herself to put her weight on her legs and began stumbling forward. It was only a few steps before she froze again.

"They're here," she whispered in horror

CHAPTER THREE

THE PROTECTOR

THE PRINCE TURNED HIS head, scanning the area. Kiora could feel the corded muscles in his arms as he continued to hold her up. "Can you stand if I let go of you?" he asked.

She nodded, reluctantly pulling back from him.

"Good." Pulling his sword, he turned to face the wood, whispering to her over his shoulder. "Listen carefully and do what I tell you."

His eyes scanned, looking for any sign of their attackers. A long low growl came from his left. Kiora froze, following Emane's gaze as he slowly turned to face it. Two sparkling black eyes shown out from the branches, intently fixed on him.

"There it is," he hissed.

Growls and snarls begin erupting from every side. Kiora whimpered, taking a step backwards. Emane reached back, grabbing her hand, and pulled her tight in behind him. Holding his sword out on front, they watched as set after set of eyes began emerging from the shadows of the trees.

"What are they?" he whispered, his hand tightening around her wrist.

The first set of eyes to appear stepped fully out from the trees and into the sun. Kiora's heart sunk as the gigantic black creature came into view. It was a hound of nightmarish proportions, taller, wider. Its face was sharp with a longer snout and enormous ears. But what was most frightening was the evil intelligence that glittered behind those black eyes.

Emane's sword swung towards it. "Why does it look like it's thinking?" he muttered. "I don't like it, dogs don't look like that."

"That is no dog." Kiora whispered, her eyes wide. Their threads were plunging through her heart, icy cold and dark. She could not ignore them

Drool dripped from the beast's wide, fang-filled mouth, as it gave another long growl. The rest of the pack emerged from the tree line, following command.

Emane crouched lower, swinging his sword back and forth in front of them, trying to keep an eye on all of them.

There were probably fifteen hounds, growling and snapping their jaws, but not one attacked.

"What is going on?" Kiora whispered, her frozen heart still managing to beat madly. "Why are they just standing there?"

The predators had boxed them in nicely against the river, but the pack kept its distance, each glancing periodically over at the largest of the pack. *Almost as if they were...waiting for permission,* Kiora realized, sickly. Emane began slowly backing up, pushing Kiora closer to the river. It was the only way left to go.

The Prince whispered over his shoulder, not taking his eyes off the hounds. "Any ideas?"

She scanned the creatures again, they were in trouble. "No."

The leader took a step forward, emitting a low angry growl. The others followed suit. "Back into the water, Kiora, now."

Kiora obediently took a step backwards, gasping as the frigid water splashed up her legs. Stepping back again, she gripped Emane's shoulder as the current whipped around her ankles. It wasn't only cold, but incredibly fast. Emane began backing up as well, keeping himself between the creatures and Kiora.

"Run, Kiora," he said calmly. It was the calm that frightened her most.

She glanced behind her at the river, and then back at the hounds, "No," she said clenching her teeth. "I am not going to just leave you here, your sword isn't going to do any..."

"DO IT, KIORA, NOW!" he yelled shoving her away from him. The hounds snarled and snapped their jaws in response to the noise.

"Emane!" she shouted.

He took one more step backwards, "Kiora! Now!"

Her gut wrenching, she groaned and turned to the river. The water splashed up against her in freezing spray. The river dropped off quickly, the shallow edges giving way to nearly waist-deep, freezing water. The current pushed back against her as her feet slipped on the smooth river rocks. Hearing splashing behind her she tried to move faster, hopefully it was Emane, but there was no time to look. The next thing she knew her head was underwater. She struggled to the surface gasping for air.

"Emane," she sputtered, before the river pulled her back under.

Her lungs screamed at her as she slid along the bottom. Desperately reaching out she drug her fingers along trying to hold onto anything, but the rocks were smooth and flat. Panic pushed in on all sides. Her lungs ached for a breath. Three fingers lodged under a stone and her heart leaped, but then she slipped free again. Then, she felt fingers close around her wrist, jerking her up out of the water. Gasping great mouthfuls of air, Emane shouted in her ear.

"Kiora, MOVE!"

Disoriented and coughing she turned to see the large black dogs leaping one after another into the water. Struggling to her feet and still gasping, she clung tightly to Emane as he attempted to drag her to the other bank. Slipping again, Emane tightened his arms around her waist, pulling her back to her feet with a grunt.

A frightened yelp came from behind them. Twisting, she looked over Emane's shoulder to see one of the hounds being pulled downstream. The others were struggling but making headway.

Kiora had to do something.

Leaning on Emane, she concentrated on the small rocks at the shore as she never had before. The rocks jerked themselves out of the mud flying towards the creatures, hitting three squarely between the eyes. They yelped. The impact was enough that all three lost their footing, each one falling victim to a river that did not forgive mistakes. Their heads vanished beneath the water and did not appear again.

Emane dragged Kiora to the bank, roughly pushing her forwards. She dug her fingers into the mud struggling upwards, her feet slipping. Finally with her feet beneath her she searched for something else she could use. The remaining hounds were not far behind.

Emane scrambled up behind her. Leaning on his knees, he panted, "I don't know how much longer we've got, Kiora!"

"Use your sword!" she yelled, scanning the bank for something larger than the few rocks she had already used.

Emane looked at the remaining set of ten snapping jaws making their way towards them and back to Kiora, "I'm good, but I'm not that good."

"I'm trying, Emane!" she yelled. "I don't know what else to use!" She spun in a circle, there had to be something, anything!

But this side of the bank was mainly mud and trees. A greedy snarl turned her attention back the bank as one of the giant heads appeared over the edge, his claws digging easily into the mud.

"Emane!" she screamed.

Emane took a step backwards, dropping into his fighting stance. He gripped the hilt with both hands pulling it back for a strike, but then the hound disappeared from sight as a flurry of white feathers landed in between them and the hound. She heard the hound snarl on the other side of Arturo.

Arturo's voice shouted through Kiora's mind, *Get on!*

Kiora ran past Emane, grabbing his arm. "Get on, Emane. We have to go!"

Following, Emane grabbed her by the waist nearly throwing her onto Arturo's back and jumped up behind her. Arturo had his wings spread and was heading back to the sky before the hounds had time to process what was happening.

Emane grunted. Looking over her shoulder, she saw him sliding backwards, arms flailing. Keeping a firm hand on Arturo, she reached out with her other hand, grabbing the front of his shirt and jerking him forward. He slammed into her as the hounds leapt forward snapping at Arturo's hoofs.

Kiora looked down at the pack of hounds snarling and snapping on the ground as Arturo rose higher. Relief rushed through her and she threw her arms around Arturo's neck. "Thank you, you saved us." Her joy was short lived as another thread ripped through her heart. It resembled Arturo's, only this one was dark, and cold, and one she swore she had felt before.

Tell Emane to hold on, but keep one hand on his sword, this is not over yet.

"Emane," Kiora sat up, wrapping Arturo's mane around her hands as she shouted back to the prince, "Arturo says to hold on, but keep one hand on your sword."

"Why?" Emane shouted back, moving his one hand to the hilt of the sword. "We left those things on the ground."

"Something else is coming," she said using her shoulder to push her wet hair back out of her face.

"Marvelous," Emane muttered.

Kiora and Emane scanned the sky. But it was Arturo who spotted the danger first. *It's Raynor,* Arturo told Kiora. *He sides with Dralazar.*

She looked in the same direction and saw a black pegasus rocketing through the sky on a collision course with Arturo.

HOLD ON!

Kiora gripped his mane, pulling her legs in tightly to his side and leaning forward as Arturo turned and rolled to the right. Prince Emane started to slide before cinching his arm around Kiora's waist, pulling himself tight against her.

"A little warning would have been nice," Emane yelled into Kiora's ears.

"I gave you warning," she yelled back, "Arturo told you to hold on."

Emane rolled his eyes but kept his other hand firmly on the hilt of his sword. Arturo and Raynor were flipping and rolling trying to avoid each other's blows. Emane pulled himself even tighter to her as the turns became tighter, the rolls faster.

Kiora couldn't help but notice how high up they were as her view alternated between the clouds and the ground. If Raynor were to injure Arturo, that fall would kill them all. This had to stop before Raynor got lucky. "Emane," she shouted, "use your sword, next time he flies past us. See if you can injure him."

Emane nodded and pulled his sword, laying it flat against Arturo's side, attempting to hide it until the last possible second.

Raynor attacked again, coming up from underneath. Arturo rolled again, missing a collision by just inches. Flying past them, Raynor turned for another attack.

"He's coming right at you, Emane," she yelled, adrenaline pumping wildly through her. She could feel Emane's heart thudding against her back as his head whipped around to find his target.

Raynor flew straight at Arturo's side. Arturo pulled his wings in, shooting down to avoid the impact. Seeing his opportunity, Emane struck, his sword opening up a wound on the dark pegasus's left side. Raynor whinnied in pain.

"You got him!" Kiora yelled, spinning around to watch Raynor.

"It wasn't very deep," Emane shouted back. "I don't think he's done."

Sure enough, Raynor positioned himself for another attack. He flew straight at Arturo's side again. Arturo again changed directions, flying towards the ground. Raynor anticipated it this time and changed directions with him. Kiora watched in horror: Raynor was going to hit them. A flood of pictures flew through her mind. They were hurtling towards the earth, then lying on the ground, dead when Eleana found them; evil taking the kingdom. She had to do something. Without understanding why, she raised her hand at Raynor.

"NOOOOO!" she shouted.

A current stirred somewhere inside her. New and unfamiliar, it rushed down her arm. A white rippling wave of energy leapt from her hand forming a large flat barrier, shimmering in the sky.

Raynor saw it, his wings flew open attempting to pull himself out of the dive, but it was too late. He slammed into the wave of magic as if it had been a brick wall. The black pegasus crumpled upon impact and dropped lifelessly toward the forest floor, hitting the ground with a sickening thud.

Kiora's mouth hung open, looking down at the crumbled black horse on the ground. "Is he dead?" she asked. "Did I..." she swallowed, grief nudging next to the cold threads of the enemy.

Without answering, Arturo circled lower a little above Raynor. They could see his side rising and falling with strained breaths.

No, Arturo answered, *not yet.* A small flutter of relief buzzed inside Kiora. *I am sure his master will come for him. We must get you back to the Hollow. Now.*

Kiora turned to Emane. "Arturo's taking us to the Hollow." Emane's eyes were wide, his mouth hanging slightly open. "What?" she asked

Pronouncing each word slowly, he said, "Did you do that?"

Kiora looked down at her hand, spreading her fingers wide before turning it over and back again. "I think so. I don't know how." She looked back up to him. "It just happened."

KIORA SCANNED THE FOREST below them, looking for the telltale signs of the Hollow. "Look," she said to Emane, pointing down into the canopy. "There's the Hollow."

"All I see is trees," Emane said, sounding as exhausted as Kiora felt.

"No, look," she said, pointing again. "See, those trees are different from the rest." Amongst the forest of pines stood trees of a different variety, with smooth trunks that arched slowly up over the canopy. Once at the top, a fan of branches sprang out. The trees surrounded the boundary of the Hollow, each one bending its branches over the top, making a natural ceiling inside.

Emane looked over her shoulder, "I don't see how hiding in the trees is going to keep those hounds from finding us again."

"The Hollow isn't just trees," Kiora said. Arturo swooped

gently to the right, preparing to come in through a small break in the otherwise dense pines. "It's enchanted to keep all threads inside from getting out. The Guardians have been hiding here since the last war. This is where Aleric brought me after we left the castle."

Arturo swooped through the branches, one of which caught Emane under the arm, pulling him up and backwards under the cracking protest of the trees around them. Grunting, Emane threw his other arm around Kiora's waist. Her heart did an awkward little skip and, minus the adrenaline, she was very aware of the heat of his palm against her stomach.

Landing gently within the magical borders, Arturo spoke to her as Emane slid off his back. *They are waiting for you in the meeting hall.*

"Thank you," she said, sliding off. "Emane, they are waiting for us in the—" turning, she nearly ran right into him "—meeting hall," she finished, jerking to a stop. He looked at her with one eyebrow raised.

"What?" she said, putting her hand on her hip, "I told you, he's telepathic." When Emane's eyebrow didn't move, she shoved past him with a huff. "Come on."

Over Emane's chuckle, she heard Arturo, *You should mention to him that if he continues to complain about my flying, next time I will leave him for the Hounds.*

Kiora stopped abruptly, whirling on Emane. "You were complaining about his flying!"

Emane's mouth dropped open a bit, before tossing an annoyed glance over his shoulder. "Not much."

"Emane! He just saved our life!"

Stopping, Emane looked skyward shaking his head, "All right!" Turning, he looked at Arturo, "I'm sorry," he said. "I'm sorry I was *thinking* that you nearly knocked me off with that last tree."

Arturo snorted before turning and flying out of the Hollow the way he came in. Kiora glared at Emane.

"What!" he asked.

"That wasn't an apology."

"Oh my..." he fisted his hands, "You really are..." Blowing out a mouthful of air, he plastered a smile on his face, "Didn't you say someone was waiting for us."

Kiora scowled, "Come on."

As they walked through the Hollow in the direction of the large red and white tent that now served as the meeting hall, Kiora had to keep slowing down to match pace with Emane. His head swiveled this way and that, taking in the beauty that was the Hollow.

Tiny Guardians flitted to and from their tiny houses that hung on silver lines from the canopy. A Guardian nearest them opened the door to his house as the sun glinted off the large ruby placed in his door, coloring the crystal walls of his home in crimson.

"These are spectacular," Emane whispered.

"I know. When you get a chance you should look at them closer."

The detail work was meticulous, and everything was done in crystal, silver, gold or precious stones. "Incredible," Emane breathed, looking intently at the nearest little home.

"Are these...fairies?" he asked quietly, but not quietly enough. One of the Guardians heard him and let out a snort of disgust.

"No" she said with an apologetic look to the Guardian. Leaning towards Emane, she muttered, "And they find that very offensive."

"Why?"

"Come on," she motioned, pulling him away from the irritated Guardian. "When the wars began, the Guardians were all fighting for good. Over time, a few began siding with evil and they started to change. Their beauty faded as their goodness did, changing over time until their outside was as ugly as their inside."

Emane had stopped again to look at a sapphire house that had been gilded with rectangular cut emeralds. Jogging to catch up to her, he asked, "How does that happen?"

"Aleric said that the reason the Guardians are so beautiful is because the greatness of their nature is too large to be contained in such a small package." Kiora smiled. "The same goes for the ones who fell. The darkness of their nature is too great to be contained, it changed their outward appearance. The villagers began calling them fairies, but the Guardians refer to them as Fallen Ones." One of the Guardians fluttered in front of them, smiling as he went past. Kiora smiled back with a little wave. "So in answer to your question, no, these are not fairies."

"You've learned a lot in a few days."

She shrugged her shoulders. "Not enough."

As she walked past the smaller tents where she and Aleric had been sleeping, she noticed a third tent had been added.

Guess it's official, she thought, *he's staying.*

Just past them stood the tent that had been erected for meetings and meals. She led him inside. A table stood in the middle of the room made of simply hewn pine planks. Around the table were four chairs made of artistically twisted vines. They were works of art, coaxed by magic into their current shape. Aleric and Eleana sat at the table with pale faces.

"Sit down," Eleana said. Her blue eyes were hard and she sat stiffly with her copper hair flowing down her back.

Both dropped obediently into chairs.

"I should have been clearer about the dangers of running off the first time it happened." She looked at Kiora, "But I was somewhat foolish and have underestimated Dralazar. I did not think he would be looking for you so quickly." She sighed. "At least you are both safe. Unfortunately, you have been spotted, Kiora. They now know who you are and what you look like. We had hoped to avoid that specific danger for much, much longer."

Aleric added, "Raynor also knows your thread and the Hounds know your scent."

Kiora bit her lip, clenching her hands in her lap, "What does that mean?"

"Just as it sounds. Evil now knows how to track you every way possible. By sight, by smell, and by thread."

Emane interrupted "The Hounds? Is that what those things are really called?"

"Yes," Eleana answered. "They are controlled by Dralazar and are the deadliest hunters we know. Dralazar is the only one on evil's side with enough magic to control the pack. But even then," she shook her head, "his hold on them is precarious. Their desire to kill everything they come in contact with is overwhelming, especially now. I am sure Dralazar has had them locked up for the last thousand years."

"Who is Dralazar?" Emane asked.

Kiora saw Aleric wilt, looking as if he wanted to drop his head into the table.

"Evil," Kiora answered.

"You should have known that, Emane." Aleric chided. "It was in your reading."

Emane shifted in his chair, before running his fingers through his hair. "Uh, Aleric, you know, I never…"

Aleric interrupted, waving him away impatiently, "Never mind, it's too late to worry about it now."

"Anyway," Emane interjected, "how can they know they found who they were looking for?"

Aleric answered. "That little display of Kiora's I am sure left them with no doubt."

"Wait," Kiora said, "how did you see that?"

Eleana motioned to a large basin set on the table filled halfway with water. "Much the way Dralazar would have seen it." She waved her hand over the top, the water rippled underneath, colors stirring just under its surface as a picture came into focus. There in the water was Kiora, her dark hair flying out behind her, stretching out her arm, power rippling outward.

The table was quiet. Kiora had fixed her eyes on her shoes feeling like she had swallowed a walnut. Her eyes flickered up to find Eleana, Aleric, and Emane, each staring at her. Her voice shook as she asked. "What do we do now?"

Eleana looked at them gravely. "The time table has been moved up. Dralazar knows you were with Arturo, and if you were with Arturo then he also knows we have you at the Hollow. It is only a matter of time before he finds it."

"How can he find it?" Emane asked. "I thought it was protected."

"There are those on his side who know how to find it. It won't be easy but it's not impossible."

"But how?" Kiora asked.

Eleana sighed. "The Fallen Ones know how to look for the holes in the threads, areas where there are none. When they find a big enough hole they will know they have found the Hollow. And then Dralazar will come for you."

"How long?" Emane asked.

"I don't know. It could be a few weeks or a few days. It depends on whose side luck remains."

"So, what?" Emane asked leaning forward across the table. "We just sit here and wait for them to show up?"

"Arrangements will need to be made for the both of you."

Eleana leaned back in her chair, evaluating the pair. "I had hoped to have more time to negotiate on your behalf, but it seems we'll have to hope instead that their curiosity gets the best of them."

"Whose curiosity?" Kiora questioned.

Eleana breezed past as if she hadn't spoken. "I will work on that while you and Emane train here."

"Train in what?" Emane asked.

"Magic," Aleric answered.

"Aleric, I don't have any magic."

"Yes, sadly that is something I am well aware of." Aleric said with a wisp of a smile.

"Then what am I supposed to do?" Emane asked.

The smile disappearing, Aleric explained, "You are now in a magical world, you must learn its rules and how to abide by them. You are the Protector of the Solus. You must learn how to do your job."

"What about me?" Kiora asked.

Aleric pulled the Book of Arian out and handed it to her. "You will work from this."

She turned it over, the old leather smooth in her hands. On the front was an image she hadn't noticed before. Two hands holding an orb, which glowed an eerie blue. Strange lettering surrounded the hands, forming a circle. Gently she touched her finger to it, tracing the lettering around the orb.

"What does it say?"

"'With you all hope lies,'" Eleana answered. Her voice was thick, Kiora glanced at her. She looked guilty. Noticing her gaze, Eleana straightened, neatly erasing whatever it was Kiora thought she had seen. Shrinking back in her chair, Kiora looked at the book. As if she didn't already have enough pressure.

"Open it," Eleana encouraged.

Flipping it open to the middle of the book, she looked at two blank pages. Thumbing through, she found more of the same, all blank.

"Try the front," Aleric coached. "It only prints what you are ready for."

Kiora turned to the front of the book, carefully moving the yellowing pages. As she reached the first page, words began scrolling across it, describing how to achieve a bubble, whatever that was.

"That's it?" Emane blurted. "One page out of a whole book, that's all she's ready for?"

Kiora's hands tightened on the book. Looking up through her hair, she glared at him. "Sorry," Emane said, holding his hands in front of him "Just surprised. I would have thought with as long as you two had been working together there would be more, that's all." Clearing his throat, he crossed his arms in front of him, leaning back in his chair.

"Don't worry, Kiora, his turn is coming quickly." Aleric grinned.

Emane's head swiveled with a frown, "What...?"

"It is late," Eleana signaled that the meeting was over. "But before you go, there is something you both need to see." Eleana waved her hand back over the basin and the picture changed. Standing in the water was a very handsome dark haired man. He was dressed impeccably with a smile that should have been warm and inviting. It wasn't. Snaking out of the basin came something that resembled a thread, although it was muted—like hearing something underwater. But even in its lessened state, it was icy, painful, and powerful.

Kiora looked up, trying not to gasp.

"Dralazar," Eleana said. "You should know what he looks like, especially now that he knows what you both look like. Now, you and Emane both have had an incredibly long day. In the morning we will begin training." She finished abruptly waving her hand back over the picture in the mirror.

As they turned to leave the tent, Eleana left them one more reminder. "Make sure that you do not leave the Hollow."

Kiora and Emane both gave a silent nod of understanding before they headed out to their own tents.

Emane walked in front of Kiora, his shoulders sagging. Slumping forward, his feet dragged behind him. Kiora trudged along in his tracks. The magic she had used against Raynor had left her empty and drained. Sighing, she rubbed at her eyes. The sun was going down sending rays of light cutting through the leaves at a much lower angle than normal. They caught the Guardians' homes at random intervals, sending bursts of greens, yellows, and reds around the Hollow.

Emane slowed as they neared the tents. "Which is mine?" he asked.

"That one," she pointed.

Grabbing the tent flap, he pulled it back, ducking to go inside.

"Emane!" she blurted.

He stopped, turning his head towards her, his eyes half open.

"Thank you," she said, looking at the ground. "You saved my life today." When he didn't say anything, she nervously glanced up at him.

"You're welcome."

She smiled, her hands fidgeting. "Well, good night." She turned quickly to disappear into her tent.

"Kiora?" she froze, one arm still holding the tent open. "Thank you for saving mine, as well."

She flushed scarlet red. "You're welcome." she dunked inside, rubbing her cheeks.

CHAPTER FOUR

TRAINING

KIORA AWOKE TO SOMETHING humming in her ear, with a groan she rolled over. Opening her eyes, she yelped as she was assaulted by light filtering through the tent and she squeezed her eyes back shut. Opening one eye slowly, she squinted out. The book she had collected, The Book of Arian, was glowing, as well as humming incessantly. She sat up on her elbow, still squinting. What was it doing? She was so tired, she didn't think she cared right now. Groaning, she flopped back on her bed, pulling the blanket over her head. The humming grew louder in obvious protest. How the book realized it was being ignored she could not understand.

Pulling up a corner of the blanket, she looked back at the book, the humming lessened. "You can't be serious," she muttered. Pulling the blanket back over her face, the humming returned, just as insistent as before. Flopping onto her back, she kicked the covers down with a huff. "All right, all right, I'm coming!" She rolled out of bed and reached over to grab the book. "You are the most demanding book I have ever met."

She opened the book to the front expecting to see, perhaps,

another page filled, but was shocked to see more than ten. She scanned the topics: bubbles, shields, summoning and calling. There were diagrams illustrating how things were to look and be done. As she scanned through the different pages, she noticed that calling had some incantations listed.

> *In the world of magic, most things are performed with your mind and your heart. We do not need the aid of spells and incantations to assist in this. However, there are certain things that are beyond the scope of what we humans alone are capable of creating. As a result, we have turned to other magical beings to assist us in these matters resulting in spells and incantations. Calling is the ability to speak to another person over long distances. There are some magical creatures, such as the pegasus, who naturally have this ability. But there is a way to talk to those who do not naturally have this ability. You will need a—*

"Kiora?"

She jumped, slamming the book shut. "Yes?"

"Oh, good, you're awake," Emane said from outside.

Kiora rolled her eyes, if she wasn't awake, she certainly would have been after his yelling into her tent.

"Malena asked me to have you meet us over at the meeting hall."

"I'll be right over." She listened to his footsteps as he walked away. Throwing on a clean set of clothes, she quickly brushed through her hair, grimacing as she ripped through sections that still had chunks of mud hidden in it from yesterday. Fumbling around, she looked for a clip to pull her hair back but couldn't find one. Her hair was long and thick, but fine. It was always flying in her face and tickling her nose. *Oh, well*, she thought, as she threw it back over her slender shoulders.

Her stomach growled. Hoping Malena had called them for breakfast, she headed over to the red and white tent. As she walked, the most delicious smells wafted towards her. Her mouth was watering by the time she entered the tent.

Emane was sitting at the table talking to Aleric, while Malena flitted just above the table. Malena noticed her first and broke into a smile, her red lips parting to reveal perfectly tiny white teeth.

Aleric looked up as well, "Good morning, Kiora. Hungry?"

Before she could answer, another growl erupted from her stomach. "Umm, yes," she said, hurrying to take her place next to Aleric. Pulling her chair in, she looked up to find Emane staring at her.

"What?" Kiora asked, wondering if she had something horrible stuck to her face.

He jolted before answering quickly, "Nothing." His ears turned red as he switched his attention to the back wall.

Before she could push the issue further, the tent flaps opened and the food came in carried by the Guardians. Each one laid their dishes on the table. But before they could eat, Malena picked up a small box and flew it over to Kiora.

"This is for you, Kiora, a gift from us. We should have given it to you earlier, but it wasn't quite ready."

Kiora reached out and took the gift. A simple wooden box with silver hinges on the back side. "What is it?" she asked.

"Open it," Malena urged.

Kiora looked over to Aleric, who smiled and motioned to the box. She nervously lifted the lid. With a slight gasp, she covered her mouth with her hand. "Malena, it's beautiful!" Inside lay a rather large round sapphire on a bed of green velvet. Reaching in, she ran her finger over the delicate silver vines and leaves that ran

around the brilliant blue pendant, a sigh escaping from her lips. A
chain slipped through the vines near the top and lay coiled beneath
it. Malena flew over and pulled it out of the box. "This pendant is
endowed with a special kind of magic," she said, placing the chain
over Kiora's head. "This will always connect you with us, no matter
how far apart we are. If you are in need of our help, for any reason,
all you need to do is call."

Kiora was speechless. It was spectacular. Looking down, she
fingered it, watching the blue dance around the facets of the stone.
"Thank you," she whispered.

Malena flew in and kissed her on the forehead. "Thank you. We
had intended to present this to you at a celebration, but things are
progressing quicker than we anticipated. And in light of yesterday's
situation, Eleana felt it was important that we be prepared. Now,
you all should eat before your breakfast gets cold."

Kiora slid the pendant under her shirt and tried to blink back a
threatening tear.

Aleric smiled broadly, "That is quite a gift, Kiora. Now, let's
eat."

Looking around at the dishes before her, she picked out some
berries that looked vaguely familiar; they were wrapped in a crust,
sugar crystals sprinkled across the top. She spooned something thick
and creamy that smelled different, but delicious. And something
she had started calling bread, it was as close to bread as she could
expect here and infinitely better than the stuff she was used to.
Picking up her cup, she took a drink, smiling as the bubbles tickled
her tongue. Looking over the rim of her cup, she watched as Emane
pulled his cup to his lips. He took a drink, nearly choking before
looking at his cup in confusion, and then cautiously taking another
sip. It had scared her half to death the first time she had tried it.
The food here was rarely recognizable but considerably better than

anything she had eaten at home. She ate until she thought her sides would burst. As she sat back in her chair trying to decide if she could fit just one more bite in, Aleric cleared his throat, placing his napkin on the table.

"Kiora, you already know what it is you must be working on. Emane, I will be working with you today." He stood and waited for the others to do the same, Kiora knew Aleric meant to get down to business.

"Kiora," Aleric said as she followed him outside, "make sure you read everything carefully. The key to learning this as fast as possible will be concentration. Do not let your mind wander."

Kiora nodded and headed toward her tent.

"Where would my mind be wandering to?" she wondered aloud.

AS THEY LEFT KIORA to work, Aleric lead Emane off in a new direction.

Emane kept glancing back over his shoulder. "Are you sure it's safe to leave her alone?"

"Quite safe. The Guardians are keeping watch for the Fallen Ones. As long as Kiora stays within the Hollow, she is perfectly protected."

"Hmmm," Emane grunted, throwing another glance backwards and tripping on a tree root. Stumbling forward, he righted himself, glaring at the offending root before finishing. "She seems to attract trouble, doesn't she?"

Aleric chuckled, "She is bound to, I'm afraid. I am surprised you care so much, considering your first meeting."

Emane's ears turned red again. "Well, I said I would protect her, didn't I?"

"That, you did," he said, turning his head to the side to hide his grin.

Emane rolled his eyes. "What are we working on today?"

"Two things. First we need to help you understand what it is you have agreed to do; and second, we will work on your combat skills."

Emane looked at him sideways, "*You* are going to help me work on my combat skills?"

"In a way, but first you must learn not to underestimate magic."

"I don't underestimate magic!"

"With all due respect, Emane," Aleric stopped abruptly, allowing Emane to move in front of him, "you have always underestimated magic."

Emane swung around, "I have never—"

Aleric abruptly raised his hand, palm out. Emane found himself being picked up in the air and thrown backwards. He landed hard and rolled. Coming up onto his hands and knees, he coughed, wiping the dirt from his mouth with the back of his sleeve.

Aleric calmly walked over to him and bent down to take his arm. "Are you hurt?"

Prince Emane jerked his arm out of Aleric's hand. "What did you do that for?!" he yelled, sitting back on his heels.

"I needed to give you a taste of magic."

Emane jumped to his feet, brushing himself off. "A taste?! That wasn't a taste, Aleric. You threw me a good twenty feet!" he yelled, gesturing back to where they had been standing.

"So I did." Aleric said, judging the distance. Giving him cold, hard stare, he finished, "but yes, Prince, that was just a taste."

"You can't be serious!" Emane said, still brushing off his pants.

"Very serious. That is only a hint of what I can do, and nothing compared to what evil will do to you. You were lucky you were dealing with only the Hounds last time."

"*Lucky*?! Those things nearly killed us both."

"Lucky." Aleric repeated, his blue eyes very serious. "The Hounds are harmless unless they get close enough to bite you. Dralazar does not need to be nearly that close to kill. If you want to survive, you must learn to combat against magic."

Emane gaped, "How am I supposed to do that?" he finally said, "You didn't even touch me and you threw me twenty feet in the air."

"First, you need to learn when to not be stupid." Aleric said holding up a finger. "There are times when hiding is the only acceptable option. Second, you will need to learn to trust and depend on Kiora. She will be able to fight magic with magic. And finally, you will need to learn to dodge magic. Those with magic can, amongst other skills, throw their magic. It can come out in a visible bolt, more damaging, or as a force that cannot be seen, as you just experienced. That is what we will be working on today."

"Dodging?" Emane repeated dryly.

"Yes."

Emane brushed his hair off his forehead. "You have got to be kidding." His hand dropped loosely back to his side.

Aleric held his gaze before answering, "No."

Emane stared at him incredulously, blood rising in his face. "How can I dodge what I can't see?"

"You learn how it works and what its limitations are, and you watch for signs," said Aleric patiently.

Emane clenched his fists before pacing over to the nearest tree and back. "Aleric, why didn't you already teach me this stuff? We had years of lessons at the castle."

Aleric contemplated a second before answering. "Prince Emane, your father asked me to teach you what I could. Had you shown more interest in your history lessons, perhaps I would have taken time to teach you more. But, you were always preoccupied with getting down to your combat lessons. I never had much of your attention." Emane stopped, his shoulders pulled up, hands still fisted at his side. Aleric sighed, "It is regrettable. Had I realized your role in all of this, I may have worked harder to make you understand."

Emane's head lowered. It was true. Aleric never really had much of his attention. "I should have listened more."

Aleric placed his weathered hand on Emane's shoulder. "Just listen to me now."

Emane looked into the eyes of his teacher and gave a slow regrettable nod of acknowledgment.

"Come, we have work to do."

BACK IN THE TENT, Kiora had decided to start with the first lesson, Bubbles. It sounded like it should be interesting.

> *A Bubble is a short-term protection against magical detection. The bubble will not only remove you from the sight of others, but also keep any magical threads inside of it trapped. Most bubbles can only be maintained for a short period, no more than an hour. It is perfect for emergencies. A bubble can be made larger or smaller depending on the needs of the person making the bubble. However, the more people under the bubble, the more energy it takes to maintain it, and therefore the shorter time you have before the bubble lapses and you are again visible to those looking for you. The bubble is made by accessing your magic and envisioning what you would like to have happen. Stay focused and do not lose sight of what it is you are trying to accomplish.*

"Accessing my magic, what does that even mean?"

Setting the book down, she closed her eyes, imagining a bubble as it grew bigger and bigger, surrounding her. One bubble turned to many as her mind wandered. Soon she was thinking about lots of bubbles, floating all around her. Sitting in a bathtub with bubbles from her head to her toes. Her mind suddenly snapped in on itself, realizing that she was far from the task at hand.

"How did he know that was going to happen?"

Shaking her arms and legs, she wiggled around the tent, coaching herself. "Okay, clear your mind, Kiora. Think bubble."

Taking a deep breath, she relaxed, holding herself perfectly still. Closing her eyes, she saw the bubble again. It was huge and beautiful. Different colors shimmered on its surface, reds and blues swum across it in a perfect water ballet. In response to the visual imagery, something moved inside of her, sliding out to her toes and her fingertips. She kept her eyes screwed shut, forcing herself to focus. The feeling was now leaving her fingertips. Cautiously, she cracked one eye to see the bubble-like film surrounding her. She followed the reds and blues swimming in front of her nose. A smile spread across her face as she stood too scared to move for fear she would break the bubble.

Slowly looking down to her feet, she noticed there was nothing under them, no bubble. The bubble came down and connected to the ground instead. She pointed out a toe, moving it around on the ground. Surely she could walk—it looked like she could at least. She took one cautious step forward, holding her breath. The bubble moved with her.

"YES!" She screamed throwing her arms in the air. The bubble promptly popped. "Rats."

EMANE STOOD FACING ALERIC, his back dripping with sweat

and his whole body ached. If he didn't get this soon, he wouldn't be walking tomorrow. Emane normally would have felt foolish facing down a white-haired old man, but after the last couple of hours he was beginning to doubt there was any result other than him slamming his backside into the ground.

"All right, Emane. You will only have a second to react once I lift my hand up. Magic moves as fast as thought," Aleric reminded him. "You must learn to anticipate what I am doing. Remember, magic moves out from the user in a fan like pattern. It starts smaller here, he tapped his right hand, at the point it leaves the body, fanning out to a larger area as it leaves. The closer you are to the bearer, the easier it is to avoid."

"I know, I know," Emane waved him on, "we have gone over this already."

"Are you ready?"

Emane eyed him warily. "I think so."

Aleric huffed, "Don't 'think so,' Emane, I don't have time for thinking." He waved his hand at him as if he were an irritating gnat. "You must be ready, and you must focus."

"Sorry." Emane snapped with a scowl. "I am ready."

Looking partially mollified, Aleric said, "Good, then let's get on with it."

Aleric and Emane stood facing each other as if they were about to duel. Neither one of them spoke. Aleric watched Emane—Emane watched Aleric's hands.

Emane focused, watching for any tiny movement. *It's just like dueling*, he thought, trying to calm his nerves, *just anticipate*. His palms were sweating, his heart raced, and then there it was—Aleric's hands moved upward. Emane dove to the side and rolled, waiting for impact. But none came. He finished his roll and came to his feet grinning.

"I did it!"

"Excellent, let's go again."

Grinning for the first time in hours, Emane trotted back to his place and readied himself for another round. He focused in on Aleric's hands, losing sight of all else. Opening and closing his fingers, he focused.

"Aleric, Emane!" Kiora's voice shattered his concentration.

Jerking his head up, he saw her running towards him a second before he felt the magic hit him square in the chest like a sledgehammer. Grunting, he found himself flying through the air again. Slamming into the ground, he bounced—landing first on his rear, then his shoulder, before sliding to a halt. He tried to raise his head but dropped it back to the ground staring at the canopy above, annoyed.

"Never, never lose your concentration." Aleric yelled at him "If that was someone who wanted to kill you, they would have."

Rolling to his stomach, Emane pushed himself to his feet. Limping back over to the dueling area, he glared at Kiora as he passed.

"Oops," she said, her green eyes wide.

"Yes, thank you," Emane replied sarcastically shaking his head.

Aleric turned his attention to Kiora, "Was there something you needed?"

"Oh, right!" she said, her excitement returning. "I need you guys to tell me if I got this. I mean, I think I got it. It looked like I got it. I just wanted to make sure that I got it."

Emane rolled his eyes. His back was aching, his shoulder was on fire and he was not in the mood. "How can we tell if you got it, if you don't get to it!"

"Oh," she jumped. "Right, sorry. Okay, here it goes." She closed her eyes and vanished.

Emane's eyes got as big as saucers. "What?" he looked around the clearing. "Where did she go?"

Aleric's smile was full of pride. "She hasn't gone anywhere. She made a bubble."

"A what?"

Kiora appeared again out of nowhere, almost bouncing she was so excited "A bubble. Oh, Aleric! I am so excited. The book told me to access my magic, and I thought it was ridiculous because I didn't know how to access my magic! But I tried anyway and then I could feel it. I felt it leave me to make the bubble. I'm so excited!" She ran over to Aleric and threw her arms around him, kissing him on the cheek. "Thank you!" She turned and skipped back to her tent.

Emane watched her go in complete confusion. He had seen a lot of sides of Kiora, but that was a new one. "What is going on with her?"

"I think she's feeling validated." Aleric smiled. "At least that would be my guess."

Shaking his head, Emane started to hobble back over to his position. "Aleric, what's a bubble?"

"A bubble," said Aleric, still smiling "Is something that makes it so you cannot be seen."

"So it makes you invisible," he clarified, turning to face him.

"Yes and no. It works in three ways. You cannot be seen or heard, but more importantly than that, it hides your threads so they cannot be tracked."

Emane processed it. "Why can't we just stay in a bubble then, when the Fallen Ones come?"

"It will most likely be needed to help us escape, but a bubble takes an enormous amount of energy to maintain. It is a short-term solution. You also have to be careful. A direct magical hit will pop the bubble, leaving you very vulnerable."

Emane shook his head. "Aleric, is it just me or does every rule of magic have an exception?"

"Most. It is not unlike the combat that you are accustomed to."

"No," Emane held a finger up. "Combat has rules that you follow—no exceptions."

"None?" Aleric asked innocently.

"No, you follow the rules if you want to live."

"So tell me then," Aleric said clasping his hands behind his back. "How far away from your attacker do you stand?"

"That depends on the length of your opponent's arms and sword," Emane explained.

"How long would that be then, exactly?"

"That depends, Aleric. I can't tell you until I meet him."

"All right then," Aleric rocked backwards on his heels, his white hair swinging at his shoulders. "What shield should you use in battle."

"It depends upon the weapon I am going up against."

"Why?" Aleric pushed.

Emane rolled his eyes. Surely Aleric could not be this dense about combat. "Because the shield I use against swords would be ineffective against clubs or heavier weapons."

"So then the shield you mentioned for swords, it always works."

"Always," Emane answered confidently.

"Never fails?"

"Never." Aleric smiled, "Unless it is against a club."

"Yes, unless it's a..." His voice trailed off, realizing he had walked right where Aleric had wanted.

"Hmmm, sounds like an exception to me. Shall we continue then?"

Before the Prince had time to answer, Aleric was raising his arms. Emane grunted as he dove out of the blast zone.

"Well done. I must say," Aleric said nodding his approval, "I thought I had you that time."

Jerking his head to toss his hair back out of his eyes, Emane said, "I think you're enjoying this, Aleric."

"Don't be ridiculous, my Prince, it is all in the name of training."

Pushing back to his feet, Emane said, "Let me rephrase, I *know* you're enjoying this."

Aleric laughed. "It looks like we are done for the moment," he said with a nod to the right.

Emane followed Aleric's gaze to see a row of Guardians flying towards them. They all carried weapons ten times their size, glinting in the light. They came forward laying the weapons at his feet. There was a sword; gold with a jewel encrusted hilt. A picture of the Wings of Arian was engraved upon the blade. The next weapon laid down was a bow and arrow. The bow was also gold with the same engraved image. The arrows were delicate with bright blue feathers and were held within a case made of the leather. Other fine weapons followed: a club, a lance, and two shields—all magnificent. Emane picked up the shield, running his finger over it. The Wings of Arian were on this as well. Instead of a simple engraving, it was outlined completely with delicate sapphires. He had never seen any weapons like these, not in all the armory of the castle. He turned to ask the Guardians what they were for, but they were all gone, all but Malena.

"What are these for?" Emane asked.

"They are for you, Emane." She gave a shallow bow in the air, her wings fluttering behind her.

"Me?" He looked awestruck at the weaponry laid before him. "These must be very special items for your people."

"They are special, but not to us. We made them for you."

"You made these?" he said, turning the shield over in his hands. "Of course."

"But why?" he asked looking up at her. "I have my own swords and shields."

Malena smiled. "Yes, yours are quite sufficient for dealing with mortal men. However, you would find them inadequate dealing with your new magical enemies."

Aleric walked closer to Emane. "Those who have magical powers have certain other benefits. We live longer and heal faster. It takes a blow from something infused with magic to impede that healing process."

"Are you telling me that it would be impossible for me to kill a magical creature with my sword?"

"Of course not. We are mortal. And a well-placed blow will finish us off just as fast as anybody else. But a blow that is less than immediately lethal will give us the time that we need to heal from it."

Malena continued, "Each of your weapons has been infused with magic. This will allow your strikes a greater chance of doing the damage you need them to do. Your shield is also infused. This will not only give you a fair playing field against their magical weapons, it will also deflect some spells."

"Some?"

"Yes, I cannot guarantee, though. With magic there are always..."

"Exceptions," Emane interrupted dryly.

"Yes." Malena looked over at Aleric, her silver hair glittering in the sun. "Covering exceptions today?"

Aleric nodded, trying to disguise the smirk on his face.

Malena smiled and turned to Emane, "I will leave you to your practicing." She flew the way she had come without a backward glance.

Emane was examining the lot laid before him, shaking his head.

"What is it, Emane?" asked Aleric.

"Are we going to be traveling a lot?"

"Yes, I assume we will be."

"Then how will I possibly haul all of this stuff?"

"Oh, that's right," Aleric said, scanning the items. "They forgot one."

Emane's head and eyes rolled in annoyance. "How is one more thing going to help?"

Aleric raised his hand and Emane lost his footing trying to scramble out of the way, landing hard on his backside.

Aleric burst out laughing. "Sorry, Emane. That was not directed at you." He raised his hand again, and a large trunk materialized next to his weapons.

"A trunk, Aleric?" Emane said struggling to his feet. "How is that going to help?"

Aleric was about to explain but was interrupted by an enormous boom echoing throughout. It sounded as if an explosion had gone off inside the Hollow. Emane and Aleric turned and ran in the direction of the sound.

They could hear Kiora's panicked cries, "No, no!"

They turned the corner and stopped short looking at the carnage in front of them. Kiora's tent had been obliterated as well as anything within ten feet of it. The trees were charred at the base and debris was scattered everywhere. Not a shred of the tent or anything in it had been spared and was instead floating down around them in tiny pieces, giving the illusion of a slightly grayed snowfall. Kiora was kneeling on the ground amongst the falling flakes holding a limp and bleeding Guardian in the palm of her hand.

KIORA LOOKED UP AS Emane and Aleric came tearing around the corner, tears pouring down her cheeks. "Aleric," she pleaded, her voice catching, "help me." She could see the horror in Emane's eyes, and turned away. She had seen that look in far too many eyes growing up, and they were always looking at her. Today though, his horror wasn't any greater than what she was feeling herself. Her heart felt like it had been replaced with lead as she looked back down at the tiny shape lying in her hand. "It was an accident; I don't know what I did."

Aleric ran to her side, placing his arms around her. Emane didn't move. The area began filling with light as the Guardians flew to the source of the explosion. Malena was in front and flew down to her fallen friend.

"I'm sorry, Malena," Kiora sobbed, "Is he dead? Did I..." She choked before she could finish, pulling the tiny figure closer to her chest.

Malena reached out her hand and touched him. "Not yet." She motioned and five other guardians flew in to collect the injured one out of Kiora's hand. They cradled their inured friend amongst them, carrying him away.

"Malena," Kiora was hysterical. "What was his name?"

"His name was Leo." She flew up, looking into Kiora's eyes. "What happened?"

Groaning, Kiora leaned into Aleric's shoulder, shaking. "I was practicing shields," her words were coming out in broken pieces between sobs. "I put out my hands to make a shield, and then this." She motioned to the surrounding area.

Aleric surveyed the damage with a new look of surprise on his face. "Kiora, you did all of this?" She nodded, shoving her head further into his chest.

"Leo must have been in front of my tent." Wailing, she grabbed at Aleric's shirt pushing her head against his chest. Her shoulders racked with sobs.

Aleric pried her off, pushing her back. She shook her head violently.

"Kiora!" he shouted. "Kiora, look at me!"

"No," she cried, still shaking her head, collapsing on the ground in front of him.

"Kiora, this is not your fault."

"Yes, it is!" she moaned. "I did it. I could have killed him, Aleric."

Malena flew over and landed on Kiora's shoulder. Within a second, Kiora felt calmness flowing over her, tangible and not her own. Her breathing slowed in response. Her gasps slowed to nearly normal breathing and she pushed herself up to sitting, looking at Malena who was now fluttering in front of her face.

"How do you do that?" Kiora sighed.

"It's a gift."

Wrapping her arms around herself, Kiora asked, "Why would you take away the pain, after what I did to Leo?"

Malena's eyes were sympathetic. "Kiora, Leo will be fine. I am sure they have him mostly healed by now. What you did was not intentional. Please, tell us again what happened."

Kiora took a deep breath, wiping the tears from her face. Grateful for Malena's calming influence, yet still feeling undeserving. She tried to focus on what had happened before the blast. "I got comfortable with bubbles and moved on to shields. I had made a few small ones, but they were so tiny compared to the one that I had made against Raynor. I thought I could do better, make a bigger one, if I just tried harder." She shuddered in remembrance. "It just exploded out from my hands. My tent was shredded and I saw Leo fly into the tree." She started to shake again, even with Malena's influence. "He hit so hard, and I watched him slide down the trunk." More tears rolled down her cheeks. "I got to him as fast as I could."

Malena touched her shoulder, "Kiora, relax."

Kiora nodded and tried to slow her breathing.

Aleric was surveying the damage. "Kiora, were you thinking about making a shield when this happened?"

"Yes, I think so, I was thinking about protecting us from Dralazar. And then..." her voice trailed off.

Aleric gently prodded her to continue. "What happened next?"

She put her head in her hands, "I was thinking about how he had sent those Hounds after us. I was scared and mad and then..." she pointed at the destruction, "this happened."

Aleric began to chuckle. Kiora pulled her head up looking at him with wide eyes. His laugh grew larger and larger until it was echoing through the trees. "Kiora, you truly are amazing."

Kiora felt anger surging, replacing the despair. "Amazing! This is not amazing! This is horrible and terrible and—"

"No, this was an accident." He walked over to her, grinning. "I am slowly learning that we have hardly begun to see what you are capable of. Malena, will you take Kiora to visit Leo? I have a feeling she will feel better once she sees that he is okay."

"Come, Kiora," Malena fluttered in front of her. "I will take you to Leo."

Kiora trudged off, leaving footprints in the ash that now blanketed the ground.

ELEANA MATERIALIZED NEXT TO Aleric, who was searching

through the rubble to find the book of Arian.

"Hello, Eleana, I never did get the hang of that," he nodded his head in her direction. "Materializing, that is."

"Humans can't, Aleric," she said dryly, evaluating the destruction.

"Yes, but it would be convenient." Aleric rubbed his hands, shaking off the ash. He turned to Eleana. "Haven't left yet, I see."

"I visited the Wings today. Dralazar has sent for them."

Aleric sat back on his heels, his bushy eyebrows drawing themselves together "All of them?"

"I believe so. I saw five signals go out. It won't be long before they arrive."

"And you will not join us in this battle?"

Eleana turned her head away, "You know I will not."

"Yes, but I do not understand why. And neither did Arian."

Eleana closed her eyes, "There are some things, Aleric, that once done cannot be undone. No matter how badly you wish you could."

Knowing that he would get nothing more, Aleric asked, "What do you think he is planning to do?"

"Kiora's shield against Raynor gave us a little insight into her potential. I am sure Dralazar saw it as well. It has made him nervous enough to move up his plans. The faster he moves, the less time she has to develop." She ran her fingers over one of the charred trees. "What happened here?"

Aleric smiled with pride. "Kiora."

"What was she trying to do?"

"A shield, but at the last second she thought about Dralazar sending out the Hounds after her, so this is what happened instead. An impressive accident, don't you think?"

"Very. That is encouraging. She is moving much faster than

expected. Drustan will be pleased to hear it. They are cautious to say the least."

"Emane?" he asked.

"That is half the problem, yes." Looking around again, Eleana asked, "Were there any injuries?"

Aleric nodded. "Leo was caught in the blast, but Malena assured us he will be fine. I think Emane was as shook up as Kiora, he left before I could talk with him." He finally found what he was looking for. "Here we go."

Pulling the book out of the rubble, he examined it anxiously, but it appeared to be unharmed. Standing back up, he waved his hand, "*eeno repar tow*." In a blur, everything was repaired and stood as it was before, the ground now free of ash. Aleric glanced over at the charred tree trunks. "I am afraid that is beyond my abilities."

Eleana glided over to the trees and placed her hands on the trunk of each one. The light spread out from her beneath her fingers, healing as it went.

CHAPTER FIVE

REVELATIONS

IT WAS WELL PAST lunch as Kiora ran through the Hollow looking for Aleric, The Book of Arian clutched in her hand. She found him in a clearing sword fighting with Emane.

Sliding to a stop, her panic was set aside for a moment as she watched them; they were both magnificent. Aleric moved with the speed and agility of a man half his age. Watching him, she noticed how much he had changed since they had met.

That first day, outside of her home, he had moved slowly with age. But now, he moved fluidly and with the grace of a much younger man, as if his use of magic had returned him somewhat to his youth. Only his white hair and deeply lined face spoke to his age at the moment.

Emane's training was evident as he easily countered every move Aleric made. His feet moved so lightly it was hard to tell if they were touching the ground at all. In one fluid movement, Aleric lowered his sword and raised his hand. Emane countered quickly moving his sword as if blocking some move Aleric had not made. There was a clang that sounded like clashing metal as something invisible hit Emane's sword. Half a second later, Aleric was knocked off his feet, hair flying back off his shoulders like white wings.

"Yes! It worked," Emane shouted, thrusting his sword into the air.

Aleric was smiling as he got up from the ground, dusting himself off. "Excellent, Emane. Your timing was perfect. It sent the spell back before I could counter it."

"Will that work with all spells?"

"Yes. Every spell," Aleric grinned, his eyes lighting up, "except the exceptions."

Emane growled, burying the tip of his sword in the ground. "What exceptions?"

Aleric moaned, "Oh, I don't know." Placing his hands in the small of his back, he stretched backwards, "but I am sure there will be something."

"Great."

Aleric became aware of their guest, "Kiora, welcome. I assume that Leo has recovered?"

"Yes, he is fine." She bit her lip. "Completely healed, actually."

"That's good, right?" Aleric asked, still smiling.

"Yes." She dropped her head in shame holding the book up, "I think I may have done something to it in the blast."

Aleric's brow furrowed, "Why do you think that?"

Kiora's voice started to wobble, "When I got back from checking on Leo, I pulled the book back out and..." She took a deep breath, determined not to cry again. "It's full, the whole thing." She shoved the book towards him, "How am I suppose to know what I can work on, or what is too hard? I might—" she paused, "I don't want to hurt anyone."

Aleric gently took the book out of her hand and thumbed

through it. "It is indeed full. And some of the spells are very dangerous," Aleric said. "Kiora, you didn't damage the book. The book just knows more about what is happening than you do." He held it back out to Kiora.

Warily, she reached out, taking the book back. "What's the matter then?"

Aleric had gone still, his eyes focused on the ground, deep in thought.

"Kiora, I want you to go back to you tent and practice your bubbles and summoning. Emane, I want you to continue working with all of your new weaponry." Aleric turned, heading back to the center of the Hollow. Kiora clutched the book to her chest watching him. Aleric stopped, looking back, but not looking at either of them. "Emane, always put your weapons back in the trunk when you are finished with them. That is very important."

EMANE AND ALERIC WERE in the dinner tent waiting for Kiora. Aleric sat, his thumb under his chin, his forefinger across his lips, tapping.

"Where is she?" Emane asked impatiently. "She should have been here by now."

Aleric stopped tapping long enough to say, "Perhaps she got caught up in practicing and lost track of time."

Emane shook his head. "Maybe we should go check on her. She is a magnet for trouble after all."

Aleric opened his mouth to answer, but Kiora's voice cut him off as she appeared in the chair next to Emane

"Am I?" she said, crossing her arms smugly in front of her.

Emane almost knocked his chair over trying to get out of it. "KIORA! What is wrong with you!? If I would have my sword and you did that…" Emane was so mad he started stuttering. "You people and your magic…I…why…" His mouth clamped shut. Glowering, he grabbed his chair pulling it out with a jerk and slammed himself back into it. Folding his arms, he stared straight ahead, his jaw clenched so tight he was liable to break a tooth.

Aleric and Kiora were both trying hard not to laugh.

"I'm sorry, Emane," she said, trying to wipe the smile from her face. "I was just practicing my bubbles. I wanted to see if I could get past Aleric."

Aleric nodded his approval. "Excellent job, Kiora."

"How long, exactly, had you been there?" Emane asked between tight lips, still keeping his eyes glued forward.

"I beat you here, but I couldn't figure out how to move the chair without you seeing it."

Emane slowly turned his entire body to face her. His lips were a thin line and she was pretty sure she saw his right eye twitch. "The *whole* time? You sat here for the last fifteen minutes? What exactly were you hoping to hear?"

Kiora's smile was now officially gone. "Nothing. I just wanted to see how long I could hold onto the bubble," she said, shifting in her chair. Moving her attention to Aleric, she asked, "How long before you could feel me?"

"I wasn't getting anything until right before you spoke. And even then, it was so slight I barely recognized it. You were here the whole time?"

She nodded, trying not to grin. Emane's glare kept it in check.

"That is extremely impressive, Kiora," Aleric said leaning back, "I can't do much more than that myself."

"Really?!"

Emane interrupted, "Doesn't anybody but me mind that she sat here eavesdropping for the last fifteen minutes?"

Aleric reached and grabbed a roll out of the center basket. "No," he said, taking a bite.

Kiora snorted.

"Perfect." Emane snatched a roll, viciously biting a chunk off the side.

Kiora ladled some of the soup into her bowl, taking a bite, "Mmm, this is wonderful."

Emane took a bite of his soup. Dropping his spoon back into the bowl, he snapped, "It would have been better warm."

Kiora scowled at him, "You didn't have to wait for me."

"Of course I did, Kiora. It's called being a gentleman!"

Fighting the urge to ask if being a gentleman included yelling at girls, she took another sip of soup before laying her spoon down next to her bowl. Sighing, she tried to catch his eye, which was yet again fixed on the wall behind her. "I'm sorry, Emane. I didn't mean to upset you." Emane just shook his head in disgust and shoveled another spoonful of soup into his mouth.

The tension in the room was getting rather thick before Aleric finally spoke. "So, Kiora, you seem to be in better spirits than last I saw you."

Kiora sighed, "I was, before you reminded me." She forced a smile. "At least before I believed that the book was only giving me what I could handle. But now, I am scared to even look at some of those spells."

"I understand your fear. Magic is a very powerful thing."

"You said you thought you knew why the book filled up," she said, taking another bite of soup. It exploded with flavor in her mouth.

"I have my ideas."

Kiora looked at him waiting for an answer. Aleric sat calmly eating his soup and bread.

"Well?" she asked.

"What?"

"Aren't you going to tell me?"

"Probably," and Aleric went back to eating.

Kiora sat and stared at him again. He continued to eat his dinner. After a minute or two, Eleana glided in through the tent flaps.

Without looking up, Aleric said, "Finally! I was worried Kiora was going to stare a hole straight through me."

Emane mumbled under his breath. "Better than blowing a hole straight through you."

Kiora's spoon dropped into her bowl with a loud clang. Her stomach twisted within her as she stared at him in horror. "What did you say?" she whispered.

Emane looked up to see Eleana and Aleric looking at him with equally horrified looks. Kiora was staring straight forward white as ghost.

"Nothing. I didn't…"

"I'm not hungry." Kiora stood slowly, trying to regain her composure before running out of the tent. Emane heard her sobs breaking shortly after.

"Kiora!" he shouted, his chair clattering to floor as he jumped up.

Aleric's quiet voice cut through him like a knife, "Emane…"

The disappointment evident in that one word humbled him in a way no one had before. Aleric didn't need to say any more. Emane had crossed the line and he knew it. He took off after Kiora.

"Kiora," he shouted. "KIORA!" He saw a flash of white and followed her. He ran until he found her huddled at the base of a large tree across a small clearing. Emane stood there motionless. His shame was growing as he thought about what he had said. There was probably not anything he could have said that would have hurt her more. He wanted to kick himself.

"Go away!" Kiora shouted, "I know you're there."

Emane rolled his eyes. These threads were a pain in his neck. He didn't even have time to think of what he was going to say. "Kiora, I need to talk to you."

"Why would you want to talk to me?" Kiora yelled back across the clearing. "I'm just the girl who ruined your life and blew up the Hollow." She broke out into sobs again.

Emane broke into a jog, crossing the clearing. "Kiora," he stood awkwardly behind her. She sat on the ground with her knees pulled up to her chest, her chin set on top, her back shaking. Emane knelt down next to her, putting his hand on her shoulder. "I am sorry, Kiora."

She jerked her shoulder away. "Sorry is not good enough, Emane."

Emane pulled his hand back as Kiora stood up and moved a few feet away before plopping back down. She curled her knees back underneath her and wrapped her arms around them, squeezing them in as tight as she could.

"Kiora, I..."

"You have no idea what I have been through," she shouted at him. "I can't..." Clamping her mouth shut, she dropped her head back onto her knees. Her tear-streaked face was illuminated by the moonlight. Emane's mouth was suddenly dry and his palms sweaty—Kiora really was beautiful. Swallowing hard, he looked away.

He stood up and moved closer to her. "Kiora, you're right. Sorry is not good enough. But I don't know what else to do to make it better." He tentatively reached over and placed his hand on her back. She tensed underneath his touch, but did not move away. He swallowed again, closing his eyes. He wanted to pull her into his arms; it was foolish. "Kiora, I'm not very good at apologizing."

She turned her head up, "You don't say."

Turning his head to the side, he nearly smiled at her bluntness. Tentatively, he reached out with a finger, brushing a tear off her cheek. Her beautiful green eyes widened before quickly turning her head away. He cursed himself for his stupidity and waited for her to jerk away from him again, but she didn't.

"I'm scared, Emane."

He knew he should move his hand, but instead he wrapped it around her shoulder, pulling her closer. "What are you scared about?"

"You saw what I did today," she paused and then dryly added, "obviously."

"It was just an accident, Kiora."

She shook his arm off her shoulder, standing. "It was an accident? What if it would have been you, Emane, instead of Leo that was outside that tent? Would you be so apologetic if it would have been you I blasted into a tree?!" Kiora's voice was getting louder. "I could have killed someone, Emane. I got lucky that it was a Guardian. How am I supposed to deal with the fact that if I think the wrong thing at the wrong time, I'm going to blow somebody up!" She broke down again, covering her face with her hands.

Emane stood awkwardly, unsure of what to do. "I don't," he dropped his head, shuffling his feet in dirt. "I'm sorry, I wish..."

She moaned. Stepping into him, she shoved her face into his chest. Startled, he looked down at her before slowly wrapping his arms around her. Standing there in the dark, he didn't say anything; he just let her cry. Her sobs began to slow after a couple of minutes and she leaned back to wipe her eyes.

"Kiora..." before he could finish his sentence, she gasped and stumbled backwards.

"It's... happening... again...," she said between gasps of air.

"What's happening?"

Kiora's eyes were blank and distant. "Kiora." Emane grabbed her by the shoulders. "What's happening?" Her legs gave out and she crumbled like a rag doll, her eyes rolling back in her head. Dropping with her, Emane put his arm under her head to prevent her from slamming into the ground.

"ALERIC!" Emane screamed. "Aleric, Eleana, Arturo... somebody help me!" Turning back to Kiora, he ran his hand over her hair. "It's going to be all right, Kiora."

Kiora didn't hear any of it. She was already deep within her vision.

SHE HADN'T HAD TIME to prepare herself for it when she felt herself falling again into the blackness. The first part was the worst, sucking blackness pulling her backward into her own mind.

When the light returned she found herself in an unknown place, so much different from the lush green forests she was used to. She slowly turned around, surveying the dismal landscape. Everything around her was charred and black. It looked as if a fire had ripped through the trees, breaking them off, leaving only their blackened stumps standing like little forlorn footmen guarding the lake before her.

The small lake was inexplicably boiling with steam rising from its surface. The smell was overwhelming, reeking of sulfur, and she crinkled her nose in response. This land was so desolate. The only color that caught her eye was a plume of purple smoke.

It looked almost alive the way it slinked and slithered its way from the sky to the earth, sliding across the charred land. The front of the smoke plume nodded back and forth, looking for something. It snaked its way up a blackened hill curling around the side and continuing on its way up the back. She followed its course around a massive hole in the ground; the smoke circled around the edge before it slid in and was gone.

As Kiora inched herself closer to the hole, she peered over, looking for the smoke. A roar exploded upward with a blast of heat. She scrambled backwards as fast as she could. Another roar came, sounding closer than the last, and then a dragon the size of a small house came shooting out of the hole and into the sky. Behind him, another dragon came hurtling out, followed by another. She watched them as their wings strained, pushing themselves farther into the sky, growing smaller and smaller before disappearing into the blackness.

The darkness enveloped Kiora again. When the light returned, she stood on the cliffs of the Garian Sea. She watched as another plume of smoke snaked its way across the sky, this one was blue. It dropped out of the clouds and plummeted straight into the sea. She nervously looked on, expectant of some other great beast exploding upwards, but instead the darkness began to close in on her again.

When the darkness began to clear, this time it swirled around her licking at her feet. Squinting, she looked ahead to make out the towering cliffs of the mountains that surrounded them. It looked familiar, two peaks, their

sides swooping in towards each other creating a pass
between them. There, between the two mighty mountains,
stood a gate of enormous proportions. Iron bars swirling
up and around, the two halves affixed in the center with a
giant lock. Standing in front of the gate was the silhouette
of a man, laughing.
The mist became thicker, obscuring him, and then faded,
sending her back to reality.
"Wait! No, I haven't seen anything yet!" she shouted at
the mist. It didn't matter. The vision was gone.

Moaning, Kiora blinked furiously trying to get the room to
come into focus. Not three inches from her nose, leaning over her
with anxious eyes, was Emane. Yelping, she scrambled backwards
like a crab, pushing herself against the head of the bed.

"Emane? What are you doing here?"

He leaned back a little, his eyes still raking over, as if checking
to make sure she was okay. "You had a vision while we were
talking. Aleric suggested I bring you here while you finished it."

Her face turned bright red, "You saw me have a vision!?"

"Yes, we were talking, remember? You just, fainted."

"Oh, no." Pushing herself out of bed, Kiora shoved past Emane.

"Kiora!" he said, stumbling out of her way, "I know you're still
mad at me but—"

"I have to talk to Eleana and Aleric." Pushing the tent flaps
open, Kiora put her arm over her eyes to block the sun. "I was out
all night?!"

"Yes, you stopped moaning after a while and Aleric figured you
had fallen asleep."

"You stayed all night?" she asked. Sheepish, Emane nodded.
Kiora blushed, turning her head away. "I have to go." She took off,

weaving back and forth between the trees as she went. She could hear Emane's feet pounding a little ways behind her.

"Kiora, where are you going?" Emane yelled.

"I have got to talk to Aleric."

"You don't even know where he is!"

"Of course I do. I'm following his thread," she shouted back over her shoulder.

They ran right past the tent where they usually ate and into a part of the Hollow they had not seen. Kiora came to a sudden halt and looked around.

Emane caught up to her. "Now what's the matter?" he asked, leaning into a tree. Rolling to the side, he put his hand on his chest taking in great gulps of air. He shook his head and mumbled under his breath, "You have got to be kidding me!"

"I'm sorry?" Kiora asked.

"You are in better shape than me, too."

"Too?" Kiora turned in a circle frowning, "I like to run." She took a step to the left, and then to the right, shaking her head.

"Of course you do." Emane said pushing himself off the tree.

"Shhh."

"What is it?" he whispered.

"Something else is here. I thought I could feel Aleric and Eleana's threads, but now they feel…fuzzy." Kiora frowned. "The thread of whoever else is here is overpowering theirs." She started walking slowly through the trees, looking around each one. Emane followed behind her. Then she saw it. She turned around to warn Emane, but it was too late. He had already seen it.

Emane's jaw fell slack, "Kiora, is that a…a…" he closed his eyes, breathing out.

"A dragon, yes. Turning back, she peered through the trees trying to get a better look at the dragon. "But it's not the one I saw in my vision."

Emane took a step up behind her, putting his face over her shoulder, he hissed in her ear. "There is more than one of those things?"

"At least four now."

CHAPTER SIX

DRAGONS

"WHAT?!" PRINCE EMANE SHOUTED jerking backwards.

Kiora cringed as the dragon turned its head toward them, letting out a thunderous roar.

"So, Eleana, you now harbor eavesdropping children?" Its voice was deep, male, and resonated with a melodic quality.

"Those children are who we have been discussing," Eleana answered calmly.

The dragon stretched its brown scaly neck around one of the trees to get a better look at the two humans that stood staring at him. His head moved past Kiora without much of glance to focus in on Emane. "This is the Solus?"

"No, Morcant, the other one."

Pulling his head back a bit, his eyes widened slightly in surprise at the sight of Kiora. Pulling back further, the dragon turned his massive head to the side looking at Eleana. "The Solus is a female?"

"Yes, Morcant, she is. Kiora, Emane, will you both please come over here?"

They picked their way through to where Aleric, Eleana and

the giant dragon were standing. Kiora was not sure how the dragon had gotten himself in there in the first place. She glanced behind the dragon at a huge section of trees that had been crushed like toothpicks.

Oh, that's how, she thought.

Eleana put her hand on Kiora's shoulder. "Kiora, this is Morcant. Morcant, this is Kiora, the Solus. And this is her Protector," she hesitated for a moment, before naming him, "Prince Emane."

Morcant raised his eyebrows as Emane was introduced. "Did you say 'Prince'?"

"I did. Morcant," she warned, "he is not his family, just as you are not yours."

Morcant humphed. Poking his massive face forward, he nearly butted Emane in the head. Emane jumped back, looking nervously back and forth from the dragon to Eleana.

"That was an interesting little tidbit you kept from me, Eleana."

Eleana pulled her head higher, sliding between Morcant and Emane. "It was Epona's decision, Morcant. You may take it up with her."

Pulling his head back to his full height, Morcant snorted in disgust.

Kiora could not get over how he sounded when he spoke. On one hand, the sheer volume was frightening. But on the other hand, it was so melodic and the tone so beautiful she didn't want him to stop talking.

"Morcant, I know it has been some time since you have had company," Eleana chided, stepping away from Emane. "But do you think you could perhaps try to recall some manners?"

The giant dragon smiled, exposing a very large row of huge teeth. He bent his head low to the ground in between Kiora and

Emane's feet. "I am very pleased to meet both of you." His eyes shifted over to look at Eleana. "I apologize for my *dreadful* manners," his voice dripped with sarcasm and amusement. "As Eleana mentioned, it has indeed been some time since I have had the need for conversation."

Kiora looked down at him, a smile playing across her lips.

Morcant pulled his head up slightly so he stood nose to nose with her. "What are you thinking, girl?"

"Her name is Kiora." Eleana corrected.

"Of course, *Kiora*. Those dreadful manners of mine." He smiled wide again exposing his teeth. "What is it that you are thinking, Kiora?"

"I was thinking what a lovely creature you are."

The dragon pulled himself up to full size, snapping a few branches in the process, letting loose a bellowing laugh. Kiora could feel her insides vibrating as the sound rippled through the forest.

"Lovely creature, she says! I like her, Eleana. I don't think anyone has ever called me that, not in at least three thousand years." His laugh was still bellowing around them. He raised a foot and stomped the ground in sheer delight. The shock wave from the impact rolled through the ground knocking Aleric, Kiora and Emane off their feet.

"Morcant!" Eleana yelled over him, "You are going to kill them all if you are not careful."

Morcant abruptly stopped, looking down at the pile of humans struggling to stand. Kiora pushed herself back to her feet, rubbing her elbow.

"Sorry," Morcant chortled. "I had forgotten the frailty of man." He clicked his tongue "Too bad, really. You could do so much more without all those limitations."

Morcant bent back down coming eye to eye with Kiora. "So,

I am a lovely creature. Why do you think that? Do I not frighten you?"

Kiora shook her head. "No."

"And why not?" Morcant sounded a little insulted.

"I can feel your thread, it is good. Much different from the others."

Eleana's head snapped to attention. "Others? What others?"

"The ones I saw in the vision. There were three." Kiora looked around, Eleana and Aleric looked alarmed, but Morcant slowly raised his head up, just watching her.

"She has the gift of sight?" He tilted his head to the side. "What else can you do?"

Eleana cut him off before Kiora could answer "Later, Morcant. I need to know what she saw."

Kiora began to expound the vision. She told them as much detail as she could remember.

"None of it made sense," she finished. "I thought the smoke must have called the dragons, but then one went into the sea and nothing happened."

"No, Kiora, it all makes sense." Eleana sighed. "You're right, the smoke signal is how Dralazar calls his followers to him. You saw only two of the signals. According to what I saw in the Wings of Arian, he has set out at least five."

"But the one went into the sea," Kiora said, "it didn't call anybody."

"I am afraid it did," Morcant rumbled. "The Garian Sea is home to both the Merfolk and the Merserpents. You also saw the gate." His eyes flicked to Eleana's. "That is most interesting."

Kiora was about to ask what was so interesting about that, but Emane said, "Merserpents? I have never heard of such a species."

Aleric choked, shaking his head violently at Emane.

Morcant swiveled his head over so that, again, he was nose to nose with Emane, clearly enjoying how the proximity between them was making the young prince extremely uncomfortable. "Never heard of them?"

Emane struggled to keep his composure with dragon teeth flashing before his nose. "No."

"Well, then," Morcant chuckled, "perhaps you have heard of the Rockmen?"

Emane shook his head.

"The Chaoses?"

Another no.

"How about the Shapeshifters?"

No again.

"Fallen Ones?"

"Yes," Emane said quickly, relieved to finally understand something.

"Well, then," he moved even closer to Emane's face. "I suppose you're not a total loss."

Kiora cringed, Morcant was horribly condescending. Emane's face had turned red under Morcant's mockery, and she watched as Emane's hand moved to the hilt of his sword.

Morcant's eyes narrowed at the movement, his voice changing from the melodic happy sound they had been hearing to a threatening low rumble with an underlying hiss. "So, the Prince wants to pull his sword?"

Emane realized what he had done and whipped his hand back to his side, but it was too late. Morcant's temper had snapped.

"You are all the same," Morcant's voice was growing louder, booming through the trees, "thinking that you are better than the rest. You humans have no idea what is in the world around you and yet you claim your superiority over it." Smoke was beginning to pour out his nose. Eleana yelled, trying to calm the situation, but could barely be heard above the volume of Morcant. "And you, because you were born into the royal family, you claim superiority above them all." Morcant's voice had grown thunderous with tiny bits of flame flickering around his mouth.

Eleana looked very alarmed. Kiora could see her mouth moving but could not make out what it was she was trying to say. Aleric was running to Emane.

"A thousand years I have been in hiding. Why? So that war would end. So that you and YOUR kind could live in peace. So that you could breed the Solus." He threw his head back into the air and bellowed. "A THOUSAND YEARS!" Fire shot from his mouth into the sky. It lit up the forest as far as the eye could see. Morcant looked back down at Emane. "We have waited for you and your kind to save us all, and you can't even tell me WHO WE ARE! We, who have sacrificed our lives, our happiness for yours, and YOU DO NOT EVEN KNOW WE EXIST!" He punctuated the last words, his voice thundering like drumbeats.

Kiora watched in horror as with the last words, fire again exploded from Morcant's mouth. The scene played out in slow motion. As the fire burned a path toward Emane, Aleric stepped quickly in front of him to throw up a shield. The shield had barely grown large enough to cover the two when the fire impacted, exploding off to the side. The fire continued its assault and it was clear Aleric was faltering; the strength needed for such a shield was putting tremendous strain on him.

Something had to be done. Acting on an instinct Kiora didn't understand, she raised her hands towards Morcant's head, pushing every ounce of energy she had in his direction. Just as before, when she had made the shield that had stopped Raynor, she could feel the magic traveling down her arms and out. The force of it slammed into the side of his head, throwing it sharply to the left. Fire scorched a line across the trees in the newly determined path.

Morcant's mouth slammed shut before he bellowed, "ELEANA!" His head swung back around and down to Eleana's face again. "HOW DARE YOU!"

Eleana held her hand up to silence him and then spoke calmly. "Morcant, you almost killed Emane and Aleric. I understand that your kind have short tempers, but that will never happen again if you are to work with us." Morcant puffed smoke through his nose, his eyes still flashing with rage. "It also might be worthy to note, that was not my doing."

Morcant just stared at her, nostrils still flaring with tendrils of smoke escaping. Eleana turned her head to look at Kiora and Morcant followed.

"Her?" Morcant asked.

"Yes, Morcant, her," Eleana snapped. "She is what prevented you from destroying Emane and Aleric with that ridiculous temper of yours."

Kiora felt her knees go weak. What was wrong with Eleana? She had just watched this dragon nearly kill two people and now she was directing his anger in her direction. But instead of breathing fire at her, his eyes softened and his face regained the calm look she had seen earlier.

No sooner had she relaxed than Morcant's head came shooting towards her. She panicked. Morcant bent down towards Kiora, when suddenly she was gone. He stopped and looked around for a second before bellowing with laughter. "Well, Eleana, I was concerned about a female Solus. But it appears I have now been outsmarted by her twice. Come, little one, show yourself. I do not wish you any harm."

Kiora appeared next to Aleric and Emane.

"Gone to protect your friends, have you?" Morcant asked.

Kiora nodded. "Your mood seems to change quickly," she said, her green eyes fixed solidly on Morcant.

"I'm sorry," Emane said a little too suddenly, and a little too loudly. "I need to go." He turned on his heels and stomped though the charred undergrowth.

Kiora turned and watched in shock as Emane left, where was he going?

"Emane," she called. He did not respond. "Aleric, what is he doing?"

Aleric moved to follow Emane, and then stopped, turning back. "Morcant, if you don't mind, I will leave you to speak with Kiora." He dipped in a respectful bow.

Morcant nodded his affirmative.

"Thank you." Aleric hurried off after Emane.

Morcant eased himself down in front of Kiora, snapping the few remaining trees near his tail. Folding his massive wings neatly on his back, he cleared his throat. "I must admit, Kiora, I find you very curious."

She sighed in frustration. "Why is that?"

Morcant's eyebrows rose. "You seem annoyed, why?"

Why? She looked over at Eleana. Eleana smiled and gestured towards Morcant as if to say, *tell him.* Then she too turned and gracefully disappeared into the trees. Kiora's eyes widened a bit, realizing that she was now completely alone with Morcant.

Morcant turned to see what Kiora was concerned about. "It is just you and me I see."

"Yes, it is." She tried to stand tall to mask the explosion of nerves.

"Now, back to what I was saying. You seemed annoyed and I asked you to tell me why."

She stared at him for a while before finally opening her mouth. "I am not sure that I would like to be the cause of you losing your temper again."

Morcant's laugh bellowed through the trees. "Curious," he grinned at her, "I give you my word I will remain calm. I wish you to speak freely."

Wondering if she had a death wish, she spoke freely. "Morcant, you almost killed Emane because you didn't like what he said. And now you act as if the incident never happened. I don't understand how you can be so casual about almost taking a life over something so insignificant. Emane and Aleric are not just my friends, but also an important part of what we are trying to do. And you almost took them from me!" The words had poured out of her before she could stop them.

"Very interesting," Morcant said.

Kiora was getting angrier by the second. "Interesting!? There is nothing interesting about it. You have a foul temper, Morcant, just foul!" She watched as Morcant's eyes narrowed, just as they had with Emane. "See!" she yelled, pointing. "You promised to remain calm and look at you, it's happening all over again."

"I am angry at your lack of understanding. But I gave you my word that I would not lose my temper."

"You did give me your word," she said softer, "but you didn't give a second thought to Emane."

Morcant puffed smoke through his nose and rose to his feet, branches popping and snapping around him. "Come, Kiora, I will show you what it is that causes these bursts of anger you are seeing."

Realizing what it was he wanted from her, a knot formed in her chest. He wanted her to go with him. Away from Eleana, Aleric and Emane; he wanted her to leave the Hollow.

"You want me to go with you? Where?"

"Do you not trust me?"

Kiora just looked at him, her mouth opening before she shut it again, nervously looking over to the section of trees where Eleana had disappeared.

"That is as much an answer as any. Eleana trusted me enough to leave you with me, did she not?"

Kiora nodded. She had a sinking feeling that in the situation, only one answer would be the right one.

"What about Dralazar? He will know if I leave the Hollow."

"A dragon's thread is strong enough to mask yours. If you stay close, we should be fine."

"All right," she ventured, "I will go with you"

"Curious, Kiora, very curious. Climb on then." He stretched himself back up to standing, his enormous legs unfolded in front of her. She was barely taller than his ankle.

"Morcant," Kiora yelled up.

Morcant flinched. "There is no need to yell, little one. Dragons have excellent hearing."

Kiora shook her head in defeat. There was no winning with him. "Sorry, Morcant, I just wanted to know how to get on."

He looked down at her and smiled. "You have not figured out a magical solution to that one yet?"

Kiora shook her head no.

"Good," he grinned. "Because the other way is much more fun."

His head rushed towards her with his lips curling back. She screamed as his mouth opened. Throwing up a bubble she vanished again.

Morcant pulled up short. "Kiora, I was picking you up."

She appeared again, "With your MOUTH."

Morcant chuckled, "All right, if you don't like that way, wrap your arms around my tail."

She lay down on top of his tail, wrapping her arms as far around it as she could. Morcant lifted his tail up into the air, depositing her onto his back.

This was a far cry from riding on Arturo. The unevenness of reptile skin was exaggerated by his immense size. Every bump felt like a boulder underneath her. She shifted around trying to get comfortable.

"I would hold on if I were you," Morcant shot back as he spread his wings.

"To WHAT?" Kiora yelled. The rush of wind from him pumping his wings was so loud she couldn't even hear herself. Despite that, Morcant heard her anyway.

"I don't know. I've never ridden a dragon before." He let out a bellowing laugh as his front feet lifted off the ground.

Kiora lurched backward, grasping at the uneven surface beneath her. Luckily, her fingers found a hold on his uneven scales. It was horribly uncomfortable, but at least she wasn't hurtling back to earth.

Morcant rose higher and higher into air. While Kiora was quickly realizing that her finger holds were not going to be a permanent solution, her fingers were already starting to throb. There was nothing to hold on to and he was too wide to wrap her arms around. She needed something else.

He had asked her about magical solutions, she thought back to the few things she had read in the book. Summoning came to mind. She had never even tried it, but it was all she had. Closing her eyes, she shut out the pain in her throbbing fingers to focus on what was needed. First she called it in her mind, focusing her energy on the item, trying to see it, feel it. Magic began to flow, pulling in instead of pushing out. Finally something rough materialized in her hands, a large coil of rope lay underneath her palm.

"Yes!" She sighed in relief, laying her head down onto Morcant's hard skin. Shifting her weight over to her left arm, she let go with her right. Wobbling a bit, she stuck one end of the rope in her teeth to prevent it from sliding down his back. With a renewed sense of confidence, she flexed her magic a bit, using it as she directed the rope out and around the side of the giant dragon. It swung easily out wrapping around his neck and back around the left side. Slowly sitting up, she took hold of both ends of the rope. She could now sit up on his back holding onto the rope like reins on a horse. She flexed her left fingers, moaning. Those fingers were going to hurt for a while.

Morcant turned his head slightly to look back. "You continually impress me, little one."

Kiora just smiled. She had impressed herself as well.

They flew due east, circumventing Meros, into a land Kiora had not seen before. This new land was quite barren and the only word she could think of to accurately describe it was… depressing. Her people never ventured outside of the forest boundaries and now she could see why. They flew past boulders and dead trees, tall brown bushes that looked like nothing more than a bundle of sticks rooted into the dirt. The land was made of one color only, brown. A hundred shades of brown.

"Well, what do you think of my home, Kiora?" Morcant asked over his shoulder.

She didn't know what to say. It was the ugliest place she had ever seen.

"Hold on, Kiora." Morcant pulled himself into a downward dive. Although grateful for the warning, she was sure was going to tumble right over the top of his head. Digging her heels into his side with a squeak, she leaned back, laying herself out flat against his back. She wanted to see where they were headed, but didn't dare lift her head in fear that it would offset the balance she had obtained.

Earth flew past her on all sides. It was a hole, just like the one she had seen the dragons come out of in her vision. The hole was enormous by her standards, but the tips of Morcant's wings nearly brushed the sides as they plummeted downwards. The dirt was packed down, smooth, with occasional deep gouges where she was sure the tips of his wings had clipped them at one time or another. As they flew deeper, the light became dimmer, the opening above her looking smaller and smaller. Then, the smell assaulted her and she coughed as it seared her throat and eyes.

"Dragon's sulfur," Morcant announced. "It's a byproduct of the fire breathing. I understand humans are sensitive to it."

"Yes," Kiora shouted. "It's a little strong."

"There is no need to shout, child, how many times do I need to tell you that?"

"Sorry," Kiora mumbled under her breath.

"Apology accepted. Now hold on, landings down here can be a little rough sometimes."

Kiora's legs and arms tensed even farther waiting for impact. As they approached the bottom of the giant tunnel, it curved, leading to an arched opening, which he nipped narrowly through before hitting the ground with a thud in a large dirt room. The walls shuddered and Kiora thought her arms were going to be ripped from their sockets as she struggled to hold onto the rope. Morcant walked a few steps to steady himself.

"There we are. Grab hold, Kiora." He put his tail up for her to grab onto.

He set her on the ground before reaching his neck out above her. Gently blowing fire, he lit a massive torch hanging from the wall. "How was your first dragon ride?"

Kiora massaged her shoulders. "Painful."

Morcant laughed. "Yes, I have heard it is not as smooth as a pegasus."

Kiora looked at him in surprise. "Do you know Arturo?"

"Of course I do. All magical creatures from the war know each other, especially those that worked with Arian."

Kiora's eyes lit with excitement. She was a bit fascinated with the writer of her book. "You knew Arian!"

"Of course. He was exceptional, especially for a human."

"What do you mean, especially for a human?"

Morcant looked at her and slowly lowered himself down to the ground, folding his wings across his back. "Most humans are not of his caliber."

Kiora sat down leaning against the cold earth wall. It was an odd sensation. The wall was cold from the damp earth and yet the room remained inexplicably warm. She could only assume the heat was coming from Morcant.

Settling in, she looked at him and waited for him to continue. But he did not. He stared at her and she at him.

Finally Kiora said, "You said you wanted to show me why Emane made you so mad."

Morcant let out a long sigh and the temperature in the room increased, along with the smell. Kiora struggled not to change her expression.

"Yes, I did," Morcant said, "and here we are, in my home for the last thousand years."

Kiora looked around the large dirt hole realizing that this is not where he had always lived.

"Where did you live before?"

Morcant's eyes filled with a wistful look, remembering better days. "Ah, such an innocent question, with so many different answers. It has varied greatly over the course of my life. Some places happier than others." He was lost for a moment in his own thoughts before he continued. "We lived everywhere and anywhere. We had freedom to live where we chose. Some of us chose mountain caves, others the forest, some were sea dwelling."

"What about you? Where did you choose?"

Morcant smiled, exposing rows of razor sharp teeth. "I chose to live in a valley between what you now call the Hollow and Dralazar's lair." His voice had taken on a lighter air as his mind took him to better days. "I made my home between two rolling hills, a river flowing between them, and lived there, happily, for some time."

She had flown over that valley with Arturo, she was sure of it. It was beautiful, a far cry from where he was now.

"Why did you leave?" she asked timidly.

Morcant's eyes hardened a bit, "Humans."

"I don't understand."

"No, you don't. Because after your race did what they did, they chose to forget that we existed." Morcant settled in further, leaning his enormous body against the wall. "Well, little one, would you like the long version or the short version?"

"The long one, of course." She smiled.

"You truly are a curious one, Kiora. You remind me much of Arian," he said before beginning his account. "Before the last war with Arian, dragons roamed the land. We lived wherever we chose and kept to ourselves, removing ourselves from the previous wars and squabbles that ran rampant amongst the magical community and your kind. When *that* war broke out, it was different; both sides were recruiting heavily, each one with their own version of events. Species by species, we picked sides. As a general rule, species stayed together with only a few exceptions."

"Like the Guardians and the Fallen Ones?" Kiora interrupted

"Yes," Morcant continued, "as well as humans and dragons. Despite what your kind believes, humans and dragons are very much alike. We are fickle and impressionable.

"The humans were split with almost a third following Dralazar. He promised them everything they desired. Money, power, riches, land. They believed his promises of glory and followed like cattle to the slaughter, and slaughtered they were. Dragons are not tempted by such things and as a result sided with whichever side could best argue their stance. Reasons and arguments changed daily, so daily the dragons were switching sides. All but one of us."

"You?" Kiora interrupted again.

"Yes. The chaos that the dragons caused in the battle was frustrating for both sides. You would be fighting a dragon on the battlefield one day, only to find them on your side of the line the next day. It is difficult enough in a battle to keep track of who is on what side without that. Imagine it, Kiora—a huge battlefield, through the fighting and the yelling you see us swooping through the lines, changing sides mid battle. They would see a member of their side do something they didn't like and they would switch, just like that. Impossible." Morcant shook his head. "I was the only one never to switch to evil. I never once believed Dralazar."

"That's amazing," Kiora said softly.

"I don't see it as amazing," Morcant growled. "I see the rest of my kind as pitiful. After the war was over and my side had won, I was overjoyed and celebrated with the victors. Unfortunately, all of the very recently converted dragons celebrated as well. If they switched sides during battle, you can imagine how fast they switched sides once a conclusion had been reached," he growled. "They cheered and blew plumes of fire into the air as if they had been fighting for good the entire time.

"The humans, however, could not forget the sight of the dragons on the battlefield. Each had been attacked in one way or another. After the battle, under order of the King of Meros, they set out to destroy any remaining sources of evil, including the dragons, all dragons. It was impossible to know which dragons had done what, so we were all to be brought to justice. I had no choice, Kiora. Those of us left were forced to flee and hide. The humans were methodical; searching everywhere a dragon had been known to live. The solution was to live where no dragon had ever lived, and here I am."

"How many of you are left?"

"I am not sure. If I had to guess, it would be under ten."

Kiora looked confused "Don't you keep in touch with others of your kind?"

"No." He shook his enormous head. "Although they were quick to switch after the victory, once the extermination began, they fell firmly onto Dralazar's side. I fear their fickle ways may have been cured with the threat of extinction."

"And yet you remain on our side?" Kiora asked incredulously.

"Yes," he snorted, as if even he found it ridiculous.

"Why have you stayed true?" Kiora asked, pulling her knees up to her chest, fascinated with the tale.

"The choices that the humans made, including their choice to move dragons into the source of myths and legends, did not change what I knew to be true."

"But you got so mad at Emane back at the Hollow.'""

He stood up and stretched. "I said it didn't make it less true. I didn't say that it didn't make me angry."

Kiora was quiet for a while. "So, what is it that you believe?"

Morcant looked down at her from his full height. Kiora felt very small.

"Arian taught me about the power of goodness. He showed me how powerful good magic was because of its source. And I saw Dralazar on that battlefield." His teeth snapped together. "He would promise them the world, but would throw them to their enemies if he thought it would benefit him." Morcant stretched his neck out and rolled his head, stretching and pulling in each direction. Then he settled back down to the ground, heaving a large sigh as an old man whose body has passed its prime. "But, little one, I did not bring you all the way here just to talk about me. I would like to hear about you."

"I am not very exciting."

"Exciting or not, you are the Solus. And as such, you must have certain qualities that qualify you."

Kiora's stomach knotted up, she still had not figured out what it was about her that had qualified her for this. And although excited about her new-found abilities, she was troubled heavily with feelings of inadequacy.

"I don't have much to tell you. I didn't know I had magic until a few weeks ago."

"Very interesting. You have progressed rapidly," Morcant began. But then his head snapped to attention.

"What?" Kiora started to ask, but Morcant silenced her with a look.

He slowly shook his head back and forth and let out a slow "Shhhhh…" Morcant stood, spreading his wings, and shot out of the hole.

Kiora watched him in utter confusion. She strained her ears to hear what was going on, but heard nothing.

DRALAZAR SAT BACK IN his throne room, waiting for a reply from his smoke summons. His mind replaying the moment Kiora threw a shield strong enough to stop a pegasus. It should not have been possible, not without extensive training at least, and yet he had watched their escape through the pack leader's eyes.

"Vitraya!" His voice bellowed through the caves. He needed to find where the Solus was hiding and flush her out. They had to ferret out the Hollow.

Vitraya flew in, her wings black as night with hair to match.

"Yes, my lord," her voice was dark and cold.

"I need the Fallen Ones' assistance in finding the Guardians."

She looked at him intently; her eyes were so dull it was difficult to tell if they were green or gray. "She is with the Guardians?" she spat.

"Of course she is with the Guardians," he spun the heavy silver ring around his finger grinning at her, "I hope your jealousy will speed your hunt."

Vitraya hissed, throwing her stringy black hair over her shoulders.

Dralazar continued. "Raynor is not picking up any magical threads and the Hounds cannot get a scent."

"That does not mean that she is with the Guardians. There are other ways of masking those things."

"Yes, Vitraya, there are," he spat back at her, his voice rising with carefully controlled anger. "I do not appreciate being questioned."

"Of course, my lord," Vitraya said, dipping her head. Her heavily jeweled dress sparkled with each movement.

"I want the Guardians found and their defenses brought down."

"We can bring them down, but only for a few minutes."

"I understand. I want you to find where they are hiding. Then I want you to come back here."

"My lord?"

He leaned forward, slowly enunciating his words, "I want the Solus." Dropping back into his chair, he finished, "After you find where the Hollow is, you will come back here, and then we will attack together. We must make the most of the few moments that we will have."

"Why does my lord not come with us now?"

His anger broke and he rose out of his chair, "I told you I will not be questioned!" Sitting down, he took a deep breath and spoke through clenched teeth, "I will not be alone when you return. Now GO!"

Vitraya bowed and flew out of the throne room.

"Insolent little monster," Dralazar grumbled. Once his forces found the Hollow, Eleana could pose a problem; one that he had already anticipated. The dragons were on their way, and would provide more than enough firepower to distract Eleana during the attack. Then Dralazar would be free to do what he needed to do— rid himself of the Solus.

As he turned to go, already celebrating his victory, a vision stopped him in his tracks. Pushing the vision outward, he watched. What he saw brought laughter bubbling to the surface. He would go to Hollow, for the pleasure of destroying it, or more appropriately, the pleasure of watching Eleana's devastation as he destroyed it. But it seemed the Solus was somewhere else entirely. A problem all too easily dealt with.

CHAPTER SEVEN

DISCOVERED

ALERIC CHASED AFTER EMANE as he stomped back through the woods. "Emane!" Aleric shouted.

"I don't want to talk, Aleric," he shouted back over his shoulder.

Aleric was beginning to tire of this game. The young prince refused to have an honest conversation with him and it was becoming a detriment to the cause. "Emane, I need you to stop or I will stop you," Aleric shouted forward.

Aleric hit a nerve. Emane stopped dead in his tracks, frozen, his shoulders rising and falling with heaving breaths.

"Emane," Aleric began.

Emane whirled around, "You will stop me! Of course you will," he yelled gesturing wildly, "because you can! Because I, " he poked himself in the chest, "am nothing but an insignificant human who can't even do magic. I am useless, helpless and now am not even allowed my own free will." He pointed accusingly at Aleric. "If I don't want to talk, you will stop me. If I say something a dragon doesn't like, he almost sets me on fire. If I get too close to Kiora on an off day, she blows me up. I can't compete with this magic!"

Emane turned, stomping away. Aleric stepped forward ready to intervene when Emane whirled back on him.

"Oh, and I am supposed to be the Protector of the Solus, so you gave me a magic sword!" he yelled, shaking his sheathed sword at his waist. "Which is useless if am picked up, thrown, blown up or any matter of magical defenses, before I get within a hundred feet of them. What do you want from me, Aleric? You have asked the impossible and don't understand why I don't want to talk?!" He threw back his head, laughing bitterly. "All I have wanted to do since the day I have arrived is to tell you 'I quit,'" Emane deflated, "but I can't. And then I ask myself, for what? So I can fight the unwinnable fight?"

"Is that what you think this is?" Aleric asked. "Unwinnable?"

His head and eyes rolled back in a look of exasperation Aleric had seen far too many times at the castle.

"YES! Aleric! Have you even listened to a word I said?"

"Of course I have, Emane, and I can understand how you feel. But I don't understand why it is that you do not understand more history than you do."

He threw his hands into the air. "Really, Alcric, I just poured my heart out to you and you tell me that I need a history lesson!"

"Come with me, Emane."

"What if I don't want to come with you?"

"You do." Aleric turned and walked away.

"Aleric, I am not coming!"

Aleric kept walking

"Aleric...I'm not!"

Aleric didn't even flinch. He prodded his way through the forest smiling, making sure not to glance backwards. It took a little longer than he thought, but he heard the Prince crashing through the foliage behind.

"Crazy old man," Emane muttered as he shoved branches out of his way.

They soon entered back into the clearing, still charred and smoking from dragon fire. "What are we doing?" Emane asked.

"Waiting," Aleric replied.

Emane was far past exasperated. "For what?"

"Arturo."

"The pegasus? He doesn't even know we're here!"

"It is truly sad how little you pay attention, you must work on that. Arturo speaks telepathically. I called him earlier."

"What! Kiora said that she was the only one who could talk to Arturo." Emane objected.

"No, Kiora is the only human with whom Arturo can speak. He can hear everyone's thoughts, human or not. You would do good to remember these things. You never know when knowledge will be the thing that saves you."

Aleric had to restrain from laughing as he could see Emane searching for one of his usual snappy retorts. Before he could find one, Aleric felt Arturo's thread approaching. "There he is," he said, pointing to the sky.

Arturo soared gracefully into the clearing and landed silently in front of Aleric. "We need to take the Prince to the Hall of Protectors."

Arturo didn't move, but locked eyes with the old man.

"I can't understand you Arturo, but I am guessing you do not agree."

Arturo nodded his head and stamped his feet.

"I think I can hold a bubble long enough to get us within range of the hall. Once we are there, the natural magic will take over and shield us for the rest of the trip."

Arturo didn't budge.

"Would you like me to make sure he doesn't see the way there?"

Arturo nodded again.

"Very well, can we go then?"

Arturo nodded again with a disgusted snort. Despite his displeasure, he turned to allow Aleric and Emane to get on. Aleric put up a bubble before muttering his second spell. Emane grabbed him from behind.

"Aleric, what is going on? I can't see."

"It's just temporary. I can't let you see how to get to the hall."

"Why not?" he said, sounding like a petulant child. "I know how to get to everywhere else."

"The Hollow and the Hall of Protectors are not exactly the same."

"You think I will tell?" Emane asked, somewhat offended, "Have I not proven my loyalty yet?"

"No, prince, I am not afraid you will tell, I am afraid someone will take the knowledge from you themselves."

Emane was silent for a while. "They can do that?"

"Yes, and worse."

They flew in silence for ten minutes before Emane spoke again. "Aleric?"

"Yes?" Aleric said weakly.

"What is this place, the one we are going to?"

"Emane," he groaned, "I will tell you when we arrive, if you don't mind. This bubble is taking an enormous amount of effort."

"Are you all right?"

"Fine," Aleric grunted, again wiping the sweat from his brow.

It was approaching fifteen minutes since they left. Aleric had laid himself down on Arturo's neck, sweat poured down his face. He clenched Arturo's mane, squeezing his eyes shut, forcing out every bit of magic he could.

"How much longer?" Emane asked.

"Soon."

Within thirty seconds, Aleric knew he was losing it. The film on his bubble was looking thinner.

We are almost out of time, Aleric thought to Arturo.

Thankfully, he felt Arturo picking up speed as they sloped downward heading into the last mountain range that held the Hall of Protectors. He looked around Arturo's head to watch for the telltale rock formation signaling the entrance into the area protected by magic. They were near the borders of the land now, mountains of ever-increasing height pushed back from this, the last passable canyon.

Two rocks jutted out on either side of the canyon, looking remarkably like the Wings of Arian. They swooped gently towards each other making a small archway by which to enter. He kept his eyes fixed upon them focusing all of his energy into the bubble. If he lost it now, they might as well send Dralazar a map. As they crossed under the arch, Aleric dropped the bubble and Emane's blindness.

EMANE YELPED BEHIND HIM as the light returned.

"Aleric," he complained. "You could have warned me." Emane rubbed his eyes, moving his hands away slowly. He blinked furiously and it was a few seconds before he could make out Aleric's shape slumped over in front of him.

"Aleric?" he did not get a response. "Aleric!" He reached forward shaking him as he yelled. "Aleric, are you okay?"

Aleric weakly nodded his head. "I will be fine," he wheezed, "I am tired, that's all."

Emane eyed him, checking for signs of distress. "You don't look tired, Aleric, you look half dead."

Aleric pushed himself up off Arturo's neck, trying to sit back up, but his arms shook with the effort. Emane put his hands on Aleric's shoulders to steady him.

"You need to rest. Lay back down until we get there."

Aleric lowered himself back onto Arturo's neck without objection.

They were surrounded by towering reddish-gold colored cliffs, stretching up for hundreds of feet. Down below was a riverbed that had long since dried up. Emane had no idea where they were.

"Are you sure you are okay?" Emane pushed.

"I will be fine. I am an old man, you know, magic helps keep me young. When I use large quantities of it, I am afraid I begin to feel my age for a time."

"Can you get it back? The magic?"

"I can't get it back, no. But my body will reproduce what it is I have lost."

"Your body 'produces' magic?"

"Yes and no. I can't make it by myself. But my body is capable of pulling it from nature to produce what I need. That is why some of us can do magic and others cannot."

"I am not capable of it?"

"Correct. Much like I am not capable of fighting in a proper knight's duel."

"I am sure you could if you trained."

"I am afraid not," Aleric corrected him. "I was always plagued by weak wrists and poor coordination. I could no more hold that lance on the back of a horse than I could fly to the moon. I was not born equipped to handle that." Aleric was starting to regain his color.

Emane snorted, "It doesn't seem like a fair trade, now, does it?"

Aleric cautiously pushed himself up. "I suppose that depends on how you look at it," he said glancing at Emane.

"You can't be serious, Aleric. You can make magic out of thin air. I can hold a lance."

"You never seem to look at the whole picture."

Emane rolled his head popping his neck as he went. "All right then, tell me what I am missing."

"You have many natural qualities and gifts which you are responsible to use. You also have been entrusted with a kingdom, a grand gift," he paused for a second, breathing in deeply as the color slowly returned to his face. "And as you well know, with gifts come much responsibility. You need to reevaluate what it is you have, and what it is you covet."

Emane was silent for a time.

Aleric interrupted his thoughts. "Hold on, we are going down."

Arturo banked sharply and headed straight down to the riverbed. Emane gripped Aleric's shoulders, squeezing his knees tight around Arturo's barreled side, while Aleric held tightly onto Arturo's mane. They were heading straight toward the earth and Emane could feel the terror rising in his throat. They were on a collision course with the ground. Emane screwed his eyes shut swallowing a scream, but impact never came. He opened his eyes to see that they were not in the canyon anymore, but in a large strangely lit cavern.

He slid off of Arturo's back looking cautiously around. "Aleric, how did we get in here?"

"The entrance was enchanted to look like its surroundings. So if you would like the true answer, we flew through the front door," he groaned as he slid off of Arturo.

As Emane took in his surroundings, he began to feel at peace.

Something about this place touched his very soul. He was feeling warm and peaceful like he had been wrapped in a warm blanket on a cold day. The whole place was glowing with light and yet he could find no source for it. Each wall was dotted with portraits meticulously painted and beautifully framed. Emane had never seen such beautiful craftsmanship in the entire kingdom. He walked slowly from one painting to the next. The artist was the same, but the subjects varied widely. There were humans, Guardians, and other species he did not recognize.

"Aleric, what…what is this place?" was all Emane could manage to ask. The questions were swirling too fast in his mind to vocalize them.

"This is the Hall of Protectors. You are looking at the Protectors of the past, immortalized in this place. The rest of the world may have forgotten them, but we have not."

"I have only heard mention of one battle, but there are probably fifty pictures here," Emane said, poring over the paintings in front of him.

"There have been many battles over the course of our history. As soon as the split was made between good and evil, there have been conflicts and battles. To keep the balance in check, a Solus and a Protector were needed. The battles used to be fierce, but short lived. There were some years where two and three Soluses were called," he shrugged. "Then there were stretches of peace. Ten, maybe twenty years, and then Dralazar would grow restless and make a bid for power again. The last battle was different.,Dralazar would not give in and the battle stretched on for years. When Arian secured victory, much of the valley's population was decimated, both magical and not. It was then that Arian made his prophecy that there would be a thousand years of peace. And now, we have you. What should be our final Protector, if the prophecy holds true.

Emane wanted to be angry—lately any mention of the Solus and their Protector usually procured that reaction. But there was something about this place that inexplicably kept him calm. He marveled at the feeling.

"Why are they all so different?" Emane asked, still looking at the pictures. "I can see no similarities amongst these portraits."

"Of course not," Aleric answered. "Each Solus is chosen based upon their individual abilities and what is needed for that time and battle. In relation, the Protector is chosen based upon the Solus's weaknesses. Therefore, it requires a different type of Protector each time."

"Are you trying to tell me that I am here to make up Kiora's weakness?"

"Yes."

Emane's voice was thick and hard as he asked with disgust, "What weaknesses?"

Aleric's eyes softened as he looked at the young prince. He motioned to a large stone bench in the middle of the cavern.

"Please come and sit." As they walked over, Aleric put his arm on his shoulder. "Do you really not see her weaknesses?" Aleric asked.

Emane plopped himself onto the bench. "No, I don't. She's…" he paused. "Incredible," he said flatly.

Aleric smiled. "Yes, she is that. I have never seen anything like her."

"Thanks, Aleric, you're *very* helpful." Emane put his elbows on his knees, shaking his head.

"Being incredible does not make her perfect. Kiora has many weaknesses, Emane. Weaknesses that she will need your help with. If you are not there to balance her weaknesses, she will fall; and if she falls, all is lost."

"I still don't see what her weaknesses are. Believe me, I've looked."

"Well, for one thing, she can't fight."

"What does she need that for?,She could do whatever she wanted with a flip of her hand."

"Not exactly," Aleric explained. "Using magic, especially high levels for long periods of time, is exhausting, as you just saw. There is only so much you can do before other methods are needed. In the past, both magic and common warfare has been used. Kiora is the first female Solus, and although she is an amazing source of magic, she lacks tremendously in other ways."

"You need me to fight for her?"

"Yes, among other things."

"What 'other things,' Aleric?" Emane's voice rose before the peacefulness of the cavern calmed him again.

"Emane," Aleric looked him in the eyes. "Kiora will need your strength in so many ways. Not just physically either. She will need your emotional strength, your capacity to deal with pressure. Your understanding of having the weight of the world placed on your shoulder without anybody asking whether you wanted it or not." Clapping his hand on the prince's shoulder, Aleric spoke from his heart. "She needs you to stop feeling inadequate. These feelings of inadequacy are crippling you. If you allow those feelings to stay in your heart, evil will use it and twist it until they have completely incapacitated you. And then you will be useless—not only to her, but to the entire kingdom."

Aleric's words pierced Emane to his core. He could feel the wall that he had so carefully constructed crumbling away.

"Aleric," a soft feminine voice floated through the chamber. It was dreamlike and melodic.

Emane looked at Aleric in confusion.

"Come, she would like to meet you."

"Who?"

"Epona. She is one of the last remaining Ancient Ones." To Emane's confused look, Aleric jogged his memory, "I would have thought you would have remembered her as she is the one that prophesied about you in particular."

KIORA COULDN'T HEAR ANYTHING from above, but she could feel a thread—dark, cold and dragon. A tremendous boom sent her scrambling to her feet as the second dragon landed overhead.

"Get out!" Morcant roared above. "You are not welcome here."

"What's the matter, Morcant?" taunted the other.

This thread was new to her, but it was clear, both by Morcant's objections and the darkness of the thread, it was not a friend. Their booming dragon voices carried easily down the hole, letting her hear every bit of the conversation.

"Jarland, I am warning you!"

"What, Morcant? Are you going to fight me?" The taunting thickened, becoming even more condescending.

"What do you want, Jarland?" Kiora could hear Morcant attempting to rein in his temper.

There was silence. Kiora strained to hear.

"Aren't you going to invite me in, Morcant?"

Kiora's heart stopped.

"No, Jarland, I'm not—" He was interrupted by the sound of wings and Kiora heard him bellow, "No!"

Jarland was coming in. Kiora threw up her bubble just as his snout appeared. She watched in horror as his enormous body filled the room. She recognized him from her vision. This was one of the dragons that had answered Dralazar's call.

His black beady eyes scanned the room, causing Kiora's knees to shake. Not only was Jarland massive, but that good feeling she had with Morcant was gone. Jarland's thread was cold and dark, squeezing her chest.

"Focus!" Kiora yelled at herself. If she allowed herself to focus on Jarland's thread, she would lose the bubble. And right now, her bubble was probably the only reason she was still alive. Jarland moved into the room sucking in air through his nose. Then he started clicking his tongue and shaking his head. Morcant came in right behind him.

"Jarland!" he roared, "GET OUT OF MY HOME."

"Tsk-tsk, Morcant, don't get so upset," he chided. "It's been so long, my friend. I've missed you." His smile was mocking and it made Kiora's stomach flip.

Morcant snapped as he circled the larger dragon. "I was under the impression that I was not welcome with my kind anymore."

Jarland clicked his tongue again. "Oh, Morcant, I was on my way to welcome you back to the herd. But..." he smiled.

Morcant rolled his eyes, "But what, Jarland?"

Jarland pulled in another deep breath through his nose.

Morcant flinched as he realized what Jarland was doing. He roared, shoving Jarland with his chest, pushing him into the wall. Jarland shoved back, his eyes flashing.

"Morcant, your house stinks. It smells like a human has been here. Can you explain that?"

"I don't need to explain that." Morcant went to charge Jarland again, but Jarland was ready for him this time. He planted his feet and puffed out his chest. They collided with a thunderous noise. The walls and the floor shook knocking Kiora off her feet. She struggled to keep her bubble from popping as she hit the ground. Morcant roared in anger.

"Where did she go, Morcant?" Jarland yelled. "I know you have the Solus. Dralazar foresaw it."

Kiora gasped. *Dralazar has the gift of sight!* She thought back to that day in the forest when Malena explained that she and Dralazar would have similar abilities. Her heart dropped. Kiora had hoped her gift offered her an advantage, but it appeared that it was just going to keep them on an even field.

"Don't you mention his name in my presence!" Morcant roared back.

Jarland snapped his jaws in front of Morcant's face. "Where is she?"

"She's gone, Jarland, you're too late."

"Are you sure?"

"YES!" Morcant snapped his jaws in front of Jarland's face. "You missed her."

Jarland's lips peeled back from his teeth in a disgusting grin. "Well, then, you won't mind if I heat this place up a little bit." He turned away from Morcant, putting his body between him and the rest of the cavern. Puffing his chest up, he turned his head to the left side of the cavern. Fire blazed into the room, moving slowly towards Kiora.

Kiora and Morcant both screamed at the same time, "NO!"

Kiora dropped her bubble, backed herself against the wall and threw up a shield with everything she had left.

Morcant watched in horror as the fire moved across the room. And then he saw the fire unable to penetrate one spot in the room, sheeting off of something invisible. It was pouring off and around the sides of a giant shield.

Jarland stopped. "There you are," he sung.

Kiora grabbed the sapphire the Guardians had given her and sent out a frantic cry for help.

CHAPTER EIGHT

DRAGON'S HEART

EMANE AND ALERIC ENTERED a chamber at the end of the passageway. In the center of the room stood a large feminine throne. Rounded edges, delicate scrolling; a throne fit for a queen. Sitting in it was a very pleasant looking woman whose face Emane had seen once before, telling Eleana who the Protector was. She stood, smiling gently, and made her way towards them. She carried herself in a way that spoke of age and wisdom. And yet, she didn't look nearly as old as Aleric. Her hair was starting to turn white, and her face held only a few wrinkles around her eyes and the corners of her mouth.

"Aleric," she said holding her arms out to him.

Aleric stepped ahead of Emane. Dropping to one knee, he took her hand with both of his, bowing his head.

"It has been a long time, Aleric," she said, smiling down at him.

"It has," Aleric admitted. Standing, he kept her hand in his. "My grandfather would be very disappointed."

Emane glanced upwards, amazed by the soaring ceiling, a perfect dome cut from the rock. The walls gently sloped down until they met with the floor; leaving the room a seamless circle. Even the multiple doorways spread around the circle were smooth and rounded in shape. Everything was lit by soft white lights that floated inexplicably through the cavern. He stared at them, they were hypnotic. Each light moved slightly, as if bouncing on the end of an invisible thread, and was surrounded by a faint outlining of pink.

"Emane?"

Emane jumped, pulling his eyes back down from the lights. Aleric was gone. He looked behind him quickly and then back to Epona, who stood before him, still smiling.

"Aleric has left us so that I might speak with you alone." Epona walked towards him, Emane shifted nervously. Placing both hands on his shoulders, Epona smiled gently before leaning in to kiss him on one cheek, and then the other. His chest burned and his throat tightened under a feeling of such warmth and peace as he had never before known. He wanted to bottle it up, keep it with him forever.

"Come," Epona motioned to him. "Sit." Turning, she headed back to the only seat in the room, her throne. Wondering where it was she wanted him to sit, Emane awkwardly made his way behind her. Near the center of the room Epona passed her hand over a circular symbol in the floor out of which silently rose a stone chair, simple in its design. Sitting down, he placed his hands on his legs, nervously flexing his fingers.

Gently lowering herself back into her throne, she asked, "I was eavesdropping on your earlier conversation with Aleric. I apologize."

Emane's eyebrows furrowed in confusion, what was he suppose to say?

"Aleric is correct, Emane, your strengths are very much needed in this war. However, I fear that Aleric and my dear Eleana may have forgotten something important."

Emane's eyes shifted nervously around the room, his fingers now tapping at his knees. "What was that?"

"My dear, sweet, Emane. Do you want to be the Protector?"

Emane stopped; slowly he brought his eyes up to hers. "It is my responsibility," he answered mechanically, the words feeling like cotton in his mouth.

"No, Emane," she said, shaking her head very gently. "No. We are not speaking of responsibilities, or titles, or what is best for Meros. We are speaking of you, Emane—a young man with tremendous potential," she leaned forward and whispered, "who needs a choice."

Emane's throat tightened even further. He had not had the desire to cry in so many years, he had almost forgotten the feeling when in his eyes began to burn. "I...I..." he stopped, frowning. Did he even know? It had been so very long.

"If you would like to go back to the castle, resume your former life, I will call another Protector for Kiora."

He looked up sharply, "You can do that? Call another one?"

"I can. There have been times where we have lost Protectors and another was called to take their place."

Emane frowned, "If another can be called, then why the prophesy, why the importance of having me here?"

"I did not say the new protector would be equal to you. Only that I could find another."

Emane couldn't sit there anymore, he practically leapt out of the chair pacing around the back. Could he leave this, go back to the castle, to his life? He shuddered a little. Placing his hands on the back of the chair, he looked up to Epona, who was patiently watching him. "I want to," his head dropped as he hesitated. Squeezing his eyes shut, he started again, "I want to be the Protector but..."

"Emane, you do not have to be like Kiora to succeed."

Emane released a breath he hadn't realized he had been holding.

"Each person is called to a different calling in this life, and they are always given the tools they need."

A peace flowed through him at her words.

She stood, making her way back to him, "This is your choice then, Prince Emane?" she questioned. "You are choosing to be the Protector of our Solus?"

Breathing deeply, he stood tall, looking her in the eye before answering. "It is."

Reaching out, Epona placed her hand against his cheek. Closing his eyes, Emane leaned into her. Epona's touch was almost like a flash of a memory. A memory he had constructed as a boy of what his mother's touch would have been like. She had died when he was born. His father had taught of duty and responsibility. But Emane had craved love and a mother's touch, and maybe a choice. His eyes continued to burn under the great love he felt here.

"Emane, this journey will take you to places you never dreamed you would be. It will change you forever. There will be times when you will not want to go on." Her hand slid to his shoulder, "But you must, Emane, you must go on."

He nodded, reluctantly opening his eyes.

She squeezed his shoulder and sighed, "We are almost out of time, but I want you to remember something. If there ever comes a time when Kiora asks you to trust her," she paused searching his eyes, "you *must* trust her, Emane, however bleak the situation may look. She is blessed with an understanding she does not yet even know she has."

A clattering of hoofs shattered the moment as Epona's hand dropped back to her side. Emane's heart objected with a thud as Arturo entered the room. Emane was not ready to leave behind these feelings.

"Yes, Arturo, I know," Epona said as Aleric came running in behind Arturo, breathing heavily.

"Now what?" Aleric wheezed. "What is going on?"

"Kiora has called him, she is in trouble. You must go now." Epona's tone was calm, even. "The Hollow is also under attack, but you must save Kiora first. I have notified Eleana that she is needed at the Hollow. Go."

Emane and Aleric climbed onto Arturo's back and the pegasus shot through the cavern at a speed Emane had never experienced before.

THE GUARDIANS FLEW TO the trees, each taking up positions to battle the incoming enemy. Malena grabbed Leo and two others.

"Kiora is in trouble. I need you to go."

Leo looked at her, aghast. "What about our brothers and sisters? I cannot just leave them here alone! Dralazar will destroy them."

Malena grabbed him by the shoulder. "Leo, if Kiora is lost, all is lost. There will be no saving the Hollow or anything else. I need you to focus on protecting Kiora."

"Where is Emane?" Leo asked.

"I don't know where Emane is. He may be with Kiora for all we know. All I know is you must go. NOW!"

"Where is she?"

Malena focused on the call, tracking its thread back to the source. "She's with Morcant, at his home," she added. "GO!"

Leo and the others disappeared just as Malena was hit with a blast from a Fallen One. She tumbled end over end in the air and collided with a tree.

KIORA SAT HUDDLING AGAINST the wall, shaking with fear
and worry. She could hear the dragons doing battle above her, each
fighting for control over the entrance to Morcant's lair. The roars
of both pain and exploding fire echoed around within the cavern
for what felt like forever. She covered her hands with her ears as
a dragon roared in agony. The volume of it shook the room, dust
spraying down around her as it shook loose from the walls. The
Guardians' threads had appeared a little while ago, she could feel
them darting and weaving and had to assume they were trying to
help Morcant. Three more threads appeared as a bubble dropped and
Emane and Aleric came swooping in on Arturo.

Jumping off, Emane ran to her. "Kiora!" He knelt down in front
of her, grabbing her shoulders. "Kiora, are you okay?"

"You must help Morcant!" she pleaded, gripping Emane's
forearms. "Please, you have to help him!"

"The Guardians are helping him. We had to make sure..."

He was interrupted by a loud roar and the sound of a dragon
crashing to the ground again. Only this time it was not followed by
the sound of giant feet getting back up.

"Oh, no," Kiora whispered. "Which one was it?"

There were only a few giant footfalls as the champion leapt into
the hole. The thread of the victor barreled ahead of the approaching
dragon, ramming through Kiora like a dagger of ice. The hole was
deep, but a dragon was fast, especially in a dive. Jarland flew into
the chamber before she could do anything.

"Hello again, Kiora." Jarland looked around at the three
newcomers standing there, appearing very pleased. He clicked his
tongue and smiled. "I am afraid these three will not be nearly as
helpful as Morcant was." Jarland's scales were blackened in spots

and blood flowed from several wounds around his neck and chest.

Aleric tried to gain the element of surprise and shot a blast of magic at Jarland before the dragon could make a move.

Jarland twitched a little, cocked his head and smiled. "Haven't been taught where to hit a dragon with magic, have we? There is a downside when you attempt to exterminate an entire race. It seems you really know nothing about them." He laughed, his lips pulled back over his still bloody teeth in a wicked sneer.

As Jarland was mocking Aleric, Arturo shoved a thought into Kiora's mind.

Summon Emane's sword.

She closed her eyes to concentrate, but before she could focus on the chest they had placed the weapons in, Arturo shoved another thought into her head. This one sounded panicked, *Kiora, Dralazar is looking for the book, you must summon it, send it anywhere but here. NOW!*

Her heart was pounding, forcing all her fear and questions aside, Kiora concentrated with all her might, summoning the book and sending it to the only place she could think of.

Did you get it? Arturo asked.

I think so. I have never done it before.

Good, thought Arturo. *Now get the sword for Emane, it needs to go right into his hand.*

Kiora closed her eyes, but was interrupted by Jarland's jeering voice. "So, Kiora, who should I kill first?" Her eyes snapped open. She looked around searching for the Guardians, but Jarland had purposely left his enormous body in the doorway, sealing it off.

"Me," she blurted. "Kill me first."

Emane yelled, "NO!"

Aleric started to run towards her, but Jarland sent a pillar of fire his direction and Aleric was forced to throw up a shield.

"You?" Jarland sneered. "The Solus?"

"Yes, but I have a request," she stammered, frantically searching for the time she needed.

"I don't usually honor requests, Kiora, although I am flattered you would think to ask."

"I would like to say a...a prayer." It was the first thing that flew into her mind.

"A what?!" Jarland's laugh bellowed off of the walls.

Aleric tried to move toward Kiora again, but Jarland shot another pillar of fire in his direction. Turning toward Aleric, he hissed with fire licking his lips. "I am warning you, old man."

Kiora saw her chance and closed her eyes, concentrating on the trunk with Emane's sword in it. She could feel it moving but was not finished yet when Jarland turned his attention back to her.

"What are you doing, Kiora?" Jarland asked suspiciously.

She did not respond. She needed a few more seconds.

"I believe she is praying," Aleric dryly answered.

Kiora's eyes flew open, she had done it. Quickly, she glanced to Emane. He was looking down clearly shocked to find a sword suddenly in his hand.

Arturo shoved another thought into her head. *Tell Emane that sword must go into Jarland's heart. It is the only thing that will bring him down.*

She glanced furiously at Arturo, *HOW?*

Arturo took off, flying straight to the top of the room before turning to a dive at Jarland. Jarland snarled as he saw the pegasus mount his attack. He shot pillars of fire into the air, searing the ceiling as Arturo dove and dipped, avoiding the deadly attacks.

Seizing the opportunity provided, Kiora ran over to Emane and grabbed him by the neck, pulling him close. Whispering in his ear she told him, "You must put the sword into Jarland's heart. It's the only thing that will bring him down."

Emane glanced down at his sword and then to the dragon who was still spraying fire through the air. Swallowing hard, he grabbed Kiora's arm and squeezed it before taking off at a dead run to the underside of the dragon. She watched him as he ran underneath, narrowly missing one of Jarland's feet that came slamming back down just inches behind him. Jarland was spinning his giant body the best he could in the limited space, trying to get a good shot on Arturo. It was making it difficult for Emane to line up the sword. Kiora covered her mouth, trying not to yell out as Emane squatted down under the lumbering giant. Emane shook his head in frustration. Peering around Jarland's legs, he looked for Arturo.

Kiora, Arturo thought. *Emane needs your help, You provide the bubble, and I will provide the distraction.* Kiora looked to Emane, who was staring right at her, giving her a quick nod.

Arturo shot off in the opposite direction of the cave, forcing Jarland to turn his head away from Kiora. Emane ran over to her, grabbing her neck just as she had grabbed his, his lips brushing against her ear. "I need to get right in front of him. Do you have enough energy to get me there?"

Kiora nodded and leaned into his ear, "We need to hurry. If he notices we're gone, he will set the whole room on fire."

Kiora pulled the bubble around them both.

Emane whispered again. "Can he hear us in here?"

"No," Kiora said without bothering to keep her voice down, "We're good."

"Let's go. I need to be right in front of his neck. I think if I go in right under there it should go into his heart."

"You think?" she squeaked.

"Kiora," Emane was exasperated, "I've never killed a dragon before. Let's go!"

They ran across the dirt floor, positioning themselves right in front of Jarland.

"Kiora, I want you to run after you let me out of the bubble. I don't know where he will fall. Ready?" Emane breathed rapidly, his knuckles white around the hilt of his sword. With one last glance up at the dragon towering over them he said, "All right. One...Two... THREE!"

Kiora dropped the bubble, letting Emane step out right in front of the target. She threw the bubble back up and ran toward Aleric.

Emane pulled the sword back and plunged it as deep as he could into the dragon's heart. The enchanted sword slid through the dragon's scales as if nothing were there at all. Jarland roared in anguish. Emanc pulled the sword out, strangely calm, as Jarland sat back onto his back legs, throwing his neck up and back. When the dragon's front legs came crashing back down, Emane thrust the sword in again. Jarland roared again and shuddered. Pulling the sword back out for the second time, Emane ran.

Jarland quivered and choked as his knees crumpled. He rolled to the right, falling into the cavern wall. The compacted earth of the wall where he struck opened up from floor to ceiling with a groan. The large crack shuddered, and then expanded. Dirt and rocks exploded outwards in a dusty shower. Emane, Aleric and Kiora threw their arms over their heads to protect themselves from the raining debris. The crack in the wall continued its path upward, reaching the ceiling quickly. From there it webbed out, racing over their heads, cracking and popping while sending more crumbling pieces to the floor. Collapse was imminent.

"Arturo, get us out of here now!" Emane shouted.

Arturo swooped down and landed in front of Kiora, Emane and Aleric. Emane picked up Kiora and threw her onto Arturo's back. He helped Aleric on and then climbed on himself. Arturo took off with some effort. Three was a large load.

Jarland's dead body was still partially blocking the opening of the cave. Arturo had to land on his back and squeeze himself through the hole before they could head for the surface.

Arturo was straining, trying to pull all three of them out of the hole ahead of the fracturing earth that was racing up behind them. The dirt was crumbling inwards, burying Jarland in the process.

The sound of the earth cracking made Kiora's stomach flip. Looking to the side, she watched fissures racing ahead of them. Dirt and rocks assaulted her and she had to shield her face with her arms.

"We're not going to make it!" she shouted.

Kiora could feel Arturo's muscles coiling underneath her as he pushed harder to clear the top of the hole. The rim began to crumble, threatening to collapse before they found the exit. With one final push, Arturo came bursting out of the hole as the entire rim gave way.

Kiora struggled to adjust her eyes to the light, frantically trying to look for Morcant.

"Arturo, please! I need to check on Morcant."

Kiora, Arturo thought, *we need to get you out of here. Dralazar will track you too easily out in the open like this.*

"I have to make sure he is okay! He saved my life."

Arturo brought them down next to the large dragon lying on his side. Like the dead Jarland, Morcant's scales were blackened and blood dripped from a large cut at the corner of his mouth.

"Morcant," Kiora said mournfully. "It's all my fault," she moaned. "If I hadn't been here..."

"Kiora," Leo had flown over next to her. "He will be fine. My friends and I will help him, but you must go."

"Leo, he almost died for me, because of me! I can't leave him!"

"Kiora," Leo said calmly, "if you do not go, his efforts will have been in vain."

Emane spoke, "He's right, Kiora, we need to get you out of here."

"But..." Kiora had tears welling up in her eyes.

"Kiora," Aleric said, "Leo and the others will work on Morcant. It looks like he needs a little healing."

Leo nodded.

"But if we don't get you out of here right now, Dralazar will send someone for you, someone who won't make the same mistakes."

Kiora laid her head on Morcant side. "You don't understand, he has been loyal all this time."

Arturo snorted and stomped his feet. *Kiora*, he rumbled.

"All right, that's enough," Emane announced. Stomping over, he picked Kiora up and threw her over his shoulder. "We are leaving now!"

"Emane!" Kiora shouted, her fists pounding weakly at his back.

"Kiora, we will talk later." Emane turned to Aleric, holding tightly to a struggling Kiora; she was too weak to put up much of a fight. "Where should we go?"

Aleric thought for a second. "Without the protection of the Hollow, Dralazar could be watching and listening. I can't tell you where to take her." He turned to Arturo with instructions. "Arturo, you and Kiora can talk on the way. I will stay here with Morcant and the Guardians. They can help get me back to Eleana."

Emane walked her over, deposited Kiora on Arturo's back and climbed on behind her, wrapping his arms tightly around her waist.

Arturo pushed into Kiora's thoughts. *How far can you make it, Kiora?*

I don't know, she thought, *I have used a lot of magic, I feel so empty.*

Where did you send the book?

To the cave, where I found it first.

Wise, he thought for a second. *It is not possible for you to bubble us the whole way there. From here back to the Hollow is a path we must take and Dralazar knows it. We won't bubble unless we sense danger. Listen for when I tell you to put up the bubble. That should only leave you with ten minutes. I want you to rest on the way so you're prepared.*

Kiora nodded. *All right.* She looked mournfully down at her giant friend as he grew smaller with the distance.

THEY FLEW BACK OVER the barren brown land of Morcant and onto the green forests. Once they had passed the Hollow, Arturo gave Kiora the command for the bubble. Kiora was weak but she obeyed.

Emane wrapped his arms tight around Kiora as she shook under the exertion. "It's all right, Kiora, you can do it," he murmured in her ear.

She just nodded, unable to speak.

They continued to fly, heading towards Arian's cave on the west side of the valley. As they passed Morcant's old home between the two hills, Kiora started to tear up thinking about him and her bubble began to grow thinner.

Focus, Kiora, Arturo thought.

Kiora snapped back, focusing on her bubble, which grew thick again.

Hold your emotions until the cave.

Sorry.

After another five minutes, Kiora was drenched in sweat and her skin was ashen gray. The mountains where the Cave of Arian was located rose up before them.

"Are we almost there?" Emane shouted forward. "I don't know how much more she can do."

Kiora answered in a whisper, "Arturo said one more minute."

Shortly after, they landed on a large boulder jutting out of the mountain. Kiora dropped her bubble.

"Are we safe here?" Emane asked sliding off Arturo before reaching up to help her down.

"Yes." Kiora still could not speak above a whisper. "Once you've landed the enchantment protects you from sight."

She stumbled over to the face and placed her hands on the wall. It shimmered, changing back and forth from a mountain to a doorway. She leaned her head against the rock with a whimper.

Kiora, I know you're tired but you are going to have to give it a little more magic if you want to get in, Arturo gently prodded her.

Kiora nodded and took a deep breath. She put her hands back upon the mountainside and it vanished, exposing the doorway into the cave. Then she passed out.

Emane barely managed to get his arms under her before she hit the rock.

"I really wish she would stop doing this," he grunted, cradling her in his arms. Once inside, he looked around for a soft place to lay her. All he saw was a desk with a candle, an inkbottle and a quill.

"Arturo, where am I supposed to lay her?"

Arturo just looked at him.

"All right, I will hold her." He sat down and positioned Kiora in between his legs so she could lean her head back on his chest till she woke up. Emane leaned himself against the cold rock wall.

"Is she having another vision?"

Arturo shook his head.

"She used too much magic, didn't she?"

Arturo nodded.

"We can all rest then, until she wakes up."

Arturo trotted over to another corner of the cave, sat down, and folded his head under his wing.

Emane sighed and looked down at Kiora. Her hair was plastered around her face with sweat and dirt. She was so pale, Emane had to rely on feeling her breath just to convince himself that she was still alive. Leaning back, he closed his eyes trying to make sense of the last twenty-four hours. Kiora shifted with a groan and Emane found himself tightening his arms around her, pulling her closer.

Even covered in dirt and grime, she was beautiful. Her dark eyelashes lay over the top of her cheeks just a few inches from his lips and he closed his eyes trying not to think about how close her face was to his. Taking a few deep breaths, Emane tried to relax. Relaxing, however, allowed all of the pains of that day to come into focus. His shoulders and biceps were throbbing with the force of piercing the Dragon, and his stomach was far beyond growling. He groaned out loud, it felt as if he had swallowed the sword himself.

Arturo perked his head up to look at him.

"Sorry."

Arturo kept looking at him. He remembered with some embarrassment that Arturo could hear his thoughts, which of course meant that he had just heard everything he had been thinking about Kiora.

Dropping his head against the wall behind him, he rolled his eyes. "Arturo, you can't tell her."

Arturo didn't move.

"Arturo, I mean it!" he said glaring at him. "Those are my thoughts. And right now I would like to keep them to myself."

It took a while, but Arturo finally nodded.

Emane shifted, trying to get comfortable. "Do you think there is any way you could stop doing that?"

Arturo shook his head.

"Really?"

No, again.

"But I have your word you will keep my thoughts to yourself?"

Arturo snorted, putting his head back under his wing.

Not sure if that was a yes or no, Emane relaxed his head back against the wall and tried not to think about anything regarding a telepathic pegasus or a certain beautiful girl that he held in his arms as he drifted off to sleep.

CHAPTER NINE

VISIONS

KIORA WAS HAVING HER first dreamless sleep in some time. No dragons or merserpents or feelings of doom. Just much needed rest. She could have slept longer if it wasn't for the pain gnawing away at her stomach. She moaned and twisted to the side hoping to relieve some of the discomfort.

Emane jumped. "Are you okay?"

Sitting up, she looked around and her stomach did a strange nervous flip realizing Emane had held her while she slept. "Fine," she said, brushing the hair out of her face. "Still a little tired…and starving."

"I know," he groaned, stretching himself out like a cat. "I'm starving too."

"I don't suppose any food has appeared?" She peered around the cave, hopeful.

"Is it supposed to?"

She shrugged, "Stranger things have happened." Pushing herself up, she asked, "Is Arturo still here?"

Emane nodded his head in the direction of Arturo who still had his head tucked under his wing.

Arturo, Kiora thought, *how do we find some food?*

I was sleeping, Kiora, he said without moving.

I'm sorry.

A sigh whispered at her mind, *Summon it.*

Summon it? I thought I had to know where things were before I could summon them.

He pulled his head out from under his wing, tired and annoyed, *Yes and no. If you want something specific, like your book or Emane's sword, you need to know exactly where it is so you get exactly what you want. If you summoned a sword you could get any number of swords. If you need food, there is any number of apples on a tree. Summon what you like and the general idea will come.*

Really?

Yes. Be cautious, the larger the item the more magic it requires. He tucked his head back under his large wing, indicating the conversation was over.

"What did he say?" Emane asked.

"He said I could summon food."

"Summon it?" he asked scrambling to his feet. "Like you did with my sword?"

"Yes."

"That was really amazing, by the way; buying time and putting in right into my hands," he shook his head. "Amazing."

"Thank you." She blushed with a bit of confusion. "He says if I summon what I want, the general idea should show up. Here goes nothing." She closed her eyes concentrating on dinner.

"Kiora?"

"Emane, I can't do this and talk at the same time."

"I just—don't do too much. That's all."

Kiora was surprised at the gentleness of Emane's tone. Peeking at him through one eye, he had turned away from her, shoving his hands in his pockets. Closing her eyes again, Kiora imagined apples and peaches, fresh cream, roast chicken and finger potatoes. She had to rein in her thoughts, and her stomach, from summoning enough food to feed a kingdom.

"Wow."

She opened her eyes to see apples and peaches, roast chicken and finger potatoes sitting on the ground. Unfortunately, cream was running over everything. "I will need to remember to summon the cream in a dish next time."

Emane and Kiora sat down to eat, devouring the feast she had summoned. Food had never tasted so good. She picked up an apple and stared in shock at the large bite that had already been taken out of it. Realizing what had happened, she began to laugh.

"I think I just summoned this out of someone's hand," she said, holding the apple up to see.

Emane almost choked on his chicken, imagining some poor man getting ready to take a bite out of his apple when it vanished.

KIORA AWOKE FROM HER second nap of the day feeling well rested, and best of all, full. The food she had summoned had tasted better than anything she could have imagined. Then again, she could have never imagined being that hungry. She smiled to herself, remembering Emane's eyes getting a little bit wider as he watched how much she was eating.

I need to go, Kiora.

She jumped as Arturo's thoughts entered hers. Why? Her stomach knotted at the thought of him leaving her.

I need to meet with Eleana and Aleric. Things have changed, and so must we. You have things to do here as well. He looked over to the book she had summoned earlier.

But what if something happens? she thought.

I will be back soon, Kiora. You are well protected here, he said, addressing the fear she hadn't vocalized. He stood up and walked closer to her. And even if you weren't, you have already become quite powerful, Kiora. Do not underestimate yourself.

That's what you all keep telling me, she thought with a hint of sarcasm.

Kiora, Arturo shouted it into her mind with all the force of a reprimanding father, you are more than what you know. Turning, he walked out of the cave entrance, spreading his wings on the ledge.

As the sun hit them, the opalescent colors of Arturo's wings bounced off and around the surrounding stone. She was reminded of the first time she saw him standing in the forest, back when she was innocent and ignorant of magic. How much things had changed since then.

With a heavy heart, she walked over to the small desk on which the book of Arian sat. She pulled the chair closer and said, "Light." The candle ignited just as it had upon her first visit here. She stared at the book, not sure where to start.

"I don't know what I need to know first," she said under her breath.

A hand on her shoulder nearly startled her out of her chair.

"Emane! You scared me half to death."

"I guess I don't need your fancy bubbles to sneak up on people, do I?" he smirked.

She laughed in spite of herself.

Emane looked over her head and noticed the book on the table. It was glowing a bright blue and humming. "What is wrong with that book?"

Sighing, she said, "It's telling me there is something I need to learn."

Emane shook his head. "This magic stuff is nuts! How about you start learning whatever it is you need to learn and I will start practicing with the weapons the Guardians gave me. That is, if you could get them for me."

"Oh, of course." Picturing where they had left the chest of weapons in the Hollow, she willed them to come to her.

Emane yelled in pain. "Ow!"

Her eyes flew open to find that chest had landed directly on Emane's foot. "I'm sorry, I'm sorry!" Kiora said jumping up to help. Emane pushed while she pulled, it slid off his foot and hit the floor with a thud.

"Emane, I am so sorry!"

"It's okay, Kiora," he said through clenched teeth. "I just need a few minutes. Go work on your magic."

Biting her lip, she backed away. She felt terrible.

"Kiora! I will be fine."

She turned reluctantly, walking slowly over to the book. Plopping down in her chair, she set her elbows on the table, dropping her head into her hands. Show me what I need to know, she thought.

The book opened and the pages flew by stopping abruptly.

Controlling Visions

Perking up a little, she leaned in closer.

Visions of the future almost always come without being asked. Although it is possible to achieve them upon request, it requires a great deal of skill. Even then, it rarely works.

Visions of the past or present can be requested by one who knows what he is doing.

You must control the vision. If you do not, the vision will control you, causing blackouts and loss of consciousness.

She read that line over again. Blackouts? She didn't know that could be controlled. Grabbing the book with both hands, she focused in on that paragraph and read on.

When a vision is coming, you must learn to focus
the vision out rather than in. When you allow the
vision to pull you inside your own mind you will lose
consciousness, making yourself vulnerable in any
situation. To focus the vision out, force the image to
appear before you. This way you can watch it as if it were
happening in front of you. At the same time, you will still
be aware of what is around you, as well as retain control
of your limbs.

Kiora was getting excited. Her visions were terrifying, mainly because she blacked out every time one happened. She needed a vision, to practice. She scanned back up the page to visions of the past or present.

To obtain a vision of past or present happenings you need
to concentrate on the event that you are wishing to see.
Relax and allow the magic to take over. The magic will
follow what it is you are asking it to do.

Biting her lip, she set the book back down on the table in front of her. Settling back into the chair, she closed her eyes. She needed to decide what it was that she wanted to see. Morcant! She was still worried about him, wondering if Aleric was able to help him or not. She thought back to that time, watching him disappear behind her as she rode to safety. It took a few minutes, but soon she could feel a familiar feeling—the rushing of the vision sucking her down and into herself.

No, no! She thought. She pushed as hard as she could trying to push the vision back out and in front of her, but it was no use, she was gone. She could feel herself fall off the chair and slam her head into the floor of the cave. Then it was all gone and she was back above Morcant's home watching Aleric move around the dragon's wounds, trying to evaluate them.

"Morcant, hold still, I am not finished." Aleric was telling the giant beast lying on his side.

"Is she okay, Aleric? This is all my fault." The giant dragon moaned in agony.

"She's fine. Arturo has taken her to safety. And, yes, this is your fault."

"Aleric!" Kiora shouted in objection, but it was no use. He could not hear her.

Morcant let out a horrible sound that sounded like a mix between a roar and a cry of agony.

"I don't know what you were thinking, taking her out of the Hollow," chided Aleric.

"I didn't think Dralazar would be watching for her yet. It's so early. And a dragon's thread is usually a good mask of magical threads."

Aleric put his hand on a particularly deep gash in Morcant's side trying to heal it. After a minute, he shook his head.

"It's no use, Morcant, I have to get you to Eleana. I can help some, but I am not a healer. Not for this size of a wound anyway."

"It's all right." Morcant stumbled slowly to his feet. "I am feeling better than before" His head still hung in shame.

Aleric put his palms with his hands facing the ground and started to rise into the air. He floated gracefully onto Morcant's back. Once on his back, he summoned what looked like a rather large chair and with magic somehow got it to stick to his back. Kiora's mouth hung open

"I wish I would have thought of that!!" grumbled Kiora.

Morcant spread his giant wings, moaning in pain before he took off.

She could feel it slipping, the vision was ending. The land started trembling.

Then she was back. Emane had a hold of her and was shaking her.

"Kiora, Kiora!" He looked frantic.

"What?" she managed to murmur.

"You're back!"

"Yes." She blinked her eyes once before the pain rolled over her. Her head was pounding like she had taken a hammer to it. Reaching up, she felt some fabric wrapped around her head that was wet and sticky. She pulled her fingers down and looked at the red liquid on her hands.

"What happened?"

"Are you okay?"

"Yes. Yes, I'm fine." Kiora tried to push herself up. "What happened?"

Emane took a deep breath, struggling to calm himself down. "You fell off the chair and hit your head on the cave floor. You cut your head pretty badly; I bandaged it the best that I could." Leaning back on his heels, he asked, "Did you have another vision?"

"Yes," she said pushing up on her elbows. "I was trying to learn to control them. The book said I could ask for visions—"

Emane interrupted her, "You did this on purpose?!"

"Yes." She frowned at his tone, sitting up the rest of the way. "It said—"

"You asked for a vision and didn't have the sense to get off the chair first!"

"Emane—"

"I can't believe you!" he nearly yelled, getting to his feet. "Are you trying to get yourself killed, Kiora! Would it be that hard to think about things before you do them?"

Kiora bit her lip, trying to hold back the tears. Not only was her head throbbing, but now Emane was yelling at her.

"Honestly, Kiora, you are going to..." He stopped mid sentence before turning on his heel and stalking off to the other side of the cave. Picking up his sword, he began running drills with his back to Kiora.

She took a deep breath and pulled herself back up onto the chair, the chair legs screeching against the rock floor.

Emane paused, "Kiora," he said through clenched teeth. "If you are going to try again, could you at least move to the floor?"

She was struck with the desire to sit there just to spite him, but out of regard for her own skull if nothing else, she moved to floor sitting cross-legged.

It was hard to pick a moment out of the past when she could pick anything she wanted. Then an idea struck her. *Arian!* She wanted to see the author of her book. She thought back to him writing the book in this very cave. And soon she could feel the vision coming—the black sucking feeling pulling her deep within herself once more.

"No, no," she groaned again, trying to push it out. The blackness halted, wobbled and started to move outward. Figures began materializing in front of her. "Yes!" she said excitedly. That split second of lost focus was all it took, the blackness rushed back in on her and she was gone.

In the vision, Kiora was standing back in the cave looking at a man sitting at the same table she had just been at. He looked remarkably like Aleric; same silvery hair, same eyes. He was taller and broader than Aleric. He leaned over his book scratching away with his feather pen, pausing every now and again to dip it back into the ink well. Arian suddenly looked up. He had a blank look on his face as he stared into the empty cave. She watched him carefully, not sure what he was doing. His eyes came into focus again and he looked like he was watching something, something she could not see.

"He is having a vision," she whispered to herself.

"No!" Arian yelled, throwing back his chair. He ran to the opening of the cave shouting Arturo's name, without a moment's hesitation he hurdled himself over the edge.

"No!" Kiora yelled. She threw herself onto her stomach and peered over the edge. Arian was falling rapidly toward the rocks below. Kiora's voice stuck in her throat. She was helpless, watching something that had already happened. He was falling toward the earth with his arms and legs in a spread eagle position. She could not believe what was happening. At the last second, a familiar streak of white came hurtling around the mountain. Arturo swooped underneath him, allowing Arian to land perfectly on his back. Kiora's mouth was hanging so far open it was beginning to hurt. She forced it closed watching Arian and Arturo shoot off into the distance.

She closed her eyes, processing what she had just seen. The unity and faith between Arturo and Arian was phenomenal.

When she opened her eyes, the vision had ended and she lay on her back looking up at the ceiling. She went to push herself up, but a hand grabbed a hold of her arm and pulled her back down. She looked over to see Emane lying next to her with his blue eyes glued to the ceiling.

His voice was forced but even, "Look, I'm sorry I yelled. Now, if you are going to keep practicing this, will you please just lay down?"

Kiora lay back down. "Did I hit my head again?"

He snorted. "Yes. Can't you tell?"

"Honestly?" She glanced at him, but his eyes were still determinedly fixed on the ceiling. "My head was pounding so hard before I can't tell much difference."

"Great. Now, if you will please promise to stay on the floor, I am going to go work with my weapons some more."

"I promise."

"Thank you." Emane stood without looking at her and walked back over to where his chest of weapons was sitting.

Kiora put her hands under her head and smiled. He did care, even when he was acting like a jerk. Without warning and without request, the darkness was back, sucking her once again back into her own head.

"No, no, no!" she shouted out loud, trying to focus all her energy into pushing the vision forward. It stopped moving just as it had the last time, wavering back and forth, shuddering. She gave one final shove and won the battle as the darkness abated and the vision rushed outwards. The vision was now clearly and easily portrayed in front of her like a moving painting, dancing around her. It took little effort to keep it there now that it had found a home.

She stood up slowly, looking around her. The picture was 360 degrees. She turned in a circle, looking at her surroundings.

She was back in her village, very close to the castle. The stone walls towered above her, the turrets stretching even higher. The houses that surrounded the outermost walls of the castle were exactly as she remembered, with the worn pathways between the villagers' homes and the bakery. The villagers milled about, going on with their daily life completely unaware that she was watching.

"Kiora, what are you doing?"

Kiora was startled; she had never been called to in a vision before. She turned slowly around trying to ascertain where it was coming from.

In front of her, and yet not fully there, was Emane. He didn't appear to be part of the vision. The vision was clear and crisp as if she were really there. But Emane looked as if he was standing behind a piece of sheer fabric. She blinked her eyes trying to make him come into focus, but he would not. It was almost like he was... she gasped.

"Emane, are you still in the cave?"

"Of course I am still in the cave, Kiora. Lay back down." He started to walk towards her.

"Stop," she yelled, "Don't come any closer. I don't know what it will do."

"What?"

"I am having a vision. It's here in the room."

"You can see me?"

"Yes." The picture started to lose its focus. "Emane, I am losing it. I need to see this." She focused her energy back to the picture before her. She could still see Emane's shadowy figure pacing around the room.

Eleana floated into the picture followed by Aleric. They stood at the edge of the village, partially obscured by the shadows in the tree line.

"Have you told her yet?" Aleric asked

"No, there is no need."

"Eleana, she is already beginning to have visions about them. There must be a reason for that."

"Perhaps, but there is not time. We must move them, we need allies."

"Have you completed negotiations?"

"Yes, I don't think they will side with him again, not after what happened last time. But they will not agree to side with us

until they have had time to examine the two of them. They are,
understandably, skeptical."

"And you trust him not to mention the gates to Kiora."

"I think he has given up on the gates long ago, Aleric.
Regardless of that, it is the only way. I will send Arturo for them in
the morning."

"And what will we do?"

"We need to continue to search for allies, as well as keep an eye
on these people. He has already been here, I am sure of it."

CHAPTER TEN

ON THEIR OWN

THE VISION FADED AS Emane came back into focus.

"Well?" he asked. "What did you see?"

"Eleana and Aleric," she frowned. "They were talking about something that they didn't want to tell me, something about a gate." The image of a gate from her visions as a child flashed before her eyes. It was a repeating theme that she could not understand. There was no such gate in their land.

"A gate? Is that it?"

"And that they are sending Arturo for us in the morning"

Emane snorted and walked away.

"What?" Kiora asked to his back.

"Nothing."

"No, it's not nothing. What?"

He picked up the club from out of his box of weapons and began testing its weight. "Kiora, it's nothing. I just have a hard time with all of this, that's all."

Kiora bit her lip. Her first impulse was to cry, but she held it back, wrapping her arms around herself. "By all of this, you mean me?"

"Well, yes... I mean, no. It's with everything, I suppose."

"Everything magic?"

"That certainly isn't helping." Emane took a few test swings with his club, "But to be honest, things weren't really all that great before I came here either." His voice came in spurts between swings. "Just...the way...things go...I guess."

"Are you trying to tell me that your problem has not always been with me?"

Emane smiled as he took a giant swing. "Not...exactly."

"What does that mean...exactly?"

Emane took a running leap at the wall, yelling, as he slammed the club into the rock. Kiora's eyes opened wide, a large piece of stone cracked and fell to the ground as Emane dislodged the club. "Look, Kiora, sharing feelings is not something I am very good at."

Nudging around a pebble with the toe of her shoe, she said, "We will be spending a lot of time together, Emane. It might be helpful if we understood each other."

Emane took another swing at the wall. "You think so, huh?"

"Yes, I do."

"Not to point out the obvious, but I don't know much about you either."

"Not much to know."

"I doubt that." He swung the club in a 360-degree spin.

"What you see is what you get," Kiora said nervously.

"No, it's not." The club came down with a crash against the stone floor.

Kiora jumped. "Do you have to do that while we talk?"

"It helps me to relax. Would you rather I use the sword?"

"No, you missed the point," Kiora sighed.

"And I think you..." Emane stopped to swing the club at some imaginary enemy, "...missed mine."

Kiora thought for a second. "I suppose I did." She had no idea what Emane was talking about.

"What you see is what you get?" he snorted while rolling his eyes.

"What is that supposed to mean?"

He slammed the club into the ground and leaned against the handle, breathing hard. "Kiora, I have never seen or heard of a village girl that had magical powers. I have never seen a simple girl go and fly off with a dragon. I have never seen a girl who cries so much, but is brave enough to risk her life for others. I have never seen anybody appear so weak," he picked up the club and threw it back into the chest, "and be so strong." Unsheathing his sword, he started running drills.

He thought she was strong? She watched him for a while, moving as if she were not there. "Why do you always change the subject?" she finally blurted.

"I...did not...change...the subject," he said between each slice of air.

Kiora could feel the fire starting in the pit of her stomach. "Yes, you did. You always do. We started off by me telling you that I don't know much about you, and then somehow you turned it back on me again."

Emane broke into a huge grin. "I suppose I did." He swung the sword hard in a deep slicing motion. "Force of habit." He sheathed his sword and tossed his blond hair back off of his forehead. "I'll tell you what. I'll try."

"Try?"

"Yes." He walked over and leaned against the side of the cave. Sliding down to the ground, he causally placed his arms over his knees. "I will try to have an open conversation with you without

WINGS OF ARIAN | 167

swinging a sword."

"Really?"

"Yes." His eyes twinkled as he looked at her.

"Why?"

He rolled his eyes and laughed. "I can't win with you, can I?"

Kiora blushed. "Sorry. I have seen so many different sides of you, I never know which one I am dealing with. I can't figure you out."

"Hmm, that sounds just like what I said." Kiora blushed, again. "I am starving, though, so here is the deal. You summon us some dinner and something to sleep on and we will talk."

"You don't want to sleep on this floor again?"

"No, I don't!"

"What sounds good for dinner, Your Highness?" Kiora bowed.

"Something warm," Emane's smile faded, "and don't call me that."

"Yes, Your Highness."

"Kiora!"

She giggled. "Sorry, dinner's coming right up."

She closed her eyes and thought about a roast chicken hot out of the oven. She felt a little guilty knowing that it would be coming out of someone's oven, but there wasn't much she could do about that. She called for a loaf of bread, some butter (in a dish this time). She imagined some apples on a tree (no bites out of these ones) and some more potatoes. She turned around and opened her eyes to see Emane tearing into a roll.

"I get dinner ready and you're not even going to wait for me?"

"Sorry, it's been a long day." He picked up another roll and held it out to her, grinning.

Kiora grabbed the roll and sat down next to him. "All right, start talking."

"I do not believe that you have held up the entirety of the bargain," he pointed out, brandishing his roll at her.

She rolled her eyes. "All right, fine, after I eat."

They ate until they thought they were going to burst.

"Not only was that delicious, but there weren't even any bites missing this time," Emane said with satisfaction, leaning back on his elbows.

Kiora laughed. "I am improving, aren't I?"

"Yes, you are." He wiped his mouth with the back of his sleeve. "I had an idea about where to get the bedding from."

"What kind of idea?"

"If you summon it, it can come from anywhere, right?"

"Yes."

"So, it could feasibly come right off of somebody's bed while they are sleeping."

Kiora giggled again, and was immediately embarrassed. She seemed to do that more around him. "That would be a shock, wouldn't it?"

"Yes. But blankets are also expensive to buy and time consuming to make. I would feel bad taking something like that from the villagers. So I want you to try to take my bedding, from the castle."

"Do you have enough?"

Emane laughed, "Yes, I definitely have enough."

"I am going to have to be very specific to get it. Can you describe it to me?"

Emane described the room, where it was at in the castle, and how many blankets, sheets and quilts were on his bed.

"Twelve! You have twelve blankets!"

"I know, it's a lot."

"A lot!? I had one, and it's two inches too short for my legs!"

"Excess seems to come with being born into the royal family."

Kiora shook her head, "All right, give me a few minutes, and no talking." Kiora closed her eyes and tried to remember the castle. She moved her mind down the hallway she knew held the Prince's quarters and tried to imagine inside just as he described. She pictured herself walking down the hall to his room and opening the large wooden door. She could see the large four-poster bed in her mind: carvings curling up and around the pillars, the gold fabric draped from the top. She concentrated as hard as she could and imagined the piles and piles of blankets and sheets moving from the bed to the cave. The magic was draining out of her; it was a lot more work than a few food items. She could see the blankets in her mind but she didn't know if they had moved yet. She gave it everything she had before she finally had to turn around, with a gasp. To her surprise, there was a pile of bedding sitting on the floor; not only the blankets, but the sheets and all the pillows too.

She looked at Emane, "How long have these been here?"

"A couple of minutes."

She couldn't believe it. "A couple of minutes! Couldn't you see that I was dying over here!"

He just smiled at her. "You didn't look like you were dying. You looked like you were concentrating. Besides, you said not to talk."

"Oohhh!" Kiora picked up a pillow and threw it at him. Looking around, she scowled, "I don't understand, why didn't I know they were here?" She examined the pile. "Did I get everything?"

"More than everything. You got the blankets, the pillows, the sheets. I even think you got the down filler." He pulled through the pile, "Yep, here it is."

She started pulling through one blanket at a time.

"What are you doing?"

"Counting."

"Counting? Why?"

She didn't answer him until she had finished pulling through the entire pile. Sitting back on her heels, she looked at him. "Eleven."

"What?"

"There are eleven blankets here."

"So?"

"So! No wonder I thought I was going to die. I was trying to summon a blanket that wasn't even there. That's why I didn't know they were here. At least I think that's why."

Emane started laughing.

"It's not funny!"

"Yes, yes, it is...very funny." His laugh was echoing around the cave. Kiora had never heard him so happy before. She couldn't help but smile.

"All right, let's get this thing set up." She tried not to let Emane see her smiling, but it was hard to hide.

Emane got up, still laughing and started to pull the blankets off to get to the down filler. It was so thick and comfortable she might as well have summoned the whole bed. Emane put it down and Kiora started tucking a sheet around the outside. Emane then took another blanket and set it on the floor across from the down filler.

"What are you doing?"

"Making my bed."

"You can't sleep with one little blanket when we have got this luxurious thing!"

"Sure, I can. You can take that."

Kiora looked back and forth between the down filler and his sad pile of blankets. "No, Emane, this is ridiculous. This thing is huge—we can share."

"Kiora, I couldn't."

"Stop it, Emane. I appreciate you being chivalrous, but you can sleep on one side and I will sleep on the other. We could even roll a blanket down the middle, if it would make you feel better."

"I will be fine over here on the floor."

"No, you won't, because you are sleeping over here. I can't have you trying to defend me with a knot in your shoulder, can I?"

Emane rolled his eyes, again. "All right, fine. But I am warning you—I kick."

"That's all right, I bite." Emane stared at her. Kiora broke into laughter, "I am just kidding, Emane." She set another blanket down on top of the down filler. "Oh, you should have seen your face."

"Very funny."

Working together, they got the mattress put together. They settled into the bed, pillows situated on opposite sides of the mattress.

"I have summoned food, blankets and the bed is made. A deal is a deal, Emane, it's your turn to talk."

"A prince always lives up to his word. What do you want to know?"

"You said your problem was not, 'exactly with me.' What did you mean by that?"

"Oh, wow, getting right to meat of things, aren't we? Umm, I choose to pass for now and come back to that later."

She leaned up on her elbows and glared at him, "You pass?"

"Look, Kiora, that needs more explanation. How about you start with something else and we will probably come back around to it. Actually, I am sure we will because I am not lucky enough for it to go away." He grinned at the ceiling, choosing not to return the stare she was giving him.

Kiora was distracted by his playful grin. He was always handsome, but with that sheepish grin plastered on his face, he was gorgeous.

"All right then, you said that things weren't all that great before you came. Why not?"

Emane sighed. "Seems like a logical place to start. Well, let's see if I can sum it up. I was born 'Prince,' which everyone thinks is great, and in some aspects it is. I have been raised to lead, to have the lives and destinies of thousands of people placed upon my shoulders. I never really asked for that. I never really asked for a lot of things," he added his voice suddenly distant. "And then there is the matter of marriage."

Kiora's heart fluttered, "Marriage?" She spoke it entirely too eagerly and fought the urge to smack herself. *What is wrong with me?*

If Emane had noticed it, he didn't let on that he had. "As the only son of my father, I am required, of course, to take the throne and to ensure the royal line continues, through marriage."

It hit Kiora what he was talking about. "Arranged marriage?" How had she not known that a match had been picked for the Prince? Surely her sister would have mentioned something like that.

"Yes, arranged marriage." He shook his head. "And she is, she is…well, she is awful."

"That bad?"

Emane nodded. "That bad."

Kiora was quiet for a second. Her emotions were mixed. She felt sadness that he had been promised, and hope that Emane thought his proposed bride was awful.

"Is she not…attractive?"

"Oh, she is very attractive."

"What?" Kiora's emotions stretched in confusion, and Emane just kept on tugging.

"She is one of the most beautiful girls I have ever laid eyes on.

She is stunning. Her hair, her face, and then there is her body. Oh, wow!" he said, putting his arm casually behind his head.

Kiora interrupted the dissertation. "I got it," she said flatly. A mental picture flashed in her mind of a girl she had met once. Blonde hair and big brown eyes, she was beautiful enough that Kiora had found herself staring. She really hoped for some reason that it wasn't her.

"Sorry, I got carried away."

"Yes, you did. So, if she was so gorgeous, then what is wrong with her?"

"She is gorgeous, until she opens her mouth," Emane groaned.

"You didn't like her teeth?"

"Her teeth? What?" Emane rolled his eyes. "No, Kiora, her teeth were fine. Perfect, actually."

"Yes, I know. Perfect like the rest of her," she said under her breath.

"Her personality. She is mean and cold and conceited and careless and selfish." He stopped and turned to look at Kiora. "I notice you are not asking me to stop on this list..."

Kiora was suddenly very interested in a tie on the blanket, twirling it around between her fingers. "Do you have to marry her anyway?"

Emane's head turned abruptly back to the ceiling, his jaw working. "My father," he ventured slowly, "would say the answer is yes."

"What about you?" she asked glancing up at him, "don't you get a choice?"

His head whipped back to look at her with an expression she could not read. "It is part of the royal responsibilities, or so I am told."

"Oh."

"No," he said quietly She looked at him, confused, before he sat up, his eyes bright with a sudden intensity. "No," he repeated, "I won't marry her." A smile crept across his face, flopping back down with a great sigh of relief he chuckled, "No."

"What will your father say?"

Emane hesitated, his smile faltering momentarily before rolling his eyes. "He will say a lot. He always does."

"Has anyone ever told you that you roll your eyes? A lot!" Kiora said, laughing.

"Yes. Aleric is very fond of telling me how often I do that."

"Aleric was your teacher?"

"He tried to be."

"Was he not very good?"

Emane laughed, shaking his head. "The questions you ask. No, he's fantastic. I have not been the ideal student. I found history and learning about ancient crafts terribly boring and a waste of my time. I would have much rather been out practicing my combat skills than listening to him go on about things I didn't feel mattered." He looked into her eyes and Kiora could see sadness and confusion. "Funny, isn't it, that the things I thought mattered are proving to be rather useless, and the things I thought I didn't need to know are now of grave importance?"

Emane took a deep breath. "Your turn." Kiora tried to object, but Emane cut her off. "I didn't say I was done talking, but I need a break. I told you I wasn't very good at this."

"You seem to be doing a good job to me."

He flashed a grin at her that melted her heart. "I am doing great, aren't I? I don't think I have ever talked so much to anybody in my whole life."

Sadly enough, Kiora completely understood. It had been a long time since she had truly opened up to anybody. She sat up, pulled her knees to her chest and wrapped her arms around them. Maybe if she were in as tight of ball as possible she wouldn't feel so vulnerable. "What do you want to know?"

"When did you know you could do magic?"

Of course it would be that question. "That depends. What kind of magic do you mean?"

"Any kind."

Taking a stuttering breath, she told him, "I started having visions when I was a little girl."

"What kind of visions?"

She squeezed herself even tighter. Talking about this made her feel like she was that little girl all over again, that she was doing something wrong. "Visions about the future, about things that would happen."

"I thought those were rare."

She thought about it. "You're right, they are. At least that is what the book said." *Seeing the future was worse than the past,* she thought. *Seeing the future made you think you had a chance at changing it.*

"Eleana's right, you are extraordinary."

"Oh, shut up! I get so tired of hearing that."

"You get tired of hearing that you're extraordinary?"

"Yes, because then I feel like I have to *be* extraordinary or I will end up disappointing everyone." *And because I'm not,* she thought.

He sat up on his elbow looking at her intently. His gaze flickered from her face, to her lips and back again. She looked away nervously, unable to hold his gaze.

"You are the most interesting girl I have ever met," he said. Flopping back onto his back again, he asked, "Back to the visions. What happened when you would have them?"

Picking at the blanket, she answered, "The same thing that you saw. I would black out, see things, and then I would come to."

Emane sat straight up, "That's it? I have been pouring my heart out to you and that's the best you can do?"

Kiora put her head on her knees and squeezed herself as tightly as she could. "This is hard." She flinched at how whiny she sounded.

He scooted closer to her and Kiora felt her breath catch in her throat as he placed his hand on top of hers. "It's all right, you can trust me."

Closing her eyes, a tear trickled down her cheek. She wanted to trust him. She wanted him close, to feel him next to her. "I would usually see bad things that were going to happen to people. One time I saw our neighbor's fields catch on fire. I told my parents, but I was so young. I think I was only eight. At first they didn't believe me. But then after it happened, my parents were terrified. They kept me home as much as possible. I wasn't allowed to go into the village." A tear slid done her cheeks. "They became so afraid of me. My sister would tell them when I had blacked out and they would push me to tell them if I had had another vision. I started lying to them—I didn't want to scare them. I didn't understand what was going on either."

"How are your parents handling it now?"

Kiora choked on a sob turning away, immediately missing the proximity of him to her. "My parents are dead. They were killed in a landslide on their way into the village."

Emane was quiet for a while. "You knew it was going to happen, didn't you?"

Kiora nodded and shuddered. "I didn't know what to do. I had been lying to them for a couple of years and I was so scared to tell them." She hadn't told anyone this, ever. The thought of others looking at her like her sister looked at her had kept her quiet. Too scared to look at Emane's face, Kiora buried her head farther into her arms. "I decided that I had to; that to save their lives, I would deal with whatever consequences would come." She choked on the words, breaking into sobs.

"That's what we saw in the wings, wasn't it?" he said softly. "You were crying as your parents drove away."

She moaned, rolling in on herself—then his arms were wrapping around her, pulling her back into him. He didn't hate her. Her heart leapt forward. Turning towards him, she buried her face in his chest.

"It's okay, Kiora. It's okay," he murmured, his lips brushing against her ear and then against her cheek.

Kiora thought she was going to explode, feeling all of the grief over her parents' deaths; grief that she never really allowed herself to feel, not with Layla watching. And now, the feel of Emane's arms holding her and the softness off his lips; beyond that, the gentleness of his voice was sending chills up and down her spine.

"It's okay, Kiora," he said, resting his nose against her cheek. "Tell me what happened."

"I told them what I had seen…they…they were…so angry. They thought I just didn't want them to go into the village without me. I had never…seen them….so angry." Kiora took deep breaths trying to calm down. "They got into the wagon to leave. I didn't know what else to do so I stood in front of the horses so that they couldn't go. My sister had to drag me out of the way so they could pass. I fell into the road screaming for them not to go." Kiora pulled her head up, reaching to wipe away her tears. Emane gently grabbed her hand, pushing it back down before he reached up himself, running his finger down her cheek, first one and then the other. His fingers left little trails of fire that were quickly lost in the heat of her blush.

"Then what happened?" he whispered, his eyes level with hers. They were darker blue than she remembered them being.

She kept her eyes locked on his, gathering strength from his support. "When they didn't come home that night, my sister flew into a rage. She told me that it was all my fault that our parents were dead—that I had caused the accident. That if I had never been born, our parents would still be alive."

"It wasn't your fault, Kiora."

She tore her eyes away, swallowing. "My visions terrified me, even more after that. I didn't want to talk to anyone about what had happened. I didn't want to see anyone. My sister didn't want anyone to see me either. She would go into town if we needed anything." She sighed. "My sister and I were never the same. We lived together more as roommates than as family. She still blames me."

"How old were you?"

"Twelve."

"I am sorry you lost your parents," he said running his finger back down her cheek. He glanced at her before letting his hand drop loosely back into his lap.

"Thank you." There was an awkward silence. Clearing her throat, she said, "Your turn, I believe."

He laughed again, lightening the mood. "After that, I suppose it's only fair."

"Why is the magical community so hard for you to be in?" she said, swiping a lingering tear from her cheek that Emane had regrettably missed.

"Is it easy for you?" Emane asked.

"See," she sniffed. "There you go again, turning it back on me."

"I will answer the question, but I really want to know if it is hard for you."

Kiora thought for a while, "It is the first time that I haven't felt like something is wrong with me. But there are things that are hard as well."

Emane nodded thoughtfully. "It is very hard for me."

"Why?"

He took a deep breath. "I am nobody here, Kiora. I have always been somebody." He looked nervous, like he was aching to jump up and begin pacing the room like a caged animal. "A somebody by force, but still a somebody. And now here I am following you. Following because I can't lead, because I can't do magic."

Kiora's eyes widen as she began to understand his behavior. "So the problem has everything to do with me."

Focusing back in on her, he seemed to calm a bit, but his gaze was intense, those eyes still darker, bluer. "I have had a very hard time getting used to you, that is true. But I have never met anybody like you, Kiora. You really are remarkable." His hand started to reach out to her cheek again, and then realizing there were no tears he stopped, bringing it reluctantly back down. Kiora's stomach ached in response. Looking down at the ground, he finished, "And not just because of your magic either."

Kiora could feel her cheeks turning scarlet, again. "But you don't like that I am the one who can do magic."

"I didn't like it. That is different."

"You like it now?"

"Mmm…" he grinned, "I am used to it now and am learning, how's that?"

"I guess it will have to do." She looked down at her feet, not sure if she should say what she was thinking.

"What?"

"Nothing."

"I can tell you are thinking something, Kiora. Don't tell me it's nothing."

Her voice came out so quiet, so unsure, it was more of a squeak. "I do need you, you know." Emane was quiet. "I would be a mess if you weren't with me."

"I was pretty sure you despised me."

She smiled at her feet, too scared to look up. "I did at first. You were an arrogant horse's ass."

His laugh bellowed through the cave. She shyly looked up at him.

"I don't think I have ever been called that." He laughed so hard, he cried. He tried to calm himself as he wiped the tears from his face. "At least not to my face anyway."

"Sorry."

"Don't be sorry. That is one of the things that I love about you, Kiora."

She frowned, "That I call you horrible names?"

"That you are always so honest in how you feel. I was taught not to let others know when things bother me. It shows good leadership, I've been told."

Kiora snorted, "How's that working for you?"

He picked up a pillow and threw it at her. "It worked great at home. It's not working so great with you. As you so eloquently put it, it turns me into an 'arrogant horse's ass.'"

She laughed. "Yes, it does."

"Kiora?" He grew serious again, leaning towards her. "There is one thing I am curious about. I know this is off topic, but whatever possessed you to go with that dragon?"

"I'm not sure. I felt like I needed to talk to him."

"Are you always going to be running off with creatures that could kill you?"

"No." She thought about it for a moment. "I don't know."

Emane flopped back onto the bed, his arms out in exasperation.

"Wonderful. How am I going to protect you if you keep running off with man-eating creatures?"

"Morcant isn't man-eating! Just man-disliking, I would say." She looked down at him, asking the question that had been bothering her from the day they had met. "Do you want to protect me?" She grimaced, hardly believing that had just come out of her mouth. Her stomach tied itself into knots in anticipation of the answer.

Emane sat back up; his eyes darkening again as he reached out and put his finger under her chin. Tilting her head up slightly, he moved in closer to her, stopping just inches from her face.

"Do you know," he asked, "that you are only the second person to ever ask me what I want?" His eyes searched hers, moving even closer. Her eyes fluttered shut, too scared to breath. "Yes," he whispered brushing his lips against hers, "I want to protect you."

She wanted to pull him into her, to feel him, and then he was kissing her. His mouth hard against hers, and the nervousness melted away in a rush of fire that ran from her fingers all the way to her toes. Leaning in, she moaned, running her fingers across his jaw. A tear slid down her cheek as she ran her fingers through his hair. Emane pulled back, looking at her curiously.

"You're crying."

She nodded, quickly swiping her tears away.

"You cry more than anyone I know," he said with a gentle smile.

"I think you have mentioned that," she whispered.

Leaning back in, he kissed her gently on her forehead. She smiled, nearly laughing with an explosion of blissful happiness. Looking down at her, he took her hand in his, "Should we get some sleep?"

She couldn't do anything but nod. Sliding underneath the

blankets, he held his arm out, "Come here." She moved over to him, placing her head on his chest as he wrapped his arms around her. She drifted off to sleep, more peaceful than she had been in a long time.

CHAPTER ELEVEN

CREATURES

EMANE WOKE TO SUN streaming in through the opening of the cave. Looking down, he smiled happily. He lay there with Kiora for some time, listening to the sound of her steady breathing, when the sound of hoofs on rock announced Arturo's arrival. The giant winged horse took a few steps within the cave and stared at the two of them lying down together.

"Welcome back, Arturo." Emane said, fighting back laughter.

Arturo walked over and nudged Kiora's arm with his nose.

"Arturo!" Emane hissed, "she is exhausted!"

Arturo ignored him and nudged her again.

"Arturo!"

Kiora started to stir from her sleep.

"Nice job, Arturo." The pegasus looked very pleased with himself.

"What's going on?" Kiora mumbled, sitting up.

"Apparently the horse wants to talk to you," Emane said, with an agitated wave of his arm.

Arturo snorted.

"Oh, I'm sorry, the *pegasus*," Emane said sarcastically.

Kiora looked back and forth between the two of them. What on earth was going on? *What are you doing?* Arturo demanded.

Sleeping and waiting for you.

Emane sat, watching their silent conversation.

You two seem to have gotten closer since I left. It came out less of a statement and more of an accusation.

Kiora blushed. Why did she blush every time Emane was brought up? *Yes, I suppose we have. You don't seem very excited about that.*

Arturo's eyes moved to Emane and back. *I am not.*

He is different from what he seemed, Arturo. Give him a chance.

He looked again at Emane. *Tell him if he ever calls me 'the horse' again I may accidentally drop him while flying.*

Arturo!

Tell him and let's go. Arturo turned and walked out of the cave.

Kiora smiled painfully at Emane.

"What?" Emane asked.

"Nothing."

TELL HIM! Arturo demanded.

Kiora grimaced. "He said if you ever call him 'the horse' again, he may accidentally drop you while flying."

"Did he now?" Emane laughed. "Perhaps you should tell him—"

Kiora interrupted, "You can tell him yourself, he is not deaf and I will not be in the middle of this."

The two exchanged a few menacing stares in which Arturo managed to very clearly express his displeasure with the situation without saying a word.

"Where are we going?" Kiora asked as Emane came up behind her, helping her onto Arturo.

We need to move you to someplace safer.

"Safer?" she said out loud as Emane climbed on behind her. "Has Dralazar found us?" *No, not yet. Although he will if I keep coming and going.*

Kiora put up a bubble as Arturo spread his wings.

No, no bubble.

Confused, she dropped it. As the film around them disappeared Emane asked, "No bubble? What about Dralazar?"

Eleana is dealing with Dralazar. It is a long flight. You would exhaust your magic before we arrived.

"Eleana is taking care of it," she relayed to Emane with a confused shrug. Arturo dove over the edge of the cliff without warning. Lurching backwards she barely had time to grab hold of his mane.

"I didn't say anything," the Prince yelled in her ear, his arms wrapping tightly around her. "And he is still trying to kill me."

"Not just you, I am on here too," she yelled back. "Arturo, what are you doing?" There was no response. Arturo was defiantly mad.

I am not mad! Arturo fumed.

Really? You haven't been your usual self since you came in this morning. she thought as he leveled out.

It's new to me, that is all.

She thought of the vision where she had watched Arian throw himself over the edge of a cliff with complete faith that Arturo would catch him. They had obviously been close, closer than she and Arturo. That relationship, she had no doubt, would develop with time. Arian never had anybody?

Arturo snorted. No, not until long after the war had ended.

Who was his Protector?

A Guardian, and he was male.

Kiora burst out laughing.

"What's so funny?" Emane asked

"I will tell you later." She was still laughing too hard to explain. "Arturo, where are we going?"

Someplace safer where we can finish your training.

They were flying in a direction she had never been before. It looked like they were headed to the far northeast. As far as she knew, there was nothing this direction. The Sea of Arian was more to the east, and they were clearly going to miss it. She watched the forest fade away as they flew further and further away from the Hollow.

"Arturo," Emane asked suddenly, "what is that?"

Kiora looked in the direction Emane was looking before jolting upwards.

Rockmen, Arturo answered.

"Rockmen?" Kiora repeated.

"How horribly appropriate," Emane mumbled. They were enormous. They towered over the trees and were ten times as wide, looking like giant walking mountains. "Whose side are they on?"

"Dralazar's," Kiora answered for Arturo. "They look like rocks!" Kiora whispered.

"Yes, moving rocks."

"Our threads!" Kiora gasped.

It's all right, they can't feel threads. They can't feel much of anything.

Their arms and legs looked like boulders stacked upon boulders, swinging freely. Their heads were enormous, and it was hard to tell if there were any eyes hidden in the crevices that ran over the surface. The Rockmen lumbered on below, unaware that they were being watched by the three as they flew over the top of them.

"They are not fast, but those clubs look deadly," Emane

observed.

Each Rockman was holding a club with three large misshapen and awkward looking fingers and an oversized thumb. The clubs were large enough to flatten several homes at once. Kiora shuddered at the thought of being underneath one of those.

"Aren't we going to do anything?" Kiora asked, spinning around as they flew over the top of them. She couldn't take her eyes of them.

No. We do not want to draw any attention to ourselves. It is imperative that where I am taking you stay secret. Everything depends on it.

Kiora watched the Rockmen growing smaller behind them until her neck burned. Turning back around,she rubbed her neck with one hand, keeping a hold of Arturo with the other. The landscape became rocky and barren with the occasional lonely tree poking up from the earth. Arturo came in and landed. The pebbles slid out from underneath his hoofs and he stumbled trying to gain a sure footing. Before them was an opening to what looked to be yet another cave.

"Another cave, Arturo?" Kiora asked sullenly.

I am sorry, Kiora. Go inside. Eleana will meet you later, Arturo thought, before spreading his wings and leaving them on the ground.

ELEANA NEARLY SMILED TO herself as she appeared in Dralazar's throne room. He was always too sure of himself to put up proper protection. Dralazar sat on his throne talking to the only other creature that made bile rise in Eleana's throat. Vitraya hovered next to the arm of his chair on her black wings. They both turned to look at Eleana at the same moment. Eleana quickly glanced around the room identifying what she was here for.

"Eleana," Dralazar said smoothing over his surprise, and his anger. He always took on a certain tone when he was trying to hide his anger, always had.

"Dralazar," she acknowledged as if she were here for a casual visit.

He leaned back smiling at her, "You remember Vitraya," he said motioning to his left. Vitraya sneered at her.

Eleana took a few steps forward. "I would like to speak with you alone," she said.

Vitraya flew at her, snarling, without warning. Eleana batted her away with an easy movement of her finger. Vitraya tumbled end over end, righting herself a few feet away. "Vitraya," she said, her blue eyes narrowing, "even I can only be pushed so far. Ridding the world of you would be far from an act of evil."

"Yet you will not do it," the Fallen One sneered.

"Stay and we shall see," Eleana said, taking a few more strategic steps in Vitraya's direction. The sight of the little monster brought back memories she wished to forget.

Dralazar laughed. "As entertaining as this is…go, Vitraya." Vitraya bowed to him, offering one last sneer in Eleana's direction before proudly flying out of the room.

"How adorable is that!" Dralazar mocked. "She still has the ability to anger you, after all this time."

Eleana breathed in deeply. Dralazar had always known exactly where to push. She would not let him see her anger, it was what he wanted, and she would not give it to him. "I am not here to talk about that, Dralazar."

"Then what are you here for?" he said, smirking. "To beg me to not hurt anyone else? To stop hunting the Solus?"

"I am here to tell you to stop, not ask you."

Dralazar laughed, first just a snicker, but then it grew louder and louder as he stepped down from his throne. "Why, Eleana? Are you going to join the fight this time? Is that what you have come here to tell me?"

She stared at him without answering. He laughed again, walking up to her, his face inches from hers. "The past cripples you, Eleana. It will always cripple you, and that will never change." Walking past her, he continued to talk. "What makes you think that you can just appear and that I will cease trying to gain what I deserve?"

Eleana moved quickly to the right, turning herself so she was leaning against the stone table that held Dralazar's basin. Keeping her eyes on his back, she put her hand behind her. Touching the base she began whispering the incantation she had come here to do.

Dralazar turned back around with his usual flourish. "You do know you could have ended this long ago?" he asked. "Saved thousands of lives?"

She stopped, narrowing her eyes. "I have heard that from you before, Dralazar." Bowing her head, she continued the incantation, her lips barely moving.

"Yes, you have." There was a pause, Eleana tensed in anticipation. "What are you doing? Eleana!" he roared, his hand flying out.

Eleana put her other hand out, throwing up as much of a shield as she could. The magic it required for her incantation was staggering. Her shoulders sagged as the magic drained out of her, but it was finished. Putting up her other hand, she used some of the small reserve of magic she still had left to throw Dralazar against the wall. He slammed hard, his knees buckling underneath him.

"What have you done?" he growled, trying to push himself back up before grimacing in pain.

"I have done what I will continue to do, protect the Solus from you."

Then she vanished.

DRALAZAR STRUGGLED TO HIS feet, staggering over to the basin. What had she done? Whatever it was had drained her. He saw it happen as she had put up her shield.

"Show me the Solus," he commanded.

The scene came into focus, showing the Solus fighting Jarland, but as the scene progressed, the picture went darker and darker until there was nothing in the basin at all. It was not as if they had bubbled. Whatever had transpired between then and now was gone. Eleana had erased it. Staring over the basin, he questioned his own conclusion. The magic required for that…but the scene continued playing, in total blackness.

Throwing his head back, he screamed, "Eleana!"

"WHERE IS HE GOING?" Emane asked, watching as their ride off this barren mountain disappeared.

"I don't know. He said he needed to take us somewhere safer, but…" Kiora turned slowly, looking into the mouth of the cave.

"What's the matter?"

"I have a bad feeling about this."

"How bad?" Emane asked, cautiously.

"Bad" She felt foolish. Arturo had told her it was safe. There was no reason she should doubt him, but something rubbed at her nerves. Staring into the void, she shivered. It was dark and cold and utterly uninviting. Water dripped inside, seeming to tap out a slow and steady message: Stay out…stay out…stay out.

Kiora took a deep breath, taking her first step towards the unknown.

Emane put his hand on her elbow. "We are going to need light, Kiora," he said, his eyes searching to make out anything past the opening.

Kiora looked around. "I think I might be able to get a light if I had something to keep it on."

Emane walked a few paces and gathered some old dead wood from one of the few trees that had been there.

"Will this work?"

"Hopefully." She focused a picture in her mind of fire burning at the end of the wood. "Light," she commanded.

Emane yelped. Kiora opened her eyes just as he threw a flaming stick away from him where it sat burning in the rocks. He stuck his fingers in his mouth. "Kiora!" he shouted through them. She cringed. "Sorry," he mumbled with a shrug of his shoulders that Kiora assumed was an apology for being an ass. "A little less next time, please?"

"I'm sorry," she slumped, moving to get some more wood. Holding onto it herself, she tried again, with a little less force. This time it lit only the tip, she handed it over to Emane.

"Much better. I am liking this magic," he nodded, looking at the torch. "And I will like it even more when my fingers stop burning."

"Do we need anything else before we go in there?" Kiora asked.

"We have wood, you can summon food. I brought my sword," he listed off thoughtfully. "I can't think of anything else."

"All right," she said. "Let's go."

Emane held the light out before them as they entered the cave. The light was helpful but only showed so far. The darkness was thick and almost palatable, swallowing up any light that tried to force its way through. The limited range forced them to walk

192 | DEVRI WALLS

slowly, picking their way amongst the rocks. The further away they got from the entrance, the thicker the black became, and the lighted circle of safety pulled in tighter around them.

She walked closely next to Emane, grabbing onto the side of his shirt occasionally, less for balance than for comfort. She was trying to withhold her fear from Emane. It had worked so far, but every step required great effort on her part to hide the terror brewing within her. It wasn't just the darkness, something kept poking at her consciousness, warning her.

She had no idea how long they had been walking, but her ankles and the sides of her feet were throbbing from the uneven terrain. Her back was aching from all the bending and crouching they had done, and her head still hurt from the overhanging rock that the torch had failed to illuminate.

"How long do you think we have been in here?" she finally asked.

"Two hours, maybe more."

"It feels like ten. Do you think Arturo wanted us to go this far in?"

"Maybe we should stop and rest. You can summon something to eat and drink and then we can keep going." Emane held the torch out to see as much as he could. "Come." He grabbed her hand and pulled her over to an area that looked as flat as any they had seen. "Here, sit down."

She eased herself down, groaning as her tired body protested.

"I can't imagine he intended for us to just sit in a dark cave, surely there is something back here," he said peering into the dark.

"This adventure just keeps getting better."

Emane laughed as he sat beside her. "You never planned to be in a cave looking for who knows what with me?"

"Nope, can't say that I had."

"What had you planned?"

Kiora stared into the darkness wondering whose idea it was to get to know each other anyway. "I'm not sure.' She hesitated. "I had two sets of plans, I suppose."

"Go on."

"One was to run away to a place nobody knew me, where I could start over. Where I wouldn't have to see my sister look at me as the one that had killed our parents."

"Run away? That doesn't sound like you. What about the other one?"

She sighed. "It does sound like me, or at least it used to."

They were interrupted by a blood-curdling scream coming from down the cavern. Emane leaped up, the scream echoed and bounced around the rocks. Placing himself in front of Kiora, Emane stood with his sword at the ready, alert for any movement. Kiora felt a thread inch its way through her heart. It was, different—magical, and yet, not good, or bad. It was decidedly neutral.

"Help me, somebody help me!' The cries sounded like that of a child. "Please, please help me," the voice sobbed.

Emane looked to Kiora, "How does it feel?" he asked holding the torch out in front of him, swinging it back and forth, searching for anything.

Kiora focused on the thread running through her. "Fine," she said, getting to her feet. There was no evil attached to it at all. "We have to help them."

They moved as fast as they could through the cavern towards the source of the sound. The ceiling of the cavern varied in height from about three feet, forcing them to crawl, to soaring ceilings that the light could not touch and seemed endless. They stumbled over the rocks that were scattered all over the floor trying to reach the sound of the child.

"Help me, help me, please! Don't let him hurt me!" The voice cried out again and again.

"I think we are getting close," Emane panted.

They entered into a large cavern within the cave. It was much larger than the light would illuminate. But the child's voice echoed around far above them, giving them a hint as to the sheer enormity of it.

"Please, help me!"

"Where are you?" Emane shouted, waving the torch around, trying to find him.

"Over here."

Emane turned to face the direction the voice was coming from. "Come on, Kiora, I think he's over here." They walked towards the voice, still swinging the torch back and forth trying to locate the child. And then they saw him, a small boy in rags huddling against a rock. He was filthy, covered in dirt and mud. The only clean parts on his body were the lines on his face where his tears had washed the dirt away. Kiora ran over to him.

"Are you okay?" she asked. Kneeling in front of him, she ignored the pain of the rocks in her knees as she searched him for any injuries.

The little boy was trembling and shook his head no.

"What is it? What's wrong?" she asked, reaching out to put her hand on his. The thread was still confusing her. It was different— not human, but magical. And the neutrality of it confused her. But the sight of the child was breaking her heart, and she pushed the thread aside to deal with the task at hand.

"Please," he whispered, "don't let him hurt me anymore."

"Who?" Emane demanded. "Who is hurting you?"

The child's arm raised and he pointed into the darkness behind him. Emane spun around, sword raised to meet whatever the child was pointing at. Moving the torch back and forth in front of his face, he searched for the perpetrator. At first there was nothing, but then a shadow stepped into the circle of light. He was tall and was wearing a long, dark cloak.

"Hello, Kiora. Hello, Emane."

Kiora froze, she knew that face.

"Who are you?" Emane demanded.

"Dralazar," Kiora said, the color draining out of her face.

The hooded man drew closer. "Very good, Kiora." His voice oozed out like poison.

Kiora reached over to grab the child's hand again, to give him comfort. But her hand fell empty. Looking over to find him, the child had vanished. She spun around, frantically looking for him, but he was not there.

"What have you done to him!?" Kiora yelled.

"Temper, temper" the hooded man chided. "I have not done anything with him."

Kiora ran to stand beside Emane. "He's just a child!" she screamed at Dralazar.

"Yes, as are you," Dralazar retorted.

Kiora struggled with what to do; her training had included bubbling, shields and lighting a fire. She was not equipped to deal with Dralazar, and she knew it. Remembering her gift from the Guardians, she went to grab it, but the thread nudged her again, and again it was off. Something was wrong, very wrong. She leaned into Emane and whispered, "Something is not right."

"Emane!" Dralazar yelled. "Why do you travel with this child? She is nothing but an impostor and a fraud."

Kiora could feel Emane bristle at the words. He took a fighting stance. "And you are a coward who preys upon children."

Kiora's mind was racing, something was wrong here, so very

wrong. The confusion drowned the anger back out of her as she grappled for the answer. What was it? She could hear Dralazar and Emane yelling at each other, but was too deep in her own world to make out the words. She had felt something about the child, something magical. She had felt threads since they had entered the cave, not good or evil; they felt neutral. She turned her attention to Dralazar's thread; it was magical and very...very...neutral. Neutral? She was trying to make sense of it but could not do it. She ran through what she had been taught in her mind. Threads were either good or evil depending on what one chose. The Fallen Ones had once been Guardians, with threads of good. After they chose, their treads turned. Dralazar was not neutral, how could he be? He could not have changed that much since her vision earlier. She looked up as Emane shoved the torch into her hand and began to circle Dralazar. *Something is wrong,* the voice inside her head was screaming. Why isn't he attacking? He could have taken out Emane already. This is not... Dralazar. This is not...

"EMANE!" she screamed, "STOP!"

Dralazar took advantage of the distraction and threw Emane across the room. Emane slammed into the cave wall and slid to the floor.

Kiora ran to him, dropping the torch on the ground as she knelt down. "Emane, are you okay? I am so sorry, Emane! Emane!"

Emane was gasping for air. "Look...out," he coughed, pointing.

Kiora turned to see this neutral Dralazar descending upon them again. She threw up a shield to protect the both of them. The shot intended for Kiora bounced off and slammed into him, throwing him across the room.

"Emane, are you okay? Please talk to me."

"Kiora," he croaked, "what is wrong with you? I had him, why did you stop me?"

Kiora's shoulders relaxed, he was okay. "If that was really Dralazar, you would not have had him. That is not Dralazar."

"What are you talking about?" he coughed. "You were right. That is the same man we saw the other night, I would remember that face anywhere." He struggled to sit up, his face twisting as he did.

"And I would remember his thread anywhere," she said, grabbing his arm to help him. "And that was not it."

"I don't understand."

"Neither do I," she groaned, pulling him to his feet.

Emane looked around, "Hand me the torch." Bending down, she handed it back to him. He took a few steps forward, waving it as he went. "Where did he go?"

"He's gone," Kiora whispered. "Just like the little boy."

Emane turned in a circle, breathing heavily, lighting the cavern as he went. "This is very strange."

Kiora summoned some water in a flask and offered it to Emane. "Here, you need to drink. I don't know what is going on, but whatever it is, it is not over yet."

"You first," Emane spoke, his eyes still searching the cavern.

Kiora drank quickly and passed it to Emane. Her senses were on fire, searching…feeling. She could feel more threads gathering. All were magical, and all were neutral. She could sense them coming from every direction. This was a test, she didn't know how she knew that, but she could feel it. It was a test of her feelings and Emane's loyalty.

"Emane, I need you to promise me something," she said grabbing his arm. "Whatever happens, you must listen to what I tell you. It's a test."

"Okay," he said, offhandedly, focused on his environment.

"NO!" She said it with such forcefulness that Emane dropped the flask. It clattered on the rocks at their feet. "You don't understand. Whatever I tell you," she said, squeezing his arm with urgency, "no matter what it is, you have to trust me."

He stilled, "What?"

"You have to trust me! Please promise me that you'll trust me."

He nodded slowly, his eyebrows furrowed. "Okay, Kiora, I understand. Do you want to tell me what is going on?"

"I don't know exactly. I can feel something coming, and it is going to be hard, particularly for you."

"For me? How do you know that if you don't know what is going on?"

"I don't know, they are questioning you." She gripped her head. It was aching from feelings that kept slipping in amongst her own. It wasn't like talking to Arturo. More like an instinct that you couldn't explain, but you can't ignore. "I can't explain it, it's just a sense I get."

The room went from black to being completely lit without warning.

Emane yelped, covering his eyes. "What is going on?"

Kiora didn't answer, but blinked furiously trying to adjust to the light. She could feel the threads continuing to multiply and they were getting very close. She wanted to see what was going on, see what was coming. And as things came into focus, she wished she wouldn't have seen anything at all. Standing before them was the most frightening thing Kiora had ever laid eyes on. She wanted to look to Emane, but was too scared to take her eyes of the creature.

This creature was created and draped in nightmares. It looked like a cross between a dragon and a serpent. Six heads, all moving independently of each other, weaving and hissing, baring long, sharp fangs. It was scaly and changed colors as the light hit it, brown to green and back again. Each head had three horns and two enormous ears. It took one thunderous step in their direction. Kiora needed time to think, and she wasn't going to get it if they just stood here. She grabbed Emane's arm and threw up a bubble. The creature screamed out in protest.

"Run, Emane!" She grabbed his arm and headed straight towards the creature.

"Why are we running at it?!" he yelled as she jerked him along.

"Because it's the last place it will look for us."

The creature drew each one of its heads back and all six blew fire out into the room. It barely missed the Kiora and Emane as they ran straight underneath it and to the back wall. The creature continued to spray the room with fire trying to flush them out.

"This isn't going to last forever, Kiora!"

"I know! I just need a minute or two to think. Watch him." Kiora closed her eyes and tried to purge her memories of what she had seen. Focus, she thought. Focus on the thread. She could feel it now, pulsing through her. And it was the same thread. Her eyes flew open; they were all the same thread—the boy, Dralazar, and now this thing.

"He can change himself," she whispered.

"What do you mean, 'change himself'?"

"They are all the same," she said, the pieces were starting to come together. "The boy, Dralazar, and now this. They are the same person...or thing."

Emane shook his head. "I don't understand, but I believe you. So now what?"

"I have to tell him that I know. I think that's what he wants. He wants to test my abilities, to see if I can feel the threads clearly enough to put aside what I see with my eyes." She stopped as the final piece fell into place. "It is a test. That's why we're here, alone. That's why Arturo didn't tell us anything."

"What are you going to do, walk out there and tell him you

know what he is?" he asked, not tearing his eyes off the creature. "And what if you're wrong?"

"That's exactly what I have to do."

"And what about me?" he sputtered, turning towards her. "You just want me to stand here and watch as he sets you on fire?!"

Kiora realized the rest of the test. "This test isn't just for me, it's for you too, Emane. To see if you will trust me." She grabbed him by both the arms, looking into his eyes. "No matter what happens," she said very clearly, "do not hurt that thing."

Emane just stared at her, wide eyed, with his mouth hanging open.

"I mean it, Emane," she glanced out into the room where the creature was swinging its heads back and forth, spurting fire in every corner and around every rock it could find. "This could look…bad."

"Look bad!" His face was turning red. "Getting blasted by that thing doesn't just look bad, Kiora, it is bad!"

This was going to be much harder for him, she could tell. She leaned over and kissed him. "Please, Emane, if you are going to be my Protector, you have to listen to me!" She grabbed his face between her hands, "No matter what, do not hurt him." Kiora didn't give him a chance to argue. She dropped the bubble and ran out into the middle of the room.

"HEY! I am over here." The creature stopped and slowly turned all six of its heads to look at her. "I don't know what you are," she yelled "but I know you are the same creature that I met earlier. I can feel your thread, and it is the same as the boy and Dralazar. I know this is a test. You are not evil, and I will not fear you."

The creature stepped closer towards her and she could see Emane step towards her as well. She held out her hand towards Emane. "Stop," she commanded, "let him come."

Emane froze but Kiora could see the panic written on his face. The creature got closer still, each step rattling stones along the ground. Growling, it brought down one of its heads to her, peering at her with one eye. She held its gaze, trying to breathe slowly despite the hammering in her chest. Looking into its eyes, she knew its intentions. There was no time to explain.

"Emane!" She screamed, spinning around to face him. "DO NOT HURT HIM! I KNOW WHAT I AM DOING!"

CHAPTER TWELVE

ALLIANCES

EMANE WATCHED AS THE creature pulled back the one head that had been staring at Kiora. It pulled itself up to its full height, opened its enormous mouth and flew down heading straight for her. Emane held his breath. Surely there would be a bubble or a shield or something. But there was nothing. Kiora sat there smiling at him with an apologetic smile as the creature came down over the top of her, and then she was gone. The creatures jaw snapped shut and tossed its head back up to swallow.

"NOOOO!" Emane screamed. "NOOO!" He reached for his sword and charged at the creature. He ran, envisioning his sword running through the creature that had just taken Kiora. Taking the life that had just taken her away from him, away from the kingdom. He had just found her, he couldn't lose her, not now. As he pulled back his sword, two memories barreled through his mind—Epona first and then Kiora saying, "Trust me." The two words wrenched him to a stop. "Trust me." The creature was now within striking distance. He held his sword up, ready to strike, his arm shaking. He wanted to kill it so bad. Every nerve in his body was trembling, wanting to strike. "Trust me." His hand loosened and his sword clattered to the ground. He looked up at the creature, defeated.

"I don't know what you are," he said through clenched teeth, kicking his sword between its giant feet. "But I promised her I wouldn't hurt you. So if you are going to eat me too, let's get it over with." He dropped to his knees, looking up to meet the creature's eyes. If this was going to be the end, he was not going to be looking at the floor when it happened.

All six heads were staring at him, but none moved to strike. The creature shuddered and started to shake. Its heads began twisting and pulling within its body. The body was shrinking and changing shape as it went. It looked as if it was unraveling at the same time, colors changing, heads spinning, popping and cracking. There was a flash of light much like the one right before it had arrived. Emane shielded his face with his arm, and then all was quiet. He lowered his arm to see Kiora standing there next to a man he had never seen before.

"What is this?" Emane whispered, his heart wrenching at the sight of her. He couldn't even trust his eyes anymore.

"Emane," Kiora whispered. "It's me."

"How do I know that?" he spat at the creature. "If you're going to kill me, get on with it. At least have the decency not to toy with me." He was tired, emotionally exhausted, and he had just watched the girl he was learning to love be swallowed by a monster.

"Emane, if I may," the man spoke. "You have been through a lot."

Emane's eyes narrowed and turned to the man. "Have I? HAVE I?" he yelled. "I don't know what I have been through, I don't know what is going on, I don't know who to trust and I certainly don't know if that is the girl I know!" He shoved his finger in Kiora's direction.

"My name is Drustan," the man spoke, ignoring Emane's rant. "I am a chameleon of sorts, a Shapeshifter, you might say. I apologize for my actions, but we had to test you and the Solus. The pair of you is a little unprecedented."

"Unprecedented?" Emane's eyebrow rose.

"Yes, surely they have told you how unusual this is."

"No, they did not."

Drustan looked over at Kiora, who also shook her head in the negative.

"That is surprising to me. I would like to invite you to stay with us for a time and I will explain all. But before I do, I would like to offer you a room in which to clean up and eat. That is, if you will accept our invitation."

"Our?"

"Yes. I apologize, Prince, I forget that you cannot feel them."

"Who?" Emane was so tired of trying to understand what was going on that he couldn't even feign politeness.

"My friends!" the man announced as if it were a most joyous occasion. "Please come forth so we can properly introduce ourselves."

Emane's eyes widened as the room began to morph around them. The boulders began to stretch and grow legs. The bats flew down from the cavernous ceiling and once their tiny feet touched the floor, they began changing as well, growing, turning, changing colors. The bugs amongst the walls and floors, every ant and centipede; people were appearing throughout the cavern—at least they looked like people at the moment. Who knew what they actually looked like? Emane swallowed, his stomach rolling with unease unlike anything he had experienced before.

"My people and I will be on our way. We will allow you and Kiora time to decide if you would like to accept our offer."

Emane looked over to the body that looked like Kiora, who was, to her credit, looking surprised herself. "You still have not told me how I can be sure that this is indeed Kiora and not one of you."

"We are masters of our own bodies," said Drustan, "we can change into anything you can imagine. But I am not a mind reader. If you would like to know if this Kiora is who she says she is, you only need talk to her." He bowed and left the cavern, his people following behind him.

Emane got to his feet as the procession left the room. As the last Shapeshifter left the cavern, she turned to him.

"Emane, I am so sorry."

Turning away from her, he clenched his fists. "For what?"

"For doing that to you. It wasn't fair."

Emane didn't want to hear any more until he knew if this was Kiora or not. "Where were we last night?" he snapped over his shoulder.

"In the Cave of Arian."

"And where did you sleep?"

"Next to you," she said softly. Emane's heart contracted. "Emane, I am so...so—"

He cut her off, breathing heavily. "Kiora, I am not ready to talk. So are we staying here or not?"

"Yes."

"Fine," he said, "then let's go." Stomping ahead, he left her standing there.

KIORA'S HEART ACHED LOOKING at the angry set of Emane's shoulders as he left. Sighing, she followed Emane out of the cavern and down the tunnel the Shapeshifters had followed. Kiora wanted to call out to him, but he was fuming, it was clear enough from the back. She was somewhat glad she couldn't see Emane's face.

A young woman stood halfway down the long passageway. She appeared to be waiting for them. As they got closer, she stood forth and bowed.

"My Lord and Lady, Drustan has asked me to bring you to your quarters if you have decided to stay."

A smile tugged at Kiora's lips, she had never been called a lady before. "Thank you, we have decided to stay."

"Wonderful! Come with me."

She escorted them through a maze of twists and turns. Rights and lefts followed by more lefts and rights. They walked until Kiora was so turned around she didn't think she could find her way out if she wanted to.

The guide suddenly stopped and said, "Welcome to the colony." She swept out her arm and Kiora could not believe her eyes.

She walked forward, Emane following hesitantly a step behind her, to an iron railing and looked over. The colony was built around a hundred and fifty foot waterfall. It had rows upon rows of doors lined upon the ridges circling downward. It resembled a sort of seashell she had seen once, spiraling in upon itself. It started where they were, and if she followed the path, level by level, it would bring her all the way to the pool at the bottom. But the most curious thing was the waterfall. It was the largest one Kiora had ever seen. It was magnificent; the speed at which it flowed over the edge and down the back wall of the colony was almost frightening. And yet despite its awesome appearance, the sound was the equivalent of a quiet babbling brook. Listening to it actually reminded her very much of the brook that ran near her old home. She used to love to sit next to it, allowing the sound of water to calm her.

"Why can't we hear it?" Kiora asked.

"Hear what?" her guide asked, perplexed.

"The waterfall, it sounds different than it should."

"It has always been that way. When they chose this location for the colony, it was decided that the sound of the falls was too great. To remedy the situation they enchanted it. Come." She turned on her heels and started down the twisty ramp that led to the bottom.

Emane trudged ahead, his eyes on the ground and his shoulders slumped. It broke Kiora's heart to see him this way.

"Where do the doors lead?" Kiora asked their guide.

"To our homes. Each door is what a human would call a 'residence,' I believe."

Kiora scanned out across this great colony, noticing there were thousands of doors. These Shapeshifters had a very large family. Approaching the falls, Kiora could feel the water splashing on her face. She was walking through the mist and it felt brilliant. She was so dirty and grimy she wanted more than anything to stand in that one spot and never move. But Emane and their guide were getting ahead of her, so she picked up her speed to fall back in place behind the trudging prince. Following behind the waterfall, they came out the other side barely damp. It was very disappointing that more of a drenching was not involved. A few feet later the guide stopped in front of a door.

"My Lady, this one will be yours."

"Please," Kiora was trying not to laugh, "There is no need to call me that. Kiora is fine."

"Very well, My Lady."

Great, now she was to be referred to as "My Lady" as well as "The Solus."

The guide opened the door with a key and handed it to Kiora. "Everything you need is inside. Eleana has sent clothes, among other things, and there is a hot bath waiting for you."

Kiora was grimy and dirty and hadn't had a bath since before she went to Morcant's lair. "I thought you couldn't read minds," Kiora challenged.

The guide looked puzzled for a minute and then tried not to laugh. "My lady, the bath was made ready not because you were hoping for one. Rather, it is quite obvious that one is in order."

Kiora looked down, suddenly very embarrassed, and mumbled a quick thank you as she ducked into the room. She could hear Emane chuckling under his breath. At least something made him laugh. She left the door open just a crack to hear where Emane was going. To her relief, she heard the guide stop at the next door down and open it for him. Shutting the door quietly, Kiora turned to look around the room.

She did not know what she had been expecting, but the room was beautiful. The stone floor had been polished to a high sheen. There were candelabras hanging throughout the room, each one lit and twinkling like a collection of fallen stars. It was bright and cheery, not at all the dull dreary cave they had entered. There was a bed. A bed! A beautiful four-poster bed. She thought she would die of joy right on the spot. It was magnificent and luxurious and Kiora had never seen anything like it. Piles of linens covered the carved bed. And on the other side of the room was the tub! It was large and deep, and the mere idea of it was heaven. She had used a small washbasin at home, but her few days in the castle had opened her eyes to the bliss that was a bathtub big enough to lie down in. She could see the steam coming off of the water and her body itched to get the disgusting clothes off. Walking over, she noticed a rather large leather satchel sitting at the dressing table. She opened it to find the things that Eleana had sent. A change of riding clothes, casual clothes and two of the most stunning dresses she ever had the pleasure of holding. There was also soap, salve for her cuts, and a comb. She dug around to see if there were any treasures she had neglected to find and found a few decorative hair combs at the very bottom.

There was a knock at the door. She ran over expecting to see Emane, but it was her guide.

"I apologize, My Lady, but I forgot to tell you that it will be dinnertime in a few hours and Drustan requested that you come in your finest."

Kiora nodded, "Of course."

How could Eleana know she would need those dresses? How Eleana knew any of the things she knew was a mystery to Kiora. She closed the door softly and practically ran over to the tub, peeling away the layers of grime and dirt as she went. Touching her toe into the hot bath, Kiora released a sigh of utter bliss.

She eased herself the rest of the way into the tub, letting her stiff muscles and sore back soak in the wonderful warmth. Leaning her head against the back, she decided that someday when this was all over, she was getting a tub. Not a washbasin, a full-size tub. If it was the only piece of furniture in her entire home, so be it.

Kiora closed her eyes and tried to not think about anything. But despite the warm water and her best efforts, Emane's face would not leave her; the look in his eyes as he watched the monster come down over the top of her. He didn't know that she had seen everything. She watched as he ran at the monster, his face contorted in rage, and then his face as he dropped his sword. He didn't know that she had stood there with tears streaming down her own face at his pain. Her eyes started to water again. Was she destined to hurt everyone in her life?

She shook her head trying to clear the memories, and grabbed the soap. Maybe scrubbing the dirt away would help scrub out the memories, at least for the moment. She scrubbed and scrubbed, she had never been so dirty in her entire life! Her hair was greasy, her elbows black and her fingernails were atrocious. The soap burned on every cut, especially the one on her head.

She pulled herself out of the tub that was now full of very warm, very black water. She rubbed the salve on her stinging cuts and sighed as it soothed all the pain. Plopping herself at the dressing table, she looked in the mirror. She looked older. She couldn't put her finger on why, but she looked older.

After Kiora had combed out her hair, pulling one side up with a hairpin, she moved over to the satchel and pulled out one of the dresses Eleana had sent. It was truly beautiful. Green and gold, intricate beadwork. Fingering the fabric, she was amazed at its softness; so different from the rough fabric her dresses had always been cut from. Gingerly she turned the dress over and rolled her eyes at all of the buttons running up the back. This dress was not made for one to be able to put on by oneself. She buttoned as many as she thought she could before pulling the dress over her head. It took a lot of wiggling with all of those buttons done, but she finally got it on. She tried to reach the rest of them, but no matter how much she twisted and turned she could not get those last buttons fastened.

"Just great." She could ask Emane for help, but she wasn't sure if he would open his door to her. He had been so angry, and she couldn't even argue with him as to why. Resigning herself to the fact that there was no way she was going to get those buttons done alone, she flopped onto the bed. She probably had at least another two hours before it was time for dinner. In case the test wasn't over, she might want to learn some new tricks. She summoned the book from the cave and began flipping through it.

Calling is the ability to speak to another person over long distances. There are some magical creatures, such as pegasus, who naturally have this ability. But there is a way to talk to those who do not naturally have this ability. You will need to know the person that you are trying to communicate with. To try this, visualize the person that you want to speak with. This is a skill that does require a small incantation to begin the process. Once you have communicated with another person's mind, the incantation may or may not be necessary the next time you try. This will depend upon the closeness of the relationship between you and the one you are communicating with. The incantation is "eh hear hena to ye la." Focus on the person, repeat the incantation, and then think the words you wish the other person to hear. Please note that this is not effective if there is a great distance between you and the person you are trying to communicate with. It will depend upon the strength of the magic as to how far one can project.

"All right, let's try it," she said, pulling herself up on the bed and closing her eyes. At least he couldn't slam the door in her face this way. Imagining Emane, she repeated the incantation aloud, *"eh hear henna to ye la."*

Pushing her thoughts into the room next door, she thought as hard as she could, I'm sorry, Emane.

She waited for a minute, holding her breath before slamming the book shut. There was really no way to know if that had worked or not. Crossing her arms, she stared at the wall wondering if she should go over and try to talk to him anyway.

The loud banging on her bedroom door scared her half to death. She jumped so high she nearly knocked the book to the floor. The banging began again. Scrambling off the bed, she ran over to open the door.

Emane came storming into the room. "What was that?" he

demanded.

Kiora shut the door behind him. "You don't need to yell."

"Why not? One minute I am getting dressed, trying to get this ridiculous brooch pinned onto my lapel," he yelled, waving a very royal looking piece of jewelry in the air, "and the next I am hearing your voice inside of my head. I almost stuck this thing right through my heart!" He pulled his lapel back to show the bloodstain on his white shirt.

She covered her mouth with a little gasp, "Oh, Emane, I am so sorry!"

"Yes," he said dryly, dropping his arms back to his side. "So you said."

Moving over to him, Kiora reached out, stopping midway. 'Does it hurt?"

"Well, yes, Kiora, it…" he deflated. "No, not anymore; it's just bleeding that's all."

"Here," she said scrambling over to the pile of things Eleana had sent. "Eleana sent me some salve, open your shirt."

Taking the jar out of her hand, Emane set it back down. "I'm fine, Kiora; it just scared me, that's all." Raising an eyebrow, he asked, "How did you do that?"

"It worked?"

Closing his eyes, Emane shook his head like she was the most exasperating creature he had ever met. "Yes, it worked. Why else would I be over here yelling about hearing voices in my head! When will you stop being surprised when things work?"

Blinking, she decided to brush off his sarcasm. "It's known as calling." She ran over to the bed to get the book "Look, it says that I can communicate with people telepathically, like Arturo."

Emane was scanning what she had shown him over her shoulder. "It says you might be able to do it without the incantation if the relationship is close enough."

"Yes."

"Try," his voice came, soft and hesitant near her ear.

Kiora thought the same thought, the one she really wanted him to understand. Emane, I am truly sorry.

"Wow."

"It worked?" She spun around, putting herself almost nose to nose with him. Swallowing, she asked quieter, "Without the incantation?"

"Yes, that is, if you were still apologizing."

"I was."

Stepping back, he looked at her, his eyes traveling from her hair, to her lips and down to her feet before trailing back up. She swallowed again, suddenly aware of how much lower this dress was than anything she had ever worn. Her fingers moved nervously to her neck, looking away. She heard his breath catch.

"You look...very nice, Kiora."

Unable to look at him, she blushed before stammering, "I can't get my dress buttoned."

"Turn around," he murmured.

Kiora turned, pulling her hair away from her back so Emane could reach the buttons more easily. Her dress was open to her shoulder blades and his fingers brushed against her skin as he fastened the last few buttons. She shivered underneath his touch.

"There," he said, "that was the last one."

Kiora turned shyly back around, dropping her hair. "Thank you," she said quietly.

Emane put his hand behind her neck and pulled her into him. He kissed her, hard. It was desperate and strong and so much different from the first time he had kissed her. He softened his grip on her neck and kissed her again.

"Emane," she whispered, "I don't want to hurt you."

"You won't hurt me, Kiora."

"I already have," she said between his kisses, trying to stop the tears. "I saw your face today, earlier in the cave. I watched everything happen."

He let go of her neck, pulling back, startled. "What do you mean, you watched everything?"

That look on his face. Horror, surprise...a look she hated and a look she never wanted to see on him. Turning away, she grabbed a hold of one of the four columns on the bed, wrapping her arms around it as if a piece of wood could protect her.

"Kiora, what did you mean?"

Biting her lip, she squeezed the column for support. "After the creature came down over the top of me, a bubble went up. It wasn't from me; I don't know where it came from." There was a silence behind her. Rushing forward, she continued, "I wanted to say something, to tell you that I was okay, but I knew they needed to see if you would trust me." Still he said nothing. "Watching you was...horrible." She leaned her head against the wood. She had seen the agony on his face in that cave and it floated in front of her in the silence he left her in. "I am so tired of hurting people," she whispered.

A chair squeaked behind her as he drug it out, she heard him drop heavily into it with a giant sigh. "What do you want?" he repeated with a vulnerability that turned her around. "Kiora," he ran his fingers through his hair. "If you watched me after I thought you had died then you know, you must know." Shaking his head, he finally met her eyes, "What do you want?"

"I want you here with me," she said awkwardly. "Emane, you're my protector! The thought of losing you..."

He made an impatient noise, "The Protector."

"You said," her voice hitched, "you wanted to be my protector."

"I do."

"Emane, I know you're angry but…"

He leapt out of his chair, "I'm angry because I thought I lost you. I am angry because they tested us and played our emotions as if it were nothing more than a game. But what I want to know right now…" he stopped rocking on the balls of his feet with nervous energy. "Kiora, I need to know if you want me as more than your friend, as more than a Protector."

She stared at him open mouthed. "Yes," she whispered it, he started to move towards her but she hurried onward, wanting to get it out before he kissed her again. "But I am so scared that I will hurt you again, like I did today."

He covered the distance between them with three strong steps. Grabbing her hands he said, "And I am scared that I will not be able to protect you, like today." A nervous smile pulled at one corner of his mouth, "I suppose we are even."

"If you changed your mind, I would understand."

"What? Like your sister? Decide to stop caring for you because of your magic?"

Kiora's eyes widened. "Caring for me?"

Emane rolled his eyes, "Kiora, what did you think we were talking about?" Leaning down, he kissed her. "You are unlike any girl I have ever met." Wrapping one hand around her waist, he pulled her tight against him.

She melted into his embrace for a few minutes and then gently pulled back. "What was all this about not being able to talk about your feelings?" Her eyes twinkled.

He shrugged his shoulders. "You bring it out in me, I guess. Now can you help me get this stupid thing on without impaling myself?"

She took the broach and pinned it onto the lapel of his jacket.

CHAPTER THIRTEEN

SHAPESHIFTER'S ALLIANCE

KIORA AND EMANE SAT together on the couch in Kiora's room looking through Arian's book.

"It says that if you try to respond immediately after I call you that you might be able to talk back to me."

"In your head? Wouldn't I need some magical ability to do that?"

"That's not what it says. As long as I start it, it might work. Let's try, I will send you a message again and then you try to say something back."

Emane shrugged his shoulders, "It's worth a try."

"All right, here it goes." Do you like being a prince? Kiora waited, but there was nothing. "What did you say? I didn't hear anything."

"That's because I didn't say anything!" said Emane. "You can't ask me a question I don't know the answer to."

"What do you mean, you don't know?"

"I don't know. Sometimes I do, other times I don't. Try again, something I don't have to think about this time."

What color are my eyes?

Green.

She looked up at him with a huge grin, "I heard you."

"Really?"

"Let's try again." Do you wish you could do magic?

Yes, I would feel more qualified to be your Protector.

They were interrupted by a knock at the door, "My Lord and Lady, if you would please accompany me to dinner."

Kiora looked around the room trying to decide where to hide the book. However, in a world full of creatures that could be anywhere at any time, she decided nowhere was really that safe. So she sent it back to Arian's cave.

Kiora and Emane followed the same guide back behind the waterfall. Only this time, instead of coming out the other side they turned and went further behind it. There was a stone box with an open front attached to ropes and pulleys. The guide motioned them to step inside.

"What is this thing?" Emane asked.

"This is how we take visitors to the bottom without having to walk the entire colony."

Kiora hadn't thought about how long it would have taken to walk from where they were to the bottom of the falls. Each turn would take at least 20 minutes. She couldn't tell how many levels there were for sure, but there were a lot. Emane and Kiora stepped inside. Their guide followed them in, grabbed the rope unwrapping it from its hold, lowering the three of them straight down behind the falls.

The box set itself gently down at the base of the falls. The wall of water crashing into the pool in front of them barely made a sound.

The three of them walked into a large hall filled with tables set for a feast. The guide pointed to the table sitting horizontally at the head of all the others.

"You are to sit there on either side of Drustan." She turned and left the way she came.

Kiora and Emane made their way to the head table. The chair in the center was obviously Drustan's, as leader of the colony. It was gold, and intricately carved. The two chairs on either side were slightly smaller, silver and adorned with jewels.

"Should we sit now?" Kiora asked. "We are the only ones here."

"That is what she told us to do. It is better to listen than risk offending our hosts."

Kiora and Emane sat. No sooner had they relaxed into their seats than the doors on either side of the stone room were flung open and the rest of the colony flooded in. The Shifters talked and chatted one with another, finding their seats.

The room quieted in respectful silence as Drustan's voice came from behind them. "Thank you for joining us for dinner." He looked almost the same as the first time they had seen him with slight differences—tall with broad shoulders and very strong features. His brows were large and bushy, and his nose looked a little larger than last time. His eyes were brown, where she could have sworn they were green earlier.

He was dressed in a white shirt and an ornate vest over the top that dropped down to his knees and simple black pants. The vest was hand woven with glittering threads in all colors. His hair was long and black with a red stripe running from his forehead back, which also had not been there before. Kiora supposed she should be grateful that Drustan looked similar enough so that she could recognize him without relying on his thread.

Drustan pulled back his chair, settled in, and clapped rather

ceremoniously three times. On cue, a procession of people entered
the room, each holding a large platter above their head. They
scurried amongst the tables, setting down platters, removing the lids
and scuttling away for more.

It smelled and looked very much like the food at the Hollow;
soups and breads foreign outside of the magical community.
Vegetables floating in broth that Kiora had never seen before,
although she was pretty sure she spotted a potato in one of the
dishes. Small slices of bread piled high with creamy toppings and
pieces of cheese on top of that. The smells alone made her mouth
water. She really would never be able to eat the way she used to and
be satisfied. The food tasted too good to ever go back.

They ate in relative silence—Kiora, Drustan and Emane—the
colony a buzz of activity around them. As dessert was served, Kiora
finally spoke.

"Do you mind if I ask a personal question?" She looked at
Drustan.

"You have earned the right to ask whatever questions you want,
My Lady."

"If you are all Shapeshifters, then why are you all in human
form? Is it something you prefer?"

"No," Drustan replied. "We all have our favorite forms. But if
we have guests, we strive to make them as comfortable as possible."

"That is very thoughtful of you, but it is not necessary. You are
welcome to take whatever form you prefer."

Drustan looked at her for a minute considering what she had
said. Clapping his hands above his head, he shouted, "Attention."
He waited calmly for the chatter to die down as all eyes turned to
him, "Thank you for coming to dinner with us on this momentous
evening. Lady Kiora has asked that you all be comfortable enough
to take whatever form you desire."

There was some mumbling throughout the crowd and then the morphing began. It was a sight to behold. Some grew larger, while others shrank. The colors changed as some grew fur or scales. Others had wings coming out of their backs. She looked around in shock. The tables were now full of Guardians, lizards, birds, animals and some creatures she had never seen before.

Drustan leaned over to Kiora, 'We do ask that those that prefer larger forms such as Dragons refrain from doing so at the dinner table."

She laughed, she couldn't help herself. "That makes sense. And what about you, you are still in human form."

He nodded. "I do prefer it. I find it very functional. The lack of wings is somewhat inconvenient, but it is nothing a little magic won't fix."

"What is your original form?" Emane asked, taking a bit of his pie. Kiora had tried it, very tangy on the bottom with a whipped sweet top.

"Original?" Drustan frowned with a quizzical look.

"What body is truly yours? What are you born as?" he expounded.

"Oh, I understand." He nodded "Nobody knows what we started as. We are born in whatever shape our mother has taken at the time." Drustan answered calmly. "I am glad you are feeling comfortable enough to ask questions. What else would you like to know?"

"Does it hurt? Changing forms like that." Kiora asked. "It looks painful."

"Not at all. It is the blessing of our species."

Kiora did have one other thing that was bothering her.

"Back in the cave...who threw up the bubble? I thought it was you, but then you pulled away from me and the bubble never left."

Emane shoved another bite in forcefully at the mention of the events in the cave.

"We did need an additional person to pull off the illusion. There was a small ant hidden underneath one of the rocks at your feet. We felt confident you would not notice him."

"Of course," Kiora muttered. "Shape shifting has many advantages."

"Many, which is why we have always been sought after during these times of war." Drustan looked at Kiora and Emane's nearly empty plates. "Are you finished? We have much to discuss."

"Yes, of course," Emane answered, laying his fork to the side.

"Yes," said Kiora.

"Wonderful. Please follow me," Drustan said, pushing his chair back.

He led them through a hall that ran behind the dining room. At the end of the hall they entered a larger room where Eleana was waiting for them.

"Eleana!" Kiora yelled and ran over to her, throwing her arms around her neck. "I am so glad to see you!"

Eleana laughed. "It is good to see you too." She pulled her back to look at Kiora. "The dress suits you."

"It is beautiful, thank you."

"No," she said, bowing her head slightly, "thank you."

"For what?"

"For impressing our friends here." Eleana motioned to Drustan. Turning her attention to Emane, she said, "I apologize for the circumstances, they were unavoidable."

"Yes," Drustan replied, "We are impressed. I am to assume their tracks were covered as we discussed?" Drustan raised his bushy brows.

"Of course, Drustan."

"Excellent. Now, there is much to talk about and little time, so please sit." He motioned to a round table with four chairs surrounding it. They each took their place. "I had mentioned earlier how unusual this pair is and they didn't seem to know what I was referring to, Eleana."

"No, they do not. I do not believe in telling people that the odds are stacked against them before they gain their footing, Drustan."

"Hmmm," he said rubbing his chin. "Appears to have been a wise decision."

Emane interrupted, "Can someone please tell us what is going on?"

Drustan smiled, "But of course. My apologies, My Lord."

"Prince," Eleana corrected.

"Prince?" Drustan's eyebrows rose, again. "That does explain a lot."

"What is that supposed to mean?" Emane demanded, shifting in his chair, trying to keep himself in it.

"Your manners are, at times, lacking. That is all."

Emane opened his mouth, and Kiora grimaced. Thankfully, he closed it with a snap, answering tightly, "I apologize for my lack of manners. This journey has been...difficult for me."

"I would imagine it has. There is a reason we have never had a non-magic-bearing human as Protector before."

Kiora and Emane both looked up and spoke at the same time. "Never?"

"Never. When we heard of this pairing, we were skeptical, to say the least," Drustan answered. "And then to pair him with a human who had just discovered her magic weeks ago—it was preposterous, impossible. And yet," his waved over the table at them, "here you sit."

It was all coming together in Kiora's mind. "That's why you

WINGS OF ARIAN | 223

needed to test us."

"Yes. Neither I nor the colony believed it possible. Needless to say, we were apprehensive about aligning ourselves with a weak pair such as yourselves. But we were happily proven wrong. You were both impressive, beyond our expectations." Leaning forward, Drustan placed one elbow on the table, "Tell me, Kiora, earlier in the cave, you sensed my intentions, didn't you?"

Kiora nodded, "Yes."

"That is why you told Emane not to hurt me. Tell me, what did you see?"

"I didn't see anything," she said smoothing her dress beneath the table. "I couldn't even really hear it. It was more like an impression. I could feel what you were intending to do."

Drustan's bushy eyebrows rose again, for the third time, as he looked over to Eleana.

"It's true. Kiora can communicate with Arturo as well."

"But you told me you were not telepathic," Kiora argued.

"I am not," Drustan said, leaning back in his chair rubbing at his chin. "But you may be."

Kiora's mouth fell open. "No, I can't be. I have never gotten anything except from Arturo."

"Humans are not capable of true telepathy," Eleana corrected. "But few, such as yourself, are more sensitive to very strong communications. It is my guess that Drustan here was testing you to see if you could feel what he was trying to send you."

"I was." Drustan smiled. "I was so curious when I heard you say that this was a test when no such thing had been mentioned. I had to know."

"So is your curiosity satisfied, Drustan? Do we have your allegiance?" Eleana abruptly asked.

"You do—on one condition. While Kiora trains further, we get to work with Emane."

"What did you have in mind?" Eleana asked as she watched Emane's shoulders tense.

"He will need some magic if he is to survive this, Eleana."

Emane objected. "Aleric told me my body is not capable of magic."

"It's not, or at least it wasn't born to be." Drustan gave Eleana a knowing glance, "But I think there are ways we can help you."

CHAPTER FOURTEEN

MINING

THE NEXT MORNING EMANE found himself practically running to keep up with Drustan. He seemed much taller than yesterday. Normally it would be an absurd thought, but considering the circumstances, it was quite possible Emane was not imagining it. They walked down at least twelve levels and Emane was left wondering what Drustan had against the contraption they had ridden in last night. Drustan turned abruptly, his bright vest billowing out behind him, and proceeded down a side passage. The passage dropped rapidly and Emane had to lean back onto his heels to keep from falling face first into Drustan.

Unable to keep quiet any longer, Emane asked, "Where are we going?"

"It took you longer to ask than I had expected, Prince."

"Please, just call me Emane. And am I to assume that is another comment about my lack of manners?"

"Not at all, just a comment on human nature. You are not the most patient of creatures." Drustan cleared his throat. "We are going to a mine deep within the mountain."

"What are we mining for?"

"Magic."

Emane stopped. "Magic?" His mind was spinning.

"Don't stop, young Prince," Drustan called over his shoulder without missing a step, "you would not fare well here if you became lost."

Emane hurried to catch back up. "I don't understand."

"Of course you don't. There are few people that know anything about what I am going to show you. This mine is rare and was thought to be a thing of myths and legends, even within the magical community. You see," he explained, his voice bouncing off the rock in the narrowing tunnel, "most magic you can feel. But what I am about to show you leaves no trace of its existence until after it has undergone a transformation, bonding it with a master. Dralazar himself does not know of its existence, nor does he know how to use it if he did find it. Unfortunately, after we are through with you, I am sure he will come looking."

Emane was fast becoming tired of Drustan's way of answering a question, forcing him to ask another. "What do you mean, after you are through with me?"

"You must have magic if you are to survive, and there are few ways of making that happen. We will be inserting you with magic."

"Inserting?" he pronounced each syllable, rolling it over in his mouth.

"Over the centuries there have been stories, most of them true, of objects that gave people magical abilities; swords, hats, stones, charms—all of them removable. These have their advantages as the wearer has the option to not wear the item if he chooses. However, they also have their disadvantages. The item can be lost or stolen, leaving the owner helpless. We have discussed giving you this magic and have come to the conclusion that the only acceptable option is to make sure that the magic cannot be lost or stolen. The only way we can think to do this is to insert the item into your body, therefore making the magic part of you, very much as if you had been born with the ability.

Emane went numb. What sounded like a good idea last night was feeling less and less appealing today. Magic was one thing, inserting magic rocks inside his body was quite another.

"You are very quiet, Prince."

"Please, please, call me Emane," he pleaded with slumped shoulders.

"Very well, Emane. You are very quiet."

"I am thinking. That is all."

"Very well, I will leave you to it. Keep up," Drustan snapped, lengthening his stride again.

Emane's legs were burning by the time they reached the mine. Drustan waved his hand at the wall and the torches ignited. Emane scanned the room. He didn't know what he was looking at, but whatever it was, it was beautiful.

EMANE'S ARMS WERE BURNING as he slung the pickax into the wall, trying to extract the vein of bright green from the stone walls. He swung over and over again at the section he had been working on for two days now. Stopping to wipe the sweat out of his eyes, he looked over at Drustan, who had been supervising.

"Tell me again," he huffed, "why I am the only one who can get this stuff out."

"If the magic is to bond with you it must be forged by you. To not forge it yourself would be risking not being able to use it at all."

"Right," Emane panted as he swung the ax again at the vein. "And after I get this out, what then? You haven't been very clear on that part." Despite the fact that he had asked Drustan multiple times.

"Then you may use it."

"I understood that part. It was the part about inserting it that you refuse to explain. *That* is what has me concerned."

Drustan sighed, "You humans really are the most impatient creatures I have ever met."

"Really?" Emane slammed the ax into the wall again, channeling his frustration through it. "I thought I was being quite patient. I have been hammering at this wall for two days with no real explanation about what we are doing after I am finished here." A large chunk of rock mottled with the green material fell to the floor. Emane picked it up and handed it to Drustan.

"Good, a couple more pieces this size and we will be ready to extract it."

"You are ignoring me." Again, he thought as he slung the pickax.

"I have told you, Emane, we want to put the material inside of your body, so that it cannot be removed or lost."

"Yes, I have heard that. What I have not heard is how you plan to do that."

"It will be explained Emane, just be patient."

Emane swung the ax into the wall trying to bash away the gnawing feeling that he should be very worried about this plan. Something about this was not right. He didn't need magic to know what his instincts were telling him.

IN THE COLONY, KIORA and Eleana were practicing blocking. Eleana would throw anything from magic to chairs at her and Kiora would block. Sometimes Kiora was to throw the item back across the room, other times, she was to hold it in place. They practiced moving things slowly and controlled, and then in forceful bursts. Kiora had been knocked on her behind more than once, but was getting more comfortable with practice. It took less and less effort each time.

"Eleana?" she asked, while keeping a chair from hurtling in her direction.

"You are comfortable enough to talk during this exercise?"

"I think so." The chair wobbled slightly but it held, "I am worried about Emane."

"How so?"

"It has been a few days now and we haven't heard from him. And I…" Kiora paused, she couldn't make sense of what she was feeling, trying to say it out loud made even less sense. "I get a feeling that he is worried about something."

Eleana was quiet for a moment, making Kiora feel even more ridiculous. Kiora focused her attention back to the chair still hovering in the room, grateful for a reason to look somewhere else.

"Set the chair down, Kiora." Kiora slowly lowered it to the floor. "You and Emane have become close, haven't you?"

"Yes," she said, her cheeks growing warm, "very close."

"What do you feel?"

"I feel…" she sighed heavily, "worried and anxious, as if something is not right."

"Are those your feelings?"

"No," she ventured slowly, looking back up to her, "I don't think so. They seem to be in addition to my own feelings. They feel as if they are Emane's feelings." Rubbing her temples, Kiora shook her head, "I don't know how to make sense of that. I can't feel what he feels, can I?"

"Come, sit." Eleana motioned to a sofa. "There are certain things that come with a relationship." She stopped. "I am assuming

230 | DEVRI WALLS

that is what we are discussing, based upon Arturo's grumbling."

Kiora laughed, "He was grumbling to you?"

"Yes, he was having a bit of a hard time with the situation." Sitting back, Eleana crossed her hands neatly in her lap. "There are certain things I should have warned you about. Although I must admit, after watching you two during your first week together, I did not see this coming."

"It was a surprise to both of us as well."

"Whenever magic is involved, things work a little differently. Things are amplified. If you have a relationship with Emane that is beyond the relationship of a Protector and a Solus, it is very possible that you are feeling his feelings."

Kiora fiddled with the edge of her shirt, not sure if this was a good or bad thing. "What if he doesn't want me to feel his feelings? What if he feels intruded upon?"

Eleana placed her hand upon Kiora's, "It is a possibility that it will upset him. You need to help him understand that it is only the strongest and most persistent of feelings that you will be able to feel. You cannot read his mind or know his thoughts. Nor can you feel all of his feelings. Most human couples can sense a change in mood from one another while in close proximity to each other. As I said, yours is amplified, and can work over longer distances." She patted Kiora's hand before grabbing it and pulling her to her feet. "Now come, we must go find Emane."

"Now?" The speed at which Eleana changed subjects always left Kiora whirling.

"Yes, something is wrong. I have been monitoring it for a couple of days now. I was waiting to see if you would sense it as well."

Kiora loved Eleana, but there were times where she felt like a caged rat that was being kept for observation.

EMANE SIGHED AS THE last chunk of rock clattered to the ground. He dropped his pickax and leaned against the wall, wiping the sweat from his forehead with the back of his arm. He was used to physical exertion, between his sword fighting and jousting training. Manual labor was an entirely different thing.

"There, that's the last piece."

"Excellent!" Drustan exclaimed. "Now, follow me."

Emane squatted down and picked up the piece of stone with a groan before adding it to the basket. Drustan picked it up as if it weighed nothing. Not only were his legs longer than when they first met, but he obviously could choose the strength of his body. Drustan turned to head back up the shaft, but stopped. Emane looked around his shoulder to see Kiora and Eleana standing there. They must have bubbled on the way down because Drustan looked surprised to see them, although Emane was at a loss as to why they would have done that.

"Hello, Drustan," Eleana said sweetly. "I see you have had Emane hard at work."

"Yes, he has removed all of the necessary material from the mountain. We will now have him purify it and then it will be ready."

"Ready for what?" Emane asked again. Perhaps with backup he could get some answers.

Drustan's eyes flickered nervously to Eleana before answering. "Ready to give you your magic, of course."

Eleana looked back from Emane to Drustan with as much suspicion as he felt. "Emane, what has Drustan told you?"

"Not much. He says they are going to insert that into me," Emane said pointing at the basket of green rock Drustan was holding. "But he won't tell me how."

Eleana turned slowly to Drustan, enunciating every syllable. "Insert it?"

"Yes, we think it's the only way," Drustan said, jutting his chin out while pulling himself to his full height.

"We?"

"The colony," Drustan said, shifting the basket to the other hand. "We have discussed it, and the danger of allowing him to carry it is too great."

"The danger of allowing him to carry it?" Eleana spoke through clenched teeth, her blue eyes flaring in a way Emane had never seen. She was always so calm, so much so he had begun to question if she was capable of feeling anger at all.

"Of course. You know the stories of creatures that have carried this magic. It was often lost or stolen. If Dralazar knew—"

"Of course Dralazar will know," Eleana snapped. "Everybody will know. The Prince who has been a non-magical being suddenly can do magic. His thread will change, Drustan, everyone will know."

Drustan stammered, looking for an answer.

She took a step towards him, her copper hair swishing around her. "You want to experiment upon our Protector, the only son of the King. You want to put this substance into his body. It has never been done before!"

"It has not, but we can think of no reason why it wouldn't work. If we insert it at the base of his neck it should work nicely."

"It could kill him, Drustan! Even he does survive the 'insertion,' as you call it. How do we know that the substance itself would not be fatal?!"

"It is the best way!"

"The best way is to not use Prince Emane as a guinea pig!"

"How are we to know if we never try?" Drustan shouted.

"Drustan!"

"ENOUGH!" Emane bellowed over the two. "Am I allowed to have a say in the matter?"

Drustan's eyes dropped to the floor.

"I choose not to have it inserted." Emane said, inclining his head, "Now, what other options do we have?"

Drustan was grumbling about it not working as well, and something about signing the papers for his death as he stormed out of the mine and to the colony above.

THE HEADS OF THE colony, along with, Eleana, Emane and Kiora were sitting in the same conference room that they had been in when Drustan had announced his allegiance with them. Now the table was larger, more chairs. Emane had stopped asking. It was very loud as the leaders of the colony and Eleana shouted retorts at each other.

"We are not inserting any magic, mined or otherwise, into Emane," Eleana said for at least the fifth time.

"How can we protect him if you will not allow us to help him?" A Shapeshifter in the form of a guardian shouted.

"You want to help him by experimenting on him! How is it helpful if it is found, by his death, that his body is not compatible with the metal?"

"We must try!" another shouted.

"No, you must try on a willing participant, which he is not. He has expressed his wishes. Why are we wasting our time arguing a decision that Emane himself has already made?"

"He does not know what is best for him, Eleana! He has never been in a magical war before. He has no idea what is in store," Drustan added.

That is enough! Emane thought, rolling his eyes. Shoving his chair back, he stood. "You're right!" he yelled. The crowd quieted and looked to the human standing before them. "You're right," he repeated in the stunned silence. "I don't know what I am in for. Regardless of that, I would like to live to figure it out. Now, the way I see it, we can all sit around arguing over a decision that I am not willing to change, or we can discuss a way to get around the problem at hand." Rocking on his heels, he turned around, placing his hands behind his back and walking the length of the table. "As I understand it, your concern is that if we put the metal into something else, I will lose the object, or that the object will be forcefully taken from me. Is that correct?"

"Yes," Drustan said with obvious annoyance.

"What if the object could not be removed from my person?"

"How would we do that," Drustan objected, "without putting it inside as we suggested in the first place?"

"My body is not a carrying case," Emane snapped. "What I meant is, what if it was on the outside of my body but could not be removed?"

"How do you suggest that be accomplished?" Eleana prodded.

"I once had a bracelet," Kiora said thoughtfully, "when I was a little girl. I loved it, but one day the clasp broke. It was so tight to my wrist that when I could not unlock the clasp I couldn't get it off."

Eleana stood, "That is brilliant, Kiora."

"He can't wear a bracelet," Dustan objected. "Dralazar will know immediately what it is."

"True. Emane, please take your shirt off."

Emane went to question why, thought better of it and began to unbutton his shirt. He took it off, laying it down on his chair.

"We need it to be concealed and yet irremovable," Eleana

explained to the table. "This is what I have in mind." Her hands moved slowly in front of her. A green mist began whispering its way across the table towards Emane. It glittered and shone just like the metal he had been mining. Under Eleana's direction it began weaving itself over and around his bicep and up to his shoulder. It went under his arm and around the edge of his collarbone, leaving room for his shoulder to move and rotate normally. The green smoke developed a head and a tail. It was a glittering beautiful snake weaving and moving its way around him. The snake opened its mouth and swallowed its tail, leaving an unbroken band. The group examined Eleana's work. It was definitely not coming off.

"I would enchant it into this position, leaving only me able to break the enchantment."

Drustan stood, walking around Emane, he examined the band suspiciously. "They will cut his arm off to get to it."

Emane's eyes narrowed, "Better my arm than my head."

"He's right, Drustan," Eleana added. "As I told you, his thread will be different. They will know something has been done. When they cannot find evidence of it on him, or with him, they will assume what you have done."

"It is hopeless then?" Drustan demanded.

"I said nothing of hopelessness. Our job is to make sure Emane is both trained and protected so that the opportunity does not present itself."

Emane looked around the group, "Are we in agreement?" The group all nodded in the affirmative; most slowly, as if they had no other choice than to agree. "Great. Now, what is the next step?" he asked as the green mist faded from around his arm.

Looking very annoyed that they were going to be unable to try his little experiment, Drustan answered. "You must finish the process to remove the magic from the stone."

"How do I do that?" Emane asked, picking his shirt back up and shrugging it over his shoulders.

"The stone must be melted down. Once it is liquefied, Eleana will separate it. Then it can be used for your intentions."

"When do we start?"

"In the morning," Drustan said. Giving Emane a disdainful look, he addressed the room, "This meeting is dismissed." The Shapeshifters filed out.

As the last one left the room, Emane collapsed into a chair. He felt more lost than anything. Leaning against the chair arm, he ran his fingers through his hair.

Eleana gave Kiora a soft smile. "Good night, you two; I trust you can find your way back to your rooms?"

"Yes, thank you." Kiora paused. "Eleana, why a snake?"

Eleana regarded them thoughtfully. "I thought it fitting that we fight a serpent with a serpent," she said with a satisfied nod before gliding out of the room.

LEANING OVER TO EMANE, Kiora asked, "Are you okay?"

"I'm fine, Kiora," he said, resting his elbow on the arm of the chair. "Just tired."

A feeling pushed at Kiora's heart: fear. It was cold, hard fear, and it wasn't hers. Then she felt a tinge of guilt that was hers. She was intruding on Emane's feelings again and he didn't even know she could.

"Emane, I need to tell you something."

"What is it?" Emane rubbed his forehead.

Her stomach flipped. "Today, well, the last couple of days, but especially today," she was rambling, "I had been getting funny feelings, nagging feelings. These feelings that wouldn't go away."

Stumbling over her words, she wrung her hands together in front of her. "I couldn't make sense of them at first. And then I did make sense of them, but wished I hadn't and...then I talked to Eleana and she told me I was right, which scared me because I didn't want to be right and I am scared that it will be horrible and..."

"Kiora," Emane interrupted, rubbing his eyes. "Are you going to, at some point, tell me what you're talking about?"

"The feelings that I had been feeling, they are," she gulped, "yours."

Emane's head rose slowly, staring blankly at her. "What?"

Tears began welling in her eyes, "I knew you'd be upset...I told Eleana..."

"Stop, Kiora. I just need to process this for a second." Emane looked at the floor while Kiora held her breath. "What feelings did you feel?"

"That something was not right; that you were worried and concerned."

"That's why you came in the mine?"

"Yes. I told Eleana that I didn't want to feel your feelings, but I guess this is common in..." she stopped. They still had not really defined what they even were, "...in a relationship, where magic is involved." She watched Emane's reaction, closely looking to see if he flinched at the word relationship. He did not.

"I see." Emane leaned back in his chair. His head tilted to the side. "I don't understand you sometimes, Kiora. If you were so scared to tell me, why did you?"

She cleared her throat. "I thought you deserved to know."

"All right," he said slowly.

"And," unable to look at him, she fixed her attention to her lap where she had clenched her hands together so tightly her knuckles had turned white. "When you told me you were fine, I felt..." she struggled for the words, "you're not."

A smile twisted at the corners of Emane's mouth. "Really, what I am I then?"

"You're afraid," Kiora spoke softly, looking up through her lashes.

"How many of my feelings do you know?"

"Not many. Eleana said that I would only feel the strongest and most persistent of feelings. Don't worry, though," she said hurriedly, "I can't read your thoughts or anything."

Emane stood up and grabbed her hand, "Let's go."

"Where?"

"Back to our rooms."

Kiora planted her feet and pulled her hand out of his grasp. "That's it?" she demanded. "I tell you that I can feel your feelings and that I know you are afraid and you are just going to pretend I didn't say anything?"

"No," he shook his head stifling a laugh. "Kiora," putting his hands on his hips, Emane looked upward, shaking his head. "You haven't been around many men, have you?"

"What kind of questions is that?" she demanded.

"Look, Kiora, I don't think the same as you. I would like some time to process the information on the way back to our rooms," he motioned to the door. "And if you don't mind, you have just accused your Protector and Prince of being afraid. If it is all right with you, I would like to further discuss this matter in private. And since we are in a 'relationship' as you put it, I would like to hold My Lady's hand." He caught her eye, "If that is all right?"

Kiora's cheeks flushed crimson, "Of course."

Walking in silence, Emane helped her into the stone box and pulled them up the back of the falls. He held her hand as they walked back to their rooms. Opening the door to Kiora's room, he escorted her inside. Silently turning, he closed the door, walking over to the sofa. Without looking at her, he patted the seat next to him.

"Will you sit by me?"

Kiora walked over and sat down, "Did I overstep my bounds downstairs?"

Emane laughed, "Of course you did, that's what I like about you."

"You like me because I have terrible manners and no idea of proper court etiquette?" she moaned. "The people are going to hate me when they finally learn who I am."

"Don't be ridiculous. They will love you because they will be able to see who you are." Emane reached over and grabbed her hand. "Now, tell me what you felt downstairs."

She looked into his eyes; they didn't look angry. She was so sure he would be angry. "Fear."

He nodded slowly, his thumb rubbing over the back of her hand. "I am afraid."

"Of what?"

He was silent for a long time. "Of magic."

"Magic, or your magic?"

Emane stood up and walked across the room. Leaning against the bedpost with his back to her he asked, "Are you sure you can't read my mind?" Kiora sat patiently, waiting for him to continue, hoping that he would. "I really thought that this would be easier if I had magic. But now...I am worried that I won't be able to control it."

She twitched, "Like me?"

He spun around, "You control yours just fine!"

"No, I don't, remember? Not always."

Emane huffed, "That was an accident. You didn't mean to hurt him."

"That is what you are talking about, isn't it, accidents?"

Frowning, Emane paced to the door, then to the bed and back again. Leaning one arm against the door, his head drooped, hair falling in his face. Kiora's fingers itched to brush it back for him.

"I suppose I am," he admitted. "But I might have a lot of accidents. This magic is not natural to me; I am not supposed to have it. Who knows how my body is going to react to it?"

Kiora hated trying to have a conversation like this. "Why do you always have to have your back to me when we talk?"

"Come on, Kiora," he said dropping his arm, swinging around to face her. "I am not beating the wall with a club. I thought I was making progress!"

She grinned, "That is true." Pushing herself up, she walked over to him. "Emane, do you think that Eleana would let this happen if it was going to be a disaster?"

"I think Eleana would let me do it if there was a good chance that it would work."

Looking up into Emane's eyes, Kiora's heart stuttered strangely in her chest, not with the old nerves but with a new excitement. Reaching out without worry, she brushed her finger along his jaw. He closed his eyes under her touch leaning into her. Raising her other hand, she ran it along the other side of his face, trailing her finger over his cheekbones and down to his lips. His eyes flashed open and her breath stopped in her throat at the look in his eyes. It was deep and intense and right now she just wanted to drown in it. Pushing up on her toes, she kissed him.

CHAPTER FIFTEEN

EMANE'S MAGIC

THE NEXT MORNING FOUND the two of them walking towards the falls on the way to Emane's ceremony. Although they were late, Emane did not seem in a hurry to make up the time.

"I need you to promise me something, Kiora. If I ever, EVER, let this magic start to change me you will tell Eleana immediately and ask her to take it off."

"Of course, but I won't need to."

"You can't be sure!"

"Yes, I can," she said, gently touching his arm, "because if you were going to allow this magic to change you, you would never have asked me in the first place."

"I am glad you have such faith in me," Emane said looking sidelong at her, "but I want you to promise."

"All right, I promise."

When they reached the bottom of the falls, Drustan was waiting for them. "Nice of you to show up, Prince, I was beginning to wonder if you wanted this at all."

"Patience is a virtue, Drustan," Emane said.

Drustan's lips pursed, obviously not amused. Kiora ,on the other hand, had to cover her mouth with her hand, looking behind them to keep from laughing.

"Follow me," Drustan said before turning down a passageway they had not been in before.

The passageway was lit by flaming torches hanging on the walls of stone. Emane turned to look at one as he walked past. They were fashioned of metal with nothing flammable on them. And yet there they were, burning.

"I don't think I will ever get used to stuff like that," he whispered to Kiora.

They walked until the passageway opened up, leaving them standing on the edge of a very large, very deep canyon. In front of them was a bridge that stretched from one side to the other. It was very old, and fashioned of wood and rope. Thin wood slats lined the bottom, tied together with thick rope that then twisted itself around to make two sides. Kiora stopped dead in her tracks when she saw it. Drustan and Emane moved forward, grabbing the sides of rope, unaware she had stopped. The bridge creaked and popped in protest under their weight, and Kiora took a step backwards. Her mouth was dry and her hands had turned to ice. She vaguely saw Emane stop and turn, but all she was looking at was the rope swinging out over the deathly blackness.

"Kiora, come on!" he yelled, his voice rolling around the empty space beneath him.

She shook her head emphatically, holding her hands fisted at her side.

"Kiora, come on, we are late!"

She shook her head again, whimpering.

Making his way back across, he grabbed her hand. "Your hands are freezing!" he exclaimed. Lowering his head, he tried to look in her eyes. "Kiora, what is the matter?"

"I don't like bridges," she whispered.

"What!"

"I don't like bridges, especially rope bridges. They are high and scary and...and..." Tears formed in her eyes as she looked desperately back at him. "I don't like bridges."

"Kiora," Emane looked to the bridge and back to her, "are you scared because it is too high?"

"Yes." She tried to step back again but his hold on her wrist kept her in place.

"You fly on Arturo all the time. That is much higher than this."

"I trust Arturo, he wouldn't let me fall. This, I don't trust this."

"Kiora, do you trust me?"

"Yes, I trust you, but—" she screamed as Emane picked her up and marched out over the bridge.

"Calm down! You said you trust me."

"I said I trusted you!" she yelled at him. "You holding me does not make me trust this bridge!"

"Close your eyes then."

Kiora moaned as she put her head onto his shoulder and tried not to listen to the bridge groaning at every step. "A magical place," she complained. "They enchant the waterfall so that it isn't too loud, and they still have this death trap of a bridge."

Emane just laughed at her. "All right, we're across." He set Kiora down and walked ahead of her, still chuckling.

"It's not funny," she hissed at his back, her hands still shaking.

The passage narrowed again as they continued further into the earth. Torches burned, lighting circles, but left slivers eerily draped in shadow. They entered a room that was oddly ceremonial looking. It was perfectly round with torches surrounding the room in even intervals. There were ornate stone inlays under their feet. Red, green

244 | DEVRI WALLS

and blue gems glittered and shone in the floor creating intricate geometric patterns. In the center was a circle of red gems and within that circle stood a large stone kettle on four squatty legs. The handle was made of iron and twisted and turned in a vine-like pattern. The room was bare except for the four high back chairs seated in a circle around the cauldron. Eleana already sat in one chair, glittering as much as the floor, waiting for them.

Eleana stood, "Please," she motioned with her hand, "have a seat."

They all took their seats in hushed silence as Eleana began to speak, "We are here today to perform an ancient ceremony. The granting of magic to a non-magical person is a great honor and a very serious responsibility. It is only bestowed in the direst of circumstances and only to persons of the highest moral character. Prince Emane has proven that he is willing to give his life to the cause and is therefore worthy of this honor. Emane, before we proceed I need to make sure that this is what you want."

He held tightly to the arms of his chair. "I want to save my kingdom, I want to protect Kiora, and I want to rid the land of the evil that threatens it. If the only way for me to accomplish these things is to do this, then I am sure."

"Very well. The concerns that Drustan expressed earlier are very valid ones. There will be those who will wish to take this magic from you by any means necessary. There may be some that wish to betray you because of it. You will need to always be aware of those around you. You will need to rely on Kiora's senses and instincts to keep you both out of harm's way."

"Will I be able to feel things as she does?" Emane asked.

Eleana's eyes softened. "I am uncertain of what you will and will not be able to do. It will certainly amplify some of your natural abilities. Beyond that, it affects every person differently. Before you do this, you need to understand that you will be nothing like Kiora. I have told you numerous times that she is exceptional. In all of my years I have never seen anything or one like her. Not in all the wars."

"Never?" Kiora's eyes widened.

"Never. Arian was amazing but it took him years to master what you master in days." Eleana turned her attention back to Emane, "It would be better if you had no expectations of what you will and will not be able to do."

"I understand."

"If you are ready, we will begin." Eleana put her hand out and fire ignited underneath the kettle. The flames burned hot and high, licking the bottom. Eleana moved around the pot whispering words Kiora did not understand, incantations she had never heard. The fire responded turning from orange, to red and then nearly white, heat poured from it in waves. Kiora and Emane flattened themselves against the chair backs, as their skin grew blisteringly uncomfortable under the assault of magical flame. Kiora could not see the inside of the kettle, nor did she dare lean closer to look, but whatever was happening within was casting a green glow upwards, lighting the ceiling. Eleana's whisperings ceased for only a second before she stretched her hand over the cauldron. Kiora could not understand how it was that Eleana could withstand the heat. More incantations followed as the green grew brighter, until with one final word it exploded outwards in a flash of light that engulfed Eleana entirely before pulling back into the kettle. The flames flickered up the sides, and then calmed themselves, returning to red, the heat also pulling itself back.

Eleana turned to Emane, handing him a very long handled stirring paddle.

"You must stir it, Emane, this is the last step before I can extract it."

EMANE CAUTIOUSLY STOOD. HE was sweating and he wasn't sure if it was from the heat alone, or his nerves. He swallowed hard before reaching for the paddle. Grasping it, he took it from Eleana. She nodded towards the kettle, urging him forward. Stepping up, he looked in.

Within, molten rock now spun. The rock he had mined had been a dark grey. It was now transformed into a bright swirling mass of silver with waves of hypnotic green which undulated, looking nearly alive. The molten rock felt alive as well, pulling at him with a strange draw he had never felt before. He wondered momentarily if this was what magic felt like. Lifting the paddle, he looked back to Eleana, unsure of what she wanted him to do. She held out her hand, indicating that he should place the paddle inside. Slowly he lowered it down and began to stir. The melted magic responded, pulling together and creating one thick wave of green that swirled from the outermost edge into the center. It was a brilliant color, brighter than the clearest emerald. Embedded within were flecks that sparkled and shone like diamond dust. He was mesmerized, connected to it. Everything around him ceased to exist and it was just him and the draw of the magic. He didn't realize he was walking closer to the flames until Eleana put her hand on his shoulder.

"That's enough, Emane, the connection has been made," she said, gently pulling him away from the kettle. "Please remove your shirt."

He stepped reluctantly backwards, looking longingly after what he knew was his, what he felt needed to be his. His fingers moved to unbutton his shirt, but he could not tear his eyes away from the contents of the kettle.

Turning her attention back to the task at hand, Eleana said,

"This magic can only be separated from its encasement by old magic. A smile ghosted across Drustan's lips at the mention of old magic, but was gone before it was noticed. "No amount of heat will remove it from its rock pairing. The next incantation is tricky, and important that it be said properly, please, I need all of you to stay very still, and very quiet."

Eleana put both her hands over the rim and once again began speaking strange incantations under her breath that rose and fell in eerie rhythms. She was tense with concentration, her hand moving slowly back and forth over the kettle. There was a thick sucking sound, like a boot jerking free from heavy mud, and the sparkling green material, now free from the rock, began to rise.

Emane's heart was pounding wildly in his chest as the material slowly rose in a thick green ribbon, twisting and turning through the air. The top formed into the head of a snake, its mouth opened and stretched. It slithered through the air moving its way over to Emane. Emane knew in his head he should be nervous at the sight of this green snake moving towards him, but he wasn't. The connection was too strong, he needed it. Reaching out to it, the snake paused at his fingers, its snout almost touching him. He ached for it. Sticking out its tongue, it started slithering up his hand, its body still warm from the process. As it slid across his arm, it sent tingling shivers through his spine that were so sharp they bordered on painful. Emane looked down fascinated, watching. The snake moved up his bicep, and then came up and around his shoulder and collarbone, and back down his arm. Moving over and under itself, knotting and twisting back again, it created a tightly woven pattern on his upper arm and shoulder. Then the snake stopped moving, poised to swallow its tail.

"I need you to move your arm, Emane, it needs to be comfortable before I seal it," Eleana said.

Emane lifted up his arm and rotated it in all directions, trying to look past the strange sensation and focus on the practicality of what he would be required to do while wearing it. "It's preventing me from fully rotating my shoulder. That won't work in a sword fight."

Eleana moved over to Emane. Touching the snake in several places she whispered to it. In response the snake began jointing itself, creating flexible areas within its body.

"Try again."

Emane raised his arm again and tested the rotation. It was comfortable. He could barely tell it was there at all. "It's good."

"Is it too tight? Can you feel your fingers?" Eleana pressed.

He wiggled his fingers back and forth and flexed his biceps. "No, it's good."

Eleana nodded and whispered the final enchantment. The snake opened its mouth, reached for its tail and bit down. The instant the two ends connected and the magic sealed itself, a force roared through Emane's body the likes of which he had never felt. It was that of fire and a million needle pricks. He rocked back on his heels with a gasp as the room began lazily swimming around him. He heard his name off in the distance, recognized it vaguely as Kiora's before he crumpled to the ground. Blinking, he looked around. The room was still rotating, and his body was on fire. There were hands grabbing his head, pulling it up and Kiora's face came into view.

"Are you okay?" she asked.

He frowned, it sounded like she was miles away. "I don't know," he mumbled, forcing his mouth to cooperate. "I feel strange." His body was screaming, fighting with the magic, rejecting it. He could feel it inside, the magic roared forward, forcing itself through him, his body resisting. More than anything it felt wrong, like it didn't belong. That feeling of ownership, of needing it was gone. He tried to hold on to the room, to Kiora's face, but he couldn't. Surrendering to the magic, he closed his eyes.

KIORA LOOKED UP AT Eleana as Emane went limp. "What's wrong with him!?" she yelled.

"I don't know, Kiora," Eleana knelt down next to her touching Emane's face. "This hasn't been done enough times to know." The band on his arm had hardened and grown cold. "Drustan, how quickly can you get him back to his bed?"

"I will get him there as fast as I can." He morphed into a creature Kiora had never seen before. It looked like a cross between a human and a wolf. He scooped up Emane and sprinted out of the cave on two legs.

"Eleana, I don't understand. What is going on?" Kiora was panicking

"Come. We will talk as we go." Kiora had to practically run to keep up with Eleana. "Emane's body is rejecting the magic. You have to understand, each person is so different, the magic reacts differently in each situation. And something like what I just did has never been done before."

"What do you mean?" Kiora's voice rose.

"As we mentioned, the other items that were made, they were all removable. Emane's band is sealed on him, it is logical that it would make a more powerful connection with him."

"Will he be okay?"

"I hope so."

Kiora wanted to scream at Eleana that her "hoping so" wasn't good enough, but the bridge looming in the darkness froze the words in her throat. Cold hard fear grabbed at her heart. Looking forward, Eleana was already crossing. Emane needed her, she couldn't just stand here. Gripping the sides of the rope bridge, she tried to breath. Closing her eyes she forced her feet forward.

"Don't look down, don't look down, don't look down," she whispered through clenched teeth.

Not soon enough, she felt her feet hit flat ground again. Gasping in relief, she hurried onward, Eleana's copper hair had already disappeared in front of her. She ran past the still burning torches and past the waterfall. By the time she reached Emane's room, he had deteriorated even further. He lay on a large four-poster bed, much like hers. Eleana and Drustan stood to the side. Rushing to Emane, she grabbed his hand; he was deathly pale and sweating profusely.

"What do we do?" She looked desperately to Drustan and Eleana.

"There is nothing else we can do. We must wait for his body to accept the magic," Eleana answered.

"What if it doesn't?"

"It will," Drustan said with a forced confidence, his eyes looking anywhere except at Emane.

"How do you know!?" Kiora snapped, glaring at him across the bed. "You are the one that wanted to put it inside him!"

"Kiora!" Eleana reprimanded her.

Kiora's anger snapped back in on her, understanding the logic of Eleana's reprimand. These were their allies; she couldn't alienate them now. She gritted her teeth. "I'm sorry, Drustan." Dropping her head, she pressed her forehead against the back of Emane's hand. "I'm worried about him." Looking over to the offending piece, she ran her fingers over the foreign magic twisting around Emane's arm. Scowling at it, she asked, "Can we take it off?"

"No, we can't. If we were to remove the magic while his body is trying to adjust, it could kill him." Eleana moved around the bed placing her hand gently on Kiora's shoulder. "I'm sorry, Kiora, I don't have any other answers for you."

Drustan's shoulders sagged slightly, his worry showing in his eyes as he turned to follow Eleana out of the room.

Kiora got little sleep. Emane tossed and turned, moaning most of the night. She summoned some water and a washrag, trying to keep him cool, but his temperature kept rising. Even sitting next to him, Kiora could feel the heat radiating off his skin in waves. She wanted to lie next to him, to hold him. But she was worried that her own body heat would make it worse. So she sat by the bed instead, holding Emane's hand, putting cool rags on his forehead and pleading with him to wake up.

The next morning a girl with fuchsia hair and large pointed ears brought her in some breakfast.

"We assumed you would prefer to eat in here today," she said, dipping her head with respect.

"Thank you." Kiora looked at the food but couldn't find her appetite.

The same girl brought in the lunch and dinner tray, but Kiora could not find it within herself to leave Emane's side. His skin was ashen, his lips dry and cracked. Dipping a clean rag in a bowl of water, she wrung it out over his lips, the liquid dripping into his mouth. Thankfully, she saw him swallow before tossing his head to the side. She ran her finger gently over his face, tracing his cheekbones that now stood prominently above his sunken cheeks. Dark circles sat under his eyes like bruises.

Sometime after dinner, Eleana came into the room. Standing in the doorway, she asked, "How is he?"

"Not good." Kiora swiped away a tear. "He just lays there and moans, and I can't bring his temperature down." She laid her head on the bed and sobbed, "I don't know what to do to help him."

Eleana made her way to the bed, looking down on Emane. "It's almost over, Kiora."

Sitting up, Kiora wiped her eyes, hope catching in her throat. "How do you know that?!"

"Calm down and feel his thread."

Sniffing, she frowned, "His thread? I don't understand."

"Feel it, and you will."

Kiora closed her eyes and tried to shove away all of the worry and the fear, allowing herself to feel the thread. It felt like Emane, but the outside was different, the outside was magic. She rolled the thread over in her mind; it was almost completely surrounded with the exception of a thin line. Her eyes flickered open looking for an explanation.

"As soon as his thread is completely encased by the magic, this will be over." Relief was evident in her eyes. "He will be fine, Kiora."

Kiora nearly collapsed onto the bed with relief. "Are you sure?"

"Yes." Looking at the trays around the room she said, "They told me you have not eaten all day."

Running her fingers back over Emane's forehead, Kiora nudged back a piece of blond hair that had fallen forward. "I haven't had an appetite."

"The colony is worried about you as well, Kiora. Please, sit with me and eat." Kiora's eyes still lingered on Emane. "Emane will be fine shortly. Eat."

Kiora reluctantly released his hand, moving over to Eleana. Dropping herself into a chair she picked up a roll and began to tentatively pick tiny pieces off. "It would have killed him, if they would have inserted it, wouldn't it?"

"Yes," Eleana said sitting across from her. "His body would have gone into shock immediately, I think. It wouldn't have taken long for his heart to give out."

The food felt like sand in her mouth and she forced herself to swallow. "Did you know that the whole time?" she asked, glancing back at Emane, checking to make sure his chest was still rising and falling for the thousandth time.

"No, I knew it was possible," she said, her gaze following Kiora's over to Emane. "But until I saw his reaction to the magic, I had no idea how serious it would have been."

Kiora watched Eleana evaluating Emane, noticing again how young she looked. She knew Eleana fought in the last war, which would make her at least a thousand years old. "Eleana, how old are you?" she asked abruptly.

"Surely you know not to ask a lady her age," Eleana said, amused.

"Sometimes you talk as if you have been alive forever." She shrugged, tearing off another small piece of bread.

"I'm not that old. But it has been a very long time; thousands of years." Her eyes looked distant. "Thousands of years watching the same cycle happen over and over again."

"How old is Dralazar?"

"Almost the same age as me."

"You two have fought against each other for thousands of years?"

"It wasn't always that way." She sighed, and Kiora finally saw the tiredness in her eyes. "I suppose it is time that you know. This is something that I would appreciate if we keep between us for the time being."

"Of course."

"Dralazar is," Eleana inhaled deeply, exhaling slowly before fixing her eyes determinedly upon Kiora "my brother."

Kiora's roll hit the ground. Embarrassed, she nearly dove off the chair to pick it back up. "Your brother?" she said, falling back into her seat. "I don't understand. You are so much more powerful

254 | DEVRI WALLS

than he is. And he...how could you possibly be related?"

"He took one path and I took another."

Eleana looked away and Kiora questioned if there was something else that she was not telling her.

"He wanted glory and honor and all the things that I did not. His choices took away what he could have been." Eleana leaned in, "Do not underestimate him, he is brilliant at what he does. The way that he manipulates people to get what he wants is flawless. His magic is strong, but the darkness he chose squandered what could have been."

"How can you bear to fight against him?" He is you brother, she thought.

"Because he is wrong. He wished to subject everyone and everything to his rule. He has chosen to go against everything that we were supposed to stand for and protect. And he will do anything to get what he wants." Eleana's voice hitched in a most uncharacteristic way. "I cannot allow that, even if he is my own brother. Being powerful does not give you the right to force your opinions on weaker species."

Still reeling from the revelation, another thought poked at her. "How will I be strong enough to fight someone that has been alive for thousands of years?" she said more to herself than to Eleana.

Eleana stood to leave. "I have told you that you are the most gifted one I have ever seen, you have unlimited potential. It is our character that helps us access our abilities, my brother has none. Because of that, Dralazar will never reach what he could be. Now, if you would excuse me." She walked to the door, but paused, "Kiora, this conversation was meant for you and me alone." Eleana reminded her before shutting the door behind her.

"I understand." Kiora leaned back in her chair, her head spinning. She could not imagine Eleana's heartbreak, having to fight

her own brother. She also wondered why Eleana had chosen to tell
her at all.

Putting the barely touched roll down, she moved back to
Emane until his fever broke. She didn't know what time it was, only
that it was late. With Emane sleeping peacefully, she finally felt
comfortable enough to lay her head on the bed and rest.

She woke the next morning to find the bed empty.

"Emane!" She sat straight up, looking frantically around the
room. She saw him sitting in a chair eating breakfast and watching
her.

"It's okay, I'm right here." He turned his head to the side. "How
are you feeling?"

Trying to shake the sleep from her mind, she said, "How am I
feeling? What kind of question is that? How are you feeling?"

He looked better than yesterday, but his hair was plastered to
his forehead and his skin still had a grayish hue to it.

"Very strange—and hungry," he said, picking up an apple, "I
have been trying to save you some breakfast but it's not working."

"Please, eat. I'm fine."

"It looks to me like you haven't eaten in some time either." He
motioned to the trays filled with old food from yesterday.

"I wasn't hungry." She padded over to the chair across from
him. Leaning forward, she evaluated him. "Do you remember what
happened?"

He shook his head, "Not really. I remember getting this," he
motioned to his shoulder, "then things started to spin and it went
dark. After that, it's all a blur. I remember hearing your voice a few
times, but I can't remember what you said. What happened?" He
took a bite of his apple.

"Eleana said your body was rejecting the magic. You were
running a fever and were incoherent." Kiora's eyes shone with tears

she was desperately trying to hold back. "I was worried. I..." she swallowed, looking down at her feet. "I was worried we were going to lose you."

"How long have I been out?"

"Two nights, one day."

"Wow," Emane said, his mouth full of apple. "Did you stay here the entire time?"

"Of course, I had to make sure you were okay. You were in so much pain."

"I feel like I have been through a war," he moaned. "Every muscle in my body is aching."

A knock at the door interrupted them. It was Eleana and Drustan.

Eleana walked in, but Drustan stood tentatively in the doorway. "I am most relieved to find you out of bed, Your Highness," he said.

"How are you feeling?" Eleana added.

"Tired, sore and starving."

"We will have some more food sent up for the two of you. It looks as if you will need it." Drustan eyed the meager remains on the breakfast platter.

"Emane, I know you have been through a lot but we do need to start using your magic as soon as possible," Eleana said. "The longer it sits without use, the less effective it will be."

"When were you thinking?" he asked.

"After breakfast, if it is agreeable?"

He nodded, "I will trust you, whatever you think is best."

"Very well, I will show you where we are to practice after you have eaten." She floated past Drustan, giving him a meaningful glance on the way out.

Drustan remained, looking as if he had something he wanted to say but couldn't quite find the words in which to say it.

Emane watched him for a minute before breaking the silence. "Did you need anything else, Drustan?"

"Prince..."

"Emane," he sighed. "Please, just call me Emane."

"That is very difficult for me," Drustan said, still not moving from the doorway. "I would prefer your proper title. It is more respectful."

"All right," Emane groaned, propping his legs up on an extra chair. "What is it that you needed?"

"I would like to offer my apologies, to both of you." He nodded in Kiora's direction. "I was stubborn and insistent about inserting the magic into you. I was thinking more of the war and less of you as an individual." He raised his chin, as if it would somehow help him barrel through this. "I sometimes forget how fragile you humans are. I was wrong, and I apologize." He bowed and stepped out of the room, shutting the door behind him. Kiora was speechless.

"I didn't see that coming," Emane said.

"Neither did I."

"I do really hate being referred to as fragile," he said, still staring at the door.

Kiora laughed looking over the breakfast tray. "You really didn't leave anything for me, did you?"

"No, I'm sorry. I am not very good at saving food." He tried to sound optimistic. "He did say they would be sending more up."

"Does it hurt?" She motioned to his shoulder.

"No," he said, peering at it. "But it feels different from anything I have ever felt before. It's almost like I have something alive wrapped around my arm. I can feel its energy." He shook his head. "I can't figure out how to describe it. Is that how your magic feels?"

Before she could answer, there was a knock at the door and the same fuchsia haired girl came in carrying four trays of food and two jugs of juice. It wouldn't have been nearly so strange had she not grown extra arms to carry her load. The strange looking fuchsia haired girl was now the strange looking six armed fuchsia haired girl. Kiora tried not to stare. She set the trays down on the table between the chairs.

"My Lady," she addressed Kiora, "Prince, the colony is pleased to hear that the magic has taken and is looking forward to a celebration in honor of you using the magic we have bestowed upon you."

"Errr, um thank you." Emane cleared his throat, dropping his feet back to the ground with a thud. "I am honored to have received it."

The girl bowed and left the room.

Kiora snatched an apple of the tray and began to devour it. Now that she was no longer worrying about Emane, she was ravenous.

"What celebration?"

Kiora shrugged her shoulders, "No idea."

"Interesting. Hopefully I can use the 'magic they bestowed upon me.' It would be a little embarrassing if they had to cancel the celebration."

"You'll be fine. I will help you."

After breakfast Kiora was so full she didn't want to move. "I don't think I have ever eaten so much at one time," she groaned.

"You did eat a lot!"

"No more than you," she objected, before pointing out that he had eaten an entire tray of food before she was even awake.

"True, but I am twice the size of you." He was trying to pull his jacket on over his button- down shirt but couldn't get his newly banded arm reached far enough behind him to get his arm into the hole. "This is ridiculous," he fumed.

"You told Eleana that it wasn't too tight."

"It's not. I told you every muscle in my body is killing me!" he groaned, trying again.

Kiora jumped up to help. She took his jacket and pulled it tighter around so that he could get his arms in it.

"There, you big baby," she laughed, smoothing down the front of his jacket.

"This morning you were worried that I wasn't going to make it, and now I am a big baby?"

She shrugged again, "I only speak the truth."

He leaned in and kissed her. "I don't believe you."

"That's too bad because…"

He kissed her again.

"Because if you don't believe me…"

He grabbed her shoulders and kissed her again.

"Are you...trying...to get me to shut up?" she asked between kisses.

"Yes!" he exclaimed, holding her at arm's length grinning. "Why isn't it working?"

Smiling, she leaned in to him, kissing him back. It was slow and sweet and exactly what she needed after the last two nights.

He wrapped his arms around her and whispered in her ear, "Thank you."

"For what?"

"For staying with me."

She didn't say anything She didn't need to. They both knew she would do it again.

"We had better get going," Emane said, kissing her one more time. "I have a feeling this is going to be a long day."

CHAPTER SIXTEEN

THE ELEMENTS

THERE WAS A LONG table in the center of the practice room covered in an array of objects and a few chairs placed around in no particular order.

"What is all this stuff?" Emane asked, walking along the table. There were small stones, a glass full of water, a dagger, a container of sand, a stack of paper, and a bug in a jar.

"I will explain, but first I need Kiora to summon the Book of Arian as well as Emane's weapons." It wasn't but a few seconds before she held the book in her hand with the chest of weapons sitting at her feet. Smiling at Kiora, Eleana remarked, "You're getting faster."

Emane stood examining the bug in a jar. It was possibly the largest insect he had ever seen, black and red and none to friendly looking. As if in response to his thoughts, the thing hissed at him. Emane jumped back.

"Kiora and Emane, please have a seat." Eleana said. "There is much about magic that neither of you understand. Before I try to teach you how to use it, I need you to understand it." She waited for the two to find their seats before continuing. "Magic affects each person differently. Outside magic, such as what you are wearing, Emane, acts differently than internal magic, such as Kiora's. All magic is completely unpredictable in how it will present itself. The best example I can think of to help you understand this is human talents."

"Everyone is gifted, some more than others," she expounded. "For some, their talents seem innumerable, others may have just one. Some may have a talent for sword fighting, but be far outmatched by someone else with a superior skill for sword fighting. Magic can be as small as being able to make an object move, to as grand as what Kiora is capable of. Magical beings are usually skilled in specific areas and weaker in others.

"Our friends, the Shapeshifters, are phenomenally gifted in changing their physical appearances. They can also slightly alter their threads. However, they are dreadful shield makers, and their bubbles are weak and short lived regardless of what form they have chosen. Aleric is skilled in many areas, yet lacks superiority in them. He also has no healing ability, so he depends more on potions to make up for his lack of gift in that area." Moving to the table, she waved her hand over the array.

"Today I have brought in different elements of nature to test where your natural abilities may lie. It is also likely that the magic you have received will work to amplify your natural non- magical abilities, such as your fighting," she added, giving a nod to Emane. "We would like to test that. We will be entering into a great battle sooner than I would like and it is important that you know where your limitations lie. It is also paramount that you understand what you can do and what you need to do it. We will start with the elements; fire, wind, water and earth. There are two groups that have been known to be able to control all the elements. The first

group is called the Chaoses. They earned their name by being able
to control all the forces of nature

"The Chaoses?" Emane said, shifting in his chair, "There are
creatures that can control all of nature?"

"The Chaoses haven't been seen here in sometime," Eleana
said. "And the other group you know quite well. The second
group has always been that of the Solus. Kiora is proving to be no
exception to that rule. The rest of the magical community is usually
left with no more than two elements; sometimes none.

"What about you, can you control all of them?" Kiora asked.

"I can, but I am an exception to many rules."

Emane sighed and rubbed his head, it was already starting to
pound and they had just started. "Have I mentioned that I hate all
these exceptions?"

"I will have Kiora show you what I need you to do, and then we
will begin."

She took half of the stack of paper and laid it on the stone floor.
"Kiora, I would like you to start a fire."

Kiora stood. "You just want me to do it?"

"Explain what you are doing while you go through the
motions."

Holding out her hand, she explained, "First, I see it in my mind,
what I want it to do, as if it were already accomplished. Then I
focus, allowing the magic to leave my body. I can feel it leaving
through my finger tips and..." the paper ignited into flames.

Emane looked at the burning pile on the floor wanting to laugh.
Those were his instructions? Grabbing the rest of the paper, he
dropped it on the floor next to Kiora's burning pile. Taking a deep
breath and closing his eyes he mumbled, "Okay, see it in my mind."
Breathing in through his nose, he cleared himself of every thought
but fire. "Then I focus on allowing the magic to leave my body,"

he repeated. Next, he became conscious of the foreign substance wrapped around his arm. It pulsed, moving through him, aching to be released. Rolling his shoulders he tried to relax, willing it to move to his fingers. Despite his anxiousness, the magic would not move. Frowning, he pushed harder, trying to force it in the direction he wanted it to go. It responded, moving down his arm several times but would stop just below his elbow and snap back. "How do I know if it's just not working or if I am doing something wrong?" he asked irritably, trying again to force his magic into submission.

"You won't at first. Once you use it for the first time, you will be able to feel the difference. Let's move on. This one will be new for Kiora as well. It may be good for you to watch her learning a new skill."

Emane fought hard not to roll his eyes. Watching her learn a new skill would do nothing other than emphasize how fast she learned. If Eleana was going for motivation, she had missed the mark.

"We are going to be working with wind. Kiora, I would like you to read with Emane how Arian suggests you control it. Let me know when you are ready."

Kiora opened the book. "Controlling Wind," she said. The books pages began to turn until it found the desired topic.

There are creatures of magic that are capable of controlling the elements. The elements of nature are a powerful weapon; more powerful than any weapons man has conceived. You must learn how to control, counteract and reverse such powers. A Solus is able to command these elements but must always do so with extreme caution. Even in situations that seem controlled, things can go horribly awry.

The first element is Wind. To control wind you must see it and understand it as a substance: something that can be molded and controlled. You must use your hands to help direct the wind in the way you need it to go. You may also use your hands to soften or increase the force. To soften or decrease a strong wind you must use your magic to soothe the force. Use your hands to make it smaller and more manageable. To increase the wind you need to imagine it getting larger, more powerful. You will need to urge the winds to increase with your hands. Once you have increased it, you may direct it where you would like it to go. You can also mold the wind into funnel clouds when needed.

"That's it?" Emane asked. "They want you to control wind and that is all the instruction you get?"

"Aleric tells me that these instructions are remarkably clear," Kiora said, shutting the book and laying it on an empty chair.

"I bet he did."

"If you are both ready, we will begin," Eleana announced from across the room. "Emane, I apologize for this," she added, "but we are running out of time."

As Eleana raised her arms, Kiora realized her intentions. Turning to Emane she yelled, "SIT DOWN!"

Emane sat down abruptly, wondering what was about to happen. He didn't have to wonder long, the wind hit him full force. He gripped the sides of his chair and wrapped his ankles around the legs to keep from being torn from his seat. Kiora did not fare so well, she went flying across the room, slamming into the wall.

"Kiora!" he yelled, but his voice was swept away by the swirling winds. He tried to get up but the wind shoved him firmly back down in his chair. Straining, he turned his head in Kiora's direction to see her still pinned against the wall. Her eyes were shut, her dark hair twisting around her face. She was struggling to get her hands out in front of her, trying to calm the winds.

Just as he thought the wind was responding to Kiora's direction and releasing him from his four legged prison, Eleana forced more wind into the room, pushing him back into his chair. There was nothing he could do as the wind lifted him into the air, flipping him out onto the ground.

Sliding across the floor, he grasped at the smooth polished stone. He too slammed against the wall with one arm wedged behind him. Kiora was pinned a good six feet above, her eyes now open and flashing in anger. Throwing one arm into the wind, she shouted something that he could not hear over the roaring in his ears, and then it stopped. The pressure was gone and he saw the wind almost as tangible as Arian had said it was, hurtling back towards Eleana. It shoved her forcefully into the opposite wall. A second later, Kiora hit the ground with a thud, crying out in agony.

Pushing himself partially up, Emane scrambled over to her. "Kiora, are you okay?"

"No," she moaned, leaning her head back against the wall. "I think I broke my foot."

"Let me see."

Kiora shied away, swatting at his hand. "No, please! It hurts too bad."

"Kiora, listen," he tried to speak softly to calm her nerves, "I know it hurts, but we have to look at it. I know what I am doing."

"How could you know what you are doing!? How many times have you broken your foot?" She snapped and then moaned again in pain.

"Kiora, I don't have time to argue with you. Medicine is one thing I did actually pay attention to in class." He gently took her foot in his hands, "Now relax. I need to get this boot off, and the more tense you are the harder it will be." Opening the laces as wide as they would go, he gently pulled it off. She winced in pain. "I'm sorry, we're almost there." He peeled off her sock as gingerly as he could. It did not look good; her foot was already beginning to swell and was turning purple. Very gently, he placed his hand underneath her heel to move it into a better position for him to wrap it. But as he touched her skin, he could feel the magic begin to hum inside of him. It moved rapidly down his arm and into his fingertips. Jerking his hand back, he looked at it dumbfounded. What had just happened? He heard Kiora exhale.

"I was not expecting that," Eleana's voice came over his shoulder.

Emane quickly forgot his hand as the anger rose within him, he wanted to jump up and confront Eleana about what she had just done, but didn't want to risk jolting Kiora's foot. Instead, he spoke through clenched teeth. "You could have killed her slamming her into the wall like that!"

"I was in control of the wind speed, Emane, she was fine."

"Fine?" his head whipped around. It was her calm that infuriated him the most. "This does not look fine!"

Eleana fixed onto him with her blue eyes, her expression the usual mask of neutrality. "She needed to know what she will be faced with if Dralazar ever gets his hands on a Chaos or if he decides to unleash the elements on her himself. Kiora did a wonderful job as usual, that is not what surprised me. You are."

Emane clamped his teeth together so tight his jaw was beginning to hurt. "I didn't do anything. I couldn't even get out of my chair." Once again, as a Protector he had proved useless, even with magic wrapped around his arm.

"No, but we have discovered one of your gifts. You, Emane, are a healer."

"What?" Emane asked.

"When you touched her injury, your magic flowed without you forcing it, and her pain stopped." Emane looked up at Kiora, who smiled and nodded. "I suspect you are a healer. I need you to touch her foot again. See it healing in your mind, the damage being repaired. Allow the magic to flow."

Staring at Kiora's foot, his mind raced. Surely what Eleana was asking him to do was not possible. But he wanted it to be. If it were true, he could take Kiora's pain away, he could heal her. Gently he laid his hands on Kiora's foot and closed his eyes. He imagined her foot whole again. No bruising or swelling. He imagined her bones mending themselves. He could feel the magic flowing again just as it had when he had touched her the first time, down his arms and out his fingertips.

"Wow," Kiora whispered.

Emane opened his eyes and looked down, her foot was perfect, no sign of damage.

She wiggled her toes in delight. "You did it! It doesn't hurt at all."

Emane pulled his hand back, staring at her foot as she wiggled it this way and that. It wasn't possible and yet...

Eleana put her hand on his shoulder. "You could not have hoped for a more useful and needed magical ability."

Kiora was walking around the room on her newly healed foot giggling at each step she took.

"How many healers are there?" Emane asked, watching Kiora prance around like a child that had just discovered her own feet.

"Very few; it is rare. The Guardians have more than most species, but even within that community there is only a handful."

"Can Kiora heal?"

"No."

"Why me?" The Prince was stunned.

"I suspect it is because of your strong desire to protect and care for her. Love will do strange things to magic."

Love...he had not allowed himself to think of that yet. "Will I be able to heal everyone, or just Kiora?"

"I suspect you will be able to heal anything you truly care about. Maybe even those you don't. There is no way to know yet."

Emane was dumbfounded. He had no control whatsoever over fire or wind, but he had just healed a broken foot in a few seconds. Kiora forced him out of his stupor, flinging her arms around his neck.

"Thank you, you are my hero," she laughed.

"And you are mine," he said wrapping his arms around her waist. "Thank you for getting that wind off of me, that was amazing."

"Truly, Kiora," Eleana said, "that was an impressive burst you turned back on me."

"It took me a while," she said scowling.

"No, it took you one time. I don't recall how many times it took Arian. To be frank, I stopped keeping track."

Kiora laughed, "Seriously?"

"Of course," Eleana said with a straight face before abruptly changing subjects. "The both of you need to eat." She ushered them out of the room, reminding them how to get to the main hall, where they had had their first meal amongst the Shifters. "I will meet you back here after lunch. I have some things I need to attend to."

Emane wondered if by "things" she had meant Dralazar. There had been no mention of what was going on above ground since they had arrived.

After lunch the work began again, this time with earth.

Eleana held out a container of sand and the handful of pebbles. "Commanding the earth element can be as simple as moving small stones to creating earthquakes."

"You can create earthquakes?" Emane asked stunned. This war was getting more dangerous by the second.

"I can, although I never would. The consequences of an earthquake spread far beyond the desired target."

"But the Chaoses would?" Kiora asked.

"Yes, although I do not expect you will come across them anytime soon. Now, I would like you to try to move either the stones or the sand. Emane, you go first."

"I thought Kiora was showing me how it was done."

"She was, until you felt the difference between what worked and what was not going to work. You have felt the difference. Now, please..." She extended her hands out to Emane.

He stood in front of the two items and tried to imagine some movement from the pebbles. He focused on the magic and willed it to raise the stones into the air. He felt the magic moving but it felt slow and sluggish, like molasses oozing down his arm. It continued past his elbows and down into his hands. The further down it moved, the thicker and slower it seemed to get until he could move it no more. It sat there, stuck right before his fingertips. Emane growled in frustration.

"How am I supposed to understand this when every time it feels different!?" He closed his eyes again and willed it onward. "It's so close, but it won't move," he grunted.

"How close?" Eleana asked.

"It's right at my fingertips." His frustration was growing. "I can't get it to move past my elbow for wind, it practically jumps out of my arm into Kiora's foot, and now I feel like I have molasses moving through me!" He had moved past frustration into anger. "This is ridiculous." He flung his hand and the stones went hurtling across the room. Emane's face fell slack watching the stones clatter to the floor.

"Did I do that?" His eyes lit with the possibility.

"You did," Eleana spoke through thin lips. "It is not something to be proud of."

"But they moved," Emane objected.

"They moved because of your anger, Emane. You are ruled by your emotions and are quick to anger. Dralazar will find out and use it to his advantage." Eleana looked him square in the eye. "Control it."

"I was angry when you used the wind to pin Kiora against that wall and nothing happened," Emane objected, trying to defend himself.

"You have no ability in that area. That leaves you just as useless as a non-magical being where wind is concerned. You have a potential ability with earth. It needs to practice, trained and honed, but the potential is there. When you allowed your anger to take over, it reacted with the magic."

"I don't understand," Kiora whispered, her eyebrows pulled together. "You told me that evil crippled Dralazar's potential. Why would anger make Emane's stronger?"

"It did not make it stronger. It gave him a quick response. A shortcut, if you will. You can use magic through anger but it will only grow so much." She looked to Emane. "No shortcuts, control your emotions."

"Isn't it my emotions that allowed me to heal Kiora?"

"Love and anger are of two entirely different worlds. Anger and hate will twist and turn the ones you love until they are not recognizable anymore." Eleana stilled, looking very lost in thought before she turned abruptly, heading for the door. "We are done for today," she said over her shoulder.

AFTER BREAKFAST KIORA AND Emane returned back to the great room to work with Eleana.

"I would like to work with your weapons today," she announced, floating into the room.

Emane perked up. Finally something he was comfortable with.

"First we will try a non-magical weapon." She nodded to the dagger. "Then we'll move to the enchanted ones."

He picked up the dagger checking its balance and weight in his hand. "What do you want me to do?"

She pointed to a small silver circle on the back wall of the room. It was no bigger than the top of an acorn. "I want you to throw the dagger from here and hit the center of that."

Emane's mouth fell open. "That is at least fifty feet away!" he objected, eyeing the distance. "Maybe more!"

"Sixty-eight."

"That is impossible! Even if I managed to reach the wall, I wouldn't be able to aim." He shook his head incredulously, "It's not possible."

"It never ceases to amaze me how closed minded you are," Eleana said.

Emane tensed before he felt Kiora's hand on his shoulder.

"Is it all right if I help with this?"

Eleana motioned her approval.

Moving in front of Emane, she took his hands. "Emane, yesterday you healed a broken foot with your bare hands. It was impossible and yet you did it. You're right," she said jerking her head towards the target, "a non-magical being could not make that shot. You are not a non-magical being, remember? Let your magic help you." She touched his forehead, "Change what's in here," she touched his heart, "and listen to what is in here," she touched the band wrapped around his arm, "and feel what is in here."

Emane's eyes softened as he listened to this young beautiful girl before him who spoke as if she were a hundred years old. "When did you change from the hot-headed sixteen-year-old girl I first met, into this?"

"She's still in there." A smile lit up Kiora's eyes. "I have just had a lot of conversations with centuries-old Guardians and a pegasus about believing in myself."

Emane closed his eyes and tried to erase all doubt from his mind. He felt the magic flowing free and easy. It seemed to fill him and hum in anticipation of throwing the dagger. A smile crept onto his face, it felt like it should. He opened his eyes and focused on the silver circle across the room. He saw the dagger hitting the center in his mind. The flowing magic increased his confidence. He pulled back his arm and threw. The dagger flew end over end not wavering or losing height. It sped towards his target with a speed Emane had never accomplished before, striking the wall just barely to the right of the target.

"That was amazing," he breathed.

"Good, we will keep practicing." Eleana flicked her wrist and the dagger pulled itself out of the wall. "Kiora, we will be training you today as well, stay alert," and with no more warning than that, Eleana sent the dagger flying in her direction.

Emane didn't have time to process what had just happened before Kiora had her hand up. The dagger hurtled across the room at lightning speed, stopping mid air inches from her face.

"Good," Eleana nodded her approval.

Emane felt the anger rising in his throat, then fear, and then...

something else. Something new and raw and blinding. No sooner had he processed what he was feeling he realized he wasn't the only one who would have felt that. Nervously, he looked over to Kiora. She had felt it, her eyes widened with a startled breath as the dagger clattered to the floor in front of her. He took a step towards her, his hand outstretched, words of explanation on his lips. But she didn't give him any time, a predictable tear trickled down her cheek and she fled past him, stifling a sob.

CHAPTER SEVENTEEN

LOVE'S FEAR

"KIORA!" HE DIDN'T KNOW what he had expected her reaction to be, but that wasn't it. He turned to follow her.

"Emane," Eleana called, stopping him in his tracks. "We need to talk."

His heart was aching and confused. "I don't understand, why did she run? Please, Eleana, I have to find her."

"You will not find her in here, not without tracking her thread."

He turned to the open door she had just run through, his body was screaming at him to follow her. But there was no way he would find her on his own, not in this labyrinth. Eleana was right, she could be anywhere. He dropped wearily into the nearest chair.

"All right, you win," he sighed.

"Emane, Kiora is very special."

"I know."

"No, I don't think you truly understand. By choosing her, you are putting your heart in a dangerous position, one that Kiora understands. I feel your anger every time she is in harm's way. You have not yet begun to imagine the situations that she will find herself in. You will be there, watching everything. You will not ever be able to truly keep her out of harm's way, for it is along harm's way that she must travel. You need to make a choice for yourself. You must decide if you will accept what she has to offer."

"What do you mean, 'what she has to offer'?"

"She offers more than any girl you will ever meet because of who she is. Her powers will increase, her knowledge and her wisdom will grow. You have only seen a glimpse of who she will become. But other things, things that you will want, she will not be able to offer."

"Such as what?" Emane demanded

"Until this war is over, Emane, she will not be free to be anything other than the Solus. Make your choice wisely." Eleana evaluated him before continuing, "She is behind the waterfall on the twelfth level. There is a small room at the back she has found." Eleana left the room, her voice floating back in after she was out of sight. "There is a celebration tonight in your honor. Please do not be late, and dress appropriately."

Emane sat there staring at the floor, his mind racing. What did he want? Could he control his anger? Was she worth the risk? He knew the answers. He had to talk to Kiora.

KIORA WAS HUDDLED INTO the corner of a small room she had found while blindly stumbling around the colony. Pushed up against the cold stone, she sobbed into her knees. How could she have been so blind, and stupid? She knew he cared for her, and she for him. But this was different. The depth of it nearly drowned her.

She took deep, gulping breaths trying to calm down, but she was shivering violently. Grateful for magic, she pictured a fire burning in the middle of the room. A warming fire erupted in front of her, the lone flames lapping happily at the stone. She smiled through the tears. Sticking her hands out to the flames, its warmth penetrated her, warming her, while the mesmerizing patterns of light and shadows calmed her mind.

As the shivers subsided, she felt a little less vulnerable. She shook her head. I could have pretended not to feel anything, she thought. Instead, she had run away crying and hid like a child. Not willing to focus on the repercussions of what had just happened, her eyes slid back to the fire, letting the flames mesmerize her into blissful numbness.

She felt his thread all too late, the price she paid for choosing not to think. Setting her jaw, she cursed herself for not paying better attention. She was not ready to talk, not ready to face him.

"Hi…" Emane's voice came.

She winced. He sounded sad, and hurt. "Hi," she said meekly without looking up.

"You're not easy to find."

"But you found me," she answered coldly.

"I had some help."

Kiora stared blindly into the fire, she didn't want to look at him.

"Can we talk?"

"I thought you didn't like to talk," she was being cruel, she knew it.

She heard him sigh and fall against the wall. Not looking at him wasn't helping. She could still imagine exactly what pose he held. The one he always held if he was frustrated and a wall was nearby.

"I don't understand why you are so angry, Kiora."

She bit her lip; she didn't understand why she was angry either. "I don't know."

"Kiora," his voice was so soft, so vulnerable. "Please, look at me."

Kiora sighed and pulled her eyes away from the flames to look at Emane. He stood there leaning against the doorway just as she thought he would be. He was so beautiful—his blond hair was casually lying across his forehead as it always did, his blue eyes shining just beneath. She felt a stab of regret as she saw the sadness in them. His shoulders, normally proud and strong, seemed to sag.

"Please, you have to talk to me. I can't make sense of this without it."

"I don't know what to say," her voice trembled.

"May I?" He gestured into the room. She hesitated before nodding.

He walked slowly over to her side as if he were scared that he would frighten her away again. Sitting cautiously down next to her, he stared into the fire with her. They sat there side by side, in silence; a thick tangible one full of questions.

"Why did you run? What did you feel, Kiora?"

Her throat tightened, pulling her knees up to her chest she said, "You know what I felt."

He sighed, heavily. The flames of her fire twisted away from his breath. "I thought I did. But your reaction is making me question whether I know or not."

Her heart began pounding so hard she thought it was going to beat right out of her chest. "Emane, I..." her voice just stopped, held back by the tugging arm of fear.

"Please, Kiora," he urged, "tell me what you felt." His hand came up as if he were going to touch her, but stopped. It wavered there for a second in her peripheral view before he lowered it slowly back to his side.

"You..." she stopped, "I mean, I—I felt..." She paused again. Why did this scare her so much? "Love," she whispered, dropping her head onto her knees, refusing to look at him. "I felt love."

Emane was quiet, his eyes fixed ahead of him. "And that frightens you?"" The lilt in his voice betrayed his pain.

Her legs itched to run, she tightened her arms farther around them. "Yes."

He cleared his throat, "That's all right, it frightens me as well…" It sounded as if he were trying to convince himself of that as much as he was her. "What I don't understand is why it makes you angry."

She wanted to tell him that she wasn't angry, but the pain lodged in her throat again prevented her from speaking. So she sat there mutely, vaguely aware of tears trickling down her cheek.

"Are you really going to make me bare my soul before you decide to talk to me?" he asked gently.

Her gaze remained unmoved, refusing to look at him.

"All right." Pushing himself to his feet, he began walking back and forth across the tiny room trying to formulate his thoughts. She watched only his feet as they paced just behind the fire. "Kiora, I don't understand why you are surprised. I thought that you cared for me as well. I thought you cared for me as much as I…"

Her head jerked up, starting to object but he put his hand out.

"Stop," he said running his fingers through his hair. "Please… stop…let me finish. I can't believe I am saying this and if you stop me now I will never get through it." He took a deep breath, lurching forward to resume his pacing. "I knew we were something, I wasn't sure what we were but we both know we were closer than friends." He looked at her with the same intensity he had when he kissed her, the same depth that made her head spin. Her cheeks flared in response before she looked away. "I believe you even referred to it as a relationship. This…love, is the natural next step for a person." She startled as he kicked a pebble, sending it clattering across the floor. "Sorry," he murmured. Turning to her, he groaned, "Kiora, I can't just make this go away. I wasn't looking for it, and it happened so fast. Kiora," he pleaded in desperation, "please look at me." Her eyes slowly rose to meet his. They were dark with desperation and something else. "Kiora," he said, leaning in as if he wanted to move forward but was riveted in place, "I love you."

Tears rose to her eyes and guilt stabbed her heart, "Emane," she pleaded, gripping her head, "don't, please, I don't deserve it."

"Why?" he demanded, lurching forward, "Why don't you deserve it?"

"Because, I can't...I mean, I'm not ready to..." she stopped and buried her head into her knees.

He knelt beside her, "Because you can't tell me that you love me?" A sob racked her body. "It's okay, Kiora." She felt his hand tentative on her back. "I am willing to wait until you are ready."

Kiora squeezed her eyes even tighter, "Why?" Her voice was muffled from being shoved into her knees.

"Because," he spoke with gut wrenching intensity, "you are worth waiting for."

She jumped up as if she had been jolted with a bolt of lightning and ran to the other side of the room, her chest heaving. "No," she pointed at him. "No, I am not, Emane. I am dangerous. I hurt everyone I love."

"You do not."

"Yes, I do! And I hurt you. I see it!" He started to shake his head in objection "Don't try to tell me I don't!" she practically screamed, her voice bouncing around the tiny room. "I feel it every time something happens that puts me in danger. It hurts you!" She covered her mouth with her hands, squeezing her eyes shut. Her chest rose and fell as if she had been running for days. Trying to calm herself, she lowered her hands slowly to her side, "And now I am hurting you again." Shaking her head, she whispered, "I can't bear it!"

Pushing himself to his feet, he walked towards her, slowly, his eyes fixed on hers. Reaching down, he grabbed both her hands, pulling them up between them. "Will you please sit so we can talk without yelling at each other?" His eyes entranced her; calm edging in around her for the first time since she had ran. She nodded.

Smiling, he pulled her towards the fire, walking backwards, as if he knew that taking his eyes off her would shatter any semblance of calm she had managed to grasp onto.

She sniffed, dropping back down in front of the fire. "When did you become the calm talking type?"

He shrugged. "One of us has got to, and I'm giving you a break. No promises though as to next time," he said, throwing one arm casually over his knee, "you might have to take over."

She wanted to kick him for being so stinking charming.

"Kiora," he said, "if we are going to be honest with each other, yes, it hurts me when you are in danger. Can you honestly tell me that you wouldn't feel the same way, loving me or not?"

"Yes, it would hurt me," she reluctantly agreed.

"Look, I know that it will be hard for me to watch you hurting, or to know that you are in danger. But the other options," he looked back to her, "will hurt me more."

"What other options?"

"I could leave," he said abruptly, "Go back to the castle. Move on with my princely duties." She felt a stab of fear at the thought of him leaving. "Or," he shrugged, "we could go back to being just the Solus and her Protector. But if I did that, if I chose that..." he trailed off.

"Emane, how can you sit here and pour your soul out to me when I can't even..." she dropped her eyes in shame. She tried to will the words out of her mouth but she couldn't do it.

"Hey." He grabbed her chin and pulled it up, "Look at me." She met his eyes. "I would rather wait a hundred years to hear you say those words, and know that you mean them, rather than hear them now and never really know."

"That's not fair to you," she whispered.

"It is. When I hear those words, I will know that you mean them. I will wait, Kiora." He tilted his head to the side, "You are the only girl I have ever met that I would wait for." A smile played across his lips as he ran his finger gently across her cheek. "And I would wait a lifetime."

The blissful burn that ran through her whenever he touched her was there, but the nagging fear that had been stabbing at her heart came blurting out of her mouth. "What If I don't have a lifetime, Emane?" she said, turning her head away. "What if I don't make it out of this war?"

He grabbed her, pulling her into his chest with a groan. "You are worried that your dying would hurt me?"

She kept her head buried in his chest while nodding emphatically.

"Oh, Kiora," he held her tighter, and she pressed into him, reveling in the comfort he offered. "What about you, aren't you worried about yourself?"

"No."

"Why not?" he asked, gently pushing her back to look at her.

"Because for the first time in my life, things feel right, I feel like myself," she spoke slowly, coming to the realization as she said it herself. Looking abruptly up at him, she blinked. "I would rather live as who I am and risk dying, than spend my whole life living a lie."

"Will you allow me the same privilege?" said Emane. Kiora furrowed her eyebrows. Reaching out, Emane tucked her hair behind her ears. "Pretending that I don't love you would be forcing me to live a lie. And I have lived enough lies."

"But what if I don't ever..."

"Say you love me?" he finished for her. "Do you have feelings for me?"

"Of course, Emane, I..."

"Then I have to believe the rest will come."

She looked at him, eyes wide with wonder. "You're really okay with this, waiting for me?"

"On one condition; you have to stop feeling guilty when I worry about you."

She let out a long deep breath, stop feeling guilty. He might as well have asked her to bring him the moon. "I will try."

"It's only natural, Kiora, that I would worry about you whether love is involved or not." He pulled her to her feet. "Come on, we need to get ready. We have a celebration to attend tonight and I was told we needed to dress appropriately." Looking down at her, he raised an eyebrow and asked, "All right?"

She nodded slowly, "All right."

CHAPTER EIGHTEEN

THE CELEBRATION

WHEN THEY ARRIVED AT their room, there were two humanish looking things waiting by Kiora's door. One was tall and much too skinny—her skin was more yellow than tan, and green hair jutted out in all directions, which almost distracted from the fact that she had four arms, with six or seven fingers on each hand. Her companion had pointy ears and enormous eyes; they were pools of the darkest blue surrounded by long black eyelashes that rested on her cheeks. Kiora noticed that the longer she and Emane stayed here, the less the Shifters tried to appear human.

"Hello?" Kiora said nervously, unsure of why they were waiting at her door.

The two bowed and the one with large eyes spoke, "Eleana asked that we help prepare you for the celebration this evening. I am Muriel, and this is Sabina," she said, pointing to the one with the extra arms.

"Um, I'm sure I will be fine...I just need...uh..." she looked back to Emane for assistance.

"Thank you so much!" Emane gushed, smirking at Kiora. "I am

sure she can use all the help you two can offer."

Kiora glared at him. With a smile, he put his hand in the small of her back and gently pushed her into the room.

"I will pick you up when it is time." He backed out with a devilishly impish grin and closed the door. She would kill him later, she decided.

The two girls circled her, clicking their tongues, "You are filthy, My Lady," Muriel said, her long eyelashes batting disapprovingly.

"I know." Crawling around in a cave sobbing usually does that, she thought.

They started pulling her clothes off despite her objections, and pitched her in the tub. Kiora felt like a two year old. She sat there fuming to herself and thinking of what she was going to do to Emane when the two "helpers" were done. The Shifters scrubbed and combed, pulled and clipped. They cleaned and buffed each fingernail and toenail and scrubbed her ears until she was sure they were bright red.

"What kind of celebration is this anyway?" Kiora asked through watery eyes as Sabina tore through the tangles in her hair with four combs at once.

"You do not know, My Lady?" Muriel cooed in surprise.

"We haven't been told much...ouch!"

"It is a celebration for the magic that was bestowed upon Prince Emane. We honor not only Emane for learning how to use it, but also the mountain for giving it freely to him."

"What does this celebration entail?" she asked Sabina, as the girl used three of her four arms to pull her out of the tub as though she weighed nothing.

Muriel, thankfully, wrapped a towel around her. "It will be grand!" she giggled. "They have been preparing for two days!"

"And we," Sabina giggled, "have been busy too...making you

this." She picked up a dress that was draped across the bed. Kiora gasped, it was beautiful. Through all the scrubbing, combing and buffing, she hadn't noticed it was there. She had thought that the dresses Eleana had sent her for the dinners were the most beautiful things she had ever seen, but this one…it put the others to shame.

She fingered the fabric, "You made this?" she asked in awe.

"Let's make sure it fits," Muriel urged. Sabina giggled as if the thought that it wouldn't fit was ridiculous.

They slid it over her head and laced up the back. It hugged tightly where it should and flared out beautifully at the waist. It had been made to perfection, not one inch of fabric was there that was not needed. Muriel and Sabina both cooed softly in appreciation.

Kiora smoothed the silken folds that surrounded her. The bottom of the dress looked to be the exact color of green as the band of magic wrapped around Emane's arm. As the dress caught the light from the chandeliers, it shone as if it had a thousand pieces of cut diamond embedded throughout the fabric. The bodice glinted with crystals that shone with all the colors of the rainbow. The top reminded her very much of Arturo's wings, it had a high collar on the back which was lined with the same green as the bottom of the dress. The front was open, with a scooped neck that accentuated her collarbones. She looked in the mirror and was taken aback.

"Thank you," she whispered, "it's beautiful."

They giggled again. "Come, sit, My Lady, we must make the rest of you match your dress."

By the time they had finished, Kiora could barely recognize herself. Her dark hair was piled on top of her head in tiny ringlets. They had managed to place little crystals throughout the curls so that when she moved they caught the light. Kiora had never worn makeup a day in her life, there was no need as she never went anywhere. But now she had soft red lips and lilac purple shadow to offset her fiery green eyes. Her lashes were black and looked longer than she had known they were. She stared at the stranger in the mirror, worried that she might disappear if she blinked.

The two Shapeshifters gathered their things.

"Thank you, you two have done a wonderful job."

Their eyes suddenly became very serious. "My Lady, is it true that you are powerful enough to defeat Dralazar?" Sabina asked.

Kiora felt the air being sucked out of her. She tried to swallow her discomfort. "I will be."

They both bowed. "We will fight with you, My Lady," Muriel added.

"Thank you," she said, humbled by their support. "And I will fight with you."

They bowed again and left the room. Turning to look in the mirror again, she contemplated if the face she saw looking back at her would be strong enough for the journey ahead.

"Oh, Ki-O-ra!" Emane's voice sung as he swung the door open. "I see your entourage has left. I thought I would just—" He stopped dead in his track,s his mouth dropping at her reflection in the mirror.

She turned to Emane, smoothing her dress, nervous to meet his eyes. "How did the 'entourage' do?"

He took one step forward before stopping again. "You look...a... amazing," he stuttered. "This dress is amazing," she said as she moved the skirt from side to side.

"No, not the dress, you." He swallowed hard. "Um, do you remember when we were in Arian's cave and I told you of the girl I was engaged to?"

How could I forget, she thought sourly, "The most beautiful girl you'd ever seen," she said dryly. "I remember."

The Prince nodded slowly, unable to take his eyes off her. "Yes, that one. You are more beautiful than she ever was. I want you to know that."

Embarrassed, she asked hurriedly, "And what about you, are you going in that?""

He looked down at the robe he had wrapped around him. "No. I don't think I would be able to walk next to you if I went in this."

She giggled. "Oh, I don't know, you do look rather handsome."

"Give me a few minutes," he said, shifting from one foot to the other, his eyes still trailing over her. "I will be back to get you."

He ran back to his own room, leaving Kiora to contemplate what the girls had asked her. She looked back into the mirror.

"Am I strong enough? To defeat Dralazar?" she asked out loud. Her reflection stared back at her without an answer, looking as lost as she felt. She had to believe that she could. If not, then why continue?

She was lost in thought as Emane came back into the room. Now it was her turn to lose her breath. She looked in the mirror back at him. He was in a full suit that looked as if it had been sewn onto him. His body was lean and muscular. The green cape he wore matched her dress and reminded her of the first time she had seen him, with his royal cape on. But now instead of haughty coldness, his eyes were full of warmth. His stance was still proud, his shoulders filling out his suit nicely, but it no longer smacked of arrogance.

Stopping behind her, he caught her eye in the mirror, offering his elbow, "Shall we?"

She smiled, "Of course." Standing in a swish of fabric, she linked her arm through his.

They walked arm in arm down the corridor, listening to the celebration drifting up through the center of the colony.

When they entered the main hall, Kiora could not stop herself from laughing out loud. The party was in full swing. The

Shapeshifters did not need costumes or fancy clothes. Instead they shifted their bodies to match the occasion. And the color! Before them was a sea of Shifters, each taking their artistic liberty with their form of choice. Hair, feathers and fur were in a fantastical array. Bright and brilliant birds flew around the room, green and blue dogs ran by, and a giant with hot pink hair pounded his feet to the music a little too hard, causing the floor to rumble. What looked like Guardians zipped around the room leaving rays of color following behind them, twisting and turning in the air. It was joyous and fun and the most amazing thing she had ever seen.

Drustan stood across the room in a glittering green jacket, which seemed to be the color of the evening, and bade Kiora and Emane come and sit.

Emane helped maneuver Kiora through the spinning and dancing Shapeshifters until they reached the head table.

Drustan bowed his head slightly, keeping his eyes on them, "Welcome, My Lady, my Prince. He stood looking as awkward as he had the day Emane awoke. "It was never my intent, had I realized..." he halted, his eyes glazing over Emane's shoulder. "My zeal sometimes does more harm than good. I do hope that my apology was understood as heartfelt."

Emane bowed at the waist, "It was."

"Excellent," he said, straightening his jacket before rolling his hand towards their seats with a flourish. "Please, sit and enjoy the festivities."

Kiora and Emane sat and watched the crowd shift and change before their eyes. The sea of color was beyond the imagination. Animals flew by in shades she had never seen. Guardians had glittering wings of silver and gold. A mini dragon made its way around the room, trailing wings of fire. A butterfly the size of a cat flew by, its wings changing with every flap. It was a wonderful kaleidoscope of color and shapes that tickled every inch of Kiora's imagination. There was so much to see, she could have watched for hours and still felt as though she could have missed something.

"Never," Emane said loudly in Kiora's ear, "did I ever imagine that I would be sitting here, witnessing this."

"I know." Kiora laughed as fireworks flew skyward dragged by two more butterflies, exploding against the roof of the cavern.

Drustan leaned over, "What do you think of our celebration?" He smiled broadly.

"It's amazing!"

Drustan stood up and clapped his hands three times. The activity in the hall stilled and all eyes in the room turned their attention to them. One of the Shifters paused mid-shift, leaving his head as a tiny guardian while the rest of his body was ballooning out in what was most likely a lion. Kiora had to look away to hide her laughter.

"Thank you all for your hard work!" he announced, his voice reverberating around the hall. "You have made this a great success. I am, as I know we all are, pleased with the two we have sitting before us, the Solus and her Protector. I know we have all been repeatedly impressed with both their skill and character. We have chosen to fight against Dralazar and I believe with them at our side we will finally defeat him!"

The crowd roared their approval.

"Many of us have suffered at Dralazar's hand and have witnessed his cruelty. This day is to celebrate not only our decision to fight against him, but more importantly the gifting of Prince Emane with magic. The mountain has deemed him worthy and so do we. May he use it in honor."

A cheer again bellowed through the room.

"The war will begin soon enough, but tonight, we celebrate!"

Drustan sat down grinning amongst the cheers of his people. "Please, eat and enjoy!" he told Kiora and Emane. "My people have worked hard preparing this."

Plates of food were set in front of them and their goblets were filled with a frothy red substance. Kiora and Emane sampled the buffet before them. The frothy drink tasted of apple and peach with just a hint of sour. Kiora tried some of everything, reveling in the flavors.

"Normal food is never going to taste as good as it did before!" Kiora said.

Emane nodded in agreement. "Even palace food doesn't compare to this. The entertainment is better too," he said, as a dog jumped in front of them and exploded into a bird, midair.

"It gets better!" Drustan said, pointing to the middle of the room.

A Shifter stood alone in the center of the floor waiting for the crowd to clear. Once he had the attention of the room, he began to change his features until Emane stood before them. The real Emane shifted uncomfortably in his chair.

"Don't worry, just watch," Drustan said, patting him on the back.

The Shifter threw his arms into the air, arching his back while his body shifted again, this time turning green and elongating. He changed himself into a giant green glittering snake twisting itself through the air. Even the Shifters were impressed—a few ahs and oohs escaped from the crowd.

The snake eyed the occupants of the room with its glittering black eyes, flicking its tongue out, tasting the air. With the sudden beat of a drum, a handful of Shifters stepped out and into the center of the room as well, each one changing into something on evil's side. There was a dragon, a Hound, and a Fallen One. Two more drumbeats thundered and a fifth Shifter, a woman, walked out to the middle, standing just in front of the snake. Turning around, it was a girl who looked exactly like Kiora.

Kiora now found herself squirming in her chair, understanding exactly how Emane felt. It was very disconcerting to watch a perfect copy of yourself standing in front of you, without being in control of what that copy does.

The snake reared up behind her as the drums began to beat faster and faster. The three evil ones circled the Solus and her Protector, hissing and growling at each other. The drums were rising to a near frantic pace, and with one final beat of the drums the Solus threw her arms out, flames and sparks flying from her fingers. The dragon roared shooting flames across the room, the Fallen One darted around as it threw sparks in response, and the Hound began to stalk. As though in protection of her, the snake struck over the top of the Solus, swallowing up each enemy in turn as it swept around the circle.

The crowd cheered at evil's defeat. The performers gave a bow, then raised their arms up to where Kiora and Emane sat, giving them recognition as well.

Drustan stood, clapping. Kiora and Emane rose to their feet as well with a standing ovation for the performers.

Drustan waited until the clapping had died down before announcing, "Let the dancing begin!"

The musicians started playing a song with a lively beat. Kiora found herself bouncing in time to the music.

Drustan turned to Kiora, "If I may, My Lady." He held out his hand.

"What?" Kiora looked frantically around. "I don't dance."

"Don't be silly, you are amongst the Shapeshifters. We dance however suits us, you cannot get it wrong."

Two mice went scampering down the table, dancing to the music. One tripped and skidded face first into her dinner plate. He shook himself, bowed, and scampered off, moving to the music.

"As I was saying…" Drustan smiled.

"It appears you will be just fine, Kiora, go on." Emane prodded her. "Just don't crash into anyone's dinner plate."

She leaned into his ear as she was getting out of her seat, "I hate you!"

"No, you don't." He grinned at her.

She took Drustan's hand and he led her to the dance floor. The music was contagious and Kiora found herself moving to it.

"The colony is quite enamored with you," Drustan said as they danced.

"With me? Why?"

"They all saw your test when you first came, and they speak of your kindness as well."

"I have been so grateful for all the kindness your people have shown to me. You are all wonderful, and this dress is magnificent."

"We do pride ourselves on our craftsmanship. Everything you find here has been handcrafted by at least one of us," he said, pulling her arm above her head and turning her around.

"My quarters have some of the most amazing workmanship that I have ever seen. You are a very gifted people."

"Thank you, My Lady," he said, inclining his head.

"And that was quite the performance."

He smiled. "They were quite proud of that, especially the part where the snake swallowed them all. It was a bit tricky."

She hadn't thought about that. "How did they do that?"

"My understanding was that they changed into gnats, before flying out his nose to escape unnoticed," he said, clearly amused.

Kiora crinkled up her nose. "I would not want to fly through anybody's nose!"

"Nor I, but they would have done about anything to impress you, I think."

She laughed. "You can tell them I was already impressed with them, they needn't fly through anyone's noses on my account."

He smirked, his eyes glittering with a joy she had not seen there before, "I will do that, My Lady."

The music changed to a slower, more melodic piece, and Emane was at her shoulder.

"Drustan, do you mind if I dance with the lady?"

"Not at all, my Prince." He bowed and moved off the dance floor.

Emane turned her around once before slipping his arm around her waist and pulling Kiora closer.

"I really, really do not know how to dance," she insisted.

"I do. Follow my lead."

She took his hand, trying to relax. Before too long, she realized that they were all alone on the dance floor.

"They are all watching us," she whispered.

"No," he murmured, "they are watching you, Kiora. I told you, you are breathtaking."

She blushed.

"Have I told you how adorable you are when you blush?"

"No, you haven't." She felt her face flush even more. Before she could say anything else, the dark began pulling her within herself. She squeezed Emane's hand. "A vision!" She wobbled as she tried to keep herself from blacking out.

"Quick, step on my feet," Emane pulled her up and squeezed her tightly around her waist. "I will dance for the both of us. Just see what you need to see."

She pushed the vision out, projecting it into the room. Kiora then watched the beginning of the end.

CHAPTER NINETEEN

THE BEGINNING OF THE END

SHE SAW TWO SQUIRRELS scampering around in the trees. A multitude of feelings and thoughts rushed through her. The squirrels were Shifters and they were lookouts.

It was a knowledge that she couldn't explain. She also couldn't explain how she knew that something was watching them, but she did. The Shifters were blissfully unaware of the spy's presence.

The one squirrel was giggling, a high pitched joyous sound. "We are supposed to be watching, Orrin."

The other squirrel pounced on her, laughing. "Relax, they are not going to find us. This is a waste of time. We have been out here since she got here, and there hasn't been a hint of movement."

"Don't underestimate Dralazar, Orrin. Remember last time," she said, taking on a sudden air of seriousness, "He will be very angry when he finds we have aligned with the Solus."

"He can't expect that we would align with him again. Not after what he did."

Kiora jolted. The Shifters were on Dralazar's side last time?

"Whether he expects it or not, he will be angry."

296 | DEVRI WALLS

Kiora could feel that whatever was coming, it was very close. She looked frantically around wanting to scream at the Shifters to run, that something was there, watching them. But it would do no good. They could not hear her.

The squirrel called Orrin pounced on the other again, "I hope he is angry! When I see him, I am going to..."

"Going to what?" a female voice asked. Kiora watched in horror as two dozen Fallen Ones suddenly dropped their bubbles, revealing not only themselves, but also the growling, salivating Hounds.

"Vitraya," Orrin hissed. The other squirrel cowered behind him.

"Hello, Orrin, nice to see you again as well. Who is your friend here?"

"She is not you concern," he said, placing his body firmly in front of his friend.

"Well, if I don't need her," Vitraya waved her hand and the second squirrel went flying into the air.

"NO!" yelled Orrin.

Vitraya left the squirrel dangling in mid air. She eyed Orrin. "I can feel you have chosen your side, Orrin."

"Let her go!"

"Very well." She dropped the squirrel. Orrin and Kiora watched as the Shifter fell from the tree and were snapped up by a Hound.

Kiora whimpered and Emane pulled her tighter. "You are doing great, Kiora," he whispered in her ear. It sounded like he was underwater.

Orrin turned around to face Vitraya. "What do you want?" He choked on the words.

"Oh, Orrin, you know what we want." She oozed evil. "We want to speak with Drustan." She flew down and stood right next to him.

"I could eat you right now," Orrin threatened, looking down over the top of her.

"You could try, but my friends here will feed you to the Hounds before you get your little squirrel mouth open all the way," she mocked. "And really, Orrin, threatening me in that form? You could have at least picked something a little more fearsome."

"I will never show you the way, Vitraya."

"Oh, Orrin," she turned her head to the side, "I thought we were friends."

"We were never friends."

"But we made such good allies, Orrin." She made a pouty face and Kiora wished she could reach into the vision and smack the sarcasm right out of her.

"We were allies until we figured out what you really were!"

"Oh, well," she sighed, "That's in the past. And now we are here, at a rather interesting crossroads. You can either lead us to Drustan or…" she motioned to the forest floor where the Hounds circled the tree, "we will feed you to the Hounds."

"You know I won't show you our home, Vitraya. We wouldn't a thousand years ago when we were allies, why would we do it now?"

"Hmm, that's what I was afraid of." As she turned around to give the order, Orrin took advantage of the moment, exploding into a bird before he was gone, disappearing within a bubble.

"No! No! NOOOO!" Vitraya screamed. "Find him! Find him, you fools! Dralazar will have our heads. Go, all of you, fan out. You know he can't hold a bubble for long. ORRIINNN!" she screamed into the wind. "When I find you, I will kill you myself! And it will not be as quick as the Hounds would have done it." She yelled back to the others, "Find something, anything!" She took to the skies scanning for the reappearance of a small brown sparrow.

The vision faded and left. Kiora looked to Emane with wide

eyes. "They are coming…" she gasped, "here. The Fallen Ones."
She stepped off his feet and turned frantically to find Drustan. She
had taken only a few steps before the doors to the hall were thrown
open and an exhausted looking boy stumbled in.

"DRUSTAN!!!" he yelled. His voice strangely magnified, it
carried over them all, pushing the hall into silence.

Drustan stood, his hands on the table in front of him. "Orrin,
what is it?"

Kiora's eyes widened, "Orrin," she whispered to herself.

"They are coming. We haven't got long before they are in range
of the threads."

"Who?"

"The Fallen Ones; they found us, they…" his eyes rose to
Drustan.

"Where is…"

Orrin shook his head before Drustan could finish. "She's gone."

Drustan stood straighter and raised his voice "All of you, you
know the plan. Out as fast you can, use all of the exits. Once you are
out, bubble as long as you can. Spread out. Leave the Fallen Ones
as weak of a trail as possible. Make your way to the Garian Sea. The
Merfolk have offered a refuge if needed. GO, NOW!"

The colony exploded into a mass of feathers, and hundreds of
birds swooped out the main door, heading out in different directions.

Drustan morphed into the largest wolf Kiora had ever seen. He
stood at least two heads taller than she. "Get on, now!"

Emane grabbed Kiora, threw her onto Drustan's back, and
climbed up behind her.

"Hold on," the wolf said. "We will be moving fast." He sprinted
towards the door and Kiora tipped backwards into Emane. He
pushed her forward and wrapped one arm around her waist, clinging
to the back of the wolf with the other.

"Wrap your hands through his fur!" Emane demanded.

She reached forward and grabbed two handfuls. Drustan ran at full speed through the colony, bounding up from level to level. Kiora thought she was going to fall to her death.

"How many exits are there?" Kiora yelled.

"Thousands, although only two for something as large as you."

He ran with such speed that the corners made Kiora's stomach flip in protest. After running for a few minutes, they exploded out of the back exit.

"Bubble, now," Drustan demanded.

Kiora threw up a bubble large enough to cover all three of them and Drustan tore down the rock-covered hill towards the forest they could see in the distance. The forest was visible, but by no means close.

"How long can you hold this?" Drustan asked.

"With all three of us, fewer than fifteen minutes."

Drustan growled underneath his breath. "Hold on tight, I am going to have to adjust or we will never make it."

Kiora gasped. She could feel the bones underneath his skin popping and moving. He was shifting beneath them, growing larger, longer, and bulkier. The new much larger wolf took off again covering the land at unfathomable speed. Emane had to lean over the top of her to prevent the wind from jerking her off Drustan's back. As the minutes ticked on, Kiora could feel her magic depleting.

Kiora! Eleana's voice slammed into her consciousness, breaking Kiora's concentration. The voice was so loud she reached up gripping her head. The bubble began to thin alarmingly.

"Kiora, focus!" Emane shouted in her ear.

"I am trying! Eleana's calling me, it's too much," she whimpered.

Eleana continued as loudly as she had started, Kiora, there are two horses waiting for you within the forest. Ride as hard as you can due south.

Kiora sent back all she could muster, All right.

They were nearing the forest and Kiora's body was starting to shake.

"Almost there, you two," Drustan yelled.

Once they entered the trees, Kiora dropped her bubble with relief. Drustan waited for them to jump off before collapsing himself. He lay on the ground, sides heaving. Kiora sat next to him, trying to keep herself from blacking out.

"Eleana said there would be two horses for us," she managed to get out between breaths.

Emane scanned the surrounding area and saw the two horses grazing not far from them.

"We need to go, now," she wheezed.

Emane ran to retrieve the horses. Drustan, still in wolf form, struggled to get up but his legs wobbled underneath him.

"No, you need to regain your strength," Kiora told Drustan. "Can you pick a form that is small and light so that we can run the horses with as little weight as possible?"

Drustan took a deep breath before he began to shudder and shrink. When he was finished there was a small brown mouse lying before her, sides heaving.

Emane came thundering up on one of the horses, holding the reins of the other. "Where's Drustan?"

"Here." Kiora picked up the little mouse and placed him into the saddlebag. She swung herself up, fighting with the impossible gown she still had on.

"Eleana said to ride due south."

"No bubble?"

"No." Kiora was grateful, she didn't have much left and she needed all the time she could to recover.

They spurred their horses forward and rode, hard.

The terrain was not conducive to speed. The forest floor was a mess, covered with fallen trees and foliage. Kiora had to close her eyes a few times, praying that the horse would clear the fallen trees that blocked their way. She urged her horse forward as the first thread touched her heart. Then there was another and another. They were coming, and fast.

"They are gaining on us!" she shouted. "The Fallen Ones." A new set of threads hit and her heart sunk further, "and the Hounds," she added.

"Just great!" Emane yelled. "I hate those things."

Kiora, Eleana's voice came again. Kiora grabbed her head in pain. Why did it hurt so badly when she did that? Are they on your trail?

Yes, the Fallen Ones and the Hounds. She waited for a response, but none came. Eleana?

Kiora, I cannot help you. I have to prevent them from finding the source of the magic we gave Emane. You three will have to handle this on your own. Remember what you have learned, and remember the elements. I suggest you turn east, there is a lake there you may find useful.

Kiora's heart sunk, they were to go this alone. It was time to fight and she didn't feel ready.

"Emane, due east," she shouted pulling her horse alongside his as they ran.

"How many are coming?"

Kiora tried to separate the threads one from another. "Ten Hounds, maybe more. Around twelve Fallen Ones." The trees flew by on every side, blurring as they passed.

He shook his head. "It's too many."

"Eleana suggested a lake, it should be ahead of us."

"A lake? What would she like us to do, drown them?" he shouted over the pounding of hoofs.

"I don't know, she said remember the elements."

"Kiora," Emane said, looking hopeful, "do you think you can control the water?"

She shuddered, not ready to have a victory dependent on her abilities. "I think so."

"I don't need you to think so, Kiora, I need you to know," he yelled, "we only get out of this alive if we all work together." She glanced at him and could see the wheels turning in his head as they rode. "I need to talk to Drustan."

Kiora wrapped the reins around one hand, reaching into the saddlebag with the other. Pulling the mouse out, she almost lost her balance as the horse thundered on.

"Drustan, when we get to where we are going, what is the largest thing you can change into?" Emane asked.

"Anything you need, Prince." It was always strange hearing his voice coming out of different creatures. But to hear his voice at full volume coming out of this tiny mouse was bizarre.

"I think I am going to need a dragon."

"I will do whatever you deem necessary, Prince."

"I am going to need you to deal with the Hounds. Can you blow fire if you change into a dragon?"

"Of course."

"Perfect. Kiora, I will need my sword and my shield. Please summon my sword first, into my hand." He said holding one hand out from his horse. She did as he requested. He sheathed his sword. "And now my shield."

"Do you need anything else?"

"No. Kiora, I will do my best to protect you, but you are the one that is going to have to come up with a way to finish this." He shook his head. "Without your magic, I don't know that we are getting out of this one." Emane secured the shield onto his arm, ready for battle.

Emane and Kiora sped through the forest looking for the lake Eleana spoke of and trying to keep ahead of the Hounds.

"How much longer before they are on us?"

"Not much longer. I can't tell for sure."

Emane glanced behind him. "Bring your horse in as close to me as you can," he ordered.

Kiora reined her horse over until the two galloped alongside of each other.

"Hand me Drustan."

Kiora reached across, dropping the mouse in Emane's outstretched hand. Emane dropped Drustan into his shirt pocket.

"Kiora, hand me your reins."

"WHAT?"

"Just do it! I don't have time to argue with you." Leaning forward against its neck, she delicately pulled the rein over the front of the horse, handing it to Emane.

Wrapping the reins together, Emane reached out his hand. "Give me your hand; I need you on my horse."

Kiora looked down at the ground flying by between the thundering hoofs of the two horses. "Emane, I…"

"Kiora! I don't have time to argue and explain every move to you. You trust me and I trust you. That's the way this works. Now, come on! You jump, and I will get you over here."

She grabbed his hand, swinging her leg over the horse, leaving herself balancing precariously on the side. She averted her eyes from the clambering hoofs.

"Good, now put one foot in the stirrup to push off. One, two, three, now!"

Kiora pushed off, throwing herself onto the other horse. But her dress kept her from swinging her leg all the way over its back and she found herself half flung over the saddle, clinging to the side, her legs dangling as the horse ran.

"Emane!" she screamed, struggling not to lose hold.

"Hold on, I got you." He reached behind him grabbing the back of her dress. He yanked hard, pulling her up so that she could swing her leg up and around.

"Curse this dress!" Kiora swore.

Emane untangled the reigns of Kiora's horse and slapped it, sending it off in another direction.

Kiora watched the horse disappear through the trees, "I hope we don't need that later."

"I hope we're alive to need it later," Emane corrected.

A few seconds later, Kiora felt some of the threads move away from them. "They are following the horse," she said realizing what Emane had done.

"How many?"

"Three Hounds."

He swore under his breath. "Not as many as I had hoped, but it's something. It won't be long before they figure out you're not on it. This lake better be up here soon or we are in a lot of trouble."

They burst through the trees into a clearing, the lake glittering in front of them.

"This is not good," Emane said, scanning the predetermined battlefield. "I was hoping for something to help protect our backs." There was nothing but a flat meadow surrounded by trees.

"Maybe we could use a dragon for cover."

"That will have to do." Emane pulled his horse to a stop and climbed off as the Hounds broke through the tree line.

"Drustan, I need you, now!" Emane said, setting Drustan expectantly on the ground. The brown mouse turned and scampered off into the tall grass. "What is he doing?"

Kiora didn't have time to answer. The Hounds had slowed their pace and begun to stalk.

"Why do they have to do the stalking thing?" Emane moaned. "It brings back bad memories." He pulled his sword, readying himself.

"I am glad to see you have a sense of humor in the face of death," said Kiora.

"Where are the other things...what did you call them?"

"The Fallen Ones, watch the tree line, they are almost here."

Bursts of light zipped out from the trees as the Hounds inched closer, growling and baring their teeth. Drool dripped down their chins coating their black matted fur.

Kiora assessed the situation. "Your bow! Emane, use your bow."

"Summon it."

Kiora summoned the bow and the quiver with arrows, handing them to Emane. He re-sheathed his sword and nocked an arrow.

"Are you ready? Because as soon as I hit one, they will be finished stalking," he said, drawing the arrow back.

"I'm ready. What about Drustan?"

"Drustan!" Emane yelled, "We need you!"

Taking aim at the closest Hound, he released. The arrow hit the hound with such force that it sent it skidding into another hound behind him. The others snarled in fury, breaking into a dead run. Emane fired the next arrow, but it flew wide. Kiora hit the targeted hound with a bolt of magic instead.

"Your magic, Emane! Remember the dagger."

Emane shook his head while nocking another arrow. "I don't know how, not now. I haven't practiced enough!"

"We need you to remember. I will handle the Hounds for now, you must concentrate!" Kiora threw wave after wave of magic, glancing over at Emane, who stood with the bow in front of him, eyes closed. The largest of the Hounds moved closer to them, Kiora raised her hand to deal with it just as Emane pulled his bow up. The arrow flew straight and true taking out the largest of the Hounds.

The targeted Hound yelped as the arrow embedded into his flesh. The other dogs skidded to a stop, focusing on their whimpering comrade.

"What are they doing?" Kiora whispered, her hand still raised.

"I think I wounded the pack leader."

The Hounds began to back up, growling and snapping their jaws. The one Emane had hit stumbled to his feet, the arrow still dangling from his side. Stumbling back to the tree line, his pack followed.

They were allowed only a second of relief before they heard a screeching voice shouting orders.

"Vitraya," Kiora shuddered. It was the same voice that had fed the Shifter to the Hounds in her vision.

"Where...is...Drustan?" Emane said between clenched teeth.

"I don't know! I can't feel him anywhere."

"He left?"

"I don't know if he—oh, no." Kiora looked frantically around the clearing. "The Fallen Ones are gone."

"Why would they leave?" Emane asked suspiciously, his eyes darting around the meadow.

"They didn't, they bubbled. They could be anywhere."

As soon as it left her mouth, Kiora felt the thread materialize behind her. She tried to turn to face her attacker but she was not fast enough. The magic hit her arm and she could feel it slicing through the skin. She screamed, grabbing at her arm that the Fallen One had just laid wide open.

Emane grunted as another Fallen One hit him, throwing him into the air. He came down with all of his weight on his arm, snapping it immediately. Kiora heard him cry out in pain.

"The Solus and her Protector..." Vitraya sneered, "they speak of your power, and yet we alone are enough to defeat you."

"What do you hope to achieve by killing us, Vitraya?" Kiora asked feigning a bravery that she did not feel.

"You really are a stupid, stupid little girl. You think I am going to kill you? I have much bigger plans for you." The hideous black-eyed creature sneered in her face. "Dralazar has been very anxious to meet you."

"Why isn't he here now?" Kiora asked, still gripping her arm. "He sends his followers out to die without him?"

"SILENCE!" Vitraya screeched. She flew closer to Kiora, raising her hand, but Kiora was faster. With a flick of her wrist she sent a targeted gust of wind, flipping Vitraya end over end.

The other Fallen Ones flew at her but stopped suddenly, their eyes fixed on something behind her.

As his thread announced his return, Kiora turned to see a giant dragon pulling itself up. "Better late than never," she said under her breath.

Drustan looked at her, and just as she had in the cave, she knew his intentions. She threw herself on top of Emane throwing up a shield to protect the both of them.

Drustan pulled his head back and let loose, igniting the meadow. There were three Fallen Ones who were too slow putting up their shields. The screams were horrible. Kiora moaned. Evil or not, their screams, and their deaths, would haunt her.

"Kiora, you're bleeding." Emane reached over with his good arm, gingerly running his fingers over the area Vitraya had cut.

Kiora winced. "I know, and your arm is still broken. Why haven't you healed it?"

"I—I didn't think of that."

"Honestly, Emane! Hurry, we need to help Drustan. They will be all over him in a second."

Emane set his hand on his own arm, healing it. Holding up his now whole arm, he looked at it in awe.

"Can we be impressed later? I need a little help." The blood was running freely down her arm.

"Sorry!" Emane scrambled to her, setting his hand on her blood-soaked arm and closing the wound.

They looked out to see The Fallen Ones zipping around Drustan's head, zinging magic at his eyes and ears. He bellowed in pain. The Fallen Ones were too small. Without the element of surprise, Drustan could not hit them with his fire breathing.

Suddenly an idea formed, it was just a hunch, but Kiora was in unknown territory. "Wings," she whispered to herself. "Emane!" she said pushing herself to her feet. "I need you to help Drustan, pull a few off of him. Use your shield to deflect their blows and use your sword if they get too close."

"What are you going to do?"

"Not exactly sure, but I need you to keep them occupied."

Kiora dropped the shield and was gone. His emotions ran through her and she knew that he didn't like it. She glanced back through her bubble to make sure Emane was running in the opposite direction.

Vitraya screamed commands, "Stay on the Shifter! You four after the Protector—and where is the Solus?" She pointed to another one and yelled. "You, find her!"

Kiora ran to the edge of the lake. She really hoped this would work. The Fallen Ones's wings, although dark, were still soft and fragile, just like the Guardians's wings, just like dragonfly wings. She looked at the water, how was she going to do this? And what if it didn't work? She shook her head, there was no time to worry about that now. Everything she was doing was guesswork at this point. She looked over her shoulder at Emane and Drustan under full attack. Emane was blocking the blows but each one would send him to his knees.

A lot of water, she thought, I need a lot of water. Perking up, she realized, I need a wave! She couldn't drop the bubble yet. She didn't know how long it would take to create what she needed. For that matter, she didn't know if she could create what she needed. The Fallen One Vitraya had sent after her flew this way and that, throwing out magic in all directions hoping to pop her bubble by lucky coincidence. Carefully, to avoid too much rippling, she stuck her hand into the lake. Focusing all her strength into the water, she pictured it rising up around her. The water began churning in response under her fingertips. Soon after, it began separating and rising around her.

"Vitraya! She's by the lake somewhere," a voice called out.

Kiora opened her eyes to see the Fallen One that had been sent after her staring at the churning lake water.

"Yes, I am," Kiora said under the bubble, pushing everything she had into this spell.

"Flush her out!" Vitraya commanded.

The Fallen One began throwing magic randomly again around the lake, hoping for a hit.

No time, Kiora thought. Dropping the bubble, she raised her arms as fast as she could, willing the water up and out. The Fallen One nearest her was swallowed up before she could shout a warning to her comrades. Kiora turned to face Emane and Drustan thrusting the wall of water in their direction. She could feel it rushing forward on both sides hurtling to its targets. Daring to look up, she was floored at the immense height towering over her. She wasn't worried about Drustan, but she called to Emane.

Emane, hold your breath!

Emane looked out from behind his shield in just enough time to gulp a mouthful of air before the water slammed into him.

Kiora watched Emane, the Fallen Ones, and Drustan be swallowed up by the entire lake of water she had just willed across the meadow. Her heart was racing, it had worked. She really hadn't known if it would. Now the worst of it—she had to get Emane out from under it. She pulled her hands back, again willing the water to recede. Drustan's head appeared first and shortly after Emane burst to the surface gasping for air. Once the water was mostly back where it was supposed to be, Kiora ran over to Emane, who was drenched and kneeling on the ground, still taking great gulps of air.

"Let's get out of here."

"Where are the Fallen Ones?" he asked.

Kiora searched for them, looking for threads but there were none. "I think they are probably bubbled, waiting for their wings to dry."

He looked at her quizzically, still breathing hard, his hair sending rivulets of water down his face.

"Dragonfly wings" she shrugged. "They can't..."

"Get their wings wet," Emane finished. "Brilliant, Kiora," he said, kissing her quickly, "Just Brilliant."

"Climb on," Drustan instructed, "I will burn the field."

Her joy was sucked out of her, the Fallen Ones were still in the field. Kiora's jaw clenched, "No!"

Emane and Drustan both looked at her, "What?"

"I said no!" Her voice shook. "I will not let you kill them while they are defenseless."

"Kiora, they just tried to kill us. And as soon as they can they will come after us again," Emane objected.

"They would not do you the same courtesy," Drustan reminded her.

"That is the difference between us and them, isn't it?" she said, her voice shaking as the screams of the dead Fallen Ones echoed in her head. "I will not allow you to kill them like this. What makes us different from them if we cannot show compassion?" she asked, motioning outwards. "If we don't have that, we don't have anything."

Drustan bowed his head. "My apologies, My Lady." His voice was soft and humble. "Thank you for reminding me why we have chosen this side. Climb on, My Lady."

Kiora closed her eyes and sighed, "Drustan, if it isn't too much trouble, I really hate riding dragons."

CHAPTER TWENTY

THE VALLEY OF NO MAGIC

KIORA, EMANE AND DRUSTAN soared over the valley below. "What are you supposed to be anyway," Emane demanded, poking at Drustan's pink fur around him.

"I am a Shapeshifter. I can be anything I want."

"Are you telling me this is an actual animal?"

"What do you think?"

He snorted, "You are a big, pink, fluffy, flying dog iguana looking…thing. It can't possibly be real."

"Not that long ago, you would have said the idea of a creature being able to change its shape was preposterous, would you have not?"

"That's not the point, Drustan. I am asking you if this is an actual creature or not."

Drustan let out a loud laugh that echoed through the sky, "Of course not, Emane! Don't be ridiculous."

"I knew it! Then why are we soaring through the sky on this pink monstrosity?"

"I was trying to cheer up the lady, if you must know."

Emane looked at Kiora who was sitting in front of him. She was staring forward, seemingly unaware that they were even speaking.

"It doesn't seem to be working."

"Perhaps you can do better?"

"Kiora?" She didn't flinch. "Kiora?" Emane nudged her gently.

She jumped, coming back to reality, "Hmm? What? I'm sorry, Emane, were you talking to me?" She turned her head to the side, but her eyes didn't meet his. They remained distant, looking out over the trees.

"Are you okay?"

"Umm, of course. Why wouldn't I be?"

"I don't know, I was wondering the same thing. We did just manage to defeat a pack of Hounds and twelve Fallen Ones. Which, by the way—Drustan, you and I will have words over your little stunt."

"Whenever you're ready, my Prince," Drustan answered with amusement.

Emane rolled his eyes, "Anyway, as I was saying, we managed to survive our first real battle. And you, what you did with that water was…well, it was something I will never forget."

She forced a smile, "That worked better than I expected."

"Better than you expected!" he exclaimed, grabbing a hold of her shoulders. "You should have seen yourself. I looked over to see you standing there—in between two enormous walls of water! And then when you sent it crashing forward, it was amazing." Sitting back, he amended. "Of course, it was more amazing after I realized I wasn't going to die."

"I wouldn't have been able to do it had you not healed my arm."

"That reminds me, let me see that arm." Emane leaned around her side to see where Vitraya had cut her. "I didn't know they could do that."

"Me either."

He glanced up at her; her voice was nearly monotone, and forced. Scowling, he looked at her blood-soaked arm and sleeve. "You lost a lot of blood."

"It was deep."

"Kiora," he asked again, "what's wrong?"

"Nothing. Drustan, where were you?"

Emane's head snapped up, he knew she was changing the subject, but this was an answer he was dying to know. "Yes, Drustan, where were you?"

"I was in the meadow, right where you left me, Prince."

"Drustan," Emane closed his eyes trying not to yell, "you are the most infuriating creature I have ever met!"

"It is an effort, I assure you, my Prince."

He took a deep breath, refusing to take the bait, "I thought I told you to turn into a Dragon as soon as I set you down. And instead, we don't see hide nor hair of you till halfway through the fight."

"It was a strategic decision based upon experience."

"How so?"

"Is the Prince asking my humble opinion?"

"No, the Prince is asking for your humble explanation, Drustan!"

"That's too bad, listening to the opinion of someone who is experienced with the enemy would be wise."

Emane took another deep breath. He was right, he knew he was right. But he really hated admitting he was wrong, especially to a flying pink iguana. "I will keep that in mind."

"Emane…" Kiora chided.

"What?"

"Just say it."

"For not being a mind reader," he grumped "you are disturbingly good at knowing what I am thinking."

She shrugged her shoulders.

"All right. You were right, I was wrong. I do want to know what it is that you were waiting for."

"I suggest that we find somewhere to stay for the night. After we set up camp I will be glad to discuss things with you."

"Where do you suggest? Kiora can't bubble us all night."

"She won't need to. They will assume that Eleana is hiding her, they won't be looking tonight."

"How can you be so sure?"

"I know."

Emane swallowed his retort and instead asked, "Where shall we camp then?"

"On the borders of the Garian Sea there is a region that is devoid of magic. It would be the last spot anybody would look for us if they chose to do so. It also makes it very easy to recognize incoming threads from a greater distance."

"Why is it devoid of magic?" Emane asked.

Drustan banked left, clearly assuming they agreed on the location, "Because the land itself is devoid of magic. We magical creatures cannot, well…" he paused unsure how to explain.

"Because once you use your magic, you need to get more, and you use the magic on the land to do so," Emane said.

"I'm impressed."

"Aleric explained it to me. What if we do need to use magic while we are there?"

"We can use what we have already, that should be enough to get us out of the area and back into magical territory."

"How far is it?"

"As the pink flying furry dog iguana thing flies? About thirty minutes."

Half an hour later, they landed in a dream-like valley framed by mountain peaks on the far side of the Sea of Garian. Emane had been to the northern shore but he knew of no one that had been to the other side. There had never been a need. Even as he wondered why, his mind slid off the question, moving instead to the beauty that surrounded them.

"How can magic not exist in this place? It speaks of magic," Kiora said as she soaked in the landscape.

"Nobody knows."

"It's beautiful," she whispered.

The grass was greener, the trees were weeping, brushing the ground. Emane reached out, fingering a leaf on the willow. The leaf was more silver than green and almost glittered as he twisted it, the now-setting sun bouncing off it. A thin layer of mist crept over the ground.

"Follow me." Drustan walked into the mist.

Emane and Kiora walked in silence, staring at the world around them. They followed Drustan's large pink backside to a weeping tree that stood towering over the rest. Drustan disappeared underneath its branches. Emane pulled back a branch, following Kiora through.

Underneath its magnificent boughs was a home made by nature, completely protected by the willow branches that laid themselves down upon the forest floor. No amount of wind or rain would bother them here. Emane watched Kiora as she leaned against the tree trunk, staring out but seeing nothing. He could not understand what it was that had her so upset, but it was like she had buried herself somewhere in her mind, somewhere he couldn't go with her.

"We had better make camp, nightfall will be here soon," Drustan reminded them.

"Kiora," Emane hoped to give her a distraction, "Can you summon us some food?"

"No, Emane," said Drustan, "She has used a lot of magic today and we can't risk her using any more. You will need to find firewood and dinner the old fashioned way."

"And you?"

"I will go fishing in the Sea of Garian, and I will be changing into something a little less pink while I am there." Drustan left their camp and took off.

"Are you going to be okay if I leave you here, or do you want to come with me?" Emane asked Kiora.

"I will be fine," she said finally looking at him. "I could actually use a little time to rest." "All right, I will be back soon."

AND SHE WAS FINALLY alone. She put her head into her hands and cried harder than she ever had before. She cried until she didn't have anything left. Leaning back against the tree, she pulled out the sapphire she wore around her neck and rolled it back and forth through her fingers. "Malena, if you can hear me, it's not an emergency but I really need to talk to you," she sighed. "But if not, I understand." She placed the sapphire back underneath the bodice of her once beautiful dress that now hung in tatters, bloodied and torn.

How could she possibly do this? Pain and death were going to be part of every battle, and she would be there to witness it, all of it. It felt like an eternity since she had watched evil in the Wings of Arian. The pain that day had been excruciating. But this, this was worse. The screams of the Fallen Ones still rang in her ears, and her heart felt as if it would break in two.

"Kiora?" a soft voice said, the same time that Malena's comforting thread reached her.

She looked up to see the tiny Guardian with long silver hair and glittering wings floating above her knee. "Malena, you came!"

"I did. You called. I should not stay for long. I used quite a bit of magic to get here. Materializing is draining." Eyeing Kiora's bloody sleeve she said, "You are a mess."

Kiora smiled for the first time since the battle. "I am so glad to see you."

Malena flew over and ran her hand along her arm. "This is Vitraya's work, is it not?" Kiora nodded. "Vitraya's taste for blood seems to exhibit itself in a most destructive way. She must have been very angry."

"She had just realized that the Shapeshifters had aligned with us, and before she could find the colony, Orrin escaped to warn us."

"I see. You saw that in a vision?"

Kiora nodded. "She killed the other Shifter before Orrin escaped." Her voice caught in her throat, she probably would have cried but there was nothing left in her.

Malena fluttered over and sat upon Kiora's knees, folding her legs underneath her as if she planned to sit there for some time. "What is it that you wanted to talk to me about?"

Kiora stared at the tiny perfect creature, "I don't know how to be okay with this."

"With being the Solus?"

Kiora thought for a second, "I don't know. I thought I had come to terms with it. But today, during the battle..." She closed her eyes, trying to forget what she had seen and heard.

"Who died?"

Kiora sniffled. "Three Fallen Ones by dragon's fire. We injured at least five Hounds. And then, of course, the Shifter I saw in the vision."

"I see." Malena flew up, fluttering inches from her nose. "Kiora,

remember after you saw evil for the first time in the Wings of
Arian?"

"How could I forget?"

"I remember how badly your heart was hurting that day, as bad
as it is now I would guess."

"Worse," Kiora's shoulders racked with an empty silent sob,
"this is worse."

"Your perceptiveness is both a blessing and a curse," Malena
turned her head to the side. "Most gifts are. It has allowed you to
achieve things that you otherwise could not."

"Like what?" she demanded. "What things has hurting this bad
enabled me to achieve?"

Malena fluttered backwards, landing again on her knee, "Eleana
spoke with me about your encounter with the Shapeshifters. You
knew their intentions, their feelings, you could feel them." Malena's
head turned again to the side, her eyes full of understanding, and
pity. "Now you feel the pain of those that were lost in battle."

Kiora felt lost underneath the pain, drowning and alone in a sea
that only she could feel. "Emane doesn't understand."

"And he won't," Malena said. Kiora turned her head away,
squeezing her eyes shut. "Kiora, you are blessed with a gift that far
exceeds his abilities. He will never understand the pain you feel
over the loss of an enemy. He will also never fully understand the
level of joy you feel. As is your pain, such will be your joy."

Kiora dropped her head back against the trunk of the tree, a few
straggling tears trickled out. "He wants me to be happy for winning
the battle. I don't know how to do that."

"You should be pleased that the work is going forward, Emane
is correct. But, feeling pain for the loss of life is part of who you
are."

"I know he is right, they tried to kill me! So why does it hurt so badly?" she looked back to Malena, pleading, "Why do I care?"

"Because to you, pain is pain and life is life. To most people, the pain of others is only valid when they feel that pain is justified. To these, preservation of life is important, but only for those they deem worthy to keep it. In regards to those who would hurt others or do any manner of things you saw that first day in the wings— the common perception is that they have voided their right to sympathy. But you can't do that." Malena shook her head, her silver hair picking up the little remaining light that was making its way through the branches. "You feel the pain of others regardless, you mourn the loss of life no matter how evil, because of your goodness. You care about them regardless of whether they deserve it or not. You love them simply because they are."

"But Emane..."

"Emane is your Protector. The Protector not only protects, but also balances. He makes up for some of your weaknesses, as you do his. Your gift of perception is also a weakness, he balances it. Kiora, there are those in this world whose evil will not be quelled. Death alone will be the end of the destruction they can cause."

She considered Malena's words, weighing them carefully in her mind. "Will it always hurt?"

"Of course it will, that is who you are. But understanding helps soothe the pain just enough to make it bearable."

"I will watch friends die," Kiora said, more a statement than a question.

Malena sighed. "I wish I could promise that it would not happen, I wish I could promise that you will not be involved, but the casualties will be great on both sides. Dralazar will not stop until he has made sure of it."

"How many were lost last time?"

"Thousands."

Kiora's chest heaved with pain, pushing her breath out. "Thousands?" she gasped.

Malena sent a wave of compassion to her. "You will always mourn, it will always hurt. But understanding the reason for their loss makes it bearable."

Kiora pulled at the glittering threads on her destroyed gown. "I wouldn't let Drustan kill the Fallen Ones I had disabled. Did I make the right decision?" she glanced up.

"Disabled?"

"I, umm...I asked the lake water to...go to them," Kiora stammered. Self recognition was not something she was comfortable with.

A smile pulled at Malena's lips. "I am sure I would have liked to have seen that. Perhaps I will ask Emane for an accurate description of what happened. In answer to your question, no, you did not make the wrong decision. You are not a mercenary and you do not kill for joy. There was no other choice you could have made. Just remember that they will never do you the same courtesy, so do not expect it," she paused, her eyes trailing over Kiora, a smile lighting up her face. "Kiora, you have grown so much since I last saw you, can you see it?"

Kiora returned to fiddling with a ripped piece of her bodice, "I think so. I see glimpses."

"Is that it? A glimpse? I can see it just looking at you."

Kiora bit her lip. "What do you see?" she asked quietly.

Malena shook her head, "It does not matter what I see, it matters what you see. You cannot act upon my knowledge. You must find the greatness that lies within you yourself."

"I have seen it," she stammered, "I can feel it. It...it is still easy to forget," she sighed. "Especially at times like these."

"The more you acknowledge it, the firmer hold it will take

within your soul. Bury it and it will die," she said firmly.

Kiora struggled with two lives, two concepts, both colliding within her. "I was always taught to be humble. How can you feel humility and greatness at the same time?"

"Ahhh," Malena nodded, understanding. "Humility is the absence of arrogance. Acknowledging the true worth of one's soul is realizing your true potential."

Kiora mulled over her words, trying to commit them to memory.

Malena flew forward, a tiny finger touching her cheek. It was so light Kiora hardly felt it at all. "I am afraid it is time."

"You need to go?" Kiora asked, sadly.

"I do. Do try to find some of that joy you are so capable of."

Malena tossed a loose strand of silver hair back between her wings and then vanished as quickly as she had come.

While she waited for Emane and Drustan, Kiora played her conversation with Malena over and over, trying to imprint her words upon her mind and in her heart.

The branches parted and Emane entered with a bundle of firewood and two rabbits.

"You caught two rabbits, already?" Kiora said, trying to sound as though nothing was wrong.

"Yes, my new dagger throwing skills are very handy."

"You used your magic?"

"I figured I am not flying us out of here, I can't bubble us, I could spare a little so that we could eat."

By the time Drustan returned, they had a fire going and two rabbits on sticks roasting for dinner. He came back in the same human form they had seen at the colony.

"Glad to see you have lost the pink fur," Emane teased.

"The things I will do to make a lady smile." Drustan looked to

Kiora, "You seem to be in better spirits than when I left."

"I am, thank you."

"I have brought fish to add to the fire."

Kiora took them and got them ready to roast. The smell of the roasting meat was making Kiora's stomach growl in anticipation.

"All right, Drustan," Emane said as he rotated the meat. "Now that we are all here, perhaps you can enlighten me. You took your own sweet time gracing us with your presence on the battlefield today."

Drustan settled himself on the ground near the fire. The red streak running through his black hair was brighter than usual and resembled a flame burning on oil. "I was gambling that you would be capable of handling the Hounds without help from me," Drustan said, looking most unapologetic.

"I am glad you feel comfortable enough to gamble with my life...again," Emane added dryly. Kiora shot Emane a look, but it went unnoticed.

Drustan hung his head. "I did not mean any harm. If I would have known how your body would react to the magic, I would not have been so insistent on inserting it."

"And what of the Hounds?" Emane pushed.

"I would have been useless against the Fallen Ones if they knew I was there, they are too fast, and too small to be caught by dragon fire. I knew I would only get one good shot in before we lost the upper hand. So, I waited for the best possible scenario in hopes that I would be able to take out more than one."

Emane nodded, "Interesting. You could have mentioned your plan."

"No time, I had to get out of range and bubble before they entered the clearing."

"I think it was brilliant," Kiora said.

"I don't know that I would call it brilliant, My Lady, especially not compared to your performance."

Kiora shook her head. "We all played a part."

After dinner, Emane stoked the fire and Kiora tried to work up the nerve to ask Drustan about the vision she had had.

"Drustan, do you mind if I ask you a question?"

"Anything you like, My Lady."

"Whose side did you fight on last time?"

Emane looked up from the fire waiting for the response. Drustan sighed deeply, a sadness washed over his face, pooling in his eyes.

"Dralazar's."

"What?" Emane's mouth fell open, aghast.

"Emane, let him explain," Kiora said, putting out her hand to silence him before he vocalized everything she could see and feel running through his head.

"Thank you, My Lady. Would you mind if I started the story from before the last battle?"

"Not at all. I could use all the information I can get."

"My species have never been able to truly decide what side we wished to follow, due to some personal extenuating circumstances." Emane frowned, but Drustan continued. "Over the thousands of years of fighting and peace, we have switched back and forth from evil to good. Once we choose, we will stay with them until the end. But during the years of peace, our resolve has always faltered and left us to choose again the next time the fighting began. We have been highly sought after, as you can imagine. Having an ally that can infiltrate an enemy's camp is a desirable advantage. During the last war, we aligned ourselves with Dralazar." His jaw hardened as he remembered. "He promised us many things that Eleana could not. All lies, of course. As the war continued, we began noticing that we were no more than pawns to him, to be used for his ultimate goal." He shook his head, his eyes far and distant.

"What is his ultimate goal?"

He snorted in disgust, his eyes focusing back in again on Kiora, "He tells his followers that he is fighting for a better world. Dralazar insists that he is trying to create a Utopia. A world where all are provided for, leading to a better life."

"But how..." Kiora started to ask.

"By making sure that everyone does exactly what he says. Without choices, there will be no mistakes," he said bitterly.

"You no longer believe him?"

"No, last time marked the first time that our people chose to leave a battle before it was finished."

Kiora drew in a quick breath. "Dralazar must have been very angry."

"I am sure he would have been had he realized. Shapeshifters are much harder to take inventory of than others. That, and the casualties were so high he had stopped counting."

Kiora flinched.

"Why did you leave?" Emane asked.

"I had become suspicious of Dralazar. I began to make a point of being wherever he was. Sometimes as something I was not, if we were in large groups, sometimes bubbled. I learned quickly that Dralazar was anything but what he had claimed to be. His wish is for power and glory and it matters not who dies in the process. He wishes for nothing but pain and misery and fear. He feeds off of fear, revels in it." Drustan spat on the ground, "I have watched him torture his own followers. He wishes to be crowned supreme ruler. And when he is, he will rule with a terror unsurpassed."

"The others believed what you had seen?"

"They had already witnessed some of it themselves and there

were whispers of more. When I confirmed what they had already suspected, we made the decision to withdraw from the battle."

"Did you join Arian and Eleana?" Kiora asked.

"To my discredit, no. Had we done that, Dralazar would have known what we had done. We could not risk making ourselves a target. Our numbers had diminished greatly during the war. It was a matter of self preservation." He bowed his head. "I am not proud of it."

"How closely did you work with Dralazar?" Emane asked.

"Very close. I was one of his top advisers."

Emane's eyebrows furrowed in suspicion, "And he didn't notice you were gone?"

"I told him that I was headed to the northernmost borders to check on the troops we had stationed there—it was near the end of the war—and we never came back. I had hoped that he assumed we were dead. But when he summoned us with his smoke signal, my hopes were proven to be false."

Leaning forward, Emane asked, "You have had strategic meetings with Dralazar?"

"Of course."

He dropped back, his wheels turning, running through the possibilities. "That could prove to be very valuable."

Kiora stifled a laugh.

"What?" Emane asked.

"I believe that's what he was trying to tell you."

Later that night, Kiora waited until the others were asleep before she stood and tiptoed past them.

"Do you mind if I join you?" Emane whispered.

Kiora almost shot out of her skin, "Emane!" she hissed, trying not to wake Drustan. "I thought you were asleep."

"Obviously." Emane sat up and grinned at her. "May I join

you?"

That grin softened her heart. "Sure."

As they went to walk through the weeping branches, they heard Drustan. "You two be careful."

Kiora threw her arms up, "Oh, good grief!"

Emane laughed, "You know, Kiora, for being so perceptive you are a terrible judge of when people are sleeping."

She heard Drustan chuckle as Emane followed her, still laughing, out into the perfect night.

The silver trees were glittering in the moonlight, even more breathtaking now, than when they had arrived.

"How could we not know that all of this existed?" she asked, looking out at the glittering landscape. "Our world is so small and within it another world has been hiding for a thousand years."

"I don't know. It just never seemed important before, did it?"

"None of us were ever given the option to decide whether or not it was important before, were we?" she said, and then felt bad for it as she saw him flinch with guilt out of the corner of her eye.

Clearing his throat, he asked, "Where are we going?"

"Anywhere. I couldn't sleep, too much on my mind."

Emane reached out and grabbed her hand. "You know you can talk to me, right?"

"I know," she drooped. "But you will never truly understand." Her voice betrayed the sadness she felt.

Emane stood quietly, looking down at her hand, his thumb running up and over hers in the moonlight. "I might understand better if you tried to explain it to me."

Kiora was flooded with Emane's feelings again. She didn't deserve to be loved this much by someone.

Emane looked up hesitantly, in time to see Kiora's eyes drop. "You felt it again, didn't you?"

"Come on," she said, pulling his hand to come with her. They walked in silence through the quiet night listening to the waves distantly working the seashore.

Emane glanced over periodically. "You are not going to give me a chance?" he finally prodded.

She sighed, shaking her head, "If I try to explain, I am just going to hurt your feelings."

"I am willing to take that risk."

Kiora bit her lip and finally glanced back at him. Dropping her hand, he held out both of his arms with a goofy grin that said, "lay it on me."

She broke, unraveling before him like a giant ball of yarn. "Everything hurts, Emane, every feeling of evil or pain or hurt. It kills me!" she said, clenching her fist at her chest. "The feelings that you are feeling, the ones I feel, are strong. But my feelings are stronger, so much more intense, about everything: love, pain, joy." She was trying desperately to make him understand. "The pain I felt when the Fallen Ones died today was stronger than anything you have ever felt."

Emane jerked backwards. "What?" He looked like she had slapped him in the face. "How could you possibly know that?"

"I know," she sighed, "that's what's wrong." She wanted him to understand so badly. "You wanted to know what is bothering me. Malena calls it my perceptiveness. Joy is so wonderful and pain is so horrible. I feel everything to an extreme that you will never understand."

"Do you think it was wrong, killing the ones we did? Is that why it hurts so badly?"

"No, we had no choice and it was for the greater good. Malena helped me to understand that, and that has made it…bearable. But it hasn't taken the pain away." Kiora looked into Emane's eyes, hoping, wishing that he would see even a glimpse of what she was feeling.

He held her gaze for a while before sighing, "You're right, Kiora, I don't understand." His eyes dropped. "I wish I did. Are you like this with everything? All of your feelings?"

Kiora nodded. Emane processed that and then slowly a smile began to spread over his face until it could go no further.

"What?" she asked.

"Nothing, just thinking."

"You can't do that!"

"Of course I can, and I will. I am not telling you what I was thinking," he grabbed her hand again, still grinning, "I can't keep my feelings from you, I should at least be entitled to my thoughts."

She couldn't argue with that. It really wasn't fair that she had known his feelings before he was ready to tell her.

"All right, fine." They started walking again. "Malena said you are supposed to balance me."

"That sounds familiar. Aleric told me that we balanced each other."

"Kiiiiooooooorraaa." Her name came whispering through the trees as if it were riding on the mist.

She stopped dead in her tracks. "Did you hear that?" Kiora asked.

"Hear what?"

"Kiioooooooorraaaa."

"That!"

"No, I didn't hear anything."

"Just listen!" Emane and Kiora stood listening. But what came next was different, it sounded like rattling. Almost like the toy her mother had made her as a child, a gourd filled with rice.

"Is that what you heard?" Emane asked, his head jerking around looking for the source.

"No. Someone was calling my name before."

"I didn't hear that, but I can certainly hear this. It's getting closer."

The sound grew louder and closer. Emane's hand inched backwards to the hilt of his sword.

Kiora grabbed his arm. "No."

"Kiora!"

"No, Emane, it's okay."

"How can you know it's okay when you don't know what *it* is?" he snapped. He shifted back from one foot to the other, eyes darting in search of the sound.

"I don't know. It's just what I feel."

Out of the mist, a sea of black moved across land. They squinted trying to make it out. As it moved closer, the sea of black revealed itself as a mass of beetles scuttling across the grass towards them. They seemed jet black until the moonlight hit them—then they shimmered a royal blue and emerald green, changing back and forth between the two colors as they scurried towards them. They had large eyes and two exceptionally long antennas, which preceded their arrival.

"Kiora, I don't like this," Emane whispered.

Kiora's heart was pounding, she never had liked bugs, and these were the size of walnuts, some larger. Despite the fear, there was an underlying sense of peace that Kiora knew was not coming from her.

"I know—I don't like it either. But it's going to be okay."

"I'm not going to have to watch as one of them eats you, am I?" he said, placing his body between her and the onslaught of beetles.

She stepped out from behind him, placing her hand reassuringly on his shoulder. "I have no idea."

"Kiora," he hissed keeping his eyes on the beetles. "What are you doing?"

"It's okay, Emane, stay here," she said, her hand trailing off his shoulder as she walked closer.

Once she had separated herself from Emane, the beetles scuttled forward, surrounding her. Emane was struggling to keep his feet planted where they were.

One of the larger beetles left the group and hurried over to Emane. Emane took a step back and went for his sword again.

"Emane, stop! It's all right, let him do what he is going to do."

"Going to do! What is he going to...?" Emane abruptly stopped talking as the beetle scurried up his leg and onto his shirt, "Kiora, what is he doing?" Emane said through clenched teeth, trying to remain still.

"Emane, I really don't know, everything is so guarded. I am only sensing what they want me to. Please just trust me and hold still."

The beetle zipped inside the open neck of his shirt and Emane turned stiff as a board. Camouflaged, it was now just a buggy shaped bump moving across his shoulder. It moved rapidly winding itself down and around his armband, pausing once, before moving its way back up. Having inspected what it came for, it emerged and scurried back down his leg. Emane remained stiff, watching it warily, as the invading bug hurried back to its comrades.

Once the beetle had rejoined the others, the entire group was still for a moment. Kiora and Emane watched silently, their eyes flitting from the beetles, to each other, and back again. Suddenly in one cohesive effort, all of the beetles closed in on Kiora. She clenched her fists tight at her side, screwing her eyes shut. But even with closed eyes, she could still feel the tiny legs grabbing at her mangled dress and pulling themselves up. They clicked and ticked as if they were talking to each other, a crescendo of sound as they climbed. Panic closed in as the weight of her dress increased exponentially, and the scratch of insect feet raked over her skin where her dress had ripped. Taking a deep breath, she tried to focus only on the calm feeling that had accompanied these beetles upon their arrival, which was difficult to find at the moment. She was also being overrun with waves of concern from Emane.

The little feet with their underlying chatter had reached her bodice. Of course, she thought to herself, through deep breaths trying not to panic. Emane gets one and I get them all.

She was worried that they were about to climb up and onto her head, encasing her completely, when all movement stopped. Breathing heavily, she hesitantly opened one cye, and then the other, finding herself staring at the largest beetle perched upon her shoulder.

Startled, she saw something in those gigantic eyes that she was not expecting. Awareness. Intelligence. A whirlwind of impressions overtook her mind. It was so different from talking to Arturo, there were no words but she knew what they were trying to tell her.

Tell no one, it will help. Time is not now, but later, secrets and trust.

They trusted her and they had a secret. She was to remember that for a later date and was to tell no one. That specific impression waved over her again and again, tell no one.

Eleana? She whispered to the beetle.

The impression came harder and clearer. No one!

"When?" She whispered back. She didn't understand how long she was to keep this secret for, and for what purpose.

Another impression came: You will know when it is time. Do not forget us.

The beetles, having delivered their message, turned at once and scurried back down the way they had come. Moving in unison, they once again became a sea of black, dissipating into the mist. But as they left, the impressions continued to wave back over her, Do not forget, tell no one, a great secret, do not forget.

Kiora watched their retreat into the mist long after she couldn't see them anymore.

Emane finally managed to unfreeze himself. "Kiora!" He ran over to her, running his hands over her arms, looking for injuries. "Kiora, are you okay?"

"I'm fine," she said, her eyes unmoving from where the last beetle had disappeared.

"What just happened?" he asked slowly.

"I am not sure," she said, finally turning to look at him. "All I know is that we can't tell anyone what just happened."

"Anyone?"

"Not anyone. I even asked about Eleana."

"Those things were speaking to you?" he asked incredulously.

"Not in words, but yes. Emane, promise me—we tell no one, ever."

She was looking at him with the same amount of intensity that she had in the cave right before Drustan ate her as a multi-headed monster. "I promise, I will tell no one."

"Thank you." Her shoulders relaxed. "I think we should get back to the tree and get some rest."

CHAPTER TWENTY-ONE

RETURN TO THE HOLLOW

KIORA AWOKE, FEELING SOMETHING wrapped around her waist. Looking down, she smiled, sliding her hand across Emane's and snuggling back into the warmth of his body.

"Good morning," he said.

Turning her head, she smiled sleepily, "Good morning, what time is it?" She yawned.

"I'm not sure. The sun's been up for a while." Leaning around her, he yelled, "Hey, Drustan, any chance you could turn yourself into a pocket watch?"

Drustan strode over carrying breakfast. "This Protector of yours fancies himself a comedian," he said, handing her last night's rabbit.

Emane stretched out like a cat after its morning nap, "It was just a question, Drustan," he said through a groan.

Kiora grinned but decided not to fuel either of their fires. Taking a bite, she grimaced. Rabbit never had been her favorite. Leftover, cold rabbit was much worse. She swallowed with some effort and had just torn off another piece as a thread came within range. She focused in, trying to recognize it.

"What is it?" Drustan asked.

Kiora didn't answer but held up her hand. A moment later, she swallowed and breathed out a sigh of relief. "Sorry, someone is coming. One of yours, I believe," she told Drustan.

One large bushy eyebrow rose in surprise, "I haven't felt anything yet."

"You will," Kiora answered, going back to her breakfast.

She watched with some amusement out of the corner of her eye as Drustan sat searching for the thread. After a couple of minutes, he shook his head. "I cannot believe you felt it that much sooner than I did. Remarkable."

"It is one of yours, right?"

"Yes, it is Orrin."

The name immediately conjured sadness. "How is he doing? He seemed close to the other Shifter that was guarding with him that night."

"Yes," Drustan said with a thoughtful nod, "It was his mate."

Kiora suddenly felt infinitely worse. Not hungry any longer, she set down her barely touched breakfast. Orrin had lost his mate trying to protect her.

"She was a wonderful girl," Drustan added. Noticing Kiora's saddened demeanor, he placed his hand on her shoulder, "They knew what they were doing when they went out there, and they went willingly."

Knowing there was nothing that could change what happened, and nothing that would make her feel better, she changed the subject. "Drustan, where did the other Shapeshifters go when we left?"

"The Merfolk had offered refuge if needed. They went to stay with them."

"Merfolk?"

"The Merfolk of the Garian Sea."

"So, when you say 'Merfolk,'" Emane interrupted, "you mean head of a man, body of fish, right?"

"Of course, what else would I be referring to?"

"I don't know, just making sure I had the right story, that's all. Your people all turned into Merfolk?"

"Some did, I am sure. But as long as it was something that could survive underwater, they would be fine. The sea probably has a larger than normal assortment of ostentatiously bright fish and sea monsters, I would guess." A sparrow burst through the branches of the tree. "Hello, Orrin."

"Drustan," the sparrow nodded in his direction and turned to Kiora. "We need you to return to the new Hollow. There has been a development and your presence is requested."

"When?" Kiora asked.

"Immediately. You are to follow me back. Drustan, I assume you have enough magic to change into something suitable?"

"Of course. Kiora, any requests?"

"As long as it's not pink," Emane interjected.

Kiora shook her head and laughed, "I give you free rein."

Drustan rubbed his hands together with glee. "Free rein?" he asked, his eyes locked mischievously on Emane.

"Whatever you want."

Drustan began to change before their eyes. Legs growing, body elongating. Wings exploded out of his back and hoofs appeared in place of feet. A pegasus.

"Thank you!" Emane exclaimed, throwing his arms to the sky.

As a final touch, Drustan exploded into color, Emane's arms dropped back to his side in defeat at the now purple pegasus.

"Purple? You had to make him purple?" Emane said in disbelief.

He stomped past Kiora, who had resorted to leaning against a tree because she was laughing so hard.

"It's not funny, Kiora, he did that just to torture me."

"I know," she said through hysterics. "That's…what makes it… so…funny!"

The pegasus smiled at Emane, "Climb aboard, Your Majesty."

As Emane pulled himself onto the purple pegasus, Drustan turned his head to look at him, "Isn't purple the color of royalty, anyway?" When Emane ignored the jab, Drustan chortled through horse lips, "Maybe not, it's just what I heard."

Kiora launched into another fit of laughter, gripping her side in pain.

"Come on, get control of yourself." Emane snapped. "They said our presence is requested immediately."

Taking a deep breath, Kiora pushed off of the tree and walked over, trying to stifle her laughter, but still couldn't manage to stand up straight.

Emane pulled her up in front of him and wrapped his arms around her as she wrapped her fingers through Drustan's mane. Orrin took off like a flash, darting out through the branches. Drustan followed behind, nearly swiping Emane off with a thick weeping branch. Kiora heard Emane grumbling behind her, something about him doing that on purpose, but she chose instead to focus on getting one last look at the Valley of No Magic, that was ironically, the most magical place she had ever seen. Glittering trees, all-too-green grass, blue and green beetles. Something was here, and she believed it had everything to do with magic.

They flew for some time back over the Sea of Garian and over the top of miles of forest before Orrin darted straight down.

"Hold on." The pegasus dipped into a dive.

The trees were set closely together here, so even despite

Drustan's best efforts this time, Emane and Kiora were both almost ripped off his back by the branches. When they landed, Aleric, Malena, and Eleana were all waiting for them. Eleana's eyebrows rose at the sight of the purple pegasus.

"Interesting choice, Drustan," Eleana commented as Kiora and Emane slid off his back.

"He did it just to tick me off," Emane grumbled.

"And it was a smashing success," Drustan added as he morphed back into his preferred human shape with a flourish.

Eleana, glittering in gold, appraised them, "You two are quite a sight." She tried to sound stern, but her blue eyes betrayed her amusement.

Kiora looked down at her torn and bloody dress. "It was a beautiful gown," she said sadly.

"I will have to take your word for that. Malena, please escort Kiora and Emane somewhere they can get cleaned up. And please find them something else to wear."

"Come with me," Malena said, floating into the Hollow. Emane put his hand in the small of Kiora's back and led her after Malena.

DRUSTAN DIDN'T TAKE HIS eyes off Kiora as she walked away, "Have you seen the battle yet?" He asked Eleana through the side of his mouth.

"No, although Malena had expressed interest in seeing it."

"I suggest that you watch it. She is growing, rapidly."

Eleana, Drustan, and Aleric gathered around a large silver basin in the meeting tent. Eleana waved her hands over the top and the water began to ripple in response. Soon the image, a mountain lake, came into focus.

They watched the lake beginning to bubble from underneath,

the waters rising, splitting around a central point. Kiora appeared
in the middle dropping her bubble. The water flexed and moved
around her, growing until it towered several feet over her head.
Kiora's hands pushed the water out, and with complete obedience
it went hurtling out into the meadow, covering everything and
everyone. She then masterfully pulled it back, restoring the lake as
it was. Nobody spoke. Aleric's mouth was agape, his eyes bulging.
Eleana had a look of surprise and pride. Drustan just shook his head
as if watching it again had been just as amazing as watching it the
first time.

Aleric finally broke the silence, "How is that possible, so
quickly?"

"How long exactly since she discovered her magic?" Drustan
asked.

"Maybe a month," Aleric said, still in shock.

"I'm surprised she hasn't had any consequences," Drustan
looked to Eleana. "Has she?"

"Not yet," Eleana said, her eyes still fixed on the basin. "But I
am sure she will." Looking up, she motioned to the chairs, "Please
sit, I need to discuss something with you before they arrive."

Aleric gladly dropped into a chair, glad to be off of his shaky
knees.

"The prophecy states that this will be the final battle; that if
evil is defeated this time, it will never return. It makes sense that
the Solus for this battle would be the most powerful of them all.
Kiora has no idea what she is capable of, and we are just beginning
to see it. Her powers will exceed anything we have ever seen."
She explained "And because of that, I believe it puts her in more
danger."

"What kind of danger?" Drustan questioned, leaning back
casually in his chair. "From what I have seen, she handles herself

well."

"She does. But…this much power…in one person?" Eleana shook her head. "It will make Dralazar drunk with desire. He will want her more than he has ever wanted anything."

"Surely he will not think that he will be able to beat her, after she has reached her potential?" Aleric said. "He could go head to head with Arian, but he was not nearly as powerful as she will be."

"He will not wait until she has reached her full potential. He will try to turn her now. Turn her and train her underneath himself," Eleana said.

There was quiet as everyone mulled over the possibility.

Drustan shook his head. "I don't believe it. I understand what you are saying, but from what I have seen, I cannot believe she would side with him."

"I agree. Which puts her in even more danger. When Dralazar realizes that he cannot turn her, he will kill her."

KIORA WALKED OUT OF her tent in a white tunic and tan riding pants, her hair pulled neatly back in a braid. Emane was already dressed and waiting for her. He leaned casually against a tree, wearing pants and a shirt that were almost identical to hers. He looked relaxed, happy and very handsome.

"Do you have to outdo me in everything?" Emane asked.

Kiora cocked her head to the side.

"The clothes," he waved a hand at her. "They look much better on you."

She looked down. "I don't think so. They look very nice on you."

He grinned, appraising himself as if the sight was new to him, "Do they?"

"Oh, you are shameless, Emane!"

He pushed off the tree with a laugh. "Is it so shameless that I would want some attention from you?" Grabbing her hand, he wrapped it around his arm, "Shall we go?"

They walked back through the new Hollow, marveling at how much it looked like the old one that had been destroyed—almost identical. The homes looked the same and even hung in the same places. As they came to the clearing in the center of the Hollow, the same tent stood waiting for them. Within, they found Eleana, Aleric, and Drustan all sitting around a silver bowl looking somewhat anxious.

"What?" Kiora asked as Emane pulled her chair out. "You all look like something is wrong."

"Of course not," Eleana answered smoothly, "we were just discussing Aleric's recent trip to the village. He went to check if Dralazar's influence had gained a foothold with the people."

"And?" Kiora asked.

Eleana looked slightly ill, "He does seem to be making progress."

Kiora didn't like the fact the Eleana was clearly avoiding eye contact with her. She was going to push for more information, when a host of Guardians floated through the door, bringing with them an array of heavenly foods.

"How is my father?" Emane asked Aleric as the Guardians hovered above the table, gently setting down plates and platters in front of them.

"He is fine. Although we do have a..." he stopped mid sentence as he became fully aware of Emane's thread. Aleric looked to Drustan and Eleana. "What have you done?"

"We have given him a fighting chance," Drustan answered calmly, taking a drink.

Aleric looked baffled as he asked Emane, "What have they given you?"

Emane opened his mouth with the beginnings of an answer—what had surely begun as a word faltered, and emerged instead a puff of deflated air. Unsure of what to say, he looked to Eleana.

"Show it to him," Eleana gestured.

Emane reached behind, grabbing the back of his shirt, and pulled it over his head to reveal the glittering green armband that wrapped around him.

Aleric stood up and walked slowly and deliberately around the table, his eyes fixated on the sparkling snake. Reaching out, he ran his finger over it, scowling.

"Eleana, what have you done?" his voice strained under controlled anger.

"Aleric, it had to be done," she said gently.

"Had to be done? You have no idea what the consequences of this might be. There has never, NEVER, been a magical heir to the throne. His father will be furious. You have to take it off!"

"Aleric," Drustan interrupted. "We had no choice. There has never been a non-magical Protector before. He wouldn't last two battles. He would probably be dead already for that matter."

Taking another approach, Aleric turned to Emane, "Take it off," he demanded. "You know as well as I do that heirs to the throne do not do magic. Your father will feel as if you have betrayed him, he will think—"

"Aleric, Drustan is right." Eleana tried to intervene. "If we allowed—"

"No, I promised to keep him safe, I promised..."

"Enough!" Emane shouted, his chair clattering to the floor behind him as he stood. He glared around the room, taking each in turn. "Why is it that whenever my life is being discussed, everyone sits around and talks of it as if I am not in the room? I chose this, Aleric," he said pointing roughly at himself, "nobody else. And I will continue to make my own choices as I see fit." He shoved his finger at Drustan and Eleana. "Had they not done what they did, we would not have made it out of the first battle alive. It was a strategic decision and one that I support."

"But, Your Highness," Aleric tried to get a word in, but Emane's voice was growing louder.

"No, Aleric. I have had enough of my life being decided for me. 'You are to be a prince.' 'You are to be the Protector.' 'You are not to have magic.' Enough!" He slammed his fist on the table. His chest was heaving and he stared, fixated on the table, his jaw working. "And you may tell my father something else as well," he said quieter. "I am entitled to make my own choices, and I will not be told who to marry."

Aleric sucked in his breath.

Turning his head to the side, Emane's eyes narrowed, "I will care for whomever I choose. I am not a puppet!" Driving his point home, he walked past Aleric to Kiora; grabbing her face roughly, he kissed her hard and fast. His eyes flashed back to Aleric in defiance. "Despite what you and my father may think, I am capable of making decisions." He stood tall and straight, with a look that dared any to dispute. Waiting a few seconds, he then gave a curt nod. "I have lost my appetite. I will be in my tent if you need me." He turned on his heel, leaving with his head held high and his shirt still gripped in a tight fist.

Kiora's body had gone rigid, her cheeks burning. She kept her eyes glued to the table to avoid meeting Aleric's, which were currently burrowing into her.

He cleared his throat. "It appears that there is a lot I am unaware of," he said as he moved back over to his chair, stiffly sitting down.

"Eleana, were you aware of this as well?" He motioned to the red-faced Kiora.

"I was."

Kiora cleared her throat. "He was right, about the battle. We would not have made it out alive had it not been for his magic."

"Kiora, we watched what happened," Aleric said exasperated, dropping his head into his hands. "We know it was you."

Tearing her eyes from the table, Kiora shook her head emphatically, "No. Vitraya cut my arm, I was bleeding badly. I had already lost a lot of blood, and then Emane broke his arm. Had he not healed us, I would have been too weak to do anything."

Aleric's head rose slowly. "He heals?"

"Yes."

"I would not have expected that," he mumbled, looking into his plate.

"Neither would I," Eleana said. "It was a pleasant surprise, and something that we desperately need. As far as his father is concerned, you may tell him that it is not permanent. When the war is over, I will be able to remove it. If that is what Emane wishes, of course."

With nothing more to say, they began eating in tension-rich silence. As Kiora nibbled at a pastry, an unfamiliar current thrummed through her. It felt like her magic, only in short intense bursts, rolling through skin and bone. She paused before taking another bite. Another came, and then another, pulsing in a new and unpleasant way. With a scowl, she slowly placed the pastry back on her plate. Each second, the current increased in size and intensity, each one more unpleasant than the last. They stretched and pulled at her as if whatever channels they were traveling in were too small and they ached to burst their bonds. Her head begin to spin and she squeezed her eyes shut, breathing deeply through her nose. It did no good. She was swimming in unfamiliar territory, her body and her mind rebelling under the current that was pulling at her.

Kiora stood abruptly, nearly knocking her plate off the table in the process. Desperate for balance, she grasped at the edges of the tabletop, "I'm sorry," she blurted. "I am not feeling very well."

"Are you all right, Kiora?" Eleana asked.

Kiora gripped her head, Eleana sounded as if she were underwater. "I think so. I think I just need to lie down." She stumbled out of the tent, her hands reaching out, still searching for balance.

As the flaps on the tent closed behind her, Eleana sighed, "It has begun."

Kiora stumbled back to her tent in a fog. Her ears were roaring like the sea, her vision fuzzy, and her thoughts disjointed. She drug her feet through the dirt to keep herself upright, but instead tripped on a rock. She could almost hear herself groan through the roar in her ears as the impact jolted her already pounding head. Pushing herself up on wobbly arms, she peered around. The Hollow was spinning like a kaleidoscope, the homes of the Guardians throwing in reds, blues, and greens. Moving forward, she headed towards what she thought was her tent. Stumbling through the flaps, she collapsed onto her bed. Shortly after, a heat began spreading throughout her body. A heat that was far too warm to be comfortable.

CHAPTER TWENTY-TWO

CHANGING

KIORA'S SCREAM PIERCED THE Hollow, sending Emane
bolting to his feet. Another scream came following on the heels of
the first. So raw and pain filled, he knew that something was terribly
and dreadfully wrong. Sprinting out of the tent, he cursed the fact
that he could not follow threads like the others. Turning towards
Kiora's tent, he took off at a dead run across the Hollow, hoping he
was going in the right direction.

"Kiora!" he shouted. "Kiora, where are you?!" Nearing her tent,
he could see Aleric and Drustan standing calmly outside. "Where is
she?" he yelled.

Her scream came again followed by gasping and crying.
Emane ran at them trying to shove them out of the way, but Drustan
grabbed onto his arm with a vice-like grip.

Emane flinched underneath the tightness of Drustan's grasp.
"What are you doing to her?" Emane yelled.

Drustan was infuriatingly placid. "Emane, calm down, we are
not hurting her."

"Not hurting her! Listen to her." He jerked and struggled to free himself.

"Emane, stop!" Aleric demanded.

"I have to help her, let me see her." He jerked again, but it was no use.

"Emane, there is nothing you can do," Drustan said gently.

"Please, let me see her. I have to see her."

Drustan looked to Aleric, who gave a nod of permission. Emane stopped struggling, looking expectantly at the fingers curled around his arm.

Drustan released him. "Stay calm, Prince, your yelling will not help her."

Emane gave Drustan an indignant glare before pulling back the flap of the tent. Kiora was lying on the bed, her skin faded to a dull ashen grey and glistening with sweat. Her clothes were drenched, as were the bedsheets. She moaned again, grabbing her head and pulling herself into a ball. Eleana sat calmly by her bedside holding her hand and muttering something under her breath.

"What is wrong with her?" Emane demanded.

With a jerk, Kiora uncurled from her ball, arching her back violently with a scream that turned Emane's blood to ice.

Emane's face went pale, the tent flap fluttered from his limp hand hiding Kiora from view again. "What is wrong with her?" his voice shook.

Drustan explained, "Kiora is different from most magical humans. She has abilities that are far beyond her physical capacity."

"I don't understand."

"Her abilities have just started to grow and already her body has reached its limit. The water at the lake yesterday put her over the edge."

"You still have not explained why she is in so much pain. She was already magical!" he argued. "She shouldn't hurt, not like me," he motioned to the armband that almost killed him. Kiora's moans were knotting up his insides. He looked back to the tent in frustration. "What is hurting her and why are you not helping her?"

"It is not exactly the same. Your body had to adjust to the magic. With her, the magic is purifying her body. It is also literally forcing itself through every cell, causing her body to mold around the magic. This has to happen to allow the magic to flow freely."

He shook his head. "That is what is hurting her so badly; the magic is forcing itself through her?"

"Yes," Drustan said. "It is very painful. And once the process has started, there is nothing anyone can do to stop it. The magic that is pulsing through her veins right now is more than was ever meant to be."

"How long will it take?"

Kiora screamed again and Emane could feel the blood drain from his face and pool somewhere in his stomach.

"It depends on the person."

"Is there nothing we can do?" Emane asked, looking between Aleric and Drustan.

They both shook their heads.

Emane stared, his fists clenching at his side. There had to something. "Please, let me stay with her."

Aleric withered at the request, "Emane, I don't think..."

"I can't let her go through this alone," he interrupted. "She didn't leave me and you can't tell me that it was easy for her," he yelled. "I have seen how she reacts to others' pains! This cannot possibly be worse for me than it was for her."

Eleana conceded the fact, opening the tent flap. "Come, Emane, if you are willing." Without hesitation, Emane entered the tent, his heart breaking at the girl that lay before him. He ached to take her pain away.

"There is little you can do for her," Eleana said gently, placing her hand on his shoulder. "Are you sure you wish to stay here?"

Emane nodded numbly.

"Very well, I will check on you throughout the night."

Emane didn't bother to watch her go, he was fixated on Kiora. Kneeling down in front of her bed, he took a hold of her hand. Every muscle in her body was tense with the pain, her face twisted into a mask of agony that had swept her consciousness far away from him. She wrenched her body upward with a scream that pulled tears immediately to his eyes and sent them pouring down his cheeks. Then, without warning or explanation, he felt magic jolting through him from Kiora's hand. It was wickedly strong, and he tore away from her with a gasp, his heart pounding at the current of magic that had just passed through him. He looked down at his hand and then back to Kiora, who had crumbled like a discarded rag doll. She tossed her head with a painful moan. He frowned, leaning closer. A section of hair as wide as his little finger was turning from dark brown to stark white. He watched in confusion, still rubbing his sore hand, as it traveled down the length of her hair turning it white from the crown of head to the ends.

OUTSIDE THE TENT, THE sun started to poke its way over the horizon.

"The poor boy has been in there all night," Aleric whispered to Eleana.

"It is what he desires, Aleric. We cannot take that away from him."

He sighed. "Do you know how long this will last? We are running out of time."

"I don't. I have never witnessed a change; days perhaps."

"We don't have days. Dralazar is running freely amongst the villagers with no opposition."

Eleana nodded gravely. "I know. We need to get her to the castle." She glanced toward the tent as another shriek was followed by Emane's mumbling. "Emane will not be happy, transporting her like this." Eleana looked up at the sky that was turning a purplish color above Kiora's tent. "Can you feel the magic, Aleric? It is flowing, centering on her. If Dralazar is anywhere in the area, he will know where she is, no matter how much protection we put around her. She is pulling magic from every direction."

"What other path can we take?"

Eleana gave one abrupt nod of acknowledgement. "I will speak to Emane. I need you to have Drustan collect some of his people— we will need an escort."

"ARE YOU CRAZY?!" EMANE shouted at Eleana. Kiora jumped in response. He lowered his voice. "Look at her! She is unconscious and burning up. Not to mention screaming in pain. We are not moving her."

"Emane, this is not ideal. But there is not time. Dralazar is already recruiting within the village. He is claiming himself to be the Solus. Having no other force to align themselves with, people are siding with him."

"How is she going to help like this!?"

"We need her at the castle so that you, your father, and I can discuss battle plans. This is a war, Emane. Sacrifices need to be made. If we wait until this process is finished, we could be days behind, and who knows how many souls will be lost to Dralazar."

"Why can't we bring my father here?" he demanded. "We can make all the plans here while we wait for this to end."

"No, Emane, I am sorry. The Hollow is fiercely protected from all outsiders."

"You let me in."

"I knew who you were before you did, Emane. You belonged here, your father does not." She said briskly. "I have called for Arturo. He will fly you both to the castle. Drustan and his top men will fly with you. Aleric and I will travel by foot watching for signs of trouble and we will meet you there. It is the only way, Emane."

Emane emerged from the tent carrying Kiora. Her face was drawn and pale, her hair and clothes wet with sweat. And with each step that Emane took, she tossed and moaned in pain.

Emane glared, holding Kiora as if she needed protecting from all of the others. "If this goes badly, I will never forgive any of you," he said, catching the eyes of each member of the group.

Arturo walked forward, the Shifters moving to the side to allow him through. Emane placed Kiora on Arturo's back, leaning her forward against his neck as Eleana whispered a few words. Glimmering ropes snaked themselves around Kiora, securing her to Arturo.

"This will help hold her until you arrive at the castle," Eleana explained. Emane climbed on behind Kiora and wrapped his arms around her waist. "Once you get to the castle, you need to speak with your father, immediately. He must be made aware of the situation. Arturo, fly as quickly as you can," Eleana instructed him, "she is pulling magic quickly. Dralazar will be able to feel her for miles."

"You failed to mention that to me," Emane said, his eyes blazing.

Eleana ignored him and turned to Drustan. "If Dralazar comes, he will either come with Fallen Ones, or dragons. I would guess the dragons."

Drustan looked around at the trees that were tightly packed. "We will have to change in the air, no room here for all of us. Arturo, we will head up to change, follow us when you see it is finished."

The Shapeshifters turned into hawks and soared to the sky. In unison the birds suddenly stopped flying and started to fall back to earth. Each plummeting mass of feathers began growing and changing in the air. Emane's heart began to pound; they were getting closer, falling faster and growing infinitely larger. They were going to be crushed.

The Shapeshifters completed their transformation moments before crashing into the canopy. With a move worthy of any acrobat, they each flipped and turned their now massive bodies, righting themselves before they could begin flapping their leathery wings. The eight, now dragons, turned back to the sky gaining altitude. As Emane's heartbeat returned to a normal pace, Arturo spread his wings and joined the dragons.

Arturo was flying as Emane had only felt him do once before. Emane kept his arm wrapped around Kiora and put his head onto her back as they shot through the sky. She only screamed once on the way to the castle, but it was the worst one yet, making his skin crawl and his heart break.

As the castle turrets appeared in the distance. Emane yelled into the wind, "Drustan! We can't land eight dragons into the castle courtyard. We will frighten the villagers."

Drustan's dragon ears pulled tight against his head. "What do you suggest, my Prince?"

"Is anybody following us yet?"

There was silence as the Shifters sensed in every direction looking for a thread. "Not yet," Drustan finally answered, "Not unless they are bubbled."

Damn those bubbles, Emane thought, "Drustan, I need to you to bubble to get beyond the castle walls. Once you're there, I need you to change into something small and hide in the gardens, at least until I can explain." That was going to be fun, explaining Shapeshifters to his father.

"Understood," Drustan shouted back.

Emane watched the ground below for any people outside the village's limits who might have spotted them. One by one the dragons disappeared, until it was just him and Kiora on a pegasus, making their final approach into the castle. As soon as Arturo's feet hit the ground, the bindings holding Kiora vanished. Emane slid off, keeping his hands on her to prevent her from falling. Gently lifting her off of Arturo, Emane cradled Kiora in his arms as he rushed into the castle.

EMANE HAD ALREADY PLANNED to place Kiora in the room next to his, with the intention of staying with her until she awoke. Instead, he found himself stalking down the stone hallway because Eleana had insisted Emane speak with his father immediately. Kiora had not left his side during his ordeal, and yet he had left her with a maid to tend to her, instead of being there himself.

He hadn't gone far when another problem reared its ugly head.

"Where is he?" A harsh female voice demanded from around the corner. Emane stopped short. How had he forgotten that?

"Beggin' your pardon, miss?" a maidservant replied.

"Prince Emane, you fool!"

Emane cringed. It was uncanny how fast word travelled amongst the staff—and from there anyone within the walls of the castle.

"Miss, I don't know where he is," the servant stuttered, "and if I did, it wouldn't be my place to say."

Emane smiled, bless her heart, a member of the staff who can hold her tongue.

"Need I remind you that I am your future queen?" The voice dripped with contempt.

Emane peeked around the corner to see Ciera looming over one of the maids.

"No, miss, you needn't remind me. I am well aware." Emane found himself smirking at the tone the maid had taken. He was not the only one dreading Ciera becoming queen.

"What did you say to me?" Ciera snarled.

Emane sighed inwardly. He supposed he should save the maid.

"Ciera," Emane said, strolling around the corner. She had once enthralled him with her beauty, but that was gone now. The long blonde hair and big brown eyes were nothing but a facade hiding a much nastier interior. And in that second, before she realized he was there, the facade was down and Ciera's interior looked even nastier than Emane remembered, it markedly resembled the evil he had seen a few times now. And then it was gone, her wall neatly rising. Ciera's face softened, turning as if nothing had happened. "Emane! There you are, darling." She wrapped her arms around his neck. "I have missed you so much!"

He gently untangled himself from her arms without reciprocating the sentiment. "Ciera, I need to speak with my father."

"Of course. I will join you!" she said, linking her arm though his, oblivious, or choosing to be oblivious to his lack of enthusiasm. Emane tried to force his shoulders to relax, but having Ciera so close to him set his nerves on end.

Emane entered the throne room with Ciera on his reluctant arm.

"Look who has come home, Your Majesty!" Ciera gloated as she flounced into the room, her blonde curls bouncing behind her.

"Emane!" The King rose to his feet embracing his son. "I am so relieved to see you home." He smiled at the vicious beauty attached to Emane's arm. "Ciera has been worried sick as well."

"I am sure she has been," Emane said dryly. He was positive that Ciera's feelings had everything to do with being queen and little to do with being his wife.

"Where is Aleric?"

"He should be along shortly. We will need to meet with you. There is much to discuss."

The King raised his eyebrows "Is the…"

"Yes, she is here."

"She?" Ciera prodded. "She who?"

"She is staying in the chamber next to my room and is not well. Aleric will explain when he arrives."

The King smiled broadly, "Have you eaten, son?" Not waiting for an answer, as usual, the king continued. "Ciera, please have someone bring the Prince some breakfast."

Emane could feel Ciera stiffen next to him. He had to suppress a smile; she preferred to give orders rather than to take them.

"Of course, Your Majesty." Her lips formed into a tight line before she turned and swept out of the room.

Emane relaxed in her absence, "We need to meet as soon as Aleric arrives. They want us to help prepare battle plans."

The King and Emane headed towards the meeting hall. "How long before Aleric arrives?"

"I am not sure. They came behind us on foot."

"On foot?" The King raised an eyebrow. "How did you arrive?"

Emane hesitated, "Aleric will explain that as well."

His father had a habit of looking at anything that was out of the ordinary as if it were a green rabbit with three heads. Explaining arrival on a pegasus would not go well. His father had practically forbidden Aleric to speak of magic at all. Just as he had forbidden Emane to speak of evil, or any prophesies.

Entering the meeting hall, they sat at a large circular table surrounded by chairs. The usual silence they shared settled in as they waited for the others to arrive. The two could not be more different, like two sides of a coin. Emane's father was steeped in traditions and custom, whereas Emane preferred to take his own road. As a result, they had always struggled to relate.

"Emane, you have been gone for weeks with no word. Have you nothing to say to me?" his father finally said.

I have plenty to say, he thought, but nothing you're going to like. "Things have been going well. The Solus is progressing quickly. She will be a valuable asset in this war."

His father leaned in. "I have been reading the history books and the prophecies while you have been away," The King looked pleased with himself, "Trying to make sure I understood everything. It came to my attention that the Solus always has a Protector assigned to them. Any idea who or what that might be?"

Emane froze, did he know already? "Why do you ask?" Emane said, searching his father's face.

"Things seem to be progressing quickly, from what Aleric tells me. I had hoped one had been chosen."

"One has," Emane ventured cautiously.

"Wonderful!" the King said slapping the table. "Will they be joining us?"

Emane squirmed in his seat. This was getting worse with every question. "father, it's…" Just say it, he thought. It was either now or later. "It's me."

At first there was silence, and then his father's eyes began to bulge, his customary redness building in his neck before rising to his face. "You?"

Keeping his eyes locked on his father's, Emane nodded.

"You? Emane, you can't possibly be the Protector. You are the heir to the throne and my only son." His voice began to rise. "You are a non-magical human."

I was before I mined it out of a mountain, Emane thought.

"Emane, I will not allow this!"

There it was again, everyone making decisions for him. Emane's teeth clenched as his temper flared. "With all due respect, father, I am of age and it is my choice to make."

The King's face turned more purple than red. "You plan to go marching off to this battle, to be slaughtered; leaving your bride here, alone." The King closed his eyes, jamming his thumb and forefinger in the corners and rubbing, hard. Dropping his hand back to the table with a thud, he challenged, "And what if I am to forbid it?"

Emane gripped the side of his chair, trying to rein in his mouth, "father, I am of age and have made this decision for myself. As heir to the throne, as you keep reminding me, it is my duty to protect the kingdom. And that is what I intend to do." His resolve deepened, determined to address the matter of Ciera before Aleric and the others arrived. Emane met his father's eyes and set his chin. "And as for 'my bride,' father, I will not marry that girl." He stood defiantly.

"Sit down," the King commanded.

"Father—"

"Of age or not, I am still your father. Now SIT DOWN."

Emane dropped back into his chair.

"We are going to talk." His father said, smoothing his robes.

"Are we talking,? Or are you?"

"I send you with Aleric," said the King, "and you come back disrespectful of your father, and forgetting your duties as future king!"

"Aleric has nothing to do with this. And as much as I would like to, I have not forgotten any duties."

"And what of Ciera?" his father demanded.

"What of her? She is no duty of mine."

"She most certainly is! As prince, you are expected to marry the girl that has been chosen for you. It is a duty!"

"No, father, it is your idea of duty. Where has it been written or decreed?" Emane waved at the shelves of books behind them. "Nowhere. It is tradition, so in your mind it must be followed."

The King's nostrils flared, "I picked the most beautiful girl in the kingdom and you are still not happy! It has been this way for hundreds of years, been a blessing for hundreds of years, allowing us to have someone who hears and knows the voice of the people; someone who was not raised in royalty to continue the line."

Emane snorted, "You think that girl gives any thought to our people. She may have been born a villager, but she cares for no one but herself!"

"She cares for you."

"No, she cares for my title."

He took a deep breath, "Emane, please be reasonable."

"I do not love her, father."

The King huffed as if that were the most ridiculous thought in the world. "You will, in time. It took time with your mother and I as well, but—"

"No, father, I will never love her."

"Emane, you are just a child," he said wearily, waving Emane off. "You do not know what love is."

Emane's anger burned deep within him and his voice trembled with the force of it. "I am not a child, and I know plenty of love. Love is wanting to be with that person for the rest of your life no matter of the consequences. Love is being willing to sacrifice your life for somebody else." He met his father's eyes, "Love is seeing the good in somebody regardless of their title or station in life. Love is so painful and yet so wonderful that it is worth it!" Emane pushed himself back up again from the table speaking deliberately. "Love is understanding that someday you might lose the person that you love, but that every day you get to spend with them is worth the risk. Love is taking the good with the bad." His voice rose with each sentiment. "Love is trust. Love is wanting to understand even when you don't." Staring at his father, Emane added, "I know of love, father, and I did not learn it from Ciera."

DRALAZAR STOOD IN THE shadows of the forest, just outside of the small cottage that Kiora had grown up in. Layla was heading back in for the night, and Dralazar smiled as he watched her go.

"She was a perfect find, Raynor," he said.

The black pegasus shifted his feet, crunching dry pine needles beneath them. Anger is an easy mark.

"Easy and useful, she has spread the word nicely."

Does she know yet, that she can do magic?

"No idea."

Will you teach her?

"I detest taking on pupils," Dralazar said, crinkling his nose, "with any luck she will garner enough support for our side that we will not need her in any other capacity." Dralazar's head swiveled to the castle, "What is that?"

My lord?

"Can't you feel her, Raynor? Kiora is here." He frowned, rubbing his fingers over his chin. "I would have expected Eleana to mask her thread, so why didn't she?" he muttered. A breeze of magic swept past Dralazar and he held out his fingers, feeling it. It was behaving strangely, sweeping past him as if it were being pulled onward.

My lord, the sky.

The sky over the castle was turning a deep purple, swirling with magic. "No," Dralazar whispered, "it can't be." His mind raced forward, if it were true...

We should attack now, while she is...

Dralazar's eyes shifted to Raynor narrowly.

That is if my Lord wishes it.

"No, Raynor." Dralazar's insides quivered with an excitement he hadn't felt in far too long; the excitement and thrill of power. A smirk pulled at one side of his mouth. "Tell Soolan to meet me just outside of Eleana's reach. We wouldn't want her picking up on our threads, would we?"

CHAPTER TWENTY-THREE

THE CATALYST

"IT'S TIME TO WAKE up, Kiora, come back to us."

Kiora heard the words floating around her, but was lost in a sea of foreignness. Her senses were overwhelmed as she wandered alone in the darkness of her own mind. She couldn't make sense of where she was. There was a current running through her veins, coupled with the most exquisite, all-consuming pain. She couldn't find where it began, for it didn't have an ending. The pain was, if possible, magnified by an intense anger simmering within her. This too felt foreign. Emane! She remembered with some relief the source, and grasped at the familiarity of his emotions, despite how nasty they were. Yes, it was his, and he was very angry.

"Kiora, come back."

She frowned, that too was familiar. She knew that voice but couldn't focus, not through the pain and the anger and whatever else was going on. Her body felt new and different, as if her mind had left, and upon waking, found itself in this foreign place. She didn't like it, this new body, and was immediately overwhelmed with a desire to have her old one back.

Something touched her. She tried to jerk away and yell but was stopped by the pain in her arm as well as the fire in her throat. Open your eyes, she thought. With great effort, she blinked two sand-laden eyelids that scratched and burned. The room was bright and she closed her eyes again to return to the darkness.

"There you are, Kiora," the voice said with some relief. "Open your eyes."

Eleana? Yes, that must be who it was. She pushed past the pain to try to feel anything else, a thread maybe. And there it was. Yes, it was Eleana. Blinking again, Kiora opened her eyes slowly.

"How are you feeling?" Eleana asked.

"Terrible," she croaked.

"Yes, I imagine you would. Here," Eleana placed a purple flask to Kiora's lips and poured the liquid into her mouth.

Kiora coughed and sputtered, the liquid was cloyingly sweet. As it went down her throat, however, it cooled the fire. She relaxed slightly.

"There, now a little more," Eleana poured more down Kiora's throat, "It won't take everything away, but it should ease the pain and help clear your head."

Kiora could feel her body relaxing in blessed relief. She still rode a wave of pain, but the swells had decreased to a point where it was bearable. "Thank you," she whispered. "What happened?" Kiora gingerly tried to push her way up to sitting.

Eleana was sitting on the edge of her bed, her copper hair forward over her shoulders. "You were pulling more magic than your body was made to hold. As a result, the magic made some adjustments. It quite literally forced its way through you, making room for more. It is not common, but very painful," she smiled weakly, "as you now know."

Kiora glanced around the room. Her eyes were still a bit blurry.

Compounding this problem was the grit that felt as if it were sanding down her eyes every time she moved her eyelids. "Am I back at the castle?"

"Yes. Emane was not happy that we brought you back in the state you were in. But the people are in need of someone to look to. Dralazar has been working in your absence. "

Kiora reached out somewhat hesitatingly, searching for threads. She gasped as they came hurtling in at her request. Hundreds upon hundreds of them, she had never been able to feel so many at once! It took her a minute to sort through them all. Her eyebrows pulled together, "How did he get to so many?" she asked, hoping that perhaps she was wrong.

"I am not sure. All I know is that he is here, working."

She gripped her head. "Why do I feel them all? I can't…focus."

"Your powers should increase dramatically in all areas. And you will learn how to shut them out when you need to, just as before," Eleana reassured.

"Why didn't you tell me," Kiora grunted, trying to shove the threads back away from her, "that this was going to happen?"

"I didn't know. Magic is a very unpredictable thing." Sitting up very straight, Eleana looked stoic and, perhaps for the first time, nearly her age. Her eyes weighed heavy with wisdom, age, and hurt. "I am sorry for a great many things, Kiora. I am sorry for what we are asking of you. But now, at this moment, your people need you to save them before they choose evil's side in ignorance."

Kiora hesitated a moment under the lingering pain and the overwhelming currents of magic before she said, "What do you need me to do?"

"YOUR MAJESTY," ALERIC SAID trying to reemphasize the

364 | DEVRI WALLS

same point that he had been trying to make for the last half an hour. "We will need everyone's help. We can't afford to spurn those that have offered to fight with us."

"Why should we trust those who fought against us last time, these 'Shifters' may not be trustworthy!" the King hollered back, despite Aleric's calm. "I have read the history books, Aleric. They detailed a great many things."

Emane was stretched out in his chair, his head resting on his hand as he drawled, "Enough, father. Yes, they fought with Dralazar last time. That was a thousand years ago," he yawned. "They are very committed to our cause, and very committed to Kiora."

"Kiora," the King sneered. "This Solus that I have yet to..." he trailed off, fixating on something over Emane's shoulder. Turning to see what had caught his father's attention, Emane saw a radiant Eleana and a rather shaky-looking Kiora standing in the doorway.

Emane leaped up from his chair, "Kiora!" he exclaimed, running to her in relief. "I am so sorry," he began, "I wanted..."

Eleana interrupted, "I insisted that he be here, instead of with you, Kiora." She finished, "You can add it to the list of things he is displeased with me over."

Kiora was wearing a rather old fashioned looking evening gown with tiers of fabric and lace from her waist to the floor, her hair was pulled neatly back from her face. It was the only thing the maids claimed they were able to find. Kiora fiddled awkwardly with the tiers, pulling and smoothing them.

"How are you?" Emane whispered, running his finger over the white stripe of hair that ran from just above her right eyebrow all the way to the end.

"Tired." Kiora absently reached up to touch the white stripe, "I have white hair, and I look like a cupcake," she whispered back, dismally.

Emane broke out into grin. "Glad to see that you are partially recovered."

"Emane, perhaps you should introduce our guests," Aleric interrupted.

Emane turned back to his father who was, oddly enough, not looking at the Solus he had just been complaining about not meeting, but rather his eyes were glued on Eleana. Her beauty alone was spectacular, but the glitter of her gown and the grace of her movements had to be of magic. And just as Emane had predicted, he was looking at her as if she were a green rabbit with three heads.

"Father, this is Eleana," Emane motioned, "and this is the Solus, Kiora."

When the King did not respond, Aleric motioned to the chairs, "Please sit, we have much to discuss and Kiora's legs are shaking. I fear the poor girl may collapse if we leave her standing there much longer."

Emane helped her over to the table, Eleana gliding behind them.

"We were just discussing with the king the decision the Shifters have made to join our side," Aleric prompted.

The King, at last regaining his composure, said once more, "I do not think we can trust those who fought against us last time."

Eleana responded. "Those who fought with you last time are either dead or sided with Dralazar, with the exception of the Guardians. Is it not reasonable to think that those who did not fight with you in the past may have learned from their mistakes?"

"Why would we take the risk?"

Eleana looked at the King steadily and, without dramatics, said simply and directly, "If you don't, you will all most likely die."

There was silence for a long while, not even Aleric knew what he should say to that.

The King finally broke, "What of this Solus?" he sputtered,

motioning to Kiora. "I thought she was supposed to save us all."

"She will, if you give her the help that she needs. No one can be everywhere at once. Dralazar has the Fallen Ones as well as all the dragons but one. He has already converted some of your people and is working to bring some other creatures out of hiding. The Shifters offer us the unique ability of fighting each species with its own. I believe the saying is, 'fight fire with fire.' And Kiora will not only aid in that, but she will be able to deal with Dralazar."

"Deal with Dralazar!? She is a child, and I have seen no proof of any magic, powerful or otherwise."

"That is enough, father!" said Emane.

"You never asked," Kiora said quietly.

"What?" the King bristled.

"You never asked." Bringing her eyes up to meet his, Kiora continued. "For reasons that I don't understand, you are angry with me. And, Emane, I am getting so much anger from you I can hardly think. How are we going to fight Dralazar if we are fighting one with another and distrusting everyone that offers to help? The Shifters have already lost lives for us—for me."

Silence again.

"Go ahead, Kiora," Eleana urged gently, "show him what you can do. The King wants proof."

Why do I have to give a visual demonstration to everyone? she thought. "What would you like to see, Your Majesty?" Kiora asked wearily.

"Summon his crown," Emane suggested.

"Where is it?"

The King scoffed, folding his arms in front of him, "The Solus should be able to summon it here without help."

"She is not a mind reader," Eleana snapped.

"Your Majesty, all magic has rules and exceptions," Kiora

explained, both to help him understand, as well as to get his anger off of Eleana. The King's face was turning red again. "Summoning means I can call things to me. If I want something generic such as an apple," a bright red apple appeared abruptly on the table in front of them, Kiora was a bit startled at how easy that had been, "I can summon an apple and one will appear." she continued. "If it is a very specific item I want, I need to be specific. Those are the rules, and no amount of power can break those rules. I must abide by them, Eleana must abide them, and so must Dralazar."

The King was staring at the apple. "How many crowns can there be in the kingdom, Kiora?"

Fine, she thought. A paper crown appeared on the table around the apple. It was worn and bent on the edges. In a child's handwriting was written: King Tobias. "At least two," Kiora responded, with great measure to keep a straight face.

Emane did not fare so well, and snorted loudly. His hand moved to his mouth, doing a poor job of hiding his grin.

The King leaned back in his chair, "So, she can summon. What good does that do us?"

"Your Majesty," Eleana said stiffly, "Your attitude and that of your forefathers is what got us into this mess in the first place. Had you listened to the prophecy and prepared the people, things would be different. She is the Solus. She will do as was foretold."

"My attitude!"

"Enough!" Kiora said, standing on still shaking legs. "We do not have time for this. I can already feel that some in the village are sided with Dralazar. We do not have time to sit and argue amongst ourselves about the past or the present. We must act. What do you need to see, Your Majesty? Would this be enough?" She reached her hand towards the window that looked out into the courtyard, the tree standing outside suddenly burst into flames. The King jumped back in his chair, looking at Kiora in shock. "Or this?" she asked again. Bubbling, she disappeared from view. Reappearing she looked desperately at the King who was shifting nervously in his chair. "I cannot prove to you that I can defeat Dralazar, you are going to have trust in me and that is all I can tell you."

Placing his hands in his laps, the King evaluated Kiora. She looked back at him, refusing to look away despite, desperately wanting to. The seconds ticked past before he seemed to wither before her eyes. "Very well," the King said, his eyes fixed on the table. "I will send out messengers to every house, telling them that we have our Solus and apprise them of the situation." He looked almost hopeless for a second. "Do not let us down, Kiora."

KIORA STOOD JUST OUTSIDE of the meeting hall in the throne room waiting for Emane. His father had asked him to stay a moment. Standing there, alone, she was bombarded by the essence of others. It was just like the first time, going from silence to a roaring tumult instantaneously. Gripping her head in frustration, she turned them off. As the threads slipped away from her and back into silence, her shoulders relaxed. Closing her eyes, she sighed in peace; it was good to just feel alone.

Taking a minute to enjoy a peace that she rarely felt anymore, she admired the throne room. It was beautiful, with its stained glass windows and interesting architecture. She wondered how much time Emane has spent in her as a boy, sitting on the throne, hiding in the alcoves that ran the length of the room. She smiled to herself. She could almost see his little blond head running around as a toddler.

A touch on her arm startled her. Whirling around, Emane was looking at her quizzically. "Didn't you know I was here?"

"No," she shrugged sheepishly. "I had to tune the threads out, there are just too many." Reaching out his finger, he tenderly ran it over her cheek, "I am so sorry, I didn't want to leave you...I—"

"Shh," she said, putting her hand over the top of his. "I understand"

Sliding his fingers behind her neck, Emane gently pulled Kiora to him, kissing her softly on the lips as if she might break at any moment.

"NO!" A scream cut through their kiss. "Get away from him, you filthy monster!"

Kiora gasped, spinning around as Emane stepped deftly in front of her, putting his hands out. "Ciera, stop!"

Ciera's hair flew out behind her, her face twisted in rage. "HOW DARE YOU! He is engaged...to me!" She slammed into Emane, her hands reaching and twisting around behind him, trying to get a hold of Kiora.

"Ciera, stop," Emane grunted, grabbing her arms and wrestling them to her sides. Ciera writhed and wriggled, still yelling. Kiora stepped backwards, sickened by the hate in the other girl's eyes. Emane took a firm grip on Ciera's shoulders, giving her a shake, shouted, "Stop!"

Ciera still struggled to free herself from Emane's grip but kept her eyes locked on Kiora, "Your sister said, and he said, you...you... monster!" she yelled, lunging at her again.

Emane still held her fast, the vein in his neck bulging.

"Let go of me!" she screamed. "How could you?" She rammed into him with her shoulder, looking at him for the first time. "How could you? She is a worthless liar! I know what you've done!" she shouted back at Kiora over Emane's shoulder. "You're a murderer! A lying monster and..."

Kiora's heart stopped and she stumbled backwards, running into a column. Putting her hands back, she leaned against the column, breathing heavily, tears gathering at the corners of her eyes.

Emane tightened his grip on Ciera's arm, jerking her within in an inch of his face. "Never, ever, call her those things in front of me again," he said through clenched teeth.

Ciera spat it in his face.

"WHAT IS GOING ON?" the King roared, exploding out of the meeting room doors and into the throne room. At the same moment, two guards had come running in through the main doors to see what all the commotion was about.

"Take her!" Emane ordered the guards. The two guards rushed over, confused, but obedient, each taking one of Ciera's arm. Emane wiped the spit of his face with the back of his sleeve. "Ciera saw something she didn't like," he answered to his father.

Ciera lunged at him, almost jerking her arms free from the guards, who were not used to being anything more than ornamental. "Something I didn't like? You are disgusting, kissing that...thing," she spat.

"What is she talking about, Emane?" the King questioned.

"I told you father, I won't be forced to marry her." Looking over to Kiora, Emane finished, "My heart belongs to another."

"You can't possibly love her," Ciera laughed bitterly. "You don't even know what she is! The town will mock you behind your back every day for your foolishness!"

Emane walked closer to Ciera, eyes flashing with anger. "There was a time where I found you beautiful. And then you began to show yourself. And now, when I look at you, I see nothing but... ugly." That last word hung in the air, thick with meaning.

Ciera lunged at Emane again, pulling the guards a step forward. "I HATE YOU!"

Emane turned back to his father. "I will not marry her," he announced pointing viciously in Ciera's direction. "If it means that am I no longer heir to the crown, then so be it." He grabbed Kiora by the hand, yanking her behind him.

Kiora thought the King would yell, follow them. But all she could hear was the screeching of Ciera.

Kiora's whole body was sore, and Emane yanking her arm down that hall was not helping. Mercifully, after they had gone a bit without anyone exploding out of the throne room, Emane slowed to a walk.

"I'm sorry," he huffed. "I should have dealt with that earlier."

Kiora could think of nothing to say, instead she gave his hand a reassuring squeeze. That was the girl he had been engaged to, and Emane was right—she was horrible. When Ciera had first exploded out of the shadows, Kiora had reached for her thread, and now that thread nagged at her. It felt off, at first, but the longer she stood there screaming, the darker it had turned. As if the sight of Kiora herself was the catalyst to her choosing evil's side. And then there was the comment about her sister, Layla...

"I'm sorry," Emane said, breathing out while rolling his neck.

"For what?"

"I know what you're feeling, what I..." he breathed out again. "I am trying to relax."

Kiora smiled, squeezing his hand again. "It's all right, you are doing great."

"Come here," Emane said, making a sudden right, "I have something to show you."

"Where are we going?"

"You will see." He stopped as they reached a set of stairs. "Do you feel well enough to climb?"

She paused, evaluating her aches and pains

"If you have to think about it, I am going to assume it's a no." Emane whisked her off her feet, cradling Kiora in his arms.

"Emane, I can walk!" she protested.

"No, you can't," he said gently. "And I fully intend to take advantage of the situation, so just relax."

She resigned herself to being carried as Emane started up the winding staircase. Leaning her head against him, she asked. "Where does this lead?"

"My favorite place in the castle."

"Hmmm, will your father be angry that we left like that?" she asked, tracing her finger over his chest.

Emane chuckled. "My father is usually angry at something, at least where I am involved, anyway."

"Why?"

"I'm not willing to bow at his every command. It has always made him angry, which is ironic really." Kiora looked up at him with one eyebrow raised, questioning. "Because that is part of what made me fall in love with you," Emane answered.

"In your whole life, no one has ever really stood up to you?"

"Not with any gusto." He turned the final curve in the stairwell emerging into one of the castle turrets. The large stone room had beautifully open arched windows. In between each open window was a smaller window fitted with intricate works of stained glass.

She was taken aback with the beauty. "It's amazing," she whispered as he lowered her to the ground.

"The view is even better." He grabbed her hand, pulling her to the window.

The main windows were so large that when standing in front of them, you almost forgot you were surrounded by stone walls. With her hand clasped in his, the walls melted away and it was just the two of them, standing above it all, looking out over the forest and mountains beyond.

Putting his arm around her, Emane pulled Kiora close. "This

is where I come when I need to escape." Leaning over, he kissed the top of her head. "I have never brought anyone up here with me before."

"Why not?"

"I was always worried I might need it."

She looked back at him with eyebrows raised.

He smiled looking past her out the window. "You met Ciera."

"Did you hide from you father too?"

He smirked looking at her sideways, "Still am."

She grinned, picking at the stone wall beneath her fingers.

"What's wrong?" he asked.

"Nothing."

"Kiora, you always fidget when something is bothering you."

"No, I—" she looked down, surprised to find that she was indeed fidgeting. She jerked her hand back to her side. "You told your father that you loved me," she said, still surprised.

He reached down, taking her hand, "I believe I told him, 'my heart belongs to another.'"

They looked in silence over the valley, leaning on one another for support.

"Have you ever wondered what is beyond the mountains?" Kiora asked suddenly.

"Sure. When I was a little boy I would dream of adventures," he stopped, tucking her hair behind her ear. "You are so beautiful."

"What kind of adventures?"

"Hmmm?" he asked. "Oh, the mountains. All kinds. You?"

Kiora looked out, remembering her childhood. "I would look at the peaks poking up over the top of the trees and wonder if there was anyone on the other side that was like me. Anyone that could…" her eyes moved to his face, he was so handsome. She reached up to touch his cheek and he asked, "That could what?"

"Could what?" she asked, her head cocking to the side. "Oh! That could do what I could." She was about to expound, but her thoughts slid away from her and she was left frowning at her feet. Suddenly more aware of Emane standing next to her, she wrapped both arms around his waist squeezing him tight. He reciprocated and rested his chin on top of her head.

His feelings of love washed over her and she reveled in them. It was selfish, so selfish! Sharply inhaling, Kiora jerked, nearly knocking them both over.

"Kiora?"

Two dark threads pierced her heart as a large dragon appeared out of nowhere in front of their window. With one large beat of its wings, the stained glass windows shattered, exploding inward in a deadly display of color. Kiora was hit with a bolt of magic before she could react, and fell unconscious to the floor. Emane threw himself over the top of her with a yell, trying to shield her from the falling glass.

THE DRAGON WAS KEEPING even with the turret with great deliberate flaps of its leathery wings. Sitting astride its back, wearing a dazzling evil grin, was a man with dark hair: Dralazar. Reaching out his hand with a laugh, Dralazar flung Emane backwards against the wall like a gnat. Emane grunted as he slammed into the stone. Before he had time to worry about the pain shooting up and down his spine, an invisible force began tightening around his throat. He clawed at it, gasping for breath, but there was nothing to remove. Despite his inability to find anything, it continued to tighten, Emane's feet dangled helplessly in the air.

Dralazar yelled something, but Emane couldn't understand it through the ringing in his ears. In response, the dragon gained altitude, bringing his feet even to the window. With more precision than an animal of that size should have, the dragon turned himself deftly to the side. One large clawed foot reached through, wrapped itself around Kiora's lifeless body and pulled her out through the stone window.

Emane tried to scream, but could only managed a strangled cry. Just as quickly as the dragon appeared, it was gone—bubbled by Dralazar—leaving no clue as to which direction it was heading.

As the dragon disappeared, so did the invisible force holding Emane to the wall. He slammed back into the ground.

"No," he coughed. "No, no, NO!" Scrambling to his feet, he ran to the window, "KIORA!" he yelled, leaning on the ledge for support. "KIORA!"

CHAPTER TWENTY-FOUR

POWER

KIORA PUSHED HERSELF UP onto her hands and knees. Wincing, she gasped and nearly dropped back to the ground. Gently she touched her side, what had happened? Pulling her shirt up she looked at the long purple and black bruises that ran from her side, all the way across her stomach. Somewhere between a groan and a whimper, she tried to rise up again, and then froze.

Magic and threads accosted her on all sides. The dark threads punched through her, grabbing hold with an icy grip and pulling her heart into a cold downward spiral, her stomach sinking with it. But there was something else, something magic and powerful and new.

Pulling her head up, she peered warily through her hair, scanning. Her view was, unfortunately, limited by the terrain. Rocks and dry scraggily bushes obscured much of what there was. She could see no one, and had no idea how she had gotten there in the first place. The last she remembered, she was standing in the tower with Emane.

Her eyes moved upwards. Mountains towered over her, the slopes coming steeply down to meet the ground where she lay.

Kiora's eyes narrowed further. The angle of the earth, the small ridges at the base, it looked somewhat...familiar. Still on her hands and knees, she turned her head to the other side and stopped breathing. Ignoring the jolting pain in her side, she pushed herself quickly to her feet. Towering right in front of her, as though out of nowhere, her dreams had magnificently emerged, fully formed, into reality. The dark threads fell away for a time as all she could see and feel was the size and power of the gate stuck between the two mountains—the same gate that she had dreamed about for years.

It was difficult to look at, her mind kept swimming in and out of focus. One second she was thinking about the behemoth structure in front of her, the next she was aimlessly wondering about whether or not she had had dinner yet that day. Shaking her head, she closed her eyes pressing her palms to the side of her head. "Focus," she whispered. It was there, she knew it was. Opening again, she focused on nothing else but seeing the gate.

The workmanship was different but equal in skill to the Wings of Arian. It stretched upwards, two separate panels arched at the top. The iron bars were intricately scrolled, some decorative, others depicting things and creatures Kiora had never seen. Beasts with bird heads and snake tails, winged people flying upwards, and more fantastical creatures beyond anything she could have dreamed.

Each side disappeared smoothly into the side of the mountain as if they belonged together. No seam or hinge was there to prove otherwise. Where the two sides met in the middle, they were sealed shut—melted, in fact. It was the only mar on an otherwise beautiful masterpiece. Stepping towards it, Kiora examined the pictures, which were beautifully illuminated by the sun that was just beginning to set. Shining straight through the break in the mountain range, the two peaks focused the light into a beam. As a result, the gate itself looked ablaze.

Acting almost without permission, her hand hesitantly reached out, trembling. She paused for a moment before taking the three steps forward she needed and then, touched the gate. Currents jumped from the gate to her, eager for an escape route. The power was shocking, but not nearly as shocking as the two distinct threads that came with it. One was dark, and familiar: Dralazar. The other was also familiar, if unexpected: Eleana.

Ripping her hand off the gate, Kiora stumbled, falling hard. Scrambling backwards, she used her hands and feet to pull her along, barely feeling the rocks and brush ripping at her hands.

"I was hoping you would touch it."

Kiora spun around, frantically pulling herself back to her feet. The lace dress she had worn at the castle caught in the brush and tangled between her legs. The threads she had felt but not seen were now standing in plain sight—an enormous dragon she was too familiar with, Soolan; a Fallen One wearing a resplendently beautiful dress to distract from her ugliness, Vitraya; and Dralazar himself. With a scream, Kiora threw out her hand, magic flying from her fingertips. She had no idea what magic she had thrown, but it didn't matter, Dralazar batted it away easily.

Vitraya, however, snarled in response and flung an attack in her direction. Kiora wasn't ready for it. She tried to throw a shield, but her tangled dress threw her off balance and she stumbled to the side. To her shock and confusion, Vitraya's attack was coolly batted away by Dralazar. Kiora didn't have time to question it,though, before Soolan released his attack. Throwing her hand up again, a shield roared forward meeting it. It was the largest shield she had ever produced, encapsulating her in a comfortable dome that merged with the rock around her. Kiora looked wide-eyed around at it. The shield was so large and easy! The silence within was shattered as dragon fire roared against the shield, sheeting off in red and orange rivulets. Then, it abruptly stopped.

Pulling her shield in on one on side, Kiora hesitantly peered out to see Dralazar with his back turned to her. Soolan and Vitraya both stood before him with heads dropped, listening. Kiora strained to hear what he was saying, but couldn't make out the words. Tendrils of smoke twisted and twirled from Soolan's nostrils, his eyes fixed not on his master, but on Kiora.

"Go," Dralazar commanded, louder this time. Soolan spread his wings, the ground rumbling as he took a few giant steps to push up in the air. Vitraya followed behind the dragon.

Dralazar turned to look appraisingly at Kiora. She noticed for the first time that he was strikingly handsome. He was just as gorgeous as his sister, but in a dark and hard way. He had high cheekbones and nearly black hair. Dralazar's blue eyes stood in stark contrast to his dark features, his nose strong and angular.

"It's all right," he said gently, "You do not need your shield anymore." Kiora scowled, pulling back further behind it. "Kiora," Dralazar said, smiling and dropping his head to the side as if she were a silly child playing hide and seek. "I know you felt our threads when you awoke. If I wanted you dead, you already would be."

Swallowing, Kiora dropped her shield.

"Dragons are widely unpredictable," he said, still smiling at her. "But it is best not to anger them unless you have something more in your arsenal than a shield."

Kiora asked warily, "What do you want?" She was unsure as to why they were having such a casual conversation.

"I want a great many things, Kiora, all of which I believe you can help me with."

"I won't help you with anything."

Dralazar crossed his arms, "Not yet." He leaned back his

head, breathing in deeply as if he were smelling something truly wonderful. "You're still pulling magic, did you know?"

Kiora frowned, her eyes flicking around waiting for something to come springing out at her. "What are you talking about?"

"Can't you feel it?" He spread his arms out. "It's intoxicating." Dropping them back to his side, Dralazar lowered his chin, looking up at her through stunning blue eyes, the color of a storm over the sea. "Normally someone such as yourself would never feel it as I do, like Eleana does. But you, you're different now—changed. And now it's your turn to feel what it's like to have and to wield so much power."

Kiora held her hands tensely at her side, "I don't need power."

"It's not just about the power, Kiora. It's about how it *feels*." He moved closer to her, speaking softer, "How it feels when magic is flowing through every inch of you, when you become it."

Kiora stood still, her mind racing, trying to understand what was going on. He kidnapped her from the tower at the castle, had her here with no protection, and was making no move to harm her. "What do you want with me?" she asked, looking at Dralazar sideways.

"I want to help you understand who it is you are fighting with," he said, snapping out of his reverie, "I think you may have been misguided."

Kiora's eyes flickered nervously to the gate.

"Yes," a smile quirked up one side of his mouth, "I was dearly counting on the fact that as powerful as you are now, you would be able to see the gate. I was hoping you would touch it. It is much easier to convince someone of the truth when they already have suspicion."

"I don't understand. What is it?"

"That," he said with a flourish, "is a magical feat unlike any other I know of. Its effects are far reaching, all inclusive. This beautiful piece of art is what has kept the occupants of this valley imprisoned for thousands of years."

Kiora stepped back, her heart hoping not to understand, but a flame growing in the back of her mind that understood. "What do you mean 'imprisoned'? We can go wherever we want, we're not—"

"Really? How many of you have ever gone past the mountains?"

"I don't know. I'm sure somebody has to have..." she stammered, trying to think of anyone.

"Think about it, Kiora, just try to think of going over the mountains."

She did, not wanting to believe. Keeping her eyes on Dralazar, she imagined herself going over the other side. But as soon as she did, her mind slipped, just as it had when she was trying to see the gate. She tried again, with the same result.

Dralazar smiled as he saw her frustration, "Nobody goes anywhere. They believe it is their choice, but it is not. You are all imprisoned here by this," he said, motioning to the gate.

"But why would you..."

"Me?" he laughed strolling back over to her. "You know it wasn't just me, don't you, Kiora? You felt the gate, you felt the magical signature." Leaning in so his face was just inches from hers, he whispered, "Who helped me, Kiora? Who?"

The memory, the feeling of the thread shoved itself to the forefront of her mind as if she had just touched it again. "Ele... Ele..."

"Yes, Eleana."

"No," she whispered, a tear trickling down her face. "I don't believe it, she would never."

Backing away, Dralazar gave her a knowing look before walking to the gate. Trailing his fingers across the iron, he glanced over his shoulder at her before leaning against it, apparently unaffected by the jolt of magic Kiora had experienced upon touching it. "But you do believe it. That's what makes it so painful."

"It doesn't make any sense," she said. "Why would Eleana want to keep us all here?"

"It doesn't make any sense because you don't know what is on the other side." Smoothly standing upright, Dralazar looked her square in the eye. "Magic you can't dream off, creatures you would not dream of. We didn't stand a chance of controlling this valley." He shook his head as if it were some great regret. "Not with the amount of magic that exists outside of these gates. It was just a matter of time before they found us, before they found this valley and took it for their own. We had no choice."

Kiora looked up, startled.

Dralazar smiled. "Yes, we," He strolled around her. "Eleana and I were going to rule side by side. It was our plan, not mine. It was not until much after that she decided to split from me, take the glory for herself, and what better way to get glory than to claim goodness and vilify me for the same choices she made." Leaning forward as if relaying some great secret he whispered, "She is a FRAUD. Kiora." He smiled a closed-lip evil smile before standing back up. "She has fooled you into fighting for her, bringing her the glory she always wanted. She is using you to get rid of me, just as she has used all the other Soluses before you."

Kiora shook her head. "No, it can't be..."

"And the proof is standing before us." Holding out his arm, Dralazar motioned to the gate.

Kiora's eyes slowly turned to follow. "But," she searched for an explanation, "why would she help me?" She shook her head, as if trying to clear cobwebs from her mind. "No," she nearly shouted. "I don't believe you. You thought you could just bring me out here and I would side with you? Did you think it would be easy to convince me that everything I have felt is wrong? I know good when I feel it, and I know evil."

"Do you? You also say you know Eleana. Did she mention this?"

Kiora's eyes flickered back to the gate.

"I didn't think so." His voice had taken on a new edge that hadn't been there until now. "Did I think it would be easy? Well, yes. Your sister was incredibly easy to convince…" he said slyly. "I thought maybe, you being family, it might be the same."

Kiora froze, a sick feeling rising in her throat. "You're lying."

"Why would I lie about something you can so easily verify, Kiora? I know you can call visions. It's true, your sister spent time convincing me how evil you were. She told me all about your evil visions, how you killed your parents."

Kiora's stomach dropped and she swayed to the side. Dralazar moved to grab her, placing his arm under her elbow. She felt magic pour into her under his touch. Gasping, she jerked her arm away.

"What do you want, really?" she demanded backing away from him. "Why did you bring me here?"

"Why are you still alive? Is that what you're asking?" Kiora nodded curtly. Dralazar smiled at her. "Because, Kiora, you and I could do amazing things together."

"You don't need me."

He gave an amused nod of acknowledgment. "You're right, I don't. But you need me."

As he reached his hand out to her, Kiora panicked. Reacting on instinct, she attacked. Her magic hit Dralazar squarely in the jaw. His head swung sharply to the side as if he had been punched.

Turning his head back slowly and deliberately, Dralazar's eyes were blazing. Reaching up, he wiped a trickle of blood from the corner of his mouth with the back of his hand, not taking his eyes off her.

The shield should have already been up, but she was so shocked by what she had just done, she stood instead, staring in childlike fashion. By the time she realized she had made a mistake, Dralazar's hand had flown up and invisible fingers wrapped around her neck. She clawed at the force but it was no use. Dralazar tightened his fingers, closing off her airway. She struggled under his grasp, choking.

"You are a very stupid girl, Kiora. I could kill you with a thought!" he snarled, before dropping her like a sack of garbage.

Rolling over on the ground, she gasped, but hadn't got more than two breaths before she felt herself flying through the air and slamming into the gate. The much-needed oxygen was knocked out of her, and she slid down, gulping for air like a fish on land, all the while the magical signature of Dralazar and Eleana ran through her. It was unmistakable, and irrefutable. There was only one way Eleana's signature would be here.

Dralazar strode up to Kiora, grabbing her roughly by the arm. "Make one move, Kiora, and I will knock you out and bind you with magic so tight you won't be able to move. I had hoped we could have a cordial conversation," he jerked her roughly to her feet. "It appears that will not be possible." Grabbing her face, Dralazar twisted it to him.

She jerked her head back, but he held fast, "Why would I side with you when you treat me like this?" she spoke through clenched teeth to prevent her cheeks from being shoved between them.

"Because," Dralazar said, dropping her distastefully, "you have been trained to think of the people over yourself. And if you don't work with me, everybody dies. Your sister, everyone. Think about it, Kiora, I can make it all go away. No death, no war. Can Eleana promise you that? She has lied to you and has no power to put a stop to anything. Work with me, and it all goes away. And," he added tantalizingly, "you won't have to be the Solus any longer. All that responsibility washes away. Just like everything else." Dralazar took a few steps backward. "Think about it, and stay put. Soolan is dying for a shot at you." He smiled and vanished, leaving her standing in front of the monstrous iron lie.

As soon as Dralazar left, Kiora grabbed for her pendant, the one that the Guardians had left her. It was gone. Sinking into a pile of torn and dirty ruffles, tears spilled down Kiora's cheeks. Her tears, coupled with the magic that hid it, made the gate's beauty swim in and out of focus.

Lies. Everything had always been a lie. She laughed a sick laugh through her tears that was anything but funny. She really had thought that she understood lies. She really thought that she could see them, or feel them, like threads. It made sense at the time—lies were evil and thereby easily recognizable. But now, there were lies upon lies, seas and levels of them. And all coming from places she hadn't seen. From people who felt good, with threads that soothed rather than froze. She couldn't help but think that there were still more, swirling under the surface that she would soon discover. And then she was sinking, drowning under the lies and the confusion and Eleana's betrayal.

It had been easier to block the thoughts when Dralazar stood before her. But now that she was alone with nothing but the lie for company...her trust for Eleana shattered.

Why would she hold back something like this? Why? But it made sense now. All the distracted empty stares she had caught Eleana in whenever Dralazar was brought up, the guilt Kiora had seen and yet not understood. She thought that it was because Dralazar was her brother. But it wasn't. It wasn't that at all. It had been this...this horrible secret. Dropping her head into her hands, Kiora realized it wasn't just Eleana. She had mentioned her dreams to Arturo; he had acted strangely at the time. Surely he knew, and had also said nothing. How many others? The Guardians? Aleric? How many had let her carry on, knowing that there was so much she had not been told.

Wiping her tears away, she sat back on her heels. She needed the truth about her sister. She called the vision to her and the scene unfolded out before her in more clarity and with more ease than ever before.

She was back in her house now, the table and chairs looked so solid she reached out to touch them, but her hand passed easily through.

Her sister and Dralazar entered from the front door, Layla looking frantic, wringing her hands in front of her. "Please, sir, sit down," Layla said.

"Much obliged," he said with a charm and a respectful nod that Kiora knew he turned on and off at will.

"You can't let the King do this!" Layla said suddenly, "He's made a mistake."

"My dear girl, I am afraid the King will need more than just my word for it. After all, I am only an adviser."

Layla's manner changed for the briefest of moments, "I don't think I have ever seen you before," she questioned.

"No, you wouldn't have. I came from the other side of the mountains."

Layla's eyes suddenly were glossy and her face blank as she tried to process the phrase, 'other side of the mountains.' Then she continued on as if she had never asked him where he had come from in the first place. "The King is wrong!" she exclaimed. "Kiora is not the Solus!"

"That is why he sent me to talk you," he said smoothly. "He hasn't actually met her yet so he sent me to find me out what I could before she returns to the village."

"She is…is…" she struggled for the word, her lips pressed tightly together.

"Evil?" Dralazar suggested.

Layla's eyes widened, "Yes! She is. She can't be the Solus. She killed our parents!" Layla shrieked.

Dralazar's hands flew to his mouth in mock surprise. "No!"

"She did! And that's not all," Layla moved to the table and sat forward, spewing forth information on all of the things that Kiora had received visions of. Only in Layla's retelling, Kiora caused it all. Burning down houses, failure of crops, accidents to neighbors, and more. When Layla had finished, Dralazar looked grave.

"I will speak with the King," he looked up at Layla in earnest. "But I don't think I can change his mind. He is convinced that she is the Solus. In fact, he is already sending out spies in search of the great evil that is prophesied about."

"But it's her!" Layla shouted as if coming to a great revelation. "She is the great evil he is looking for."

Dralazar frowned, rubbing his chin and looking very thoughtful indeed. "I suppose it's possible."

"It's the only explanation; look at what she has done." Layla gestured widely as if proof of Kiora's deeds were sitting just outside the door.

"I need your help, Layla. You must tell the people, all of them. Convince them that she is evil, and not to be trusted. Otherwise," Dralazar said, his head hanging sadly, "evil will win and the peace we have will be lost forever."

Layla sat back in her chair and shook her head in agreement. "I will, we have to stop her."

The vision faded and Kiora felt a new feeling engulf her. Anger. She wasn't mad, or frustrated, she was fuming angry. It slid through her body like a dark snake, engulfing the good and poisoning the peace. She wanted to leave it all behind. Leave Dralazar, Eleana, everyone. Striding over to the gate, she opened up her magic as she never had before. White magic poured up and around the gates, flowing over the ironwork, flitting around the edges. Throwing her head back, she let out a scream of rage that echoed through the canyons.

The gate was glowing white at this point, absorbing all the magic she could throw at it. The more she let loose, the more she understood what Dralazar had taunted her with, the feeling of magic, and power. It flowed through every inch of her with powerful intoxication.

"Kiora!" A deep, vibrating dragon voice came from behind.

Kiora spun around, her chest heaving, hair flying and the metal behind her glowing white hot. "Morcant? How?" she looked around. But dragons could not bubble.

"I had help," Morcant rumbled, looking at her with great curiosity. "Something has happened, your thread is altered." He accused, moving into a defensive position.

"What? What do you mean?"

His eyes narrowed, "Do not pretend you do not feel what is in your heart. It is darkening your thread, little one."

The mention of the name 'little one' brought her slamming back to reality. "This gate, can you see it?" she demanded.

"I can. You shouldn't be able to."

"I shouldn't...be able to?" she sputtered. "You all knew, all of you!" she accused.

"Of course. All of us with magic were trapped in this valley when it was erected. We are acutely aware of it."

"But how can you?" she looked back and forth between Morcant and the gate. "Did you know Eleana helped him erect it? DID YOU?" she screamed.

Morcant's eyes narrowed again, dangerously this time. "Do not yell at me, child. Solus or not, you are teetering on a dangerous precipice, both for your safety and the rest of ours."

Taking a strained breath in through her nose, "Did you?" Kiora asked again.

"I suspected."

"Then how can you side with Eleana!?"

"Kiora!" Morcant's voice rumbled through the canyon, demanding her attention. "You are listening with your ears and that is not good enough!"

"How did you find me?" she asked.

"You are still listening with your ears. As a matter of fact, you are not listening at all," Morcant said, tendrils of fire escaping from his nose, his eyes scanning the sky. "We do not have much time. Feel my thread, Kiora, feel it! Not with your ears, your heart. What do you feel?" It was not a request.

Kiora tried to feel it, but could not swim past the anger.

"Close your eyes!" Morcant demanded again. "Concentrate."

Kiora closed her eyes, taking deep breaths in, and searched again for Morcant's thread. It eased into her, pushing aside the pain, the betrayal, the anger. As it pierced her heart, she felt his goodness, she felt peace and love. The anger seemed to recoil from it, spinning away as if repulsed by his goodness.

Morcant and Kiora let out a breath of relief in unison.

"There you are," Morcant said in a grumbling whisper. Moving his head closer, he stood nose to nose with her. "Never, ever listen to the words of Dralazar. Sometimes his words may be truth, but mostly they are truth mixed with lies.

"Do not listen with your ears, Kiora. Never listen with your ears, only with your heart. You asked me how, all those years ago, I stayed true. It's because I listened only with my heart. The threads of Eleana and the Guardians only inspire peace and kindness. There is no anger and agitation, no pain and misery. Are they perfect? No. I cannot tell you why Eleana did what she did; only she can do that. But I tell you this, whatever her reason, she did not do it out of anger and a thirst for power like Dralazar. After what you have seen, I am sure you will ask Eleana what those reasons are. But wait until the time is right, focus on the feelings, and let the rest go unanswered, just for now."

Kiora nodded with a soft smile, "You are a very wise dragon," she whispered.

"I am a very old and experienced dragon who needs to get you out of here."

The thread appeared much too quickly, "Morcant!" Kiora yelled. Soolan dropped out of the clouds, his wings pulled tightly to his sides in a deathly fast dive. No doubt he had hidden his thread by sheer height, dropping in as fast as he could. He was closing the distance fast.

Morcant reached out and grabbed the front of her dress nimbly with his two front teeth before taking off with her. Behind him, Soolan opened his jaws and sent fire spewing in their direction. Morcant took the hit on the right side. He bellowed in pain, all the while keeping his teeth firmly clenched. Kiora's hands flew to her ears. She could feel the vibrations of his roar jangling through her. Flying straight up, he dropped her on a ledge far too high up the mountain for her to go anywhere. Kicking back off with his hind legs, he flipped his massive body around to face Soolan.

"You may have gotten the best of me last time, Soolan, but will you not be so lucky again," he roared.

"You are a traitor to you own kind! I will kill you first," Soolan roared, "and then I will kill the girl."

The two dragons dipped and dived in front of her ledge, roaring. Soolan shot at Morcant, who deftly flipped himself upside down, his great claws slicing at the underbelly of Soolan. Soolan bellowed, blood dripping from the gashes.

"You should have kept this fight on the ground Soolan," Morcant bellowed. "You forget my flying skills exceed yours."

Soolan growled and banked for another attack.

Dralazar materialized next to her on the cliff. Weary, Kiora just turned to look at him.

"What?" he said, clearly amused. "No feeble attempt at bubbling or attack magic?"

"No."

"It's a beautiful sight, isn't it?" Dralazar asked, pointing to the two battling dragons spinning in front of them. "Two powerful creatures fighting over you."

A vision freely exploded into view, easier than ever. Kiora smiled at what she saw.

Dralazar misread her expression. "Ahhh, you are finally beginning to see what I have been trying to show you."

"If I work with you," she said, "the village will be spared?"

"Of course," he oozed, looking pleased.

He was not listening with anything but his ears. Had he, he would have realized her thread was pulsing with anything but ice.

"And if I say no?" Kiora asked. Soolan's wing scraped the mountain on his last pass, sending a large boulder tumbling down just to the left of her.

Dralazar's smile faltered for a second. "We don't need to worry about that, Kiora, do we?"

"I suspect you would have to kill me."

"Of course."

"Well, then, my answer is no." Kiora caught a glimpse of the shock on Dralazar's face before stepping off the cliff. She was sure he was yelling, but the wind rushing by her ears muffled it. Looking around frantically, she spread her arms and legs as wide as they would go. When nothing happened she thought, I really am going to die.

Don't be ridiculous, Arturo's voice came. Look to your right.

Kiora looked over, nothing. And then he appeared, the white pegasus dove, coming up underneath her. She slammed onto his back.

Shield NOW! Arturo yelled.

Kiora threw up a shield just as a bolt of magic connected with it. She gasped in pain, the magic was red hot and sizzled against her shield. This was not a warning shot. Kiora resisted giving the shield more magic, frightened of the surge of power she had felt when she opened up on the gate.

Do not hold back! He will kill us both. Arturo banked to the side.

The magic was burrowing through her shield, burning her. She had no choice. She opened up and let the magic flow through her. The shield grew and thickened. She felt it again, the power, the euphoria. She twisted her head around to see Dralazar standing on the edge of the cliff. He had both arms extended, red bolts flying from his hands.

Kiora's body took over, acting on impulse. She opened up a small hole in the shield and stretched her own hand out. White lighting flew from her fingertips, red meeting white in the void between her and Dralazar. Kiora forced more power forward to meet Dralazar's attack. Dralazar's eyes widened at her response.

"You will pay for this!" he screamed over the wind. "When you look at your burning village and count your dead, know that it is your fault. Soolan! Deal with them!" Dralazar vanished a second before Kiora's white fire slammed into the side of the mountain.

Kiora whirled, looking for Soolan, but Morcant beat her to it. As Soolan turned to obey his master's orders, Morcant flew straight at him, crushing him into the side of the mountain. Soolan's head smashed into the rock, his eyes rolling back into his head before tumbling end over end to the ground below.

"Bubble, Kiora!" Morcant demanded.

She did so before collapsing onto Arturo's back, magic rolling through her. She tried to breath, to relax, but there was so much of it pulsing through her, causing her head to spin. Focus, Kiora, you need to pull it back. Arturo's voice sounded weak.

Kiora pulled at the magic, trying to close it down, to control it. Arturo was drenched in sweat, trembling beneath her and losing altitude fast.

Kiora! His tone was severe. I need you to control this magic, now. And we need a bubble or we will lead Dralazar straight to the others.

She looked around; realizing that in an attempt to shut down the magic, she had also dropped the bubble.

Kiora sat up and pulled with all her might, shutting down the current of magic that was electrifying her body. She could feel it slowing to a trickle before Arturo began gaining altitude.

Bubble, Arturo reminded.

Morcant flew up and over them as Kiora bubbled and he headed back out in the direction of the Sea of Garian.

"Where is he going?" she asked.

Arturo was silent for moment before he replied, He is making sure no one else is on their way here, leading them off the path if necessary.

"How did you both get in there?" she asked. "Without bubbles?"

The guardians bubbled us; it was the only way to get close enough to you. A lone Guardian is vulnerable, he explained in answer to the question she hadn't been able to ask yet. They returned to the hollow once their job was completed.

Looking forward as they headed back to the castle, her mind replayed everything that had happened from the time she met Aleric until now, trying to piece together a puzzle that was surely missing a few pieces. Anger flared again and she struggled to push it away again. Why had Eleana not told her about the gate? How could Eleana have worked with Dralazar in the first place to erect such a thing? Despite Morcant's speech, she still felt betrayed. Lies. She thought gritting her teeth, *so many lies*. Making everything worse was the sudden realization that Dralazar would surely be headed toward the village, the village that she had just condemned.

That is not true, Arturo thought. This path was laid long before you stood up to Dralazar.

"Since you have been listening to me think, Arturo, is there anything else you would like to expound upon?" she asked tightly.

No, I am sorry but that is something Eleana must do for herself.

"Can you tell me if I am justified in feeling betrayed at least?" An angry tear leaked out of one eye, she hurriedly swiped it away. "I have risked everyone's lives on a feeling."

There was a longer silence this time, not the silence of Arturo reading thoughts, but the silence of him trying to compose his own. Kiora, feelings are all we really have to go on. Making decisions by them is the only way to ensure you are not being deceived by the silver tongue of another. Regarding your sense of betrayal—it is an understandable reaction to what you have learned. All I can tell you is that her reasons were not that of Dralazar's and that in the beginning, she thought she was doing right. Beyond that, I am afraid you will have to wait until she chooses to tell you more. It is not my secret to tell.

She sighed deeply. "So now, I fight Dralazar?"

I am sure that is what is coming, yes.

"What if I can't defeat him?"

Then we are no worse off than if you wouldn't have tried at all. But you have become powerful, Kiora, I don't think you realize. Arturo's sides shook beneath Kiora in a chortle. I don't think Dralazar realized fully either. It was a foolish risk leaving you there without any concealment. And when you finally let him have it, he was very shaken with the amount of power you issued.

"But he knew I had changed, that's why he took me."

Yes, he knew that. But he had no idea exactly how dangerous you had just become. Of course, now that he knows...Arturo trailed off.

"He will be here even sooner, won't he?"

I am quite sure.

CHAPTER TWENTY-FIVE

THE EXODUS

THE SUN HAD SET, leaving the world in the dark, which was oddly appropriate. Arturo and Kiora flew back over the land. Trees had turned into seas of black beneath them, mountains silhouetted against the night sky, and the lights of the castle twinkled like distant beacons.

Soon they were flying over the roofs of Kiora's village. Below them, tiny disembodied lights bobbed along the paths.

She peered at them, "What are those?" Kiora asked.

The king has sent out messengers again, via Eleana's request, trying to assure them that you are indeed the Solus.

Kiora started to reach out for the threads, but the results were so varied she tuned them back out. Far too many had listened to Layla.

Arturo dropped gently out of the sky into the back courtyards of the castle. Kiora jumped off before he had fully come to a stop, heading straight inside. Pushing open the back gates, Kiora dropped her bubble.

She hadn't made it far down the first hallway before Eleana appeared a few feet in front of her. Kiora screeched to a halt. She was as beautiful as ever—a glittering gold gown, copper flowing hair, and those knowing blue eyes. She lit the space from the inside out and the thread that emanated from her was as calming and peaceful as it always had been. Despite all that, the flame of anger Dralazar had so carefully lit within Kiora flared in response to Eleana's presence. Eleana flinched and Kiora was quite sure she had felt Kiora's anger as well.

"I sent Morcant to find you," Eleana said softly, her eyes lingering on the ground at Kiora's feet. "I suspected Dralazar might take you there."

Kiora thought she had control of the anger, she thought that she was fine. "You sent MORCANT!" she shouted. "You knew I was there, KNEW I was with Dralazar and you sent Morcant?" She took a step closer, one shaking finger pointing accusingly. "Why didn't you come? How could you leave me alone with him? He could have killed me!" She was practically screaming now. "You let him take me to that...that...horrible gate that YOU helped...you let him take me and you didn't stop him...you didn't..." She stood gasping, fists balled and shaking at her side. Finally, she shouted the only phrase that was clearly coming to mind. "HOW COULD YOU?"

Eleana bowed her head further. "I'm sorry." Those two words carried more pain and conviction than should have been possible, and it washed over Kiora's anger like a bucket of water, extinguishing the flame. "I'm sorry," Eleana repeated, a tear trickling down her cheek.

Usually when Eleana spoke of the past or was feeling an emotion deeper than the calmness she usually exuded, she looked older, as if the years had caught up to her. Her face darkened, the lines deepened. But today, at this moment, she looked so much younger, like a child who had done something they hadn't meant to do and realized all too late the harm they had caused.

"Kiora," she continued, folding her hands in front of her. "I knew if I went to help you that Dralazar would use it to feed your anger. I knew if he took you to the gate that he would tell you parts of the truth he wanted you to hear, having me there would have only made it worse. I needed to send someone who would not make you feel..." she gestured to her, "the way you are feeling right now."

Kiora was still breathing heavily despite her efforts to calm down. "I still don't understand how you could..." She couldn't even form the words.

"I will tell you everything," her voice cracked, "but I need to ask for your understanding."

"For what?"

Eleana's head finally rose, pleading, "I need your understanding in why I did what I did. And worse, I need your understanding that an explanation must wait."

Kiora's mouth open and shut in stunned silence. "You-want-me-to wait?" she punctuated.

"Yes. Dralazar will be here by morning, I suspect. The Rockmen have already begun moving this direction. There are things I need to show you, things that need time." She sighed, looking wilted, looking ever so much younger. "So I need to ask you," she said, wringing her hands together in front of her, "no, I need to beg you...will you fight for your people on faith alone that what we are doing is right, despite any grievous mistakes I have made in my youth?"

Kiora stood, not moving. She had given Eleana her full faith once, and what good had it been?

Eleana looked up at her silence, "Out of everyone, I had hoped you could understand that sometimes things are not as they seem...I thought maybe..."

Kiora held up her hand. "Stop...please." Holding Eleana's gaze,

Kiora asked, "Do I have your word that as soon as this battle is over, you will tell me everything?"

"You do."

"Everything!" she insisted more strongly, "Not just what you think I need to know."

Eleana looked at her with a peculiar look in her eye as she said, "Yes, I think you will need to know everything."

Breathing in deeply, she closed her eyes. "Listen to your heart," is what Morcant had said. Her mind was screaming at her, but her heart was calm, and even. Kiora had to do this. "All right. I will fight." Standing to her full height, she announced, "We need to make plans, have everyone meet me in the throne room."

Eleana's face cracked into a smile and the peculiar look changed for a second to one of curious excitement. "I will call Drustan and the Guardians. Aleric and Emane are there already speaking to the King."

EMANE STOOD STIFLING A yawn. He hadn't slept the night before—Kiora's screams had kept him wide awake. And he certainly wouldn't be getting any tonight, not until Kiora was home. His father and Aleric were talking, but Emane had tuned them out forever ago, hearing only a droning in the background. Staring out the window, he wondered where Kiora was, pleading internally that she was safe. Emane had begged Eleana to let him go with Morcant to find her, but she had insisted he stay here.

A tap on his shoulder jolted him, "What?" he blurted, looking around.

Aleric was smiling and jerked his head towards the door.

Turning, his heart thudded in pure relief. "Kiora!" he yelled running over to her. Skidding to a stop, he whirled her around before pulling her tightly into his arms. "Are you okay?" he murmured, his face in her hair.

"I was," she said with a grunting laugh, "but now I can't breathe."

Pushing her back from him, Emane's eyes ran from her head to her feet, examining her for damage. "What happened to you?" he asked, running his fingers through her hair, separating the white strands from the dark.

She shook her head. "Not right now. We have a problem that needs to be addressed." Her voice was firm, resolve set in every inch of her. With a loving pat to Emane's shoulder, Kiora made her way to the King. Emane turned, watching her as she walked away. Something had happened while she was gone. She stood taller, straighter. And that underlying current of determination he had seen was now as visible as if she were flying a banner.

"Dralazar will be here, probably in the morning," she announced. "Eleana is sending word for Drustan and the Guardians to meet us here. I expect they will arrive shortly." The King stiffened and Kiora addressed it without fear. "Your Majesty, if you do not think you can support us in working with the magical community, I would ask that you not be here when they arrive."

Emane's eyes widen at Kiora's bravado. The sole hint that she was nervous was visible only to him. Her fingers, hidden behind her back, pulled at the lace of her dress. A smile crossed over Emane's face, whatever Dralazar had done had clearly backfired.

The King's chest puffed up and he opened his mouth before Aleric grasped his shoulder.

"I know that you are not used to taking orders," Aleric said firmly, "but she is right." Aleric glanced back to Kiora with a bit of pride. "If you cannot openly support those we are working with, you will offend the only hope we have in saving this people, your people. Your Majesty, choices were made that must now be amended, and that responsibility falls on you. You must be supportive or not be here at all."

"I have already removed Ciera from the castle and sent word of the Solus to the people," the King blustered. "What more do you expect me to do!?"

"We need you to not be disgusted by magic, Your Majesty." Aleric clarified.

"I am not disgusted by…"

"Yes, you are." Emane called from the back of the room, striding forward. "And you always have been." Emane crossed his arms in front of himself "Why?"

Before he could get his answer, the doors opened and in flowed a host of somewhat humanish looking Shifters. "Humanish" because they all had added a bit more flare to the human shape and coloring. Their hair was too bright, legs a little too long, eyes too big, and so on. For some, the adjustments had made for an exquisitely beautiful human. Others had created a bizarre beauty that made one stop and stare. Flying above their heads and intermixed between them flew the Guardians.

The King shifted uncomfortably. Rolling his eyes, Emane grabbed him, steering him to his throne. If there was one place that made his father more comfortable, it was sitting on his throne.

AS THE SHIFTERS POURED in, they barely noticed the king. Instead, they gathered themselves around Kiora, congratulating her on her survival, which was a bit uncomfortable of a sentiment to say thank you for, but she did anyway.

Eleana flowed in a few minutes behind them, and silence draped the room. She wisely acknowledged the King, who relaxed slightly with the gesture. The King wore a stiff smile; Kiora assumed it was the best he could fake.

"Thank you for coming," Eleana said, her voice silencing the room. "Kiora," she said, reaching her hand out to her, "has some things she would like to say."

Kiora made her way through the crowd, looking to Eleana questioningly.

Quietly, Eleana urged her onward, "Tell us what you would like us to do." She moved away, leaving Kiora standing with all eyes on her.

She cleared her throat. "Dralazar is coming. He has already sent the Rockmen to surround the village, and we expect the rest of his forces to follow by morning." There was a murmur throughout the room.

"Who will fight," Drustan asked from the crowd, "besides us?"

Kiora faltered, "No one."

Another murmur moved through the room accompanied by a few gasps.

"What of your people?" one of the Shifters questioned. "Will they not fight for their own homes?"

Kiora hesitated, searching their anxious eyes. "My people know nothing of magic, of fighting, or the lies." Praying they would understand she continued, "My people would be at such a severe disadvantage that they would be slaughtered."

"So you want us to fight for them?" yet another Shifter questioned in near disbelief.

Kiora could see the King squirm in his chair. "Yes," she said loudly. "I would like to spare my people from fighting in this battle in order to preserve them for the next, for one where they could be properly trained." She saw the Shifters moving, murmuring one to another. "But, no," she continued, "you are not only fighting for them. Regardless of if they fight or not, you know as well as I do that you are not just fighting for my people. You are fighting for your families and your freedom from a man whose reign of terror you have witnessed. A man who was so vicious and cruel that you left his side the last time before the battle was even over. You know as well as I do that this people are in no shape to fight, and I apologize that we did not have time to train them so that they could add to the ranks, but with or without them, it does not change what is at stake for you and yours." Kiora scanned the crowd to judge their reactions. Most were nodding, albeit reluctantly, in agreement with her words. Drustan was looking at her with a glint of pride. Breathing out slowly, Kiora smoothed her dress and tried to not let them see her ragged breathing.

Drustan cleared his throat. "We agree with your argument, but we will not save them all, Kiora. I know you must feel their threads. Some have sided with Dralazar."

"How is that possible?" a Guardian asked midway to the ceiling, her long hair fluttering gently in her self-created breeze, "If Dralazar would have been in the village, we would have felt him."

"Dralazar isn't here," Kiora explained. "He is using…" she hesitated, knowing somehow that speaking the truth would bring it crashing into a horrible reality, "my sister." The words stung. "He is using my sister." She had expected a murmur to move throughout the crowd, or maybe a gasp of disbelief. Instead, she was met with silence. "Layla has been telling the people that I am not the Solus, but that I am the Evil that had been prophesied about." She finally forced herself to let in the threads that she had been blocking since the change. They slammed into her with the force of oncoming wall of water. Her heart sunk further, there were more than before. Layla had been busy.

"But how…" a Shifter with orange and red striped hair asked, "would she possibly convince them of that?"

"Because..." there was no use being embarrassed or ashamed about it anymore, she understood it now for what it was, and so would they. "When I was a child I used to have visions. Nobody understood it. They didn't know magic, all they knew was that I would say bad things would happen and then they would." The words come out in a rush. "I saw my parents' death before it happened. I tried to warn them but they left anyway, and they never came back." Kiora wrung her hands together in front of her, feeling the pain all over again. "Layla never forgave me. She thought and still thinks that it was my fault, that I killed our parents. That is what she is telling the villagers, and some believe her." The murmur she had been waiting for ran through the room.

Of course they believe her, Kiora thought, she is telling the truth. Blinking, Kiora nearly laughed out loud. The truth! She had been so worried about the lies, but Dralazar wasn't using those. He was using nothing but the truth, and twisting it in a way to suit his fancy. He hadn't lied about Eleana, and Layla wasn't lying about her. Not really.

The murmur died down before Drustan again spoke up, "What would you like to do, Kiora?"

A plan had been quietly formulating as she had been speaking—one that she hoped they would agree to. She started to bite her lip before mentally yelling at herself to stop. No one wanted to take orders from a scared little girl. Pushing her shoulders back, she said, "I want to remove the people who have not been convinced by Layla to a safe location until after the battle is over."

The King blustered at this and Eleana addressed him, "You cannot assume that your people are incapable of lies, now that evil has been reintroduced."

"How are we going to do that?" the King asked, sputtering,

"There is no way of knowing what side they have chosen!"

"Yes, there is." Kiora said, "All we need to do is listen to their threads." She could see the King ready to object and she hurried onward. "We go tonight, before the sun rises, and move from house to house. If those inside have chosen to believe Layla and Dralazar, then we leave them behind. If not, then we escort them out, bubbled to a safe location."

"And where would that be, Kiora?" Aleric asked earnestly.

"There is nowhere that Dralazar will not feel their threads."

"I was hoping that Eleana might be able to help us with that, something along the lines of the Hollow."

"Of course," Eleana agreed immediately.

"And what of the people we leave?" The King demanded. "What will happen to them?"

She knew the answer, but could not get it to come out of her mouth. She tried, opened her mouth in hopes that it would somehow fall out, but the thought made her sick. Drustan could see her pain and rescued her, "They are Dralazar's people now," he said. "We will leave them for Dralazar, and if they are lucky he will see a need to keep them alive."

"And if they are not!?" the King demanded.

"They have chosen their master," Drustan said quietly "and where their loyalties lie. We cannot change that and we cannot change what Dralazar chooses to do with them. To take them with us would risk exposure and death of a good majority of your people."

"Your Majesty," Aleric said, "we have sent out people to every house in Kiora's behalf. They all knew her as a child. There is nothing more we can do."

The King nodded reluctantly, his eyes glassy and unfocused.

Kiora watched with curiosity as Drustan moved his way

through the crowd to the throne. The King was unaware of
Drustan's advance until he took the first stair. The King started with
the realization that a former enemy, and a magical creature to boot,
stood not but a few inches from him.

Drustan dropped to one knee in a painful act of submission. His
movements were stiff and forced and Kiora understood what it took
for him to offer this gesture. "Your Majesty, I know what it is like
to love a people so fiercely that in an attempt to offer happiness you
inadvertently cause pain instead," he stopped, looking down. Kiora
glanced to Emane. Both could fill in Drustan's pregnant silence, he
had led his people to Dralazar's side last time, and his people had
been decimated. He understood the King's dilemma better than his
Majesty would ever understand. "I understand that the thought of
losing them is unbearable." Raising his head to the King, Drustan
continued, "But you must understand, these people of yours are not
one. They are individuals with choices to make, just as you are. You
cannot control who they are, or who they are to become, any more
than they can control you. They must be free to make their own
choices. If not," Drustan dropped his head, "then we, as rulers, are
no different than Dralazar." Standing, Drustan gave a slow nod of
acknowledgement before retreating back to his own people.

The King sat staring at the spot Drustan had vacated, thinking
for some time before he finally raised his head. With pain in his eyes
that all too many in the room understood, he said, "I agree. Proceed,
Kiora."

Needing confirmation first, she questioned the King "You are
sure that every family has been told everything they need to know?
About the prophecy, the history and me?" she prodded.

"Yes."

Eleana's voice floated through. "Your people know each other,
Kiora; they knew you growing up, and they know Layla. If the word

has been sent out and they chose your sister, then they have not chosen blindly."

Kiora swallowed hard. That was the problem, she knew them too and now she was about to leave them to a questionable fate.

"It would have been preferable to have you introduced earlier, so that the people could have witnessed your transformation. But it is too late for that now," Eleana continued. "And good or evil does not come down to a matter of magic."

Kiora moved forward in reluctant agreement. "We will go out, tonight. I will need the help of the Shifters. If you accompany me from house to house, those that need to be evacuated can be taken by you, via bubble, out of the village." She looked to Eleana, "That is, if it is close enough that they can." Shifters were the not the best bubblers, Kiora remembered.

Eleana hesitated. "Why the Shifters?"

"Because they can look human, it will lessen the people's fear."

"Of course. I will find a place within range."

"Thank you. The Shifters will quietly take the groups to the place that Eleana has designated. Once they are safely hidden, we will all come back here and wait for Dralazar."

"What of the people we leave here?" demanded a Shifter whose purple hair stood up in spikes on his head. "They will fight us from inside our defenses."

Emane finally spoke up. "No, they won't. This people, they know nothing about battle. Although sided with Dralazar, they are not accustomed to violence. My guess? They will run."

Some of the Shifters looked unsure.

"He is correct," Eleana assured them. "Evil and murder do not spring forth overnight, it is reached in increments. These people are not there, not yet."

"But what if one attacks us!?" a Shifter demanded.

"Then," Kiora paused, her hands shaking, "you do what you must." As the words spilled forth, her stomach lurched and she thought she would be sick.

ALTHOUGH THE SHIFTERS HAD all taken human form, to ease the villager's fears, Kiora did have to make a few last minute adjustments. "I know you like pink," she was telling one of the Shifters, "but humans don't have pink hair."

"Not ever?" the Shifter asked innocently.

"Not ever. We don't want someone to start screaming in the middle of the night and alert everyone. Now, please, a normal color."

"But you all have such ugly hair," the Shifter whined. "Black, brown, yellow."

"There's red," Kiora said, trying to be helpful.

The Shifters face brightened. "Red! I like red." Her hair changed to a brilliant crimson red.

"Not that kind of red," Kiora moaned. "I suppose you better switch to one of the ugly colors, just to be safe."

The Shifter grumbled, switching her hair to a raven black.

Drustan was standing back with his arms folded looking very amused. "Well played, My Lady. She never takes criticism well."

Kiora shook her head. "You left her for me on purpose."

"Of course, one must see where your skills lie. You are proving to be an exceptional leader."

Kiora sighed, "I am no leader, Drustan."

"On the contrary, My Lady," he gave her a bow then he motioned to another Shifter that was walking by them, "I don't think that those ears are to regulation either."

"Oh, for heaven's sake!" Kiora sighed as she went after the

pointed-eared human moving through the room.

Drustan watched Kiora, smiling. He didn't take his eyes off of her when Eleana gracefully approached.

"She is remarkable, Eleana. I have never seen a Solus like her," said Drustan.

"Nor have I. It begs a few questions," Eleana sighed.

Drustan's head snapped back to look at Eleana, an old hope springing forward, "You don't think that she is…"

She searched his eyes. "Time will tell. Although, as you know, things will be changing one way or the other."

He nodded gravely, but a spark of excitement ran through him. "The old magic."

"Yes."

Drustan's eyes found Kiora again. "I didn't think I would see it in my lifetime. That would be remarkable if it were true." His eyes sparkled with possibility. "If the gate could be opened, it would mean…"

"Yes. IF." Eleana floated away to take her place at the front of the room.

"If I may have your attention, please." Eleana's volume did not rise above a normal speaking voice, and yet, somehow her voice swirled and twisted through the room, silencing the rumble.

"As Kiora has told you, we will be bringing the people to the back courtyard of the castle. It is not visible from any part of the village and you can then drop your bubbles, reserving as much magic as possible for the morning. From there, we will be leading them to their new home. Do not move anyone unless they are bubbled. Shifters, you will take turns. You should be able to move one family before having to let your magic return. Have them bring only necessities, and move quickly."

Kiora spent the night going from house to house, standing

outside first and assessing the threads. Once she identified that they were good, she would quietly knock at the door, explain the plan, and assure them that they would be fine. The people's reactions varied, but all came.

The houses that contained threads that were good thrilled her and gave her some relief that she so desperately needed, but the homes belonging to the followers of Dralazar shredded her.

She stood in front of the door of San and Gwen, who had been friends of her parents. San used to come and help her father with a number of chores, and her father in turn would help them. She remembered him as kind and smiling, and his wife baked the most delicious sweet rolls she had ever eaten. But, standing in front of their door, the threads came through as some of the clearest she had come across. They had sided with Layla, and thus with Dralazar. It was Orrin who stood behind her waiting for the next family. He finally interrupted her thoughts, "Are we taking them?" he asked.

"No," she said dismally, "we are not." She wanted to talk with them. Maybe if they saw her...but if she was wrong they would alert Layla, or Dralazar. She couldn't risk everyone's life for those of her friends. Despite that, she didn't move, continuing to look longingly at the door.

Orrin placed his hand on her shoulder and squeezed. "We all lose those we love in war." Despite the strong set of his shoulder, his eyes were filled with pain.

"Orrin," she whispered, "I am so sorry."

He squeezed again, "It is not your fault. Come." He nodded his head forward. That was enough to get her feet moving, although it didn't make her feel any better about what they were doing.

Almost at the end of the night she carried a little boy in her arms that couldn't have been more than three who kept asking her if they were, "Really, really indivisible." It took her a second to figure out that he meant invisible. She assured him that they were and couldn't help wasting a little magic once they arrived at the castle. She set him down and bubbled for him. He screamed in delight and clapped his hands as Kiora vanished.

"Again, again!" he shouted. "Make me indivisible again."

Kiora bent down and put her fingers to his lips "Shh. I can't tonight. But next time I see you, I will make you invisible, I promise," she whispered.

The little boy threw his arms around her neck. "I wuv you!" he announced.

It was very early in the morning when the last family arrived in the courtyard. A little over two thousand men, women and children waited for what was next.

Eleana came up next to Kiora, Emane walking behind. "I need to speak to the both of you for a few minutes before I move the people." She continued walking with complete assurance that she would be followed.

Kiora and Emane did follow, as expected, weaving into the surrounding forests and disappearing from view. Eleana walked silently ahead, stiff backed. Finally, without warning she stopped and turned. "I train Soluses," she said suddenly, "and Protectors. I do so because not to would be sending this people and its defenders to slaughter against something that they do not understand. And also perhaps," she paused, "to amend for my mistakes. However, besides that, I do not interfere with the affairs of your people and Dralazar."

Emane looked a little flabbergasted. "You're not fighting?" he said, a little stunned.

"No."

"But...but..." he stuttered. "Why would you allow him to do this, and do nothing?"

She looked to Kiora instead as she answered. "Because I

learned a long time ago that others' lives are not to be interfered with. Sometimes the consequences of interfering can be worse than it otherwise would have been."

"Is that your explanation!?" Kiora exploded. "You promised that you would tell me everything!"

Emane looked lost.

"No," Eleana said. "It is not. When this battle is over I will explain everything, just as I promised. But I wanted to let you know…"

"That you would be vanishing during the battle," Emane interrupted.

Eleana exhaled. "There is so much you do not understand. Kiora, you are more powerful than any other Solus before you. Dralazar's defeat is in your hands. Emane," she stretched out her hand, "come here, please."

Emane walked forward, looking very betrayed.

Eleana pulled up his sleeve, exposing his arm piece, and waved her hand over the top muttering words that Kiora could barely hear.

"What was that?" Emane asked looking suspiciously at the snake.

"Extra protection," she ventured cautiously, "for things that cannot be undone."

Emane's suspicion grew, "What did you do?" he pushed.

"All that I could do to right a wrong." She smiled at both them "In your words, Kiora, do what needs to be done, and follow your hearts."

CHAPTER TWENTY-SIX

BATTLE FOR MEROS

THE PEOPLE, INCLUDING ALERIC, were safely hidden away
in the forest. Emane agreed that Aleric and half of the Guardians
should stay with the people. They needed some protection, in case
the worst were to happen. The other half of the Guardians were with
Drustan, dispersing themselves around the tree line of the village.
Kiora now waited with Emane within the castle's grand entry.
Although they had made all the plans they could, she felt woefully
unprepared.

The Rockmen were plodding on towards the village, the rising
sun shining behind them, turning them into large black shadows.
With each one of their steps, the castle windows shuddered. Emane
had suggested sending the Shifters out to stop them, but Drustan
worried that separating the few forces they had so early would not
be a wise decision.

While Kiora paced, Emane peered out one of the stained glass
windows that flanked the main doorway. In order to see, his face
was pressed hard against it, squinting. Kiora had already called the
weapons the Guardians had made him. His sword was belted around

his waist, quiver on his back, his bow and shield leaned against the door. He had also chosen to wear a piece of shoulder armor they had found hidden in the castle, used in battles long past, to camouflage his armband as best he could. Kiora wore nothing but a plain tunic and riding pants, as the only shield or weapons she would need were the ones she could produce herself.

"They are coming out now," Emane announced.

It wasn't but a few seconds later that the first scream pierced the air. The Rockmen had been spotted by one of the villagers. More and more screams came as door after door opened, and one family after another stumbled into the square to see the monstrosities pressing in upon them.

One man ran, pulling his horse out from the stall, he threw himself onto its back without bothering to saddle it. A clatter of hoofbeats echoed out as he tore out of the village. The man shouted something over his back that calmed the crowd.

"Where is he going?" Emane mumbled aloud.

"They are going for Layla."

He looked at her over his shoulder. "What makes you so sure?"

"They are looking for a leader. They will look to her," she said with resignation.

Emane turned back, frowning.

Kiora moved over to a velvet tufted chair. She needed to regain as much strength as she could, last night had been long, and she had used a lot of magic and still had not slept. The magic was pouring in, attempting to fill the empty reserves. She wished it would move a little faster. She had refused to let Emane use magic of any kind last night, fearing that he was going to need more than he had.

A few minutes later, Emane sighed, "Well, you were right. Here comes Layla. At least I think it's her." He shrugged. "I don't know who else they would be bringing back, and she is with," he pushed his face closer to the window, "...Ciera?"

"Layla must have taken her in."

Emane shook his head, "Unbelievable."

"I hope she was the only one staying there," Kiora said scowling, "I didn't bother to check my house for threads."

"It doesn't matter. Anyone that was staying there would surely..." he was cut off by a familiar voice screeching at the front of the castle.

"KIORA!"

Kiora dropped her head, wincing at the tone. She didn't know why it still bothered her, it wasn't new.

"She apparently wants to speak with you," Emane said, finally swinging around.

"Kiora! I know you're in there!"

"No, she doesn't," Kiora said with a groan pushing herself to her feet. "She just hopes I am."

"It's time then?" Emane asked, his eyes searching her. "Are you sure you're ready for this?"

"Yes."

Emane went to grab his shield, but there was something she still needed to tell him and unfortunately couldn't put it off any longer. "Wait," she said hurriedly grabbing his hand. "Emane, I need you to work with Drustan on this."

Emane jerked back like she had bit him. "What!"

"This battle will be in the air," she scrambled to explain. "Drustan already pointed that out. If we can keep the dragons and the Fallen Ones fighting in the sky, then we can maybe prevent them from destroying the village. Arturo won't be able to maneuver with two on his back, especially not with you being so weighed down by armor and weapons."

"He has flown with two before," Emane objected. "Three

once!"

"Emane—flying, not fighting. Trying to maneuver in a battle
is entirely different, you know that. Drustan will be fighting as a
dragon and I need you to ride with him." She said it with a forced
finality. Her eyes, however, looked nervously to the floor.

"No!" he said emphatically, jerking his hand away and gripping
her shoulders. "I am your Protector! How can I protect you if I am
nowhere near you?"

"It is the only way to protect the village."

"I agree with you on keeping the battle to the skies, but surely
there is another way! We can both ride Drustan."

"No," she shook her head. "We are already outnumbered,
Emane. Staying together puts us at a disadvantage and makes us an
easy target. You know I am right." She reached out, gently cupping
his jaw in her hand. "The only reason you haven't suggested it
yourself is because you didn't like what it would mean."

Layla screamed again, "KIORA!"

"Kiora, I..." Emane bit his lip, turning his head away.

"Trust me, please, Emane," she pleaded. Emane dropped his
head in defeat, his arms falling limply to his sides. She nodded
in relief and squeezed his arm reassuringly. Closing her eyes, she
called Arturo. *I am ready. Meet me by the front gate.*

Growling, Emane snatched his shield, shoving his bow over his
shoulder before throwing open the door, letting it slam into the wall
with a bang. Arturo landed just in front of them, looking annoyed at
Emane's little outburst. Emane looked annoyed right back.

Kiora took in the scene. Layla and Ciera sat on horseback with
the villagers cowering behind them, as if the two silly girls would
somehow know what to do. Ciera took her role nicely, looking smug
atop her horse. Layla was next to her, staring at Arturo, aghast.

She is wondering how there could be two of us, Arturo

informed Kiora.

"Yes, Layla, there are two of them. One fights for Dralazar, and the other fights with us."

Layla's head turned towards Kiora equally shocked that Kiora knew what she was thinking. And in a flash, it was clear why Dralazar chose Layla. Kiora had thought it was because she was her sister. But that wasn't it all.

"Pegasuses are telepathic," Kiora announced in both explanation and exasperation that she had not thought of this earlier. "They can hear your thoughts. Which means Raynor could hear yours." It explained everything! She was chosen for her thoughts. Raynor heard all the anger, all the bitterness, and then ran and told his master.

Ciera nudged Layla, looking at her expectantly.

Coming back to herself, Layla snapped, "I don't care what they can do. What have you done?" she demanded, pointing to the Rockmen who were no longer just shadows, but clearly defined with the sun shining just above their heads.

Kiora had usually felt shame, guilt...sadness when her sister had spoken to her like that. The blame always made her question if, perhaps, the blame really did reside with her. But today that new anger jolted inside her. "Those are not mine, Layla," she said jutting her chin out, "They belong to you, in a way."

"Liar!" Ciera shouted.

Before she could explain, another scream went up from the crowd. Dralazar had sent his first round of cavalry. "Dragons!" came the cry from the villagers.

Not good. They had hoped that Dralazar would lead the attack. Honestly, Kiora should have known better. There were six dragons. One broke off from the others, landing on the far side of the villagers. His wing clipped the side of one home, sending the entirety of it clattering to the ground like a mere bundle of twigs. It was Soolan, of course. His eyes locked onto Emane. Kiora was surprised at first, but she saw something in his eyes, and felt a wave of intention—revenge. Emane had killed Jarland. Soolan was not going to let that go.

Everything happened too fast. Soolan puffed and Kiora screamed. The people are all going to die, right now! They all were in the path between Soolan and his intended target, Emane. Releasing all the magic she had access to, she threw up a shield, willing it to cover them all. Soolan released too, his fire sheeting up and around the protective barrier Kiora had just produced.

The villagers scrambled backwards with screams, getting as far away as they could from the source of destruction; all except for one. Gwen stood right next to the barrier, unmoving. She turned slowly, her brown eyes taking in Kiora. The two stared at each other for moment, Kiora remembering all the time she had spent with her. A tear trickled down Gwen's face and in that moment Kiora felt her thread drastically alter, it was no longer dark. Gwen knew. Kiora's heart leapt with a joy unsurpassed, she knew!

Layla dismounted from her horse in the chaos and ran straight at Kiora, "I won't let you hurt them!" she screamed. Emane bolted to stop her, but was not fast enough.

Kiora was racking her brain trying to figure out how to get Gwen out of danger, when she was shoved to the side by Layla. Falling off Arturo with a scream, the shield faltered as Kiora hit the ground. The domed shield dropped. Kiora scrambled to her feet, and although Soolan had already begun to pull back the fire in defeat, the last of it exploded through with a roar of heat. The world seemed to move in slow motion as a ball of fire licked in and swallowed Gwen whole. Kiora reached her hand out, but Gwen's thread had already fallen silent. She was gone.

"No!" Kiora screamed, bending over, her hands fisted in her stomach. "NO!"

San ran through the crowd, pushing his way to where his wife had fallen. His thread turning darker with every step.

Emane had thrown Layla onto the ground where she was screaming at Kiora, "How could you! How could you call that dragon?"

"Are you insane?" Emane yelled down at her. "She just saved you all!"

Kiora searched for the threat; surely another molten attack would be on its way. But Soolan glared, and took off with grunt.

"Why is he leaving?" Emane asked without taking his eyes off Layla.

"Dralazar," she had felt him before he dropped out of the clouds on Raynor.

Emane pushed himself up off Layla, looking around.

Kiora, get on. Now.

The people stood like confused sheep not knowing where to go. They looked to Layla as their leader, who scrambled back to her feet, looking very much relieved at the mention of her master's name.

Kiora pulled herself back onto Arturo and hissed to Emane. "Go, find Drustan."

Looking fiercely at her, Emane whispered, "You had better be safe, Kiora. If anything, anything happens to you while I am not there to protect you, I will never forgive you!"

She smiled weakly. "That is good to know."

"Or myself for listening to you!" he finished.

Just kiss him and send him on his way before Dralazar lands, Arturo grumped.

Kiora bent over to give a final kiss, "Now GO!" she said,

pushing Emane's shoulder.

Emane growled under his breath but went. Sprinting off to the side he disappeared through the trees.

Dralazar landed a second later, grinning. "Your Protector running away already, Kiora?"

The dragons were circling the village waiting for orders. She couldn't see the Fallen Ones but she could feel them circling as well. The Rockmen had come into position and stopped. Dralazar's smile faltered and faded as he felt the threads of those villagers around him. "What have you done?"

"I have left those that follow you, and that is all." She paused trying to bolster courage. The people noticed for the first time as well that many that should have been there were not. Kiora could hear them calling out names, searching through each other for those that were gone. Dralazar's eyes sparked with fury.

"They are yours now, Dralazar," Kiora said, motioning to the people.

Dralazar's eyes narrowed and he sat straighter, calmly calling her bluff. "Come now, Kiora, you don't mean that. You can't intend to leave them here at the mercy of the creatures we find ourselves surrounded by."

"Dralazar," Layla asked, taking a step forward, her face pinched together in confusion. "What are you doing?"

Smiling at Layla, that same disarming smile he had tried to use on Kiora, he said, "This is proof that she is not the Solus. The Solus would have cared what happens to this people, no matter whose side they are on."

Layla was satisfied. The people stood oddly quiet, with the exception of San, who knelt alone, sobbing loudly over his wife's dead blackened body.

"I guess there is only one question, then," Kiora said. She

feigned bravado, hoping that her instincts were right, hoping that his anger over losing her would override his need for this people. Arturo tensed underneath her in anticipation. "If these are your people, what is more important to you? Will you stay to protect them," she motioned to the circling dragons. "Or chase me?" Arturo spun on his hind feet taking to the sky. "Now, Drustan!" she yelled, looking over her shoulder.

Dralazar sat unmoving on Raynor, his eyes following Kiora. With no emotion, he raised his hand, motioning to one of the Rockmen. The giant raised the club above its head, slowly reaching the peak of its arc before slamming down into four or five of the homes on the furthest edge of the village. The wooden roof and walls were no match for the force. The other two Rockmen followed suit, each raising a club. The crowd fled in different directions trying to stay clear.

It wasn't going to work. Kiora panicked. What was she thinking? Playing a battle of wits with Dralazar? He would let her fly away, while he destroyed the helpless village. "Go back!" Kiora screamed to Arturo, "Go back!"

No, that is what he is hoping you will do. Let Drustan deal with it, he knows his job.

No sooner had he said it than trees begun snapping all around the village as Rockmen and Dragons seemed to, with Shifter magic, appear out of nowhere. Emane had instructed them that they were to match Dralazar's forces tit for tat. Shifters in the form of dragons and Guardians flew out from the forest, while three Shifter-Rockmen strode in long slow steps to stop the three real Rockmen that were smashing their clubs into the village.

Another motion from Dralazar, and dragons fell from the sky, opening their jaws in terrific roars. Most collided midair with the dragon-Shifters that had already taken to the skies. One slipped through the lines, spewing fire as he flew over the housetops. The roofs ignited immediately.

"Arturo, please!" she screamed.

He will come, Kiora. He is playing your weakness like a fiddle.

"Is caring for others a weakness!?'

Right now it is. They have chosen Kiora, he reminded her. *You cannot protect them without losing those who have chosen properly.*

Layla and Ciera's horses reared, screaming in fear of the flames, and dropped both girls unceremoniously on the ground. Kiora couldn't see their faces, but they turned running, following the people into the forest.

"Yes, run," Kiora pleaded to the people, high above them. "Run!" All around her, the battle raged in the glow of morning, dragons dipping and roaring, magic flying from Fallen Ones. The Shifters were doing a fine job of keeping the shots clear of her and Arturo. Emane flew by, riding Drustan on a saddle Kiora had provided. Her attention moved to him, making sure he was still safe when Arturo warned.

Kiora!

Dralazar and Raynor had left the ground and were heading straight for her. Kiora's heart began hammering. She hadn't fully decided what she was going to do next—all she had been focused on was getting Dralazar out of the village.

You really don't have a plan? Arturo demanded.

"No! I am making this up as I go." She looked over her shoulder to see a bolt of red magic leaving Dralazar's outstretched hand. "BANK LEFT!" she yelled.

Arturo banked as the magic slid past his right wing, barely missing it.

Hold on, Arturo directed.

Kiora turned her head to the front, realizing that their evasive maneuver had placed them directly into a dragon's line of fire, its flame spewing in their direction.

Shield, shield, shield! Arturo yelled into her head.

Kiora threw up a shield and the dragon fire sheeted off of it, but not before one of Arturo's wingtips was singed.

A little faster next time!

Arturo swooped underneath the dragon with Raynor closing in fast. The sky was a mess of dragons, fire and red magic bolting across it.

"He's gaining on us, Arturo!"

Of course he is. He's faster.

"What!?"

Yes, something you should have asked!

"Arturo!"

Don't panic, I maneuver better.

Kiora turned to see another shot coming towards them. "Right!" She threw up a shield as well to protect Arturo's left flank during the turn. The magic missed them cleanly, but dragon fire from another one of Dralazar's horde slammed into the shield. They flew over Emane, who was trying to maneuver a shot with his bow and arrow.

"Take us higher," Kiora said, spinning her body around, trying to see all sides at once. "I can't watch Dralazar and the dragons at the same time."

Arturo flew straight up, almost pulling Kiora off his back.

You need to return fire, Kiora, or he will destroy us both, Arturo ordered.

Kiora had been so busy thinking defensively that offense had escaped her entirely. She turned and fired a shot back. It was weak, and Raynor barely flinched as it connected.

You better commit yourself to this, or surrender, Kiora, Arturo chided.

Arturo had taken over steering, maneuvering neatly through the skies. He was right, Raynor was faster, but he couldn't turn as well. Every time Raynor had to follow one of Arturo's evasive maneuvers, he lost valuable time.

Kiora opened up, letting the magic flow within her. The power, the euphoria of being one with the magic bore down on her, which she probably would have enjoyed, had Dralazar not tried to use those feelings against her. Stretching out her hand, a bolt of white lightning, reminiscent of the one she had used to escape Dralazar, cracked across the sky. Raynor was forced to roll hard to one side, almost unseating Dralazar. Kiora was shaking.

That's better. Now, focus it on them and keep it out of me.

Kiora and Dralazar fought and rolled through the sky. Red and white flashed between the two of them. Kiora connected with Dralazar's shoulder leaving blood flowing down his arm. She watched as he reached over, placing his hand on his shoulder. A few seconds later he had grabbed back ahold of Raynor's mane.

"He can heal!" she screeched, whipping her head back around as Arturo maneuvered hard to the side.

Yes.

"Why doesn't anybody tell me these things?" she shouted.

Focus! He told her as Raynor tried to come up underneath them. Try another approach. Less surface damage, more force.

Kiora threw another bolt of magic at Dralazar. This one was not visible, but hit Dralazar mid chest with full force. He tumbled backwards off Raynor and went hurtling towards the ground.

Good girl.

Raynor turned and shot downwards after his master. She watched in disappointment as Raynor came up underneath Dralazar, catching him neatly.

Smoke was clogging the air, providing dark plumes and one

more thing to maneuver around. The two combating pairs rolled
though the sky throwing magic, blocking with shields, all while
dodging dragon fire and attacks from Fallen Ones. The sky was, as
Kiora had hoped, the battlefield.

Dralazar yelled up to her, "If you want to play, we can play,
Kiora!" He reached out his hand, not towards her, but towards the
nearest Shifter-dragon, Drustan—the one Emane was riding.

"NOOOO!" Kiora screamed.

Dralazar shrugged his shoulders in obvious amusement. A flick
of his wrist and Emane was flying off the dragon.

Thankfully Emane had ahold of the rope slung around Drustan's
neck, it snapped taut as he fell, jerking him to a stop. Emane yelled
in pain, dangling by one arm that was twisted at an awkward angle.

By the expression on Dralazar's face, that was not what he had
intended. No doubt he had hoped to make Kiora watch Emane fall
screaming to his death. Raynor turned, coming around for Dralazar
to make another shot.

"We have to help him!" Kiora yelled, putting up a shield to
protect herself and Arturo while the white pegasus maneuvered
himself underneath Emane. "Let go!" she yelled up to Emane,
watching Dralazar bear down on them.

Emane dropped onto the back of Arturo, groaning in pain,
cradling his arm. Kiora braced herself for the next hit. Red magic
slammed into them with ferocity, rippling across her shield. Her
hands were on fire fighting to keep it stable.

"Arturo! I can't hold it much longer!"

Without explanation, Arturo turned and flew straight at Raynor.
Dralazar's attack was blistering Kiora's hands and draining what
magic she had left very quickly.

"Arturo!" she screamed.

He flew on, aiming a head-on strike. She was giving it

everything she had, but Dralazar wasn't holding back either. He aimed to kill. At the last moment, Raynor finally yielded, going into a deep dive to break the connection.

Bubble! Arturo demanded, also dropping into a dive.

Kiora threw up a bubble as Arturo ingeniously hid the three of them underneath Raynor. Dralazar screamed in rage, firing shot after shot at random into the sky hoping to hit them.

"We have to get him to the ground," she pleaded, looking over her shoulder at Emane. He looked sick, his eyes dulled with pain. "Now!" She heard him moan out behind her as Arturo dove steeply down.

When they landed, Kiora jumped down first, carefully helping Emane off Arturo's back. "Is it just dislocated?" She asked, trying to be as ginger as possible.

"No." His face was ashen. "Something tore, I think."

She glanced up through the trees warily, as a dragon roared. "Hurry, Emane, heal it."

He shook his head, sweat dripping down his face, "I tried already," he said breathing every few words, "I used too much magic fighting the dragons...there isn't enough left."

Kiora's mind was racing, she couldn't leave him injured. There had to be a way to get him his magic faster so he could...she looked at Emane's armband.

This is not a good idea, Arturo intruded on her thoughts.

Setting her mind to it, she thought back, I don't have a choice. Ignoring Arturo's concern, she walked over to Emane. Carefully, Kiora removed his shoulder armor. He grunted, gritting his teeth as she pulled it off. His shirt was wet with sweat and blood.

"What are you doing?" he asked, eyeing her warily.

"Shhh," she said, placing her hands over the top of where Emane's armband wrapped underneath, she imagined her magic flowing out of her and into Emane. She felt it flowing, cooling...she didn't know how much he would need, so she gave him as much as she thought she could spare. After she let go, she could feel only a faint glimmer of magic left within her.

"What did you do?" Emane asked, his eyes wide.

"I can't heal you," she said pushing her hair out of her face, "but I can at least help you heal yourself."

Emane reached his hand over to his shoulder and sighed with relief. "Thank you," he murmured.

"This is so very touching," Dralazar mocked, appearing a few feet above them on Raynor.

Turning with a yelp, Kiora raised her hand as Emane reached for his sword, but with one swift movement Dralazar picked them both up and threw them in different directions. Kiora was pinned against one tree, Emane against another. Kiora grunted as she hit, the force knocking the wind out of her. She gasped for air.

"Stupid," he continued, "but touching."

Arturo stepped forward, to which Dralazar snarled, "Arturo, one twitch out of you and I will kill them both." Relaxing, Dralazar looked back to Kiora with a smile. "You do realize, of course, that you have just condemned yourself."

Kiora struggled against her bonds, her heart sinking. Arturo was right; it had not been a good idea. She was nearly helpless.

Raynor landed and Dralazar dismounted, walking towards Kiora as Raynor headed for Arturo. "That was very foolish, Kiora, pouring magic into Emane. Why would you do such a silly thing? It is not as if he is magical." He mocked her, crossing his arms in front of himself. She turned her head away, she would not cry. Not in front of him.

"At least that is what I thought. But," he paraded in front of Kiora, crossing around until he was standing beside her, looking across the clearing to Emane, who was struggling against his invisible bonds, "unless my eyes deceived me, it looked as if he healed himself. And I am left asking myself: How is that possible?"

"Leave him alone!" Kiora screamed.

"Hmmm, very interesting," Placing his fingers on his chin, Dralazar spun to look at her. Kiora's heart constricted, his eyes were dangerous. "Emane's thread has changed. That is very interesting." Dralazar took slow, deliberate steps towards Emane, examining him as if he were a piece of meat. He walked around the tree, scanning him as Emane struggled helplessly, eventually focusing in on his shoulder. Reaching up, he ripped Emane's shirt open exposing the armband. The brilliant green sparkled in the sunlight. "What is this?" he murmured, running his finger over the metal. Dralazar looked Emane in the eye. "Where did you get this?"

Emane set his jaw, looking straight forward.

"I assure you, I can make you talk, Emane," he said, flickering red magic from the tips of his fingers.

"Stop it!" Kiora screamed, struggling against the magic that was still holding her in place. "Leave him alone. It's me you want."

Dralazar rolled his eyes in feigned exasperation. "Kiora, you are so narrow-minded. I want whatever I can get." He grinned. "Now," he said rubbing his hands delightedly in front of him, "back to the problem at hand." Turning his head to the side, Dralazar gently stroked the snake, whispering magical enchantments under his breath. Once or twice, the snake seemed to move, but then became still again. Dralazar studied the piece thoughtfully. "This is a very nice piece of work you have here. I am sure I must credit Eleana." He stroked the snake's head, whispering more enchantments, coaxing it to unlock.

Kiora's breath caught in her throat as the snake unexpectedly responded. It opened its mouth, releasing his tail. The glittering green snake pulled its head back, stretching its jaw.

No, she thought. Only Eleana was suppose to be able to remove it.

"That's right," Dralazar coaxed.

He began more incantations and reached his hand up to stroke it again. The snake turned its head to look at him with glittering eyes. Then its eyes narrowed and the creature struck, clamping its jaws down on Dralazar's hand, sinking its fangs deep within his flesh. Dralazar swore in pain, ripping his hand back. The snake promptly bit back down on its own tail and went still once more. Emane was looking down at the band as if he had never seen it before.

Dralazar was infuriated. "That's enough!" he roared. "I should have disposed of you already!" He opened up his hands and red fire exploded from within him bolting straight at Kiora.

"Kiora!" Emane screamed from across the clearing. She tried to raise her hands but it was no use, she was pinned and helpless. Closing her eyes, she thought of death, but none came.

A second later the magic that had held her to the tree released her, dropping her to the ground. Breathing heavily, she looked around to see her salvation. Dralazar's magic popped and sizzled in front of her, trying to burn its way through a shield thicker than one she had ever been able to produce. Kiora looked down at her hands, and back to the shield, it wasn't coming from her.

The attack abruptly stopped and Kiora could see across the clearing Emane encased in the same type of shield she was under.

"ELEANA!" Dralazar roared.

Eleana emerged from behind a tree. "Dralazar," she acknowledged.

"How dare you interfere!" He was fuming.

Pulling her chin up, Eleana said, "Because I have chosen not to interfere in the past does not mean I do not have the right."

"You seem to be making a habit of it this time." Dralazar inclined his head, eyes glistening. "It doesn't matter," he laughed. "You cannot defend them and yourself at the same time, Eleana. Three shields is one too many." He held his arms out. "Who shall I kill first?"

"Perhaps you should take your anger out on who it is directed towards," Eleana said. "Although, I am sure you plan to kill us all, regardless."

"It doesn't matter what order then, does it?" Dralazar yelled while extending his hand toward Eleana. Red fire spewed out closing the distance between the two.

Kiora watched the shield from Emane drop, leaving him unprotected as Eleana threw one up for herself.

"No," Kiora gasped, her eyes fixed on the now helpless Emane.

"That's what I thought!" Dralazar roared. He reached out his wounded hand as soon as the shield was down and directed a shot at Emane.

"Emane!" Kiora screamed, running towards him. Eleana's shield might as well have been a wall, she slammed into it and fell to the ground. Pulling her head up frantically, she looked for Emane.

Dralazar's red fire flickered and sputtered but would not cross the distance. He looked at his hand in horror.

"Your snake bite seems to be taking effect," Eleana said calmly.

Dralazar looked to Emane's magical piece and then back to Eleana. "You did this!"

"I enchanted the snake, yes. I am not sure of how much time you have before its venom destroys all your magic."

"You lie!" Dralazar grabbed his wounded hand and tried to heal it, but nothing happened.

"You can choose not to believe me, but I would not recommend it. The old magic is potent. And being a Witow would be a terrible fate for someone like you."

A Witow? That was a term Kiora had never heard before.

"Old magic?" Dralazar glared at Eleana. "You wouldn't."

"I did," Eleana said, her eyes blue and steady. "I am sure you can find the cure somewhere, if you hurry. I assure you, though—you are running out of time."

"You wouldn't dare use the old magic," Dralazar took a shaky step back. "I don't believe it." Kiora could see the fear flicker in Dralazar's eyes that he did indeed believe it.

"Try using your magic again, if you would like proof."

Dralazar flung his hand out towards Emane again with a yell. Eleana didn't bother to shield him. There was a little sputter and then Dralazar's magic was gone.

Dralazar glared at Eleana, clutching his hand in front of him. "You dare to open up the old books?" His face was hard and dark. "After everything you have done to protect this pathetic species?"

"Dralazar, take those that follow you, and go," Eleana demanded.

Raynor walked over to his master, nervously watching the three that stood between him and Dralazar. Dralazar's eyes flickered back and forth from Eleana to Kiora, she could see him frantically thinking. "You have chosen the wrong time to interfere."

"No, I do not think I have."

A bitter smile passed over Dralazar's face, lighting a spark of excitement in those dark blue eyes. The excitement scared Kiora the most, because she could not understand what it was that would have caused it.

"Know this, Eleana. You are responsible for what I do next," Dralazar snarled as he mounted Raynor.

"Dralazar, you can't," Eleana said, holding her hand out to him. "Please, listen, we don't know what's happened since it was closed."

Dralazar laughed, shaking his dark hair. "You are the one that opened the old magic. This is on you." He smiled a devilish smile, his eyes going distant. "Everything is about to change." Raynor took off towards the dragons, leaving Kiora and Emane wondering what it was that just happened.

"Why did you let him go?" Emane asked, sounding utterly bewildered, watching pegasus feet soar over the top of them.

Kiora shook her head giving him a look that said, Not now!

Eleana stared into the sky with a stunned look on her face. "He's going to open the gate," she muttered under her breath. "What if I'm wrong?"

It was so quiet, Kiora barely made out what she had said. "What?"

Eleana didn't seem to have heard her. "His magic will be affected for quite some time." She turned and glided away without another word.

"What is going on?" Emane demanded. "What gate?"

Kiora stared after Eleana, "I can't tell you, not yet."

"And what is a *Witow*?"

Suddenly there was a loud roar, and the sun was blackened by a large dragon flying overhead. Not following Dralazar, but on its way to the village. A second body flew over in pursuit, Kiora could tell by the thread it was Morcant. Dragon after dragon shot over the top of them. Some were Shifters, the rest were Dralazar's, all headed for the village. She heard the crackle of dragon fire followed by the screams of those left in the village.

"We let him go and he sent the dragons after them anyway," Kiora said numbly.

Kiora, focus. You still have work to do, Arturo said. Dralazar will only surprise you if you expect something from him. There is no honor among evil.

Drustan had told her, that day in the meadow when she had allowed the Fallen Ones to live, "don't expect them to do the same for you." What did she really expect? "We need more Shifter-dragons," she announced. "Emane, I need you to go up with Arturo, take out as many dragons as you can."

"Wait, what!? You think I am leaving you, again!?"

"Listen," she sighed, hanging her head. "I don't have any magic left; I gave it all to you."

"All of it?"

"Nearly. It's coming back, but I need some more time. I will run back and send the rest of the Shifters left on the perimeter up. You go and stop those dragons from burning down everything we have. I don't have time to argue about it, please!"

Grabbing her, Emane kissed her, hard. "I swear, Kiora," he breathed roughly. "My threat still stands. If you die, I will never forgive you." Turning, he ran and leapt onto Arturo, whose front feet were off the ground nearly before Emane was seated.

Turning back towards the village, Kiora ran, leaping over fallen logs and rocks, the branches tearing at her face. People were streaming out from the village seeking refuge from the fire. Some carried possessions that they had saved from their homes before fleeing. Others carried their children on their backs. Some just ran. In all the chaos, no one noticed Kiora.

She ran faster, pushing herself to her limits. The closer she got, the thicker the smoke and the more her lungs burned trying to extract oxygen. A shape emerged in front of her, a Shifter by the thread. Breathless, she grabbed the Shifter girl's arm, who was still in human form. "We need help," she gasped. "Take the rest of your people up, as dragons."

"Yes, My Lady," she bowed before taking off into the smoke.

Coughing, Kiora turned to head back out. She needed to breathe, but her breath caught in her throat as the first evil threads she had ever felt came back to haunt her. "The Hounds," she gasped. "No!" Her yell echoed through the smoke. "No, no, no, no!" She punched the air in frustration before breaking back into a run. The villagers were all out, running themselves— completely unprotected and unaware of the predators that were speeding their direction. She had to save them. She couldn't allow them to be torn apart by the Hounds. She couldn't. Maybe if she could find the villagers, warn them, she could save at least a few.

Eleana's voice slammed into her mind. *Bubble, Kiora.*

She gripped her head, nearly falling head over heels. Why was Eleana's voice so much louder?

I don't have enough magic left to bubble and save the village, she thought back.

You will not be able to save the village if you are dead. Bubble!

Angry at her predicament, Kiora threw up a bubble, zagging to the side to clear herself of her previous scent trail.

Nearly negating her efforts, a Hound exploded out of a bush, barely missing the edge of Kiora's bubble. Landing heavily, it looked around, sniffing the air. The Hound issued an almost human sounding sigh of satisfaction as it settled into a crouch. It waited for someone. Kiora looked around, there were so many threads it was hard to keep track of them all, but she soon realized that one thread was coming right at them. Kiora turned, yelling out a warning, which the bubble kept neatly contained.

The Hound leapt forward, anticipating his next victim's arrival. His large hairy body flew through the air at a teenage girl who came running around the trunk of a tree, looking frantically behind her. Before she had enough time to realize what was happening, the Hound collided with her. Kiora screamed out, sinking to her knees as the bodies of Hound and human rolled over one another, coming to a stop a few feet away. The girl moaned, trying to pick herself up off the ground, her long blonde hair hanging down full of dirt and twigs. The Hound was already on its feet, ready to pounce again. Unwilling to witness the imminent carnage, Kiora turned away. But nothing could have muffled the scream as the Hound sunk his jaws into the girl. The scream itself forced Kiora's head back around in time to see the girl go limp as the Hound tore her to pieces. Kiora dropped her face into her hands, her heart aching as she felt the girls thread go silent. The rest of the Hounds, frenzied with the smell of blood, bounded past unaware of Kiora's presence. She heard whimpering and assumed it was the girls, but she had felt the thread vanish, the girl was gone. A moment later she realized the whimpering was her own.

The Solus. Never had the term felt more ridiculous to her as it did right now; lying on the ground, underneath a bubble, unable to save even one person from falling victim to the Hounds.

Get up, Kiora! Eleana's voice returned. Your magic is running out. You must go!

She was right. If she ran out of magic here, she was dead. She needed to get back with Arturo and the others. Keeping her eyes averted, she clumsily stood. There were threads everywhere, the villagers were spread throughout the forest, but so were the Hounds. And where the two threads crossed, she could feel villagers' threads being extinguished.

Kiora screamed, placing her hands over her ears and running, as if that would stop her from feeling the threads. She ran and ran, back towards the village, stopping to catch her breath. She hadn't taken more than two breaths when Ciera and Layla broke through the trees also stopping not but ten feet in front of Kiora.

"What was that thing?" Ciera exclaimed, leaning over with her hands on her knees and breathing hard.

"I don't know, but it just killed Sarah," Layla said, also breathing heavily, looking back over her shoulder.

Kiora's heart wrenched, she had grown up with Sarah too. She was sweet and kind, although she had idolized Layla. Now she was dead.

The giant Hound must have been stalking the two girls, because it seemingly leapt out of nowhere. Crouching down in front of them, it bore its teeth, red with blood. The girls whimpered, backing up, gripping each other's arms.

Kiora took a step in their direction. She's my sister! I can't just leave her! The swelling of pain and fear Kiora had been shoving down all morning pushed upwards, tightening her throat, and threatening to pull her all the way underneath it.

The Hound took another step forward as well, its muscles tight. Snapping like a tightly coiled spring, it leapt into the air.

Once again her world reverted to slow motion. The Hound crossed the distance, teeth bared, drool dripping down its blood-matted muzzle. Ciera leaned behind Layla, throwing her arms over her face, screaming. Layla reached behind her, grabbed Ciera's arm and threw her into the Hound's path. The jaws of the Hound connected with a sickening crunch around Ciera's skull. Her scream was cut off as her body instantly went limp. Layla turned and ran through the forest, disappearing from view.

Kiora turned away, sickened not only by the violence, but also by her sister. Clutching her side, Kiora wretched, her back heaving from the force of it. Breathing hard, she wiped her mouth with the back of her sleeve before taking off at a dead run back to the village. Her sister had thrown Ciera to the Hounds to save her own skin. Layla truly did belong to Dralazar.

Kiora's magic was nearly gone. Skidding through the tree line she looked frantically for anyone on her side, when a roar came just overhead. With a glance up she dove to the side to avoid being hit by the monstrous dragon that slammed into the ground just inches from her. Soolan scrambled to his feet shaking his head violently from side to side, trying to dislodge an arrow that protruded from his eye. Morcant landed just behind Kiora unaware that she was there.

"Go home, Soolan," Morcant growled.

"You traitor," Soolan snapped at him.

Kiora was trapped. She had a dragon in front of her and behind her. The village was on fire to her left and the forest was filled with Hounds that would devour her the second her magic ran out.

Soolan rolled his head in the dirt still trying to dislodge the arrow. "You let that human kill Jarland. You are a disgrace."

"Go home, Soolan," Morcant repeated. "The others have all left you."

Soolan looked to the sky with his good eye to see the Shifter-dragons circling him. All the true dragons had fled.

"Are you going to let them kill me too, Morcant?"

"Only if you stay."

Soolan pulled himself up to his full height. There was blood running down the side of his head. "There will come a time when your luck will run out Morcant. And when it does..."

Kiora's bubbled flickered, and was gone. Sick, she slowly turned her eyes to Soolan.

"Well, hello," Soolan finished.

Morcant rose up on his hind legs with a roar, wings flapping, trying to place his body between her and Soolan. Seeing his opportunity, Soolan slashed upward with his front claws as Kiora dashed back between Morcant's hind legs. Soolan's claw entered Morcant's body, in the exact spot where Emane had sunk his sword in Jarland, he pushed deep, slashing open Morcant's chest. A roar, and Morcant went limp crashing to the ground.

"MORCANT!" Kiora screamed.

"As I was saying, Morcant," Soolan's head moved down to Morcant's drooping ear. "When your luck runs out, I will be ready." Soolan's eyes flickered up to Kiora. "And now for you…" Multiple roars sounded from above them and Soolan's head jerked up to see a horde of Shifters and Guardians pouring down on them.

Soolan's head swung back, eyes narrowed. "Next time, perhaps." Then he jumped over her, spread his wings and shot to the sky.

"Help me!" she shouted. "Somebody help me!!" Frantically, she climbed over Morcant's back leg that lay skewed at an awkward angle. Blood was pouring out from underneath him, soaking the dirt and turning it black. She ran through the mud and blood, she had to get to Morcant. She could still feel his thread, but it was barely there. Falling next to him, Kiora placed her hand on his snout.

"Morcant?" she whispered.

The world had gone quiet. She couldn't hear the fighting, the yelling, the crackling of fire. All she could hear was Morcant's strained breathing. Leaning back, she yelled both out loud, and in her mind. EMANE! I need you!!

"Little one," Morcant wheezed.

"Oh, Morcant, hold on," tears slipped down Kiora's cheeks as she ran her fingers over Morcant's snout. "Hold on."

"Don't forget what I told you, little one."

"Hey, now," she said, rubbing her hand along his jaw. "Don't talk like that. Emane is on his way. He can heal you, I know he can."

"I have lived a long life, Kiora, it is all right."

"No, it is not all right. I need you, Morcant, you always know the right thing to say,"

Morcant wheezed a laugh. "I don't think anyone has ever said that about me before."

"It's true."

He rolled his head to the side, looking her in the eye. "When you go through the gate, visit my home for me."

"What are you talking about?" she said through tears. "Your home is here."

"No," he blinked slowly. "My childhood home is an island, past the oceans. They called it Toopai." He breathed it out as if it were heaven itself, his eyes fluttering. "Promise me you will visit, promise."

Forcing a smile, Kiora agreed, "Of course, Morcant, but...the gate is sealed, I can't..."

"Take a scale," he coughed, blood dribbling out the side of his mouth. "It is what we do." His voice weakened even further, the beautiful booming base having left him. "When we die, there is a place where a scale is left," another cough racked his body, "in remembrance of those who are gone. Please, leave it there."

"Morcant," she placed her hand on his head trying to smile, "You are going to be fine, you..."

"Good bye, little one," Morcant gave a serene smile and exhaled one final time as his thread went quiet.

Letting out a wail of agony, Kiora collapsed against him.

Arturo and Emane came in behind her. Emane dropped to the ground before Arturo could even land, and ran to her.

"What's wrong, Kiora? What's wrong?"

Looking up frantically, she pleaded. "Heal him, please, heal him, Emane."

Arturo stepped in between Emane and Morcant, shaking his head at Emane while speaking to Kiora, There is no bringing back the dead, Kiora. He is gone.

Drustan landed in dragon form, quickly morphing back to human. "What is wrong with you people!" he demanded. "You don't just give up the chase and let him GO!"

"Not Now!" Emane yelled at him. "Look around before you start yelling at people!"

Kiora had thrown herself back over Morcant's nose, sobbing hysterically. One by one the Shifters and the Guardians returned to the ground, paying their respects to one dragon who never gave in to Dralazar.

Emane finally placed his hand on Kiora's arm. "It is finished, Kiora, we need to go," he said as gently as he could.

She nodded, knowing what she had to do. Hesitantly, she reached out to Morcant's body, pulling one brown scale gently from the underneath of his jaw. It was smaller than she had expected it to be, fitting within the palm of her hand. Wiping her eyes, she looked around. The group before her was battered and bruised and barely visible through the smoke. "The Hounds?" she asked.

"Dralazar must have called them back," Drustan informed her. "We went to deal with them but they were already heading out of the forest."

She nodded solemnly.

Come, Arturo said. You must get everyone to safety and they will not leave without you.

Leaning over Morcant one last time with his scale clasped in her hand, she kissed his nose. "Thank you, for everything" she whispered.

CHAPTER TWENTY-SEVEN

AFER THE BATTLE

ARTURO LED THE WAY for the villagers, during which the Shifters and the Guardians gave inventory of the casualties they had witnessed. Drustan had lost six Shifters that he was aware of. The Guardians had sustained no losses. Kiora told Emane of Ciera, and although there was no love lost between the two, Emane was visibly saddened. No one deserved to die that way.

Eleana had established the camp within the forest to the west of what remained of Meros. A large natural clearing was being used as a place for the people to eat and meet together, while the tents for individual families were scattered throughout the trees, giving them as much privacy as possible. Eleana had shielded this clearing as she had shielded the Hollow, maintaining all threads safe within its borders.

When Kiora entered the camp, the people were clapping and cheering the return of the Solus and their Prince. Kiora looked around as she clung to Emane's arm. She was so horribly numb that even that had begun to hurt. The people crowded in around her, smiling, frowning, buzzing with questions. Her eyes slid from face to face in a daze unable to say anything. Outside the crowd, a few groups stood gathered along the border looking up at the pillars of thick black smoke billowing up through the sky. Her life, their life, it was gone, all of it.

Kiora slid out from Emane's grasp, smiling weakly at his question as she tried to slip out of the crowd. Hands ran over her, people tried to stop her, all asking questions. She just smiled, shaking her head, blinking back tears.

I'm sorry, Emane, I can't do this, she thought to him. Please, you are much better at this than me.

Go, he thought back. I understand.

Slipping past the last of the group, Kiora bubbled. Turning, she watched Emane holding his arms up, trying to quiet the group. "One at a time, one at a time!" he shouted. "Please. We will tell you everything you want to know."

She knew they would ask who had died, how many of their friends had been lost. She couldn't watch the expressions of joy switch to those of mourning and despair. Turning, she ran through the mess of tents looking for one that was not occupied. She mourned for her people, for her home. But right now, more than anything, she mourned for a dragon, the pain of which none of the villagers would understand.

Pulling back the flap, she sagged under her grief. Slumping across the tent, she took only enough time to kick off her bloody shoes before collapsing onto the bed. Burying her face in a pillow, she cried out as much as she could, weeping and screaming and pounding her fist into the bed. The thick blanket of exhaustion carried her off to sleep. She went willingly.

Had she known how tormented her dreams would be, she would have fought sleep harder. She dreamed of Hounds and dragons and death. The faces of those she knew had been lost rolled through, demanding remembrance, and thereby forcing her to relive the pain of their loss. She tossed and turned, yelling out, but nothing could change what had already passed. She watched Layla throw Ciera to the Hounds, watched Gwen die after she had realized the truth with no time for Kiora save her, and watched Morcant's eyes close for that last time, over and over again.

And then, mercifully, the scene changed and she was back underneath the weeping willow tree with beetles whispering to her. "Don't forget, don't forget." And then it moved back to the gate, smoke and shadows swirling around it. In her dream, she reached out to touch it—only the fear of feeling that betrayal again finally ripped her from the nightmare. She woke with a start, breathing hard.

"Good morning." Emane was sitting at the foot of her bed.

She blinked, rubbing the sleep from her eyes. "How long have I been sleeping?" she groaned, pushing herself up. She hurt everywhere.

"Quite a while. You slept through dinner and breakfast. It's almost lunch."

She moaned again, flopping back down on her bed, wrapping her arms around her head. The battle had left her sore, but beneath that the new magical current flowed underneath her skin, feeling like a rain-swollen river fighting to leave its banks. She tried to look past it, but it was stronger than before. "I feel terrible," she moaned.

"Tell me where it hurts."

"Everywhere!"

Emane scooted closer and put his hands on her back. Comfort spread out from his palms, soothing every muscle and ache. Kiora relaxed under his touch as he moved up to her neck and shoulders before asking, "Where else?"

Sitting up, she held out her arms that had been scratched to pieces running through the forest.

"How are the people?" she asked, watching him take her forearms.

"As well as can be expected; many are mourning those that were left behind. Others are already asking how long before they can rebuild." Inch by inch, he wiped away all evidence of the battle she had been through.

"Thank you, that was amazing," she sighed.

Taking her hands into his, he asked, "How are you?"

"I don't know," she grimaced. "It's hard to think past all this magic running through me."

"I can't heal that," he said with a crooked grin. "But I could offer a little distraction." Leaning in, he kissed her. Her whole body went fluid, and pliable. Falling into him she wrapped her arms around his neck. It was like the first summer's breeze flowing through her, wiping away some of the remaining pain, the kind his healing magic couldn't reach. His kisses were so tender, she lost herself in his embrace, feeling her magic slip for the briefest of seconds before she reeled it back in.

Emane jumped off the bed with a yelp, "What was that!?"

Kiora's hand flew to her mouth. "I don't know—I...what happened?"

"You shocked me!" He rubbed his lips. "Hard."

"I am so sorry." She dropped her head into her hands. "It's all this magic. Every time I think I understand what is going on, there is more!"

Emane put his finger underneath her chin, pulling her face up to. "No, it's okay. It's not your fault." He kissed her again. "And I am fine." He smiled at her and sat down, leaning forward with his elbows on his knees. Clasping his hands in front of him, Emane was quiet except for a couple of rather large, frustrated breaths.

Kiora shifted awkwardly, "What?" she finally asked. The other option was to let him sit there and huff at her all day.

He gave one more, large sigh. "There is something I wanted to talk to you about."

"Is this about me sending you with Drustan? Emane, I did the best I could. I..."

"No," he interrupted getting to his feet, "just listen." He paced back and forth across the tent. "I am your Protector," he started, his hand at the hilt of his sword as though he going to start swinging it around the room. "How am I supposed to protect you if you are sending me off to fight somewhere else?"

"You protected me," she objected.

"No, I didn't. As I recall, you saved me," he gave her a look, "twice. I was a perfect target that Dralazar could use, and did use, to pull you out of the fight. And then," he stopped in front of her, gritting his teeth, "you poured your magic into me leaving yourself helpless! Had Eleana not intervened..." He stopped, shaking his head. "We both know what would have happened had Eleana not intervened."

Kiora closed her eyes as she saw the bolt of red magic leave Dralazar's hand, in what she was sure was to be the last moments of her life.

"What was I supposed to do?" she asked softly.

"I don't know." He kicked at some imaginary stone on the floor. "We are at a disadvantage. Fighting with magic is still new to you, and I grew up learning strategic lessons in *history* classes, all of which are proving to be completely useless among the enemy we are facing. But I do know this: I cannot protect you if I am not near you."

"I understand." Pushing herself off the bed, she took his hands in hers, looking at him intently. "But, Emane, there will be times

446 | DEVRI WALLS

when we will have to separate. And there will be times when I will protect you as well. I need you to be okay with that."

He looked down at her hands, his lips pursing forward. She could nearly see what she had said rolling around in his head. "I will trust your judgment," he finally said, squeezing her hands.

Jerking her hands away from him, Kiora stepped back. "Why are you so willing to trust my judgment!?" she cried, turning away from him. "My judgment nearly got us both killed. And it cost Morcant...I mean, I..." she covered her face with her hands as if she could hide from it.

"What are you talking about?"

"It's my fault Morcant's dead," she wailed, "My magic ran out, that's why Soolan attacked. Morcant opened himself up to an attack trying to shield me." Tears poured down her face.

"Hey," Emane said turning her around, "look at me." He peeled her hands back from her face, searching her eyes with his. "It's not your fault Kiora. It is Dralazar's fault," he said firmly. "Morcant knew what he was doing; he chose what he wanted to do. He was willing to risk his life for yours," he put a finger under her chin, "as am I."

She sobbed, turning her head away. "I don't want any of you to."

"Listen," he said, wiping the tears from her eyes, "although I did not like being ordered to leave you, watching you these last couple of days has been eye opening. You have a gift, an ability to know what needs to done. Kiora, you truly were born for this. The further into this we go, the more I see that. You will be a force to be reckoned with, my Solus." He kissed her forehead. "Morcant already knew that, and he would want you to remember it."

She took a deep, shuddering breath, trying to calm herself, but the mention of his name had brought back the tears. She leaned on

Emane's shoulder, letting them flow freely down her face.

Emane half smiled. "Kiora, if he knew you were blaming yourself for his death, he would be so mad he would have started spraying fire already." She smiled in spite of the grief. "And burned down my tent too!" Emane laughed.

Kiora couldn't help but laugh herself.

"All right?" Emane gently asked, squeezing her hands.

She tried to say all right, but all she succeeded in doing was opening her mouth before nodding instead.

"Now, you need to get dressed and have some lunch. I would hurry. A little boy keeps asking to see you. Something about being invisible?"

"You mean indivisible."

"Yep, that's the boy," Emane laughed. "You better eat first, though, you need your energy."

"Yes, Your Majesty."

"Kiora! I think deep down you like the arrogant prince attitude." Chuckling, he pulled back the tent flap to leave.

"Emane?"

"What, no 'Your Majesty'?" He asked sarcastically.

"I..." she hesitated. "I..." she looked in his eyes, hoping desperately he could see it, what she was feeling.

The annoyance was replaced with a grin from ear to ear, "I told you I would wait, Kiora. But for what it's worth, I love you too."

He was so devastatingly gorgeous when he smiled like that. It made Kiora's heart flutter and her stomach twist as if it were the first time she had ever seen him. Emane ducked underneath the tent flap and she collapsed back onto her bed with a sigh.

AFTER LUNCH, KIORA SPENT the rest of the day amongst the

people. Eleana had erected tents throughout the camp, one for each family. In the middle stood several large tents where meals were served, nd an empty area where the people would gather to talk one to another and the young men could practice their swordplay.

The Guardians and Shifters had already returned to their homes with the promise that they would return if needed. The people had many questions for Kiora, although none asked of those that were lost. She had a suspicion Emane had instructed them not to. But the most repeated question of the day was, "Are we going to have to stay here forever?" It was the worst question because Kiora really didn't know.

Emane came to her after dinner with two swords and handed her one.

"What is this for?" she asked, as the weight of the sword jerked her arm to the ground.

"I have decided you need to learn how to fight," he said, laying his blade across his hand, examining it.

"You have, have you?" She grunted, trying to wrench the sword back up.

"Well, Aleric and I decided." Emane shrugged, dropping the sword back to his side. "If I do get separated from you and you happen to run out of magic, you need to be able to defend yourself. I have already spoken to the Guardians and they have promised to make you a sword that is your size. But for now, we will practice with these."

"Emane, I don't even know how to hold one of these things."

"Lesson number one, it is called a sword."

"All right, a sword," she said, placing a hand on her hip. "Problem number two, I can't lift it."

"Try," he said, jerking his head towards her sword.

Rolling her eyes, she grabbed the hilt, struggling under the weight of it, managing to pull it up a few inches before the weight dragged her back down to the ground. Emane burst out into laughter, taking it out of her hands.

"Well worth it!" he grinned, shouldering her sword. When she looked at him confused, Emane leaned forward as if telling her a secret, "I really just wanted to watch you not be able to do something."

"Are you serious," she sputtered. "You gave me that sword just to laugh at me? Did you even talk to Aleric?" Her face flushed.

"Of course I talked to Aleric." Emane was trying to stifle his laughter but it wasn't working. "And I am going to teach you to fight." He buried the swords into the ground so that they were standing straight up. "But we normally don't start with those. He pulled out two wooden swords he had stashed behind a tree. "Normally we start training with these," he said, spinning them around in an arc before presenting her with the much smaller, much lighter wooden sword.

She snatched it out of his hand. "You really are a jerk, you know."

"Hmmm," he said smirking, tossing his sword from one hand to the other. "I'm happy with jerk. It's much nicer than what you used to call me."

"You're that too," she half grinned.

"Nope, we have downgraded to jerk and I am keeping it." He started circling around her. "First things first, you need to protect yourself. I will try to get past your guard. If you block me, you win. If I get past your guard, I win. And," he drug out, "I will expect to be paid with a kiss."

"What do I get if I win?" she asked.

Emane took advantage of the question and jabbed in quickly, connecting with her arm. "One kiss for me," he winked, backing out again.

"That was cheating!" she objected. Emane swung around the blade, lightly connecting the flat side of the sword between her shoulder blades.

"Two kisses for me."

"Oohhh," she growled. "You are an arrogant horse's ass!" She took a protective stance and blocked the next blow.

"Nice job." He danced around her and connected with her opposite shoulder. "Three kisses for the horse's ass," he gloated. "Come on, Kiora, you have to move your feet." His eyes glinted mischievously.

She started to move and circle, following his lead. She blocked blow after blow, but missed at least one out of every three. "Come on, Emane," she complained, "take it easy on me. It's my first day."

"I am taking it easy on you," he laughed. "You're terrible!"

"Thanks a lot," she said, trying to force a glare at him. "You're not exactly encouraging." She lifted her sword to block another shot.

Pushing his sword down over hers, he leaned in, "I actually like the fact that you're terrible, more kisses for me."

Kiora heard a few snickers from behind her and noticed that the camp was turning up to watch the training session. Pushing back, Emane jabbed in and caught her in the stomach.

"HEY!" she yelled, doubling over.

"That's at least 15 kisses, I am losing count." Spinning in a wide lazy circle, he asked the spectators, "Anyone want to keep track for me?"

"You...are such a..."

"Uh-uh," he said, shaking his finger at her, "we have little ears amongst us, watch your language."

"JERK!" she yelled.

"That's better." Emane swung again and she soundly blocked. It went on like this for longer than she had wanted. The crowd cheered when she blocked a shot and they counted kisses when Emane made it past her guard. And they laughed at every joke he made, which only encouraged him.

"Please," she gasped. "I am dying, can't we take a break?"

"Breaks are for girls!" He taunted her, dancing around her with the stupid, albeit gorgeous grin, plastered on his face.

"I am a girl, Emane." He moved in to take another shot, which she barely blocked. "I mean it, Emane, I am going to cheat if we don't stop." He raised his sword over his head. With a flick of her wrist she swept his feet out from under him. He reached for his sword, but with another flick of the wrist, the sword slid across the ground out of his reach. She dropped to her knees, putting her sword to his neck, "Do you yield?"

The crowd was in hysterics. Emane stretched his neck looking around. "How many kisses am I owed?" he shouted to the crowd.

"Seventy-two," the answer came.

"Hmmm, seventy-two kisses," he put both arms behind his head. "That should be enough. Yes, I yield."

"Thank heavens!" Kiora collapsed on the ground next to Emane as the crowd cheered and laughed with approval.

Emane rolled over and leaned on his elbow, looking down at her through half-open lids. "I think the Lady should pay up." He leaned down and kissed her "One down, seventy-one more to go." Emane jumped to his feet and offered her a hand up. "All right, folks, that's it for today." There were some moans and groans as the crowd dispersed.

"You are shameless, you know that?" she said, brushing off her pants.

"So you tell me." He threw his arm over her shoulder. "Let's go get something to drink."

That evening she sat and talked with Aleric at the campfire. Emane sat beside her, holding her hand. "Where is Eleana?" she asked.

"She and the Shifters are evaluating, making sure that things stay quiet," Aleric replied.

"She made me a promise" she sighed staring into the fire. "I was wondering when she was going to keep it." Looking up she asked, "What is 'old magic'?"

Aleric furrowed his brow, "Where did you hear that?"

"Eleana. She enchanted Emane's snake with 'old magic.' It bit Dralazar and his magic started failing."

"That would explain the silence," Aleric mumbled. "Are you sure that is what she said? 'Old magic'?"

"Yes. Dralazar seemed shocked."

Aleric stared into the fire. "I am shocked myself."

Kiora waited, hoping for more of an answer.

Aleric took a deep breath, "Old magic is powerful and dangerous. It is filled with incantations and depends less on the magic of nature and more on the power of the user. Old magic is rumored to have created some very powerful sorcerers that almost could not be controlled. It is my understanding that a spell was placed, preventing old magic from being used.

"By who?"

Aleric pulled his gaze away from the fire to look at Kiora, "By Eleana."

CHAPTER TWENTY-EIGHT

THE GATES

THE NEXT FEW DAYS were swirls of the same—questions, the little boy Rayen's invisibility trips, and sparring with Emane. Nights by the fire were quiet as both Kiora and Aleric avoided any more conversations of old magic. As the days passed, Kiora's anxiety, as well as her irritation ,grew that Eleana had not appeared to make good on her promise. The Guardians claimed to not know where she was, and Kiora's calls to her had gone unanswered.

Heading to bed, Kiora noticed the sky was abnormally dark. The stars were nowhere to be seen. She scowled. It didn't look natural, which meant it probably wasn't. Kiora found Leo and Malena conversing on a tree branch on the border of camp. Even they weren't sparkling as much as usual without the evening light.

"Kiora," Malena said, turning, "How are you?"

"Fine. I was wondering about the sky," she said pointing up. Leo and Malena gave each other a meaningful look. "Something's not right, is it?"

"No, I don't think so." Malena answered cautiously.

"That...is debatable," Leo added, looking at Kiora as if he had never seen her before. Spreading his wings behind him, he inclined his head. "Have a good night, Solus."

That night she dreamed of the gate.

It was just as she remembered it, beautiful scrolling iron, pictures of creatures she had never seen, the two halves melted together. And standing before it was Dralazar, his hand still red and inflamed, two puncture wounds oozing liquid.

Putting forth his good hand, he laid it on the gate and began muttering words that she did not understand. The melted iron that had held the two halves together split with a thunderous crack and the gate began to creak open. He yelled to the sky, "This is on you, Eleana!" Thunder boomed and lighting clapped as the sky overhead offered an ominous warning.

Kiora awoke with a start to thunder and lightning pummeling the camp.

Dralazar opened the gate, she thought. But what did that mean? Kiora had no idea what was on the other side, and neither did anyone else. A fear seeped through her. She needed answers, now. Shoving her feet into her shoes, she ran out into the rain weaving around tents and trees until she passed the magical boundary. Worried she would wake the others, she ran further before throwing back her head and yelling, "ELEANA!" She turned in a circle staring up at the purple, rain-dripping sky. She was already soaked to the bone, her hair stringing together and feeding little rivulets of water down her face. "YOU MADE ME A PROMISE!" she shouted.

She was answered with nothing but the sound of rain falling around her. She kicked angrily at a rock, spraying mud and water in the process. Was there really no one she could trust? She had put aside her anger, her confusion, to fight this battle—and now, another lie.

"Kiora?"

Whirling around, she saw Eleana, standing dry in the rainstorm.

"Kiora, here," she said, reaching out her hand. "You're sopping wet."

"I don't want your help!" Kiora yelled, her ferocity surprising even herself. "I don't want your help," she repeated softer. "I don't care if I am wet, or cold. Dralazar opened that gate." She waited for a reaction; there was none, "I don't know what it means, or if it's good or bad, because you have told me nothing!" she shouted. "You promised, Eleana, I trusted you, even after…" she pointed in the gates direction. "And you lied to me! I have called you, and you ignore me! People died! Morcant died! For what?"

"I'm sorry, Kiora. I have been watching Dralazar."

"Wh-what?" Water stuck to Kiora's eyelashes, blurring her vision.

"I needed to know if he suspected why I opened the old magic."

Kiora stared at Eleana through the rain, shoving a wet and dripping piece of hair behind her ears before swiping the water out of her eyes the best she could. "Why did you?"

"Kiora, I promised you answers. But I," she drooped, "I can't give them to you."

"What do you mean you can't give them to me?" Kiora burst out; wanting to run at Eleana, shake the answers out of her.

Eleana held up her hand, "You will have your answers, but I cannot…" she stared at the sky. "Kiora, things have changed since I made that promise. There is much more you need to know. I have called Arturo to take you. But, please, if you can find it in your heart, know that I ask for your forgiveness, for everything." She bowed her head and vanished.

Kiora stared at the spot where Eleana had disappeared, shocked. She didn't turn around when she felt Arturo approach.

Are we going? Or shall we stand out in the rain all night?

"She left," Kiora said, dazed. "She promised me answers, and she left."

She is giving you answers. Just because she is not telling you herself does not mean she is not keeping her promise, Kiora.

"But why wouldn't she just tell me herself?"

Guilt can be a powerful gag.

Finally, Kiora turned to look at Arturo. Lacking whatever magic had kept Eleana dry, he was dripping wet. His normal colors were muted, white feathers sadly beige.

You don't look so great either, Arturo answered her thoughts.

Maybe it was the stress or the grief, or Arturo's dry tone, but whatever it was, she started to laugh. Harder and harder she laughed until she was hunched over holding her stomach. "I'm sorry," she wheezed to Arturo, who stood silently dripping water, "I'm sorry!" Trying to calm herself, she climbed onto Arturo, still chuckling, "I'm ready."

You need to bubble. Dralazar must not find where we are going.

She obeyed, finally calming down as they flew. "Where are we going?"

The Hall of Protectors. It is where we honor the memory of those who have protected our Soluses. But you are going to meet Epona. She is an Ancient One. Very few have ever met her.

"Have you?"

I have.

"She is going to tell me about the gate?"

And more.

She frowned, "Why can't you just tell me, if Eleana can't?"

You are under the impression that Eleana has told me why she did what she did. As I said, grief can be a powerful gag, and one that becomes thicker and harder to dislodge if you allow it to remain in place.

The two flew for some time before entering a canyon between two rocks shaped like wings. Kiora looked around in wonder. Arturo dove straight down, nearly pulling her off his back.

"A little more warning next time," she yelled into the wind.

Close your eyes.

She looked down to see the ground rushing up to meet them. Pinching her eyes shut, she screamed. The impact never came. Cautiously, she opened one eye to find herself flying through a large cavern.

I told you to close your eyes. I would have expected a little more calmness from you. Emane didn't scream.

"Emane's been here?" she asked, her eyes trying to take in everything all at once.

Against my better judgment, but Aleric insisted.

Arturo landed softly, and Kiora slid off, gazing at her surroundings. It was beautiful. The light was everywhere, and yet seemed to be coming from nowhere. There were exquisitely detailed portraits hanging up and down both walls in an oversized, soaring hall. Besides those and a stone bench sitting in the center, it was otherwise empty. She walked, looking at the pictures, trailing her fingers over the frames.

"Are these the Protectors?"

Yes.

She looked at the different faces, all from different times. She was examining a portrait of a Guardian that vaguely resembled Malena when a soft angelic voice floated into the cavern.

"Kiora," it beckoned her to follow. She looked to Arturo, who nodded his encouragement.

Kiora's wet clothes were sticking to her and she pulled her shirt away from her skin, trying to smooth down her hair as she made her way to the back of the cavern. Passing through a stone archway into a smaller, yet more elegant room, she gasped, taking in the beauty of it all. The ceiling arched high above her in a perfect circle with orbs floating around giving off a soft, beautiful pink light. The smoothness of the walls, the grace of the archways, it was one of the most beautiful spaces she had seen, even surpassing the craftsmanship of the Shifters. In the middle of the room, an ageless woman with shoulder-length hair that had just started to turn white sat upon a delicate throne.

She spoke, "You have come at last." Her voice was so, melodic. The only other time Kiora had noticed that quality so distinctly was when Morcant had spoke. Yet where Morcant's was booming and baritone, hers was that of a soft soprano, calming.

Kiora didn't know what to say, so she said nothing.

"You are so young." Her gentle eyes appraised Kiora. "So young to bear so much: you and your Protector." Motioning, she said, "Please, sit." Kiora didn't have time to ask where she was to sit before a delicately carved chair rose from the floor. Kiora mutely walked to it, and sat. "I am Epona," she said warmly.

Kiora forced a smile, "It is nice to meet you." She bit her lip, shifting in her chair. "Why am I here?"

"You are here because it is the only place where you can see what you need to see," Epona waved her hand towards the wall. There was a muted grinding as two large stone wings began emerging to the right of them, pushing themselves straight out from the wall between two of the archways. Once they had freed themselves from the stone surround, a small dot of liquid light appeared in the center, growing larger and brighter. It swirled and moved, very much like the Wings of Arian, but instead of gold feathers these matched the silver grey stone they had emerged from. Kiora looked to Epona, but she was watching the wings.

The light snapped into place, turning Kiora's attention back
to it, and without explanation the pictures began flowing. There
were creatures she had never seen before; plants and landscapes
which were foreign to her. The scene moved from place to place,
each different, each unknown. Waterfalls and plains, mountains and
streams, oceans and islands. The inhabitants of which she vaguely
recognized as many of their figures had been immortalized in the
swirling ironwork of the gate.

When the pictures ended, Kiora turned to Epona. "That is what
is on the other side of the gate, isn't it?"

"Yes. It is the only record we have left of the place we came
from. The Wings of Arian were constructed after the gate."

Kiora stared back at the wings, "But why?" she asked, "Why
did they put the gate up?"

Epona settled back into her throne, placing her hands in her
lap, one on top of the other, much like she was settling in for a long
story. "Before I can tell you that, you need to understand a few
things. The other side of the gate is much different from the world
you have lived in. It is based entirely on magic."

Kiora looked to the floor, trying to process that. "You mean
outside the gate, they all have magic?"

"Almost without exception, yes. There were legends of a race,
humans, which were nearly devoid of magical ability. We Ancient
Ones worked hard to make sure that you remained a legend."
Kiora leaned forward in her chair, elbows on her knees. "Before
the gate, we tried to keep you hidden ourselves; your kind was so
vulnerable. But word spreads quickly, especially among the magical
community."

"What happened?" Kiora asked, scooting even further forward
on her chair.

"In response, we took two of the more powerful youngsters of the time, a brother and sister, and brought them here, charging them to look after your people and protect you from any who might prey on your weaknesses."

Kiora was beginning to understand where Epona was taking her. Dropping backwards, she said, "Dralazar and Eleana."

"Indeed," Epona nodded, looking over the top of her head as if remembering. "It went well for some time. But Dralazar began to enjoy his power more than he ought to have. He thirsted for more and wanted his sister's help to get it." Epona looked down to Kiora. "He came to her with the plans for the gate, presented under the guise that it would offer complete protection from outsiders." Epona sighed, "Eleana came to me, and I advised her against it. They were both so young," she shook her head, "but she heeded my words and refused her brother's plan."

Kiora frowned, "But then why…"

Epona motioned to the wings. "Watch."

The void in the wings snapped, more quietly than the Wings of Arian, and a picture came into being.

A very young looking Eleana sat underneath a tree with a handsome young man, holding his hand. His dark hair was cut short, emphasizing his strong jaw and beautiful brown eyes. Those eyes looked at Eleana, much like Emane looked at her. She laid her coppery hair on his broad shoulder and smiled.

"I'm not hurting you, am I?" she asked shyly.

"No, I can't feel any magic at all today," he said sweetly, running his fingers through her hair.

Snuggling closer, she smiled, "I have been practicing."

Epona narrated the scene, "My poor Eleana was in love with a human. He was a wonderful soul, kind and gentle. A perfect match for her in every way," Epona sighed, shaking her head tragically, "but entirely non-magical."

The picture switched to the handsome young man walking alone through the forest. He was armed with a bow and arrow and crept slowly forward, hunting most likely, when something hit him from behind, throwing him forward. Scrambling to his feet, he looked down at his broken bow that lay beneath him. Grabbing the arrow alone, he spun around, holding it out in defense and turning on the spot, looking for his attacker.

A Guardian flew down from the trees, pelting and slashing with magic. Cuts opened around his face and body, blood seeping through his clothes. He flailed, trying to fend off the attack with his arrow, but the small weapon was useless against the magic. Sinking to his knees, he slowly succumbed, and after one final shot, fell dead in the forest.

Kiora inhaled sharply, covering her face.

"So was the first Fallen One," Epona whispered.

Dralazar then appeared, unbubbling himself at the scene. He also looked incredibly young. "Let's see how Eleana feels about protecting her precious humans now." He grinned at the lifeless body at his feet. "Good work, Vitraya," he addressed the Fallen One whose transformation had not yet begun. She was still beautiful and fair-haired with sparkling blue eyes. "Hide where we discussed. I will come for you after the gate is up."

Epona added, "Eleana was devastated. She blamed herself for not keeping a closer eye on the magical creatures that inhabited the region. So when Dralazar came to her, you can imagine her weakness."

Dralazar walked over to a sallow and sunken Eleana. "We can still protect the rest. Sister, there is no need for any more to die."

"I don't know, Dralazar," Eleana said.

"I know what Epona said, but you saw what happened. He was attacked for no other reason than that he was non-magical, and by a

Guardian, no less! If they will attack, what do you think is going to happen when other things start wandering into the valley? The word is spreading. A group of Shifters crossed the pass just a couple of days ago."

Eleana started, "Shifters? Are you sure?"

"Yes. And you know there is more—dragons have already come and there is bound to be more on the way. And we have been lucky. There are much worse things that haven't found us yet. Some of the species are growing very bloodthirsty, power hungry." He placed his hand on her shoulder. "I know you love them, Sister, I love them too. But they are weak, and our presence is not enough to protect them. Please, help me protect this people, help me erect the gate."

"All right," Eleana said with a sob. "All right."

"The day her love was killed, a piece of Eleana died," Epona said as the wings grew silent. "She caved to her brother's wishes in her grief, and they erected a gate to block the only way in or out of the valley. They used old magic to enchant the valley to ensure everyone in stayed in, and all others stayed out. It was her attempt at protecting the people that she had grown to love so deeply."

Kiora's breath leaked out in a slow and steady stream as she leaned back in the chair. "But, if she wanted to protect us," Kiora began slowly, "then why does she refuse to fight with us, to put an end to Dralazar?" Sitting straight up, she blurted, "Does she know what he did?"

"She does." Epona nodded tragically. "She realized too late his betrayal. She tried to open the gate herself, but Dralazar, anticipating her regret, had altered it. Trying to right a wrong she could not truly undo, she laid some enchantments of her own, forbidding old magic. Try as he might, Dralazar could have no access to it. This meant he could not use the old magic. It was a rather brilliant spell and the only thing that kept Dralazar from coming into power centuries ago.

"But, she could have stopped him, couldn't she?" Kiora asked, searching Epona's expression. "She is more powerful than he is."

"She is," Epona conceded. "But she feels that the last time she interfered, she changed the destinies of all who live here, in more ways than one. Sometimes old magic can have unforeseen consequences." Epona raised her eyebrows at Kiora, looking like she was waiting for her to understand something.

"What?" she finally asked, feeling foolish.

"The gate had an unsuspected response to what it was asked to do. Can you think of nothing strange about this valley you live in?"

Kiora shook her head no. Not any stranger than being locked in a valley by a gate.

She leaned back into her chair. "This valley is small," she prompted. "And yet Meros never gets any bigger."

It bubbled to the surface like tar, slowly. "That's why we can't have very many children." she replied, more of a question than an answer.

"Yes. The old magic controlled all the populations, both magical and non-magical, to prevent the valley from being overrun and its resources depleted. This is one more thing that Eleana blames herself for. She has watched more than one woman cry and plead to the heavens for more children, children that would never come."

Kiora stared at the ground. Her mother had been viewed as exceptionally lucky for having not one, but two children. She had no idea. It had never been strange to her that there were so few children in Meros; it just, was.

The conversation at the battle played through Kiora's mind. "When Eleana used the old magic, it broke the enchantment," she said.

464 | D E V R I   W A L L S

"Yes."

Shifting awkwardly in her chair, Kiora struggled to keep her voice even. "But why would she do that? If there really are horrible things on the other side of the mountain, things that could destroy the people, why would she allow him to open it now? And why would he do it? He shut it to keep them out in the first place."

"After you went through the change, Dralazar recognized that he may lose this battle. According to the prophecy, if he loses, it will be final. Evil will be banished forever. He is searching for help from the outside."

"He is going to recruit the creatures that you showed me?"

"I am sure that is his plan, yes."

Kiora sat, trying to reconcile everything she had heard.

Epona rose from her chair, making her way down the steps, "Kiora, once a path is chosen, things align themselves in order with it. When Dralazar locked the gate securing the valley as his own, magic intervened. It began calling Soluses and Protectors to keep things in balance to keep Dralazar's evil from overrunning everything. But now that the gate has been opened," Epona ran her fingers over the grey stone wings. "Things are changing."

"Will we not need a Solus anymore?"

Epona turned, "Kiora, there is so much you will need to see and understand, much more than I can show you in one night. But you need to know of your calling. You asked why Eleana would open the old magic. She suspected your true calling from the day you went through the change. You are not a Solus, you are The Solus. There are prophecies about you, out there in the world, that date back thousands and thousands of years," she stretched her arm out, "You will unite us all."

The wings shuddered and once again rushed over a world that Kiora had never seen. Foreign faces flicked through, one after another, each whispering her name.

"What are you telling me?" Kiora asked, pushing herself back into her chair, desperate to deny the knowledge that was resonating within her.

"Kiora, it was said that the Creator gifted the people a collection of jewels that shone brighter than the sun. And from them sprang the source of light and joy." Walking back to her chair, Epona explained, "One by one over the years, some of the jewels were stolen. Nobody knows who took them, or where they went. Whoever took them was powerful—powerful enough to prevent themselves from being seen. Not even by wings, or visions. The only thing that has ever been seen is a dark shadowed figure."

Epona continued, "When the treasure was lost, darkness spread over the land. Some, such as your own people, were able at times to withstand the darkness and find peace and harmony despite this, but others lost themselves to the evil. It was prophesied that one day a child would come to restore what was lost. A child, and a Witow," Epona said with a nod to Kiora before sitting herself back down.

"Eleana used that word," Kiora interrupted. "What does it mean?"

"A Witow is an ancient word for those without any magic." Tilting her head to the side, Epona continued, "I was intrigued when I learned your Protector was a human, a Witow, in fact. It had never happened before. I could see how well he complemented you, but it was a dangerous choice. And then when you went through the change, Eleana and I began to wonder. Now that the gate is opened, I can feel the magic calling you."

Kiora tried to imagine herself going through the gate, but her thoughts were still slippery. "If the gate is open, why can I still not think of crossing the mountains?" she asked.

"The enchantment was strong and has been in place for

thousands of years. It is pulling back as we speak, but it will take time before the entire residue is gone. The magic that calls you is stronger. Surely you feel it."

Kiora stared at the ground in front of her, anywhere but in the eyes of the woman who sat before her. "What about Dralazar?" she asked. "What if he has already gone to get others?" "Dralazar is going to be distracted for a time. The spell Eleana used on him was particularly potent." The old woman smiled. "Dare say he deserved it."

"Did it really affect his magic?"

"Oh, yes. It will take him some time to repair the damage. That hand may never be the same again. Dralazar has no intention of risking an attack on you in his weakened state. Especially now that the gate is open, he will think time is on his side."

"Does he know of this prophecy?"

"I am sure he does. But I would be surprised if he had given it a thought any time in the last three thousand years." Epona chuckled. "He never was very good at looking at anything besides what was right in front of his nose."

Kiora's mind was eased at the possibility of a reprieve from worrying about an attack from Dralazar. But as it did, she felt a tugging, something pulling at the rivers of magic that already flowed through her. Something was calling her. Closing her eyes, she squeezed her hands into fists. It would have been so much easier to think that Epona was wrong, or lying, but she couldn't. Something was calling her, and a terrible weight settled onto her shoulders.

"I think that it is time for you to return to Emane; he is worried about you."

Kiora opened her eyes, staring out into the room.

Epona rose and walked to Kiora, gently taking her hands and pulling her to her feet. Kiora reluctantly looked into Epona's gentle eyes. "Kiora, I know it is difficult to understand. I know that this is not something you would have chosen. The magic calls you because it knows your heart. Your heart is incorruptible, a rare quality indeed."

Patting Kiora's hand, Epona said, "I will not burden you with any more tonight. Please, go back to your Protector. Talk with him—he understands more than you know." Epona leaned in and kissed Kiora on the forehead as a grandmother would her granddaughter. "Drustan will also be an invaluable friend on your journey."

"What about Aleric?"

"Aleric has been called in a different direction, for now."

"I don't understand."

Epona shook her head firmly. "You have so many questions and not enough energy left to listen to the answers. You must learn your limits, child. Arturo will take you back now."

Kiora heard the gentle clopping of Arturo's hoofs walking slowly into the room. Pulling herself onto his back, she looked to Epona, who was watching her with a mix of pride and sadness.

"Kiora, please try to understand Eleana. What she wishes for most of all right now is your forgiveness."

Kiora nodded wordlessly, laying her head down on Arturo's neck. She closed her eyes as he left the Hall and she didn't open them again as they flew home.

Arturo came in at the border of the camp. Kiora slid off, still damp and cold, inside and out. The sun had risen, painting the sky in fantastic pinks and oranges, but was unable to paint her emotions.

How are you? Arturo asked.

"Not now," she said softly. Her hand dropped off his back, falling heavily to her side. Without a glance backwards, she walked numbly into camp.

Almost making it to her bed, she was pulling back her tent flap when a wave of raw emotion slammed into her. Emane was coming. She sat herself down on her bed in anticipation of the onslaught.

EMANE CAUGHT A GLIMPSE of Kiora's dark hair disappearing into her tent and he stormed after her. Throwing back the flap, he marched in. "Where have you been?" he demanded. "I have been looking for you for over an hour. I wake up and you are gone! No one has seen you, no one knows where you are!" he said ticking off the offenses on his finger.

"And would it be too much for you to call me? I know you can do it, you have used it before." His voice grew louder, pacing back in forth in front of her. "So why is it that you do not feel the need to notify me when you choose to go missing in the middle of the night? Kiora! How am I supposed to protect you when I can't keep you within twenty feet of me?!" He looked around frantically. "And why is it that there is not a single hard surface in here for me to hit!?" He took to pacing again. "Do you think you could enlighten me as to what was so important that you almost gave me a heart attack?"

Before Kiora could answer, Emane continued his rant.

"And it's not just me anymore, Kiora. Aleric was worried sick, as were the people." He stopped yelling, and turned his back to her. "I don't think it's too much to ask for you to take me with you when you leave. And if nothing else, at least notify us."

"I am sorry," she whispered.

He spun around. "Sorry isn't good enough, Kiora!" He looked at her, eyes flashing.

It was the first time since entering the tent he had actually taken time to really look at her. As soon as he saw her, he wished he hadn't said anything. She was still damp. Her eyes looked cold and empty, her shoulders hunched. There was a hollowness about her that he had not seen before.

He deflated, "What happened?"

She looked up at him with pleading eyes, and what was left of his anger dispelled. Plopping down on the bed next to her, he put his arms around her and pulled her into him. "What happened?" he asked again.

She shook her head, "I can't—not yet." Burying her face in his chest, she murmured, "I am sorry I scared you."

Pushing Kiora's wet, matted hair out of her face, Emane kissed her forehead. "Will you promise to tell me?"

"I will," she said, her voice still muffled from his shirt. "It's as much about you as it is about me. But right now, I just need you to hold me. Do you think you could forgive me long enough to do that?"

"Come here," he said, pulling her onto his lap and wrapping his arms tight around her. "I will hold you as long as you need me to."

Emane felt Kiora relax against him, her breathing slowing to a steady even pace. Breathing her in, he leaned his forehead against hers.

CHAPTER TWENTY-NINE

FREEDOM

KIORA AWOKE TO THE heat of the sun beating on the side of her tent. Staring at the ceiling, she smiled at herself, she had taken it better this time than last. At least she hadn't run out of the Hall of Protectors screaming, and a dreamless sleep had left her better prepared to accept the enormity of what she had been told last night.

Trying to think about going over the mountains, Kiora found that for the first time in her life she could. Thinking on that, she felt the pull deepen. The magic was indeed calling her. She was ready to tell Emane what she had learned, but she needed to find Drustan first. It only took her a few minutes to track the Shifter down and set her plan in motion before she was off to find Emane.

She found him in a small clearing away from camp, running drills with his sword. Bubbling herself so as to not disturb him, she leaned against a tree to watch. He moved gracefully around the clearing, sparring with an imaginary enemy.

She envied his grace. It was not a gift she possessed. When she fought, she was awkward, her movements stiff. Emane promised her that fluidity would come in time, but she doubted it. Some people were just born with gifts, this was one of his.

Letting all of her worries melt away for a time, Kiora's heart swelled for this prince whose path had just changed as much as hers. She felt guilty and grateful at the same time—guilty that she was responsible for taking him away from his kingdom, and grateful that he would be at her side throughout this.

With one more wide swing, Emane shoved his sword into the ground, breathing hard. Kiora dropped her bubble and begin a gentle applause. He whirled, hand still on hilt, before he realized it was her.

"Kiora!" He beamed, running to embrace her.

She hugged him back fiercely. "I have something I need to share with you."

"Is this in regards to where you disappeared to last night?" he asked, raising one eyebrow.

"It is, but it's something I would rather explain somewhere else," she reached out taking both his hands in hers. "Will you come with me?"

"I would go anywhere with you, don't you know that by now?"

She truly hoped he would. "Come on then," she said, pulling him.

"What about Dralazar?"

"I have been assured that Dralazar will be out of commission for a little while."

"Really? By who?"

They walked across the camp hand in hand. "Epona."

Emane's brow furrowed as if trying to remember why he knew that name. "Epona? You went to the Hall of Protectors?"

"Yes. It was beautiful." She glanced at him sideways. "Why didn't you tell me that you had been there?"

He shrugged. "I don't know. Aleric and I came straight from

there when you were attacked by the dragon. After that, it didn't seem as important as what we were dealing with."

Emane and Kiora left the protection of camp and Kiora stopped. "Where we are going is not close. I have asked Drustan for a ride."

"Drustan? Why not Arturo?"

She took a few steps before answering, "I have so many thoughts swirling around right now, I would really like, just this once, to keep them to myself."

Emane nodded, "I completely understand." A large pegasus stepped out through the trees. Emane inclined his head, "Arturo?"

"Hello, Drustan," Kiora said with a chuckle.

Rolling his eyes, Emane went to help Kiora on, "Why did you have to look exactly like Arturo?"

Drustan stretched his neck back to look at him, "I really like to mess with you."

Emane pulled himself up behind Kiora. Leaning over her shoulder, he said, "Have I mentioned how much I like this guy?"

Kiora and Drustan both burst into laughter as his wings took them high into the sky.

"Where to?" Drustan asked as they soared.

Kiora took a deep breath. "The mountains."

Drustan's bellowing laugh rolled over the valley. "I was hoping you would say that!" he yelled, picking up speed.

As they flew, Kiora tried to prep Emane for the news he was about to receive. "Have you ever thought about going over the mountains? I mean really going over?"

"Sure, I have. We talked about it, remember?"

"No, we talked about what we thought was on the other side." They tried to talk about it at least, neither one of them had been able to get through the sentence without getting distracted. "But why haven't you ever tried to go see?"

Emane thought for a minute. "I don't know."

"Has anyone in the kingdom ever tried to go over the mountains?"

"Not that I know of."

"Don't you think it's odd? We live in this valley surrounded by mountains on every side. And not once has anyone ever even attempted to cross."

Emane was quiet. "What are you trying to tell me?"

"I will explain when we get where we are going, but I want you to think about it."

Kiora's heart was racing. The closer they got to the mountains the stronger the pull became. Her magic felt like it was jumping underneath her skin, anxious to go.

Drustan flew higher and higher heading for the peaks. The air was colder up here and Emane wrapped his arms tightly around Kiora to combat her shivering. Landing on top of the mountain ridge, they looked out over to the other side. The land stretched out before them in an uninterrupted expanse. Speechless, the trio took it all in.

"It's been a long time," Drustan finally spoke.

"You have been on the other side?" Kiora asked.

The pegasus morphed back into human form and Drustan stared over the great expanse of land. His eyes began to water. "I didn't think I would ever see it again." He looked over to Kiora. "I was traveling with a group of Shifters." He shook his head as he looked back out, "Our timing could not have been worse. Not long after we entered the valley, the gate was shut and we were trapped. We had no choice but to settle here and make a home for ourselves."

"You know this land," Kiora said, beginning to understand why Drustan was to be with them on this journey.

"Yes, very well."

She looked over at Emane, who was looking at the two of them utterly lost. "Drustan, do you think you could give me some time alone with Emane?"

Drustan nodded. "Call for me when you are ready. Do you remember the incantation?"

"I do. Wait, Drustan, why does calling use incantations? Isn't that old magic?"

"No. Some of nature's magic just needs a little help, that's all."

"Hmmm, interesting," Kiora said.

"Exceptions," Emane said dryly. "There's always exceptions."

"Well, he gets some things right." Drustan smiled, morphed into a hawk, and shot off into the new countryside.

Kiora sat down on a large cold rock, pulling her knees to her chin. With a jerk of her head she motioned for Emane to sit. "I am afraid this is a long story, you better sit down." Launching into her night, Kiora recounted everything Epona had told her. When she was finished, they both were silent for a time, looking out into the great unknown.

"They locked everybody in here, all this time," Emane finally mumbled, shaking his head. "Are you sure that this prophecy is about...do you think they are right?"

Kiora sighed, "I have wished that they were wrong. But when you feel the truth, you just know it." She laid her head on his shoulder. "You said you would follow me anywhere, did you mean it?"

"I would follow you to the ends of the earth, my love."

"That's good, because I think that is exactly what it's going to take." She chewed on the edge of her lip. "How do you do it?"

"Be so charming? Gee, I am not sure. Born with it, I suppose."

Kiora couldn't help herself, she laughed out loud before playfully shoving Emane to the side. "This is no time to make jokes!"

Laughing, he pulled her close, pinning her arm against him. Kissing her on the forehead, he asked, "Do what?"

She looked out over the land that Epona claimed was waiting for her. "Have everything riding on your shoulders."

"My father calls it the 'yoke of one's calling.' I would suppose yours is heavier than mine."

"I don't believe that. You have the weight of being the Prince and of being the Protector. And don't try to tell me that didn't add weight to you."

"You're right," he said, glancing down at her. "I still would argue that you feel your burden heavier than I feel mine. You are too sensitive and caring. I imagine it makes the load heavy."

"You are caring."

"Not like you, Kiora. Your heart is something beautiful and rare."

She fiddled with a wrinkle in his pants. She felt the river of magic flowing beneath her skin. "What if I start seeking power, like Dralazar? I can feel how powerful I am becoming."

"But the power scares you, Kiora, not like Dralazar."

"But it feels good too," she squeaked.

"But it scares you," he repeated. "People who crave power and glory are not fearful of it." Squeezing her, they both looked silently outwards. Emane slyly looked at her sideways.

"What?"

"You know, we haven't been able to be alone together for a while." Emane hinted "And you still owe me at least sixty kisses."

Kiora turned her face up to his. "Sixty sounds like a lot," she teased. "Are you sure?"

His eyes darkened and he kissed her with a hunger. Her body was thrumming with feelings for this man, as well as magic that was threatening to spin out of control. Breaking away from Emane, Kiora held him at arm's lengths, breathing hard.

"What's the matter?" Emane asked.

"Nothing is the matter," she said breathing heavily, "It was wonderful, but I am trying not to shock you again."

He moved in to kiss her again anyway. "I can stand a little shock."

She put her hand up to his chest and shook her head. "No. The way you're kissing me, it will be more than a shock. I'm afraid I will knock you off the mountain."

"That good, huh?" He smiled, leaning back on one arm.

She was too busy trying to keep things under control to keep his ego in check. "Yes," she nodded breathlessly, "it was that good."

GET READY TO BUBBLE! Drustan's voice came screaming into her head.

Her head jerked upward, scanning the horizon. A hawk exploded out of the tree line, heading straight for them. Emane noticed her distraction.

"What is it?"

"I don't know. Drustan told me to get ready to bubble and he is coming fast." The hawk swooped in and landed before them.

BUBBLE NOW! the hawk demanded.

Kiora pushed a bubble out around all three of them, grateful for the release of magic. "What's the matter?"

"Just watch," Drustan said. Emane and Kiora stared out into the distance looking for anything, and then there it was—a gigantic animal, unlike anything they had ever seen before, came bursting through the treetops. It was the size of a large horse, but looked somewhat like a bird with large feathered wings. Ending, however, its birdlike resemblance was its serpent's tail. The juxtaposition of scales and feathers was a strange sight. It was brilliantly colored—reds and blues gleamed in the sun. It flapped just enough to hold its position in the air as its giant head scanned the area.

"What is it looking for?" Emane asked.

"Us. That is an Aktoowa. I must admit in all the excitement of returning home, I had forgotten some of the dangers."

"Are you going to tell us what an Aktoowa is?" Emane asked, rolling his eyes.

"An Aktoowa," Drustan said, pausing for dramatic effect, "is a creature who quite enjoys the taste of magic."

Kiora paled. "The taste?"

"Yes. It feeds on magical beings. The more magic the being, the more he desires it. He probably would have picked up on me, but by the time I saw him he was intently hunting something else." He shot a look at Kiora.

"He was hunting me," she groaned.

"Yes, your thread has become very strong. He picked it up some time ago, I'm sure. Don't worry, once we get over there you will learn the threads to watch out for. Bubbles are very effective against an Aktoowa." As if in response, the creature screamed a horrible screechy sound and disappeared back below the tree line. "See, gave up already. Not the most patient predator."

"How many more creatures like that are over there?" Emane asked.

"Like that?" Drustan nodded to where the creature had disappeared. "Not many. But I do not wish to mislead you. The world on the other side of this mountain is not like anything you can imagine. It is filled with dangers, both apparent and not."

"You realize, then, that Emane and I have to go?" Kiora said.

Drustan's eyes widened. Although he managed to keep his voice level, his chest was rising and falling rapidly. "I suspected. Has Epona confirmed it?"

"She says I am the one to restore the light."

Drustan morphed back to his human form and knelt before her, "The True Solus."

"No, please don't do that." Kiora tugged at his arm. "Please don't bow to me. I can't bear it."

Drustan remained on the ground. "You should get use to it. When people realize who you are, it will be custom to bow."

"No please, Drustan, please get up."

"If My Lady commands it." He rose to his feet. "I never thought I would see the day when the one who would restore the light would be born."

"Will you go with us? Guide us?"

Drustan looked at her with excitement, "My Lady wishes me to join the quest?"

She smiled, nearly laughing at his excitement. "I think there is no one better. You have knowledge of this land that would be invaluable."

"It would be my honor," he said solemnly and bowed.

"Drustan, you can only come if you stop bowing!"

"Yes, My Lady," he said with one more short bow. "Now, we need to get you back to Eleana. There is much to do before we can go." He looked around at the bubble, "Can you make this bubble bigger, that Aktoowa is still close."

Kiora stretched and pushed the bubble out giving him room to shift back into a pegasus. As they headed back to camp, Kiora kept the bubble up, not out of necessity, but as a means to drain a little magic. Her magic seemed to be increasing nearly every day, and something about Emane's touch today was sending her magic into a flurry. It bounced around, pushing at its boundries. Now, with Emane's arms wrapped around her, Kiora felt as if she were about to explode.

END OF BOOK ONE

WINGS OF TAVEA

Book Two in the Solus Trilogy

CHAPTER ONE

THE MORNING CAME ALL too soon for Kiora. Eleana had said they needed to leave immediately, before Dralazar realized who Kiora and Emane really were. Kiora stepped into a comfortable pair of pants and her usual white tunic before reaching under her pillow to pull out a brown scale. Exhaling, she plopped onto her bed, looking at the scale in her hand, remembering the wise dragon who had, quite literally, saved her at the gate.

It was happening, they were going through. And Morcant would never see it. "Toopai," she whispered, remembering his last request. Looking around, the leather cords dangling from the tent flaps caught her eye. Perfect.

A minute later she walked out to meet Emane, a dragon scale hung by a leather cord under her shirt. They walked together past the magical barrier just as the sun was peeking through the trees.

They found Eleana, Aleric, Arturo and Drustan waiting in the clearing with three horses.

"We have packed the horses with as many provisions as we could," Eleana said. "We have food and clothing, as well as some books on old magic. If you would summon the book of Arian, we will send that too."

"Isn't it too dangerous to take?"

"It is not known outside of this valley. It should be fine."

Kiora handed Eleana the book, which was promptly slid into the saddlebag.

"Drustan will be able to help you with the old magic for now. Please listen to him and follow his advice; he knows of the dangers that await you."

Dangers like the Aktoowa, Kiora thought.

Eleana then held up three long cloaks with hoods. "You will need to wear these always, with the hoods up. Being recognized as humans will draw the attention of those that we do not wish." Moving to Drustan, she said, "I need you to lead them to Lomay."

Drustan's eyes widened. "The Ancient One? Eleana, I do not know where to find him. His location was kept secret long before you—" he stopped "—before I came to stay in the valley."

"He is in the Morow region. I trust you know how to get there."

"I do."

"The magic of the gate is still fading," Eleana explained to them all. "Epona could not speak with Lomay directly, but she has sent him a message requesting that he send someone for you." Turning her attention to Kiora, she continued, "Lomay will teach you what else you need to know concerning the prophecy. He will teach you and arrange for some training for the both of you. I wish I could help you more, but I must stay here for a time and fix the mess that I created."

The three travelers climbed onto their horses. It felt strange to ride an animal without a magical thread.

"Kiora," Eleana pulled out a glittering blue sapphire pendant with silver vines surrounding it. "Malena was concerned that you needed another one of these."

Kiora gasped. "How did she know?"

"This pendant links you with the Guardians, and consequently with me. When Dralazar destroyed it, we felt the link break. They have been working since the battle to make you a new one. As you travel, you can call us if you need us. Just be aware that the further you are, the longer it will take us to come. So in essence, it is up to the three of you." Kiora slipped the pendant over her neck, sliding it under her shirt to sit next to Morcant's scale. "The link will also help if we ever need to find you." Kiora fingered the necklace. It was almost identical to the one she had lost. "The Guardians have also made weapons for you as promised. They are in your packs." Eleana looked to Emane and Drustan, "Work together and keep her safe." They both nodded their agreement. "I will go with you on Arturo until the gate, and then I must leave you."

"Arturo is not coming?" Kiora asked, jerking her head up.

"He will be near. As I said, you do not need to draw attention to yourselves, and pegasus are rare, even on the other side. You will be able to communicate with him if you need to, but you will not see much of him."

Kiora felt better knowing that he would at least be near.

Eleana continued. "We will be passing closely by Dralazar's territory. Kiora and I will take turns bubbling to get us through."

Aleric stepped forward. "I have something to offer before you leave. Holding up an oval shaped amber amulet, he held it out to Emane. "I would like you to take this." Emane reached out, taking it by the chain. "It will alert you to the intentions of those you interact with. Amber is a friend, red is not. I don't have much use for it here, not with threads. But for you..."

Emane turned the amulet over in his hand. "Are you sure, Aleric? This was your grandfather's, wasn't it?"

"I am sure. You are in need of it much more than I am. My grandfather made it to be used, not to be remembered by."

Eleana looked around at the group. "Are we ready?"

There were no words, just solemn nods of heads. Everyone felt the danger that awaited them on this journey.

The sound of the horses' hoofs was the only sound amongst the band of travelers. All were silent as they plodded across the valley. Eleana was bubbling all of them to keep their travels from being known. They had moved through the remaining forest and onto the meadow-like grasses, and then finally into the rocky covered land that preceded the mountain range.

Kiora, Eleana called her.

Again, Kiora gripped her head. Why are you so much louder than the others when you talk to me like this? she thought back.

I apologize. The voice came much softer this time, bearable. Kiora let go of her head and sat back up. I didn't realize I was hurting you. There was a long pause and Kiora looked sideways to Eleana. Her shoulders were hunched forward, head down. Kiora, I am so sorry for everything. If you could find it in your heart to forgive me someday, I would be in your debt.

Eleana, I do not need to forgive you. This is not your fault.

It is my fault! Epona must not have explained.

No, she did. She told me of the man you loved. She glanced over at Eleana who was riding with her eyes forward. Grief is powerful.

A single tear slid down Eleana's cheek.

You made a mistake, Kiora thought gently. When you realized your mistake you did everything within your power to fix it. I could not ask any more of you than that.

Turning her head, Eleana finally looked at her. *Truly, Kiora, you are remarkable. I find you more remarkable every time we speak. It will be an honor to see what the years will bring.* As they approached Dralazar's lair, the landscape continued to change. The earth here was rocky, to say the least, covered in large black rocks and boulders, some the size of houses. They glanced nervously around, waiting for a dragon or Fallen One to fly into sight. Kiora took over the bubble; Eleana had held it for well over an hour.

"We are getting close," Eleana announced to the group. The mountains were looming in front of them.

A flurry of movement caught Kiora's eye. Glancing around, she saw a figure moving between the rocks. Squinting, she tried to make it out, but it kept appearing and disappearing into the rocky landscape. And then, just for a moment, it was out in the open, a small dark haired girl. "Layla," she whispered.

Her sister turned and ran behind another rock and was gone.

Shortly after, the group turned the final bend coming to the great iron gate that had occupied so many of her dreams. The lines were fading now, the two halves shrouded in mist.

"The spell is fading," Eleana told her. "Before long, they will be gone."

Where the gates had once stood was now a canyon, stretching out before them. Cutting neatly through the two mountain peaks, it marked the way out of the valley and into the unknown.

"This is where I must leave you. Go with speed and caution." Eleana shimmered and was gone.

Don't stray too far from me, Kiora thought to Arturo.

I will stay as near as possible.

"Are we ready for this?" Kiora asked Emane and Drustan.

"I have been waiting for this day longer than you can possibly imagine," Drustan said, throwing a wicked grin back at Kiora as he spurred his horse forward.

Kiora looked to Emane, "What about us? Are we ready for this?"

"Does it matter?" He smiled. "The Solus is going through that pass, isn't she?"

Kiora stared forward at the new path before her. "Yes."

"Then her Protector is going, too."

"All right," she sighed. "Let's go." Kiora took one last look back before urging her horse forward, leaving the valley that had held them hostage.

CPSIA information can be obtained at www.ICGtesting.com
Printed in the USA
LVOW08s0935161114

413957LV00002B/456/P